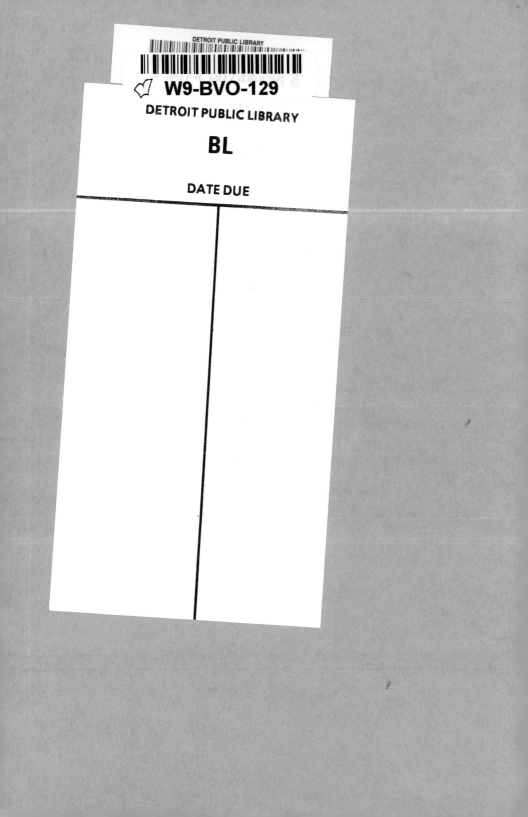

BOOKS BY RUTH HARRIS

THE LAST ROMANTICS
THE RICH AND THE BEAUTIFUL
DECADES

THE LAST

ROMANTICS

RUTH HARRIS

SIMON AND SCHUSTER • NEW YORK

c₁ /

Published by Simon and Schuster
A Division of Gulf & Western Corporation
Simon & Schuster Building
Rockefeller Center
1230 Avenue Of The Americas
New York, New York 10020
SIMON AND SCHUSTER and colophon are trademarks
of Simon & Schuster

Designed by Eve Metz

Manufactured in the United States of America

1 2 3 4 5 6 7 8 9 10
Library of Congress Cataloging in publication data

Harris, Ruth.
    The last romantics.

    I.   Title.
PZ4.H3159Las   [PS3558.A655]   813'.54   79-29753
ISBN 0-671-24595-3

Grateful acknowledgment is made for permission to quote
lines from the following lyrics:
    "Five Foot Two, Eyes of Blue" by Sam Lewis, Joe
Young, and Ray Henderson; © 1925 Leo Feist, Inc; ©
renewed 1953 Warock Corporation; International
Copyright secured. All rights reserved.
    "I Want to Be Happy"; © 1924 Warner Bros. Inc.,
copyright renewed. All rights reserved.
    "Brother, Can You Spare a Dime?" © 1932 Warner Bros.
Inc., copyright renewed. All rights reserved.
    "By Myself" by Howard Dietz and Arthur Schwartz;
copyright © 1937 by DeSylva, Brown & Henderson, Inc;
copyright renewed, assigned to Chappell & Co. All rights
reserved.

BL

AUG 2 5 '80

TO MICHAEL, WITH LOVE

Against the background of Paris between the wars, Nicole Redon, an internationally acclaimed couturiere, and
Kim Hendricks, an avant-garde novelist,
share a fiercely passionate love that
threatens to consume them both.

Even though it happened in France, it was all somehow an American experience.
                                        —Gerald Murphy

CHAPTER ONE

1.

Paris
11 November 1918

*How do you say "I love you" to a stranger?
How do you describe a thunderbolt? A gift from the gods?
A kiss from destiny? How do you tell her you've been
overcome, overwhelmed, carried away, transfixed, transported and hypnotized? How do you find words to express
feelings you've never felt before?*

Kim stood there on the rue Montaigne, rooted to the
sidewalk, immobilized by the sight of her—glowing
golden, ravishingly perfumed, holding a broom, looking
at him as if she'd never seen a man before . . .

What could she say? "Je t'aime"? *She had never seen him before in her life! How could she describe the* coup de foudre *that had stolen her speech and bewitched her, turning her, in the flash of one second to the next, from a busy and purposeful young woman into a creature enchanted and bedazzled? How could she describe what she felt when she had never felt it before?*

Nicole stood there in front of the door to her shop, fixed to the sidewalk, the broom forgotten in her hands, struck by the sight of him—lean and tall, elegantly and extravagantly handsome, looking at her as if he'd never seen a woman before . . .

He was McKim Hendricks. He was twenty years old; a war hero with pieces of the Kaiser's shrapnel in his knees to prove it; a professional journalist with published bylines to prove it; he was on the side of democracy, progress, peace, truth, justice, honor and art. He had a fiancée and a once-in-a-lifetime job waiting for him back home in New York. A return ticket—for the day after tomorrow!—was in his pocket, and in his right hand was a bottle of champagne, remnant of the night-long celebration he'd shared with writer and artist friends in the cafés of Montparnasse.

Still the words spun recklessly through his mind: *I love you! But more than that! You will be my everything and I will be yours! Together we will be everything we want to be and do everything we want to do . . . not only now but now and forever and always . . .*

Extravagant words produced by extravagant emotions swirled through him, and Kim knew that if she could read his mind she would think him crazy. Everyone had always told him he was too intense and too romantic; had warned him to think with his head and not his heart. But she was—well, she was unique! Extraordinary! Spectacular! Ravishing! Dazzling! And the heavens had meant her for him.

Now, if he could only think of something intelligent to say . . .

Kim had been on his way, along with the rest of Paris and, it seemed, the rest of the world, to the Champs-Elysées for the official announcement of the Armistice —the war to end all war was finally to end—and the parades when, having crossed the traffic-choked rue Montaigne in the middle of the block, preoccupied with the story he would write—it would be the best one to come out of Paris!—he had almost walked straight into her and knocked her over. She was young, his own age, her hair the color of honey with glints of gold, and her eyes were the color of topaz. She gave the impression of existing in her own burnished golden aura. She wore elegantly simple clothes of striking style and she was, of all things, sweeping the sidewalk.

Standing so close that he could have touched her if he had reached out his hand, Kim suddenly smelled flowers. But it was November! There were no flowers here in the middle of Paris! The Armistice would be announced at eleven—it had been decided there was something lucky about the eleventh hour of the eleventh day of the eleventh month—and Kim, face to face with her, smelling the scent of flowers which he soon realized was her perfume, thought that the day was not only lucky but magic. The bolt of lightning that had struck him on the rue Montaigne kept him rooted to the pavement, silent and bereft of speech. He wondered if he would ever be able to speak again and, if he could, what words he would say to her, when, suddenly, the words came to him.

"*Vive la France! Vive la paix! Vive l'amour!*" he said.

11

He held out the champagne in a salute and an offering. "Will you drink to that?"

"At nine-thirty in the morning?" She smiled a dazzling and intelligent smile—just the kind of smile he knew she would have!—and continued to sweep with a very European twig broom bound round with sturdy twine. The janitor had gotten drunk to celebrate the Armistice; he had not shown up that morning and so Nicole was doing his job.

"Your boss must be a real ogre to make you sweep the sidewalk on the most important day of the century," Kim said, reading the elegant sans-serif letters inscribed in gold on the black plaque to the right of the iron grillwork door with its brightly polished knob: Nicole Redon. "Redon must be a real battleaxe," Kim said, "but even she wouldn't begrudge you a festive sip of champagne . . ."

Nicole continued to sweep, trying to keep her eyes away from him but failing . . . failing. He wore lean tan twill trousers that made his legs look even longer than they really were, a soft grayish-blue chambray shirt, the color of his eyes, a heavy belt with a massive metal buckle captured from the Germans, and a heathery tweed jacket. A trench coat, all flaps and buckles, was thrown over his shoulders. He was tall—just over six feet —and his body was beautifully balanced with just the right amount of muscle and flesh over perfectly proportioned bones. He was tanned and his features were even, strong and refined at the same time. His clear blue eyes were sensitive, filled with life and curiosity, and his generous mouth was sensual and expressive. He spoke good, fluent French with a distinct American accent he wisely made no attempt to hide. Nicole liked Americans and had a strong prejudice in their favor.

"You smell just like spring. I thought I had walked into

a garden. In November!" Kim said, more confident now that she had smiled and spoken. "What's the name of your perfume?" he asked. He would buy Sally a bottle of it before he left Paris. "What is it called?"

"It doesn't have a name. I take a little of this, a little of that," she said. She had finished with the sweeping and had turned toward the door, ready to disappear inside. She didn't want to go. She was pulled in one direction by her overwhelming attraction to this magnetic American; she was pulled the other by the mountain of work waiting inside for her. She stood there on the sidewalk, her hand on the door, torn by indecision, hoping he would say something that would persuade her to forget work and stay with him . . .

Suddenly, the bells from the small church across the street began to peal, joining with the bells of all the other churches in Paris, ringing in celebration. Muted, from a distance, under the soprano sound of bells was the masculine roll of drums. People shoved past them, waving tiny flags and shouting. *Vive La France! À bas les boches!* Tears of joy ran down the face of a boy still in his teens, a veteran, his legs gone, condemned by the Kaiser's bullets to live out his life in a wheelchair. A taxi driver stopped to let off passengers. He honked his horn to join in the noisy festivity and, on the front seat next to him, his dachshund wore the *tricolore* on its collar. All Paris was moving inward, toward the Champs-Elysées. Kim and Nicole, forced into silence by the bedlam, watched the bands of happy Parisians and their allies, the Americans, the English, the Australians, the tall, exotic Africans, the wounded and the whole, old and young, wives and widows, fiancées and sisters, shopkeepers and lawyers, intellectuals and sportsmen, waiters and scrubwomen, and the *clochards*, drunk this time with an excuse. All Paris was a party.

"Come with me to the Champs-Elysées. I'm a journalist. I'm going to cover the announcement and the parades for the American newspapers. It's still early, and if we hurry, we can get a good spot right up in front. If you come with me, you won't miss a thing," Kim said when the noise abated enough that he could be heard. "Poincaré is going to speak. There'll be parades, celebrations . . ."

"I'd like to—I truly would—but I have to work. We're terribly busy!" Nicole said, not even trying to conceal her regret. The interval when the din of Paris had prevented them from speaking had been just long enough to sober her up, to bring her back down to earth, to the thought of the clients she had struggled so hard to draw to her shop, to the realities of the rent and the wages she owed, to the piles of dresses, half-finished, waiting inside for her. "Everyone who can has ordered a Redon dress in anticipation of the parties and dinners and balls that will mark the Armistice," Nicole said, exaggerating the extent of her business just as Kim had exaggerated when he said that he was covering the Armistice for the American newspapers; he was, in fact, in Paris on trial, and he always crossed his fingers when he sent off a story. He was looking forward to the security of a regular job. "It's going to be a very long day," Nicole continued. "Very long and very busy . . ."

"Play hooky," Kim begged. "Madame Redon will make do without you for a few hours."

"Not really," she said, and smiled again, that lovely, remarkable, vivacious smile. She smiled with intensity, with great energy, with headlong abandon. Kim had never seen such a transforming smile. In repose, she was exceptionally pretty. When she smiled, she was unforgettable.

"Then later," he begged. "I won't give you up. I won't

let you get away!" Kim spoke with passionate intensity, as if his life depended on her answer. "What time will you be finished with work?"

"At eight," she said, deciding at that moment not to stay until midnight as she so often did. This was Armistice Day. She deserved time off, too, just like the rest of the world.

"At eight," he confirmed. "Here, keep the champagne," he said. "It's my personal guarantee that I'll be back!" He gave her the bottle and as she took it from him, she suddenly looked at something in the street behind him. Kim turned to see what it was. A gray-and-black Rolls Royce had pulled up to the curb and a distinguished-looking man in his early thirties emerged.

"Monsieur Xavier," she said. "Good morning."

"And a good morning to you, Mademoiselle Redon," the man said with an anxiety in his tone that Kim tried to interpret. "The world is at peace now," the man said. "I propose we decree our own private armistice as well."

She let him take her by the arm and usher her into the shop. The heavy door closed silently behind them. Kim, realizing his mistake, blushed scarlet. She was the *owner* of the shop! *She* was Nicole Redon!

"Oh, hell," he muttered to himself, looking at the limousine, the uniformed chauffeur already busy with a chamois, removing invisible specks from the long hood. "How can I compete with that?"

2.

Kim spent the day walking around Paris, observing and listening. It was cold and frost clung to the twigs of Paris's famous chestnut trees, bare now in November, and to the blades of grass in the squares and *places* and parks, glinting like millions of tiny diamonds in the thin winter sunlight. Along the parade route on the Champs-Elysées the reviewing stands, erected by carpenters who had worked all night long sawing and hammering, were each named after a town or province in Alsace-Lorraine, once again French after the blood of thousands of young men had been spilled across the width of the continent. In the place de la Concorde, where the fountains spurted forth for the first time in a long time, Kim noted that the sandbags which protected the statues of Renown and Mercury were studded with rusted German helmets and bayonets, and that behind the walls of the Tuileries captured German airplanes stood in a straight formation as if lined up ready to take off. Every statue and every monument of Paris, all its lampposts even, were festooned with flags and bunting and garlands of greens. And the noise! Squadrons of planes wheeled overhead, the roaring of their engines competing with the pealing of church bells and the blaring of horns and the joyous shouts of the citizens and guests of Paris.

In an expensive restaurant near the Bourse, Kim overheard stockbrokers talking about how peace would cause the value of shares to go up. In a butcher's shop on the rue Mouffetard a housewife and the butcher talked happily about the end of the wartime specialty Parisians called Belgian *paté*. The recipe called for horse meat and rabbit meat in equal proportions: that is to say, one horse to one rabbit. On the rue St.-Denis the bored expressions on the faces of the streetwalkers seemed to say that, Armistice or no Armistice, it was business as usual. A woman sat on the curb in the Jewish quarter near the place des Vosges. When Kim asked if she was all right and if he could do anything to help, she simply handed him the black-bordered announcement of the death of her son, which had arrived in the mail that very morning, the morning of the first day of peace. In the Marché aux Puces dealers spread out their wares on blankets, drank red wine, and ignored business.

At four o'clock, starved, Kim stopped by the Deux Magots, where he ran into Gus Leggett, who offered to buy him lunch. Gus, scion of a midwestern banking family, a tall, solidly built man in his twenties, already running to well-fed flabbiness, was establishing a literary press in Paris and he asked Kim how his stories were going.

"Fine! Just fine!" Kim said, not mentioning the rejection slips that were piling up. It was against his principles to tell the truth to publishers. He might have been very young and very inexperienced, but *that* he had already learned.

"When are you going to let me read them? Remember, you promised I'd have first look."

"Unfortunately, I have to earn a living," Kim said. "I always have to interrupt myself to do journalism."

"You shouldn't waste your talent on journalism," Gus said. Gus had always been bookish, much to the disappointment of his banker father. More than anything, Gus wanted to be like Kim Hendricks: literary but also totally male.

"You've never read a word I've written," Kim said. "How do you know I have any talent?"

"For one thing, I can smell it," Gus said, tapping his nose with a forefinger. "For another, it's obvious even in your journalism."

Kim shrugged, uncomfortable as always at direct praise. Most of the time he was totally convinced of his own talent, had an absolutely religious faith in it. At other times, though, he thought he was a fraud, no better than the "poets" and "novelists" who sat around in cafés complaining that the world didn't recognize the genius of the poems and books they never quite got around to writing.

"Where are you living?" Gus asked. "I'll come by and read your stories. You won't even have to take them out of your apartment."

"I'm staying in a hotel. A real fleabag. Anyway," Kim said, patting his jacket pocket, "I'm returning to New York day after tomorrow. Sally and I are getting married Christmas and both families expect me back in time for Thanksgiving."

"Too bad," said Gus. "You really ought to stay in Paris and find out what life is all about."

"*The Sun* finally gave in and agreed to hire me. I intend to live in New York and find out what life is all about right there," Kim said. Since he'd left Yale to volunteer for front-line service in 1916, he'd had no place to call home. He was looking forward to a spell of stability.

"New York isn't Paris!" Gus said. "Paris is the only place for literary men."

"Maybe one day, if I can afford it, Sally and I will live here," Kim said. "Anyway, thanks for lunch." He had had garlic sausages and potatoes and white wine—all delicious. "I've got to get along. I'm doing an article on Armistice Day here in Paris and there's still a lot I want to see."

"By-by," Gus said. "Don't forget to look me up if you and your wife ever get to Paris. I've rented an office on the Left Bank, the rue du Dragon, so drop by . . ."

Kim promised he would, and as he soaked up the sights and sounds of the celebrating city, he began to compose mentally the story he would send back to New York. As the words came to him and the story began to take shape, conveying the sights and sounds and emotions of the day, he began to feel confident and strong, and he revised his opinion about being able to compete with the suave gentleman in the Rolls Royce. With his talent and his ambition, he decided, he could compete with anyone. And the more he thought about her, the more he was enthralled and mesmerized by this dazzling, sweet-smelling, golden Mademoiselle Redon, who at such an early age already had an elegant shop, was not above sweeping her own sidewalk, and had let him flounder around in his own mistake, making a fool of himself. Calling her a battleaxe! He blushed every time he thought about it.

From time to time he thought about Sally and felt guilty, but the exhilaration of the day, the confidence he had gained from Gus's interest in his work, and above all and irresistibly, the power of the rapturous emotion that Nicole Redon had evoked in him made it easy to brush away the dampening fingers of guilt.

This was Paris, the city of love! The war was over and the world was celebrating. He was young and he was still single and his whole life was ahead of him—a life he planned to share with Sally. A once-in-a-lifetime romantic fling with a bittersweet ending built in from the beginning wouldn't hurt. In fact, as a writer who wanted to experience all the richness and all the pleasure and the pain of life, he owed it to himself. He would make everything more than even to Sally and, at ease in his soul, Kim spent the day on a cloud, a lovely, invisible cloud scented with the memory of her perfume. It made him inexpressibly happy that every time he looked at his watch it was a little closer to eight o'clock.

3.

Roland Xavier was a rich man and the war had made him even richer. His mills all over France manufactured the materials that had clothed the troops of Europe. Since the beginning of the war the mills had worked twenty-four hours a day, spinning out a river of fabric and an ocean of gold, and Nicole wondered what kind of armistice he had come to propose to her. They had, after all, stopped speaking to each other a year ago.

In 1917 Nicole had started a small shop in Biarritz. Before that she had been employed at a milliner's shop there and she had made herself a dress of jersey adapted from the linen duster she wore to protect her own clothes while working with the feathers, plumes, ribbons and flowers. The milliner's clients had admired Nicole's simple little dress and had asked her to make copies for them. Nicole, who was hardworking and ambitious, had decided to try. But she needed fabric and she needed to buy it at wholesale.

She went to Paris, making her way through the countryside at some risk to herself, since the war was then at its height, and brashly knocked on the door of Tissus Xavier, even then one of the biggest mills in France. Roland Xavier spent a minute and a half with this girl from the provinces and then turned her over to one of his salesmen—not even, Nicole was acutely aware, to his *head* salesman—and she was shown all the bolts no one else wanted. Nicole, who had always lied about her past from the moment she left home, was accustomed to castoffs, to making do with what others did not want.

A knitted woolen fabric called jersey was one nobody wanted. The inventor had thought it might be used in underwear, in nightshirts. It was cheap enough to make with the newly invented knitting machine, but cheapness seemed to be its only virtue. People complained that it was too scratchy, that it itched; they feared it would hike up, that it would bag at the seat, that the elbows and knees would stretch. The color was considered ugly, a beige that reminded people of the drab clothes of ditch diggers and truck drivers. No one wanted jersey. It did not sell but lay in bolts, taking up space. Nicole wanted to buy Xavier's entire stock; the salesman hesitated. Nicole Redon was unknown to the House of Xavier. More to the point, her credit rating was unknown to them. A little boutique in Biarritz, probably bought by a lover as a hobby for his mistress, was hardly impressive to Roland Xavier, who was used to supplying the important couture houses of France: Doucet, Worth, Poiret. No, the salesman informed Nicole, she would not be able to place an order for the entire lot of jersey. She insisted. She insisted to the point that she was once again ushered into the presence of Roland Xavier.

"I want to buy the entire inventory of your jersey," Nicole said.

"Do you have the money?"

"I will have it in ten days."

"Good. Then in ten days you may buy the fabric."

"But I will be in Biarritz in ten days," said Nicole. "I have my shop. I have to be there to serve my clients."

"Your clients are women?" asked Xavier, a solid man with a distinguished mustache and clear brown eyes.

"Of course," said Nicole, not comprehending the meaning behind Xavier's question.

"This jersey was intended for use by men," he said. "It has not been the success we imagined. Men won't wear it. The hand is too hard; it is considered stiff. What makes you think women will wear it?"

"Because I wear it myself and what I wear my clients want to wear." Nicole had bought a few yards of the jersey at retail and had made the dress for herself from it, lining it with silk to make it hang properly and to give it softness on the inside. She had cut it cleverly in such a way that, with the stability lent by the silk lining, it fell naturally and becomingly on the body, without bagging or hiking.

"Well, perhaps in Biarritz," said Xavier, not at all convinced. "Maybe in a resort for a short season."

"Then you'll sell me all the bolts?" asked Nicole.

"Oh, but no," said Xavier. "We have already established that you don't have the money."

"I told you I will have the money. In ten days."

"Then in ten days you may have the fabric." Xavier was irritated and bored with the argument. It involved such a small amount of money and it was taking up such a large amount of his valuable time.

"You're a coward, not a businessman!" Although her words were insulting, her voice was light and feminine. The effect was oddly charming. "You're really afraid to take the slightest risk, aren't you?"

"Look, mademoiselle—" He stopped. He didn't remember her name, didn't even remember if his secretary had introduced them. "How much money do you have? Right now, I mean, not ten days from now."

Nicole took her wallet out. There were forty francs, not counting her fare back to Biarritz.

"It's enough for three bolts," said Xavier. "and at that I'm giving you a bargain."

"What bargain?" asked Nicole. "That fabric, that jersey, sits there unsold. You're not giving me a bargain. You've found money out of what would otherwise have been a dead loss."

"Look, mademoiselle," Xavier said, exasperated and not even making the polite pretense of trying to remember her name, "do you or don't you want to buy the fabric?"

For an answer, Nicole put the franc notes on his desk. "I'll be back," she said.

She was. Six weeks later. And again, two months after that.

22

"I'm glad you have been so successful with your dresses," said Xavier. "And I'm glad you've finally worn one to Paris. I've been curious about what kind of dress you could make from wool jersey."

Thousand-pleated bodices and point d'esprit veiling, waists nipped in to the choking point, ruffles and ruching, embroidery and lace—that was the fashion. That was what women wanted. Not a drab and unglamorous woolen jersey originally intended for men's underwear! How could you bind a waistline in a fabric that stretched like jersey? And how could the bust darts be placed in such a fabric? Not to mention the problems of ruffling and ruching it, of embroidering and decorating it? Well, now he knew the answers! There were no ruffles and no ruching on the bodice because there was no bodice; instead, the neckline was cut into a vee that showed more skin than was really considered respectable. The question of bust darts had been similarly solved: there were no bust darts! Daringly, the jersey dress showed the shape of the wearer's breasts. The problem of the waistline had been solved more or less the same way—the dress simply followed the body, curving in slightly to indicate the waist of the wearer beneath, but no seam, no tight indentation, marked it, and further, from what Xavier could see, there was no corset beneath! Poiret, of course, had dispensed with the corset, but Poiret's creations, extravagant and opulent, with an exotic Oriental feeling about them, distracted the viewer's eyes from the absence of that essential undergarment. Not so the dress of Mlle. Redon—by now Roland Xavier knew her name well—the jersey dress, undecorated, unembroidered, unruched and unruffled, focused the attention on the body of the woman who wore it.

And that skirt! Poiret, who was Xavier's idol among designers—the most imaginative, the most daring, the most modern, the most inventive—had raised skirts. He had allowed the foot to show. Mlle. Redon's skirt bared not only the foot but the ankle and the calf of the leg as well. Shocking! But on Mlle. Redon, also intriguing . . .

"Your dress is certainly—" Xavier groped for a word "—different. But I still have a question. That color. It's so . . . plain. Don't your clients object?"

"Oh, no, not at all. I gave it an exotic name. I call it 'kasha.' It's a Russian word for a kind of buckwheat grain," explained Nicole. "And when I point out to them how neutral the color is and how it goes with everything they already own, they immediately see how practical it is."

"Very clever," said Xavier, admiringly. "And I am certainly glad you have been so successful with it," he repeated, "but I can not sell you any more jersey. As you know, I have no more left to sell. You have already bought all of it."

"Then manufacture some more on your knitting machines," said Nicole. "I will buy as much as you can make."

"We have beautiful fabrics—flannel and worsted, taffetas and gabardines, jacquards and hopsacking. Make your dress out of other fabrics."

"I am famous for my jersey dress. I don't *want* any other fabric," Nicole said. "Why should I use the same fabrics other designers do? I was the one who bought up your whole inventory of jersey. I was the one who made it fashionable. I bought it when you couldn't give it away. Now you are in a position to return the favor. I'd like you to make more—to my order. I would like the weight made heavier for winter and I would like to have some samples dyed—rose, garnet, coral—before I place my final order."

Roland Xavier was impressed by her confidence and also highly dubious of her claims. Fashionable? Perhaps among her seasonal clients in Biarritz, but in Paris

24

no one had ever heard of her. And then to make demands— A heavy gauge for winter! Colors! The expense of readjusting the machines and the costs of dyeing, no doubt, to be assumed by the House of Xavier. It was too much! And in any event, the war was on! Tissus Xavier was selling fabric to the army, tens of thousands of yards. He would have to be insane to start production of a small order of woolen jersey for Mlle. Redon. And he was not insane. He was a Frenchman; he was a businessman.

Roland Xavier held up his hand, palm out, to stop her in midsentence.

"The answer is no. It is not worth my while to manufacture for you. You're not big enough and you're not important enough for the House of Xavier. We are outfitting an army. I will not stop everything to make a few bolts for you."

"I bought fabric you couldn't give away!" Nicole was furious. Above all, she detested being treated like a nobody. Being told she wasn't big enough or important enough—it brought back all the insults and taunts she had endured as a child. It flooded her with a feeling of insignificance, and she became outraged. "You take my good money for a fabric you can't give away. I turn it into a success and now you won't make me more. Money! It's all you care about! Money! You're throwing away your future for money! You're an ingrate! A coward! Small-minded and unimaginative!" Nicole hurled her anger and her accusations at him. She did not notice him ring a bell at the side of his desk.

"Please show Mlle. Redon out," said Xavier to his secretary, speaking as calmly as he could in the midst of her outburst.

"I'll never speak to you again. I'll never buy from you again. You'll be sorry," were her last words as the secretary escorted her to the street.

And for a year, Nicole Redon and Roland Xavier did

not speak. She was busy making her little dress, cutting until her hands ached and sewing until her fingers began to bleed, keeping her own ledgers, supervising a few employees when she was able to afford to hire them, working day and night, struggling, succeeding and failing and then working some more until she succeeded again. And he was busy—busy with the tidal waves of his millions.

Roland Xavier did not give her a thought until 1918. A man who took his business very seriously, he subscribed to all the fashion magazines. The French magazines, *La Gazette du Bon Ton* and the *Journal des Dames et des Modes*, had stopped publishing in 1914 when the war began, and in the interim Roland took the American publications instead. In the September 1918 issue of *Harper's Bazaar*, he had seen the sketch the Paris fashion correspondent Margaret Berryman had sent to the New York editorial offices. Nicole Redon's "charming chemise" dress was, Roland saw, essentially the same dress he'd seen on Nicole a year and more before. In the interlude it had come to look less peculiar.

Now that the Armistice had been signed, there would no longer be armies to clothe. Roland Xavier decided it would be well worth his while to call on the stubborn but charming Mlle. Redon.

By Armistice Day Nicole was just establishing her Paris shop on the rue Montaigne, still struggling along from month to month but having her first taste of success in the world's most fashion-conscious city. Thanks to the sketch in *Harper's Bazaar*, women were going out of their way to seek out Nicole's small shop to order a "charming chemise dress." When they got there, they found a second Redon invention, a specialty Nicole had begun to make since moving to Paris. At the end of the war, Paris was under bombardment by German long-range cannons. The Big Berthas shelled the city at night, under the cover of darkness. The sirens sounded and the inhabitants of Paris fled from their beds to the shelters, the *abris*, that dotted the city. Nightgowns were too flimsy, too revealing, impractical and dangerous besides, with their long voluminous skirts, for clambering up and down poorly lit cellar steps. Nicole, responding to the problem, designed a functional and chic garment adapted from men's pajamas and, daringly, called it just that: pajamas. The trouser bottoms were clear of the ground, allowing women easy movement, even climbing down steep, dark cellar stairs. The tops preserved modesty and were also flatteringly cut. At first Nicole made her "pajamas" only in black, but soon enough—since they were immediately successful—in scarlet, sapphire and magenta. Thanks to Nicole Redon's pajamas, Parisiennes, who had always set the style for the world, continued to set a style while fleeing from German attack. By the time of the Armistice, Nicole and her elegant, practical pajamas were being noticed and talked about.

Bringing a gift of impossible-to-buy real coffee, Roland Xavier complimented Nicole on her new shop, on the originality of her designs, and told her that Tissus Xavier depended on the creative genius of the designers of Paris. He told her he wanted to forget their past harsh words and expressed the hope that she would reciprocate in a spirit of compromise. Nicole, in turn, proudly showed off her new pajamas, accepted Roland's gift and compliments, and ultimately agreed to overlook the insults they had once traded. Firmly forgetting that they had vowed never again to speak to each other, Nicole and Roland began to do business again.

As she spoke to Roland Xavier about samples and dye lots, Nicole's mind kept returning to the American she had met that day, whose name, it occurred to her, she didn't even know. He exuded an almost tangible energy. He was the kind of man who could do anything he set his mind to. He seemed masculine and strong, but sensitive too. He was captivating and intriguing and Nicole was captivated and intrigued. Her own lover, Cyril, a White Russian émigré, was in America and she had no idea when she would see him next. She had been lonely for months, devoting herself like a nun to her work. And now she had spent most of Armistice Day on a seesaw, sometimes certain she would see her American again at eight, other times equally certain he had simply been caught up in the feverish celebration and that she'd never set eyes on him again.

Nicole worked hard all day long, pinning and fitting, dealing with clients and seamstresses, negotiating with Roland, approving each and every garment that left the shop carefully swathed in white tissue, giving orders and taking them, too, talking, joking, gossiping, bargaining and all the time eight o'clock was never very far from her mind.

She wondered whether she'd see him again or not. She honestly had no idea.

4.

At the stroke of eight he stood on the doorstep of her shop, almost staggering from the weight of the gifts he'd brought.

"Here's more champagne," he said, "so we won't run out!" His left arm cradled several bottles of champagne —at least half a dozen of them!—and his right arm clasped masses of red and white carnations—at least a field of them!—bound by blue ribbons. The colors of France—and America. "And a few flowers too."

"Oh!" said Nicole, speechless.

"May I come in?" he asked, practically hidden behind his offerings.

"Yes, yes. Please," she said, still overwhelmed. She held the heavy door open for him and for a moment as he crossed the threshold they looked at each other, wondering what they had gotten themselves into.

"You're even prettier than I remember," he said.

She smiled at the compliment, her heart racing.

"And you're even prettier when you smile," he added, setting the champagne and the flowers down on a glass-topped table. He glanced around at Nicole's shop. The clients had all gone and the small showroom, carpeted in ivory and mirrored on three sides, was empty. From the workroom behind the velvet-curtained door to the rear came the clack of sewing machines as the extra seamstresses Nicole had hired to take care of the sudden rush in business worked far into the night to finish the dresses due for delivery the next day. They were alone in the small showroom but aware of the presence of others nearby. It made them less self-conscious with each other.

"It's very elegant," he said, "but comfortable. When I was young and my aunts took me shopping with them, I was always uncomfortable." He remembered small, spindly chairs and fragile tables and compared them with the generously sized, deeply upholstered divans and solid tables painted white with fitted glass tops and great big ashtrays.

"Men usually feel that way. I specifically decided to make my shop comfortable for men. After all, men are important to my little business. Husbands, lovers, admirers who pay the bills . . . I wanted them to feel at ease, too," said Nicole. As she arranged the carnations in every vase and pail she could find, they filled the room with their spicy scent and Kim opened one of the bottles of champagne. The cork came out with a slight *pop* and he poured the sparkling wine into two glasses. He already knew what the toast would be.

"*Vive la France!*" he said.

"*Vive la France!*" she repeated, and they sipped.

"*Vive la paix!*" he added.

"*Vive la paix!*" she repeated after him, and again they sipped the pale, sparkling wine in a toast.

"*Vive l'amour!*" he said, looking directly at her. He noticed that in certain lights her topaz eyes seemed to turn gold. This time she did not repeat his words but flushed and looked away.

"Now, let's go," Kim said when they finished their champagne. "Paris is waiting for us!"

He took the two glasses, holding them upside down by their stems, and took the bottle, holding it carefully by the neck so as not to warm the wine with the heat of his hand, and stepped toward the door, ready to leave.

"You're bringing the glasses with us?" she asked, amazed. She had never heard of such a thing! "And the wine?"

"Naturally! Who wants to celebrate without champagne?" Kim said. "Anyway, from tonight on, you'd better get used to it. We're going to open another bottle every day."

"And when we run out?" she asked, astonished by this unpredictable American.

"We'll never run out!" he promised, and held the door for her with his elbow.

Paris was a feast set out for them, happy people on every street, the sounds of joyous celebration coming from every bar, every café, from every lighted window. Paris had the electric air of a city that had survived a terrible ordeal and was now settling down with exhilarated anticipation to the comforts and pleasures of peace.

Kim took Nicole to the places he knew: to the Dingo Café, where they met Picasso, ruggedly handsome with his dark hair, strong features and animal magnetism; to the Closerie des Lilas, where Ezra Pound announced that he was already drunk and intended to get even drunker; to the rue de Fleurus, where Miss Stein and Miss Toklas welcomed Kim and fussed over him as if he were a favorite son, pouring clear mirabelle into his glass and offering one delicious small tidbit after another to please him. Nicole took Kim to the places she knew: to Fouquet's, where they had icy oysters—Kim ordered a second dozen and, to Nicole's amazement, ate them all himself; to Maxim's, where they couldn't afford a table but had a drink at the bar, and where Nicole, although she couldn't afford being a regular, was, because of her chic, welcomed by the owner, who understood the importance of elegant women to the success and glamour of his restaurant; and to a private party given by a White Russian Princess, a client introduced to Nicole by Cyril.

A buffet laden with *zakuskie* of caviar and smoked fish, cold and warm meats and poultry, beets, cucumbers, potatoes, eggplants and cabbage in spiced and seasoned salads, fruits and pastries, reminded the guests of the Imperial Russia that had stopped existing with the storming of the Winter Palace. Entire bottles of vodka had been frozen into blocks of ice and it was considered bad manners, Nicole told Kim, not to eat as many of the *zakuskie* and drink as much of the vodka as humanly possible. Kim, who said he didn't want to insult the hostess, proceeded to taste all the food and to drink a staggering quantity of vodka without showing the slightest effect. The party was noisy and crowded and Russian was heard more than French.

"Everyone I've been introduced to has a title," Kim told Nicole when they were alone for a moment. "Prince this. Count that. It's like a Tolstoy novel."

"Titles, yes, but no country of their own. No roots. No legitimacy any more," said Nicole. "I don't envy them. They've lost their past."

As Kim, who despite himself was impressed with all the nobility, was about to comment on Nicole's clear-eyed logic, the hostess appeared with another guest, a lean, supremely elegant Englishman.

"Nicole, this is the Duke of Mellany. He complimented me on my evening pajamas and said he wanted to order some for his wife. I told him I'd introduce him to the designer immediately."

The Duke, tall, blond, blue-eyed and fair-skinned, was very, very handsome in a very, very English way. He gave off echoes of polo fields and croquet lawns, huge country houses and exclusive men's clubs, Gainsborough portraits and the royal enclosure at Ascot. He bowed slightly from the waist and kissed Nicole's hand. He made the courtly gesture seem perfectly natural, politely correct, and yet intimate all at the same time. "Nicole Redon," he said. "I'm pleased to meet you. You're very talented."

"Thank you," said Nicole, thinking, irrationally, that it was disappointing the Duke was married, although she couldn't imagine what possible difference it could make to her. "And this is . . ." She turned to Kim to introduce him to the Duke.

"McKimskovitch," Kim said, bowing slightly from the waist and speaking before Nicole could finish the introduction. "Professor Feodor Ivan McKimskovitch."

"A professor," repeated the Duke. It was impossible to

tell from his tone exactly what he thought but Nicole imagined that he seemed impressed. "Of what?"

"I'm an authority on freshwater biology," Kim said. "Frogs and tadpoles. Their life cycles are fascinating. They duplicate the life cycles of humans but in a much shorter time span. The future can be read in the life cycle of a frog."

"Really?" asked the Duke, almost drawling. "Has a frog in one of your laboratories ever turned into a prince?" There was an edge to the question and Nicole sensed with pleased surprise that the Duke of Mellany was attracted to her and that Kim also sensed it. Kim Hendricks and the Duke of Mellany were fighting over her and it warmed her enormously, as it always did, to be found desirable.

"I work in American laboratories," answered Kim. "there are no titles in American laboratories. We're very democratic."

"I'm sure," said the Duke, not the slightest bit ruffled. He turned to Nicole. "Mademoiselle, I will send my wife to you for one of your beautiful pajama outfits. Perhaps our paths will cross again." He bowed slightly once again and left Nicole and Kim alone.

"Professor McKimskovitch!" Nicole said. "You were outrageous!"

"I thought it was time to bring the party back down to earth," Kim said. "Now let's have a final vodka and find something more egalitarian."

Nicole agreed and they left the party as several of the guests, sufficiently fueled by vodka, began a noisy saber dance, brandishing real sabers. Nicole and Kim abandoned themselves to the city and to each other. Between dances and drinks and snatches of conversation with others they encountered, they told each other about themselves.

Kim spoke of his father with love and of his mother,

who had died when he was ten, with adoration. He told her about his childhood: summers in Maine, the thrill of fishing for bass and landlocked salmon in Moosehead Lake, canoeing on the mirror surfaces and sudden white waters of the Allagash; he told her of his current job as a newspaper reporter and of his dream to become a famous novelist. He told her he had left college to volunteer for General Pershing's American Expeditionary Forces, but when she asked him about his slight limp he evaded the question.

Nicole spoke about herself: she told him that her father was a real gentleman, a man who had lived on his inherited income and had never had to work a day in his life, an avid sportsman who had taught her to hunt and fish, and a man devoted to charity. Her mother, she said, was religiously devout and a strict disciplinarian. She told him that she had first revealed her talent for design when she decorated hats for her mother with veiling and egret plumes, and how her mother's friends had asked her to make hats for them too. She described her parents' opposition to her going into trade and how she had strong-headedly risked their disapproval by opening a shop in fashionable Biarritz, where they spent the season. She confided her dream that she would be the only designer in Paris to make modern clothes. No one, she said, made clothes that were appropriate for liberated postwar women. All the important designers were men and, since they didn't wear the dresses they designed, how could they know how they fit and how they functioned?

All the things they talked about revealed them a little more to each other, one petal of confidence unfolding after another.

There were also things they did not speak of. Kim did not talk of his engagement to Sally Cushman or the big wedding planned for Christmas, the invitations already sent out, the acceptances and regrets already counted. Nicole did not talk about Cyril, her lover and best friend, the man who had lent her the money to start her Biarritz shop and later her Paris shop, who was now in America but who wrote constantly to say that he couldn't wait for the war to be over so that he could return to Paris and to her. It was too soon for certain assumptions to be made and too much emotion had passed between them too quickly for every intimate fact to be revealed.

At four o'clock in the morning they found themselves in les Halles, the great city market already beginning to stir with deliverers of fruits and vegetables, eggs and poultry, lamb and beef, fish and shellfish, butter and cheese, bringing in their fresh produce from every corner of France. Over bowls of onion soup topped with strands of savory melted cheese they admitted to each other that they didn't want the evening to end. The thunderbolt that had struck them both that morning still gripped them, mesmerized and enthralled, in its thrilling sway. They had come too far with each other just to say goodnight and part.

"I'm living in a real dump," Kim said, "a hotel just off the Madeleine, and it's not too far from being a *maison de passe*. I'd be embarrassed to bring you there . . ."

"I live on the Ile St.-Louis. We can walk there from here," Nicole said, and when they finished their meal they walked through Paris, the dawn just beginning to break. They walked separately, acutely conscious of not touching each other, not speaking very much, crossing the rue de Rivoli and continuing along the Right Bank of the Seine until they came to the pont Louis-Philippe. Midway across the bridge, Nicole shivered involuntarily and Kim took off his jacket and put it around her shoulders. Then, moving as if propelled by the identical, no longer resistible impulse, they reached for each other's hands in the same motion and at the same moment as the Quai de Bourbon became the Quai d'Anjou and, holding hands, walked silently until they reached Nicole's building on the rue de Bretonvilliers. As she reached in her bag for her key, they suddenly found themselves in a deep embrace, clinging to each other as if to life itself, and they abandoned themselves to the haunting emotions each had bottled up all day and all night long, sharing their first kiss. Then, gradually tearing themselves away from each other, their lips still tasting of the other's, they let themselves into her apartment.

Nicole's apartment occupied the third floor of the building and overlooked the treetops of the garden below and, beyond them, the waters of the river itself. The apartment's best feature was the high, balconied windows that received direct light from the sun as well as reflections of the gently rippling waters of the Seine. The living room had a golden glow all day long which turned to apricot and red and finally mauve as the sun set in the evening. The room had been lacquered a glossy cream, most effective for capturing the beautiful morning-to-evening light of the sun and the river.

"What a beautiful view!" said Kim. "It's like being on a boat right in the middle of the city!"

"I took the apartment because of that view and the light," said Nicole. "I need light and sun. I can't live without it. The furniture, though, is best forgotten."

"You're right!" said Kim, sitting in an uncomfortable late-Empire sofa with a carved, gilded frame that poked him in the back of the neck if he leaned back too far. The chairs, some overstuffed and fringed, others pseudo Louis-the-something, were obvious leftovers, and an immense oak table that looked as if it weighed a thousand pounds was too big for the room and stuck out into the middle of it. "Whose furniture is this? Not yours . . ."

"The landlord's," laughed Nicole. "All I can say in its favor is that it's cheap enough. I really can't afford any more right now. All my money goes into my business and I don't have much to spend on myself. My parents don't approve of my being in business and refuse to send me a penny. So I struggle along—not that it bothers me. I hardly spend any time here except to sleep and change my clothes. I'm at my shop all day long."

"It reminds me of a lot of apartments in Greenwich Village. I guess landlords' furniture is the same the world over. Anyway, poverty is a respectable stage for creative people and I personally approve of it," he said. He did not tell Nicole that his father was a respected estate lawyer with a well-connected Wall Street firm and that, although hardly rich on the scale of the Goulds and Vanderbilts, his family was certainly comfortable enough to have sent him to private schools and to Yale, where his father had been educated. "But one day I'm going to be rich. Not that money itself means a lot to me, but freedom does. I want to be rich enough to write exactly the way I want to write without having to change a word for anybody!"

"One day you'll be rich and famous. You have the talent. I can sense it," Nicole said. Her words echoed Gus Leggett's. Even people who didn't know Kim very well sensed he was destined to be someone special. It glowed out from him like a beacon.

"But I'm not now. Not famous and not rich," Kim said. "Does that matter to you?" he asked. He was thinking of the man in the Rolls Royce. The Duke of Mellany. The Grand Duke Cyril he had overheard the hostess mention to Nicole.

"It doesn't matter," said Nicole, and they really couldn't have said how they got into each other's arms but that didn't matter either. It was something destiny had ordained and there was no point thinking about it, talking about it, or questioning it.

Much later, in the warmth of her bedroom, lightly perfumed with her scent, Kim said, "Nothing like this ever happened to me. When I first saw you it was . . . well . . . I don't know how to explain what I felt. My breath was taken away. My heart stopped. I felt as if the earth had stopped."

The same thing happened to me! thought Nicole. *I thought I'd been struck by a thunderbolt. I couldn't think. I couldn't speak. I couldn't swallow.*

"I was afraid of being too forward," Kim continued, "I thought you'd tell me to go to hell. I thought you'd think I was crazy. But I knew I had to talk to you, to get to know you although I felt I already knew you even though it was obviously impossible . . ." he trailed off, still not knowing how to put into words the feelings that had overwhelmed him. "I hope you didn't think I was an obnoxious American."

"Not at all," said Nicole, smiling her lovely smile. "Although, frankly, I could have done without the 'battleaxe.' "

"Can you feel me blush?" Kim asked, guiding her hand to his cheek. "I still blush when I think of it. You really must have thought I was awful."

"Not for one second," said Nicole. "I didn't think you were awful at all. Not for one second. I thought you were . . ." She paused to collect her thoughts, not wanting to give away too much of the feeling that still threatened to carry her away in a rushing, irresistible current of emotion. If she did, she would be lost forever. "Well, I thought you were . . ."

"Were what?" Kim prompted, wanting to know what she thought of him, knowing that his candid solicitation of a compliment was charming.

"Oakie-doakie!" she said, pronouncing with her French accent the all-purpose word the Yanks used constantly. It made them both laugh and, once the laughing was done, surrender once again to the astonishing passion that neither could nor wished to escape.

The steamship ticket became his enemy. Without even telling Nicole it existed, Kim went to the steamship company's office on a street just off the Champs-Elysées and exchanged it for a new one: he would leave Paris on the second of December. It was as much time as his conscience would permit him. He sent Sally and his father the same cable: everything was fine but his work was taking longer than he had anticipated. He regretted missing Thanksgiving but would be home in plenty of time for the wedding and Christmas. With an easily made payment of guilt, Kim bought himself three weeks with Nicole.

Every evening at eight he picked her up at her shop on the rue Montaigne. Paris was coming back to life: there were taxis, lights, flowers, parties, an air of ease and gaiety. Nights, Kim and Nicole explored the city and each other; days, inspired by their nights, they explored themselves. They were both talented but young and inexperienced people; under each other's magic spell, they both blossomed.

Nicole burst with new ideas. Faithful to her wool jersey, she designed a cardigan jacket and two skirts: a narrow one and a pleated one. With a blouse, the three pieces made two complete outfits. Comfortable, easy-to-wear and unpretentious, the jersey suit was a grand success. And when Nicole quilted her jersey to make a warm but light coat, it seemed that every client had to have one for the coming cold weather. Nicole's little shop hummed with clients and orders and samples and extra seamstresses. In the two weeks following the Armistice, Nicole's business almost doubled.

While Nicole designed, Kim wrote. He had a brand-new idea and he had gotten it from Nicole. She had been telling him about the way she designed: "I made a rule for myself. I leave out everything everyone else insists on." Her words struck Kim with the force of a revelation, and he applied her rule to write his *Sun* articles and to rewrite a story that had been rejected several times. He left out everything writers—including himself—regularly insisted on. He left out lyrical descriptions of landscapes and sunsets, melodramatic examinations of emotional states, fancy language and high-flown philosophy. The adjectives went; the nouns and verbs stayed. Sitting all day long in a café, nursing a single cup of bitter coffee or a glass of wine, Kim honed down his stories until they were all action, all character, all movement. Gradually his stories became as strikingly and uniquely his as Nicole's designs were strikingly and uniquely hers. Kim pursued his experiment in a growing fever of creative and romantic excitement and he became addicted to the fever. He did not want to leave Paris; he did not want to leave Nicole. He never told her about the ticket that would take him away from her on the second. He had convinced himself that the second would never come.

"Who's the man in the Rolls Royce?" Kim asked at the end of their second week. The big car had been parked outside Nicole's shop when Kim had come by to pick her up that evening.

"Roland Xavier," Nicole answered. She was in the bathtub, her hair in a knot on top of her head, bubbles around her shoulders, her face shiny with the steam of the hot water. "I buy fabric from him. Although I don't know why. He charges me outrageous prices."

"And who's Cyril?" Kim asked. There was a chaise longue in Nicole's bathroom and Kim liked to keep her company while she bathed and dressed for the evening.

"How did you know about Cyril?" Nicole asked, the drift of Kim's questions now clear.

"Princess What's-her-name mentioned Cyril at her party. She said he's leaving America and returning to Paris. Is he . . ." Kim paused, knowing he had no right to ask what he was about to ask. "Is he someone special to you?"

"Yes. As a matter of fact, he is."

"How special?"

"Very special. Although it's really none of your business," Nicole said. "After all, I had a life before you arrived on my doorstep."

"You're right, of course," Kim said. He was silent for a moment and Nicole was unable to guess his mood. "The Duke of Mellany was interested in you," he finally said. When Nicole didn't answer, Kim said, "I guess I have a lot of competition."

Nicole didn't answer for a long time. Then very deliberately she said, "There doesn't have to be. Not if you don't want it."

Kim had had an extraordinary effect on Nicole. He behaved as if anything were possible, and that was a revelation to her. Perhaps it was because he was American and she was European, but she had taken it for granted that certain boundaries, certain defined limits, existed. Nicole had always thought in the back of her mind that one day she would give up her shop and get married. Her bold dream of being an important couturiere with her own *maison* frightened her; after all, no woman had ever done it alone. The things Kim said and the way he encouraged her made her think she was a fool to be frightened of her own dream.

Kim's personal extravagance was also a revelation: he did nothing in moderation. He either skipped meals or ate stupendous quantities; sometimes he wouldn't drink at all but once he started he'd drink all night long; he never made love to her just once but over and over as if he couldn't get enough of her; when he was writing he concentrated so fiercely that he didn't hear if she spoke but when they conversed he listened to her every word as if she were the only person in the world. To Kim, things were wonderful or terrible, irresistible or repulsive, black or white. With Kim limits did not exist. With Kim she had the universe to choose from. With Kim she could be anyone or do anything she wanted.

"There doesn't have to be any competition, Kim," she said in her soft, certain tone. "If you don't want any, you only have to tell me."

It was Kim's turn to be silent. She was offering herself to him and he wanted her. But he wasn't free. He had never told her about Sally. At first because it was too soon and there was no reason; later because too much had happened between them and he didn't know how. Besides, all along he had kept reminding himself that his adventure with Nicole was just that: an adventure. He had known about the bittersweet ending from the very beginning.

"It never dawned on me that . . . this . . . would happen," Kim said finally. He spoke slowly, carefully, afraid of the words of love he was on the very brink of speaking. Words, once uttered, from which there would be no return.

"What do you mean, 'this'?" Nicole prompted, trying to make it easy for him. She loved him—*Je t'aime* were the first words that had crossed her mind the very moment she had laid eyes on him—but she would never say it first. She wanted him to say it. She sensed—she *knew* —that he yearned to say it, that he yearned to tell her that he loved her. In a moment now, he would say the words. She waited, quietly.

"Us," Kim finally said after a long, thoughtful pause. He longed to say *"I love you"*—he almost said *"I love you"*—but he forced himself not to let the words escape. It wouldn't be right. Love was what he felt for Sally. *"I love you"* was supposed to be for Sally and only for Sally.

"And is 'this' so terrible? 'Us'?" asked Nicole. The sharp disappointment she felt at the harmless word "us" was physically painful. She was surprised that she could make her tone of voice so normal. "You sound as if it's a tragedy."

"No. Not at all. It's wonderful," Kim said, firmly shutting Sally out of his mind. "Wonderful!"

He held out a bath towel as Nicole stepped from the tub, and wrapped her in it, kissing her hot, shiny face, picking her up in his arms and carrying her into the bedroom, making love to her, knowing in his heart and soul *this* was love. Not the straitlaced emotion he felt for Sally. *This* sweet, magic, compelling, powerful, fragile, rapturous emotion was love. *I love you*, he thought, looking at her, drawn into her golden aura. *I love you.* The words pushed at him, battered at him, insisting on being said. He fought them, struggled against them, finally defeated them. Once said, they would carry him away, engulf him in a torrent of feeling in which he might lose himself and spin away, drowning.

"What are you thinking?" Nicole suddenly asked.

"Oh, nothing," he said. "Nothing."

Love, Nicole, the thunderbolt—whatever had happened to him had unleashed a gale of creativity. More pleased with the articles and the story he had written than with anything he had written before in his life, Kim decided to try a brand-new story. When he followed Nicole's rule the very act of writing was transformed for him. Before as he wrote he had imagined the praise and the compliments, thinking about what people would say and how impressed they would be. Now when he wrote he thought of nothing except the words and the story, losing himself in them. He would find himself moved, tearful, angry, excited, aroused, surprised, in response to the words he put down. "Kim Hendricks" disappeared; he became in turn a man or a woman, a teacher, a housewife, a child, a husband, a businessman, an artist, a criminal, a ship's captain. He thought that if he continued he would find a thousand people inside himself. He was excited, exhilarated, barely able to sleep at night.

"This must be good for me," he told Nicole. " 'Us.' "

"You say that as if you'd thought it might be bad for you."

"I always had the idea that . . . romance . . . would distract me from my work," said Kim. He would *not* say the word *love*. "I thought I wouldn't be able to think straight, never mind be able to write a coherent sentence. But it's just the opposite. I can concentrate better than ever."

"You had some strange ideas," Nicole said. She had known Kim for almost three weeks. They had spent days and nights together, never apart at night. She wondered what was going to happen. She thought about the future . . . their future. She waited for him to say something. He would, soon. It was the normal next step.

In the beginning, Kim had imagined the bittersweet moment of parting, the acidly romantic, aching farewell. Then he had forgotten, abandoning himself to an infinite present, an endless now. But just as he could not control a thunderbolt, he could not control the passage

44

of time. The first of December dawned, a bludgeon. Kim was quiet and withdrawn. He did not want to leave. He had never said a word about it to Nicole and he did not know how to tell her. Destiny had brought them together, necessity would tear them apart.

"You seem unhappy," Nicole said. They were walking —a familiar walk by now—from the rue Montaigne, across the Seine, to the Ile St.-Louis. Nicole had adopted the habit of wearing Kim's tweed jacket. She loved its warmth, its comfort, the way it made her feel protected and physically close to him even when they weren't touching. "Is something the matter?"

"No. Nothing," he said.

Nicole was about to say that she didn't believe him when he cut her off. "Something *is* the matter. I have to go home and I don't want to. I have to leave Paris and I don't want to. My father expects me home for Christmas. I'm running out of money. I start work at *The Sun* the first of the year. I practically begged for the job and they finally hired me and now I have to go and I don't want to leave. When I leave you it will be like dying."

"Leave?" Nicole repeated. She was shocked, barely able to comprehend what he was telling her. "When?"

"Tomorrow."

"Tomorrow!" Nicole looked as if she had been struck. Her eyes were flat and unfocused.

"Yes," said Kim. He got the ticket out of his pocket and showed it to her.

"You've known from the beginning! You've known all along!"

"Yes." Kim had not mentioned Sally. He felt slimy and shabby. Despicable.

"And you never told me! Why didn't you tell me! You knew right from the beginning that 'this' . . . 'us' . . . was just temporary. What you Americans call a fling! you could have told me! I could have protected myself. I would have known, too! Why did you let me think about a future? You led me on. Now you're going to leave me . . . just like that!" Nicole's amber eyes had come back to life. They glinted a dark, glittery gold and flashed with hurt and outrage. "What kind of man are you?"

"I was a coward," Kim said, ashamed, stung by her accusation, knowing he had no defense. "I believed in magic. I convinced myself that if I did not talk about today, today would never come."

"You've had your fling in Paris and now you're going home where it's safe and cozy and you have a job and a family waiting to take you in!" She moved away from him, walking parallel to him but refusing to look at him. "You'll waltz away and I'll be left. You'll have your memories and I'll have mine and we'll never see each other again! Is that it?"

"Don't say that!" Kim said. His voice was hoarse and tears stung his eyes. "Don't even think it!"

"What am I supposed to think?" Nicole asked, contempt and anger strangling her voice.

"Nicole!" The curt authority in his voice stopped her. He took her in his arms. She was stiff and resisted him. In broad daylight, on a public street, he crushed her to him until she stopped resisting his embrace. He thought if he held her tightly enough he would never have to let her go. When he had found Nicole, he had found himself. He would have to go home. He would have to find the words to tell Sally that, on the eve of their wedding, he had met someone, fallen in love . . . more than love . . .

"I'll come back to Paris. I'll come back to you. I swear . . ."

Early the next morning they were at the Gare de l'Est. The train would take Kim to Le Havre and the steamship

46

for New York. The conductor was making the final announcement of departure. The engine puffed, the whistle blew, and steam rushed out from the tracks. Kim and Nicole had run out of time. They had run out of words. Silent as a condemned man waiting for the executioner, Kim stood on the steps of the train, waiting for the inevitable moment of parting.

"Here! Take this!" he said suddenly. Swiftly, he pulled off his tweed jacket. By now it smelled of them both—masculine and feminine—and he put it around Nicole's shoulders. "Like the first bottle of champagne," he said. The train had jerked once, stopped, jerked forward a second, time. "It's my personal guarantee. I'll come back to Paris. I'll come back to you . . ."

The train lurched, sure of its motion now, picked up speed. He was gone and she was alone again.

The uncertainties of 1919 were over. America was going on the greatest, gaudiest spree in history.

—F. Scott Fitzgerald

CHAPTER TWO

1.

SALLY CUSHMAN WAS the first person Kim saw as he descended the gangplank of the *White Star*.

"Kim! Darling!" Sally waved excitedly and Kim waved back. She was wearing a beaver coat and her round face was rosy in the cool December air. Tendrils of hair had escaped from underneath her hat and blew freely in the open, windy docking area. She looked very young to Kim although she was only a year younger than he, very healthy and very American with her cornsilk blond hair and sky-blue eyes. As soon as Kim saw Sally she became real to him again and he understood why he had fallen in love with her. Nothing was going to be simple.

Sally held up a newspaper but she was too far away for

Kim to read the headline she pointed at. He wondered what had happened in the eight days it had taken the *White Star* to plow across the winter-gray Atlantic.

"*Allo, cherie!*" Kim called back, speaking French because he knew how much it pleased her and because it also pleased him. He liked to feel cosmopolitan, worldly. "*Allo, Sally, mon amour!*"

"Welcome home, Kim!" Lansing Hendricks, Kim's father, was next to Sally. He was an older version of Kim: the same height and the same graceful proportions; the remarkable blue eyes; the same strong, refined facial planes. Lansing Hendricks' hair had turned a distinguished gray, while Kim's was a dark blond that bleached to straw in the summer sun; there were attractive character lines around the older man's eyes. Lansing Hendricks had aged well and so would Kim. Lansing was proud of Kim and Kim more than loved his father; they were more than parent and child—they were best friends.

"Dad! Hello, Dad!" Kim called out. As soon as he was alone with his father he would tell him about Nicole.

"Look, Kim!" Sally shouted, and pointed again to the newspaper. He was still too far away to read the headline and his attention was distracted by the customs official poking through his luggage. Finally the official okayed Kim's baggage and waved him through the customs barrier, and in another moment Kim was in Sally's arms.

"Oh, the time went so slowly! I thought you'd never get back!" she said, tears and smiles intermingling on her face. "The hours just dragged by . . . and look what we have for you!"

Kim's article about the Jewish woman near the place des Vosges was on the front page, under Kim's by-line. The front page!

"*The Sun* has run your articles from Paris on the front

page every day!" said Lansing. "The phone hasn't stopped ringing. Every newspaper wants to hire you— you have your pick of jobs in the entire city." The pleasure and pride in Lansing's face was reflected, multiplied and amplified in Sally's.

"We're so proud of you . . ." Sally and Lansing spoke the same words at the same instant and turned first to each other and then to Kim and laughed with happiness and excitement. "We're so happy to have you back!"

His right arm around Sally and his left around his father, a porter following with his luggage, Kim left the customs shed for the row of waiting taxis at the curb. *The Sun*, folded so that Kim's by-line and article were all that was visible, was in Kim's right hand. He brought his arm more tightly around Sally and she leaned into him, interpreting the extra squeeze as a special, private caress. Kim, with something else in mind, was unaware of her, and held his right hand up so that he could gaze at his name in print. The words he had written in the cafés of Paris, in type! So the phones were ringing! So he had his choice of jobs! And no one knew about the two stories he had rewritten! They were in the inside pocket of his trench coat, carefully folded next to the letters he had written Nicole on board the *White Star*, which he would mail here in New York.

Kim could not tear his eyes away from the magic of his name and his words in type. The front page! For the second time in a year he was returning to New York from Paris as a hero! The world was his oyster! There wasn't anything he couldn't do!

Lansing Hendricks had the taxi let him off at the Yale Club. "You take Sally home," Lansing said. Kim was anxious to see his father alone. To tell him about Nicole, to ask him what to do about Sally. "I have a meeting here with a client. I'll see you later. We'll have dinner at Sherry's. Terrapin and pheasant—anything you want! We'll have a special celebration!"

As the taxi took off down Vanderbilt Avenue, Sally threw herself into Kim's arms. *"That's* the way I wanted to kiss you before," she said, kissing him deeply and passionately. They had begun making love before Kim had left for Paris, and Sally, who was very proper publicly, had learned under Kim's loving guidance to be privately passionate. He had forgotten. "I missed you, I missed you," Sally said. "Did you miss me as much as I missed you?"

"More." Kim paused a moment—just one imperceptible moment—before giving Sally the answer he knew she expected.

"Now we never have to be parted again. Not ever," said Sally. "And wait until you see the surprise I have for you!"

"Another surprise!" Kim still had not had time to get over the thrill of seeing his by-line on the front page. Even through Sally's passionate kisses and declarations, he had compulsively glanced at the folded newspaper over and over. He could hardly wait to mail a clipping to Nicole. "Don't you think I've had enough surprises for one day?"

"But you were the man who told me you could never get enough of anything!" Sally reminded him. "Now kiss me again. I can't get enough of your kisses." In the taxi, she kissed him, locking her mouth to his, her arms wrapped around him. "I can't wait until we're alone. Really alone," she said, and she felt herself flush a little because she knew—and he knew—exactly what she meant.

Sally Cushman from Saint Louis had come to visit her cousin Flora Wilson in the spring of 1918. She had been invited for a fortnight and had stayed the entire summer. The reason was Kim Hendricks. In May 1918, the same day Sally arrived in New York, Kim had limped down the gangplank of the troop carrier *Générale Lemoine*, still suffering the effects of the wound he had sustained in France. The deputy mayor of the city had presented Kim with a bouquet of red roses, and *The New York Sun*, where Kim had worked summers as a copyboy, had sent a reporter and photographer. Kim, leaning on a black-wood cane, cut a dashing figure in a military trench coat with great lapels and flapping buckles, and a captured German garrison belt with an enormous buckle of silver, binoculars hanging from a strap around his neck. He was asked about the part he had taken in a daring raid on a bunker of Big Berthas which had shelled Paris from the nearby Saint-Gobain Forest. The next day the photograph and accompanying article, which referred to Kim as "a journalist, Yale man and military hero," appeared on the front page of *The Sun*. Kim accepted the compliments of his friends modestly but he was secretly flushed with pride at how heroic the newspaper made him sound.

The same evening Kim and Sally Cushman met at a dance at the Knickerbocker Club. Although it raised more than a few eyebrows, Kim cut in on Sally during every dance and was part of the group that went on to Delmonico's for a late supper. Much later that night, as Sally and Flora got into the twin beds in Flora's pale-yellow bedroom in the Wilson brownstone on Washington Square, Sally said, "Do you remember Kim Hendricks?"

"Who doesn't?" said Flora. "He's the handsomest man in New York."

"Well, I'm going to marry him."

"Sally, how can you say that! You just met him!" The determined silence from Sally's bed spoke volumes. "You really mean it, don't you?" said Flora, amazed at her usually conservative and proper cousin. "You really mean it!"

"I really mean it," said Sally, and it was a long time before she fell asleep because she couldn't forget how she felt when Kim Hendricks' hand touched hers.

While she thought of nothing but McKim Hendricks, Sally kept up with the New York social whirl of balls, dinners, lunches, enjoying the gossip and the clothes. Kim, whose father had been the Wilsons' family lawyer for two generations, went to all the same balls, dinners, lunches and parties Sally did, and though other girls may have been prettier, none pleased him as much as Sally, who took his dreams seriously, who applauded and encouraged him the same way his father did, who, unlike other girls, who tried to be sophisticated and blasé, never hid her admiration of him. In no time at all Kim's name was written in for the last dance before intermission and they spent those quiet interludes in candlelit drawing rooms, and on romantic staircases, in conservatories sweet with potted plants. Sally made herself pleasing and available but she did not make the mistake of throwing herself at his feet. She never let Kim take her home; there were always other beaux to accompany her; there were always other beaux to bring her plates of food and refreshments from the buffets; there were other beaux to take her to Sunday afternoon concerts and Tuesday evening musicales.

"Why won't you let me take you home?" Kim asked five weeks after they'd met. They were at a *thé dansant* at the Plaza Hotel.

"I'll let you take me home tonight," Sally answered.

"You never let me take you home before. Why now?"

Sally shrugged delicately and mysteriously and charmingly. She had kept him at arm's length long enough.

That evening, in the Wilsons' drawing room, the

house silent except for the ticking of a grandfather clock in the downstairs hall, the gaslights from Washington Square casting a soft glow, Sally let Kim kiss her. From that night on, it was Kim and Sally. Sally and Kim.

Kim Hendricks was not the least bit like the young men Sally had grown up with—young men, whether from New York or Saint Louis, whose futures were planned from the moment of their birth, in their fathers' law firms, in stockbrokerages owned by cousins, in banks to which they were attached by a network of family connections. Kim was different: he was a hero of the raid on the Paris Guns, a published journalist, he wanted to be a novelist, he called her "darling" in French; he brought her armfuls of flowers while other boys brought only a corsage; he wrote poems for her while other boys only offered a box of chocolates; he arranged a ride over Manhattan for them in a single-engine, open-cockpit biplane while other boys were lucky to borrow their father's Model-T for a special occasion. By the time, in midsummer, that Kim proposed, there was no doubt in Sally's mind or in his what her answer would be. Kim went to Saint Louis—sweltering, humid, drowsy—in mid-July to meet Sally's parents, who were no more immune to his charm than Sally had been. The combination of his personal attractiveness and the fact that he was from a good family known to the Wilsons won the Cushmans over totally. Lansing Hendricks, whose only reservation was that Kim might be a little young to marry, completely approved of Sally, who had, he said, everything a man would want in a wife. Lansing gave Kim his mother's diamond engagement ring for Sally, and while it was at Black, Starr & Gorham being reset, Sally wore a fragment of the metal that had been dug out of Kim's legs on a chain around her neck, as a mark of their pledges to each other. At the end of July their engagement was officially announced, with the wedding date set for Christmas Day, 1918.

While Sally's mother ordered flowers and champagne and musicians and caterers, and while Sally's father complained pleasantly about how much it was costing him to marry off his daughter, Kim and Sally, back in New York, where they would live after they were married, got to know each other. Sally, Kim learned, was intelligent and sensitive and tended to hide her private feelings. Kim, Sally learned, presented an exuberant, confident face to the world but there was a part of him that could be moody and depressed, and when he was in one of his blue periods he refused to go out or to see anyone.

"You're the only person I can let see me like this," Kim said when one of his stories came back, rejected, for the third time.

"You can let me see you any which way," she said. "Because I love you . . . all of you."

"I'm not worth it. I'll never amount to anything," Kim said. It was three in the afternoon and he was still in pajamas and a robe. When he was blue he refused even to shave and dress.

"Don't say that! You'll do everything you want—and more!"

"Do you really think so?" he asked.

"I *know* so!"

"Sally, Sally," he said, embracing her, her reassurances having the power to restore his faith in himself. "I'll be your eternal fiancé. Your knight. Your protector. Your lover. Your husband. I promise."

"And I'll be your lover, your wife . . . forever and ever. I promise."

They sealed their promises, as they sealed all their promises to each other—promises to be honorable and truthful, to be loving and tender—with a kiss. There had been a hundred promises, a hundred kisses, and no reason at all to think they wouldn't keep each and every promise. They made love then. It was so natural, so right, the way it had been for them since the beginning, that they felt no embarrassment, no guilt, no shame; it was as if the earth, which had been disturbingly out of orbit, had just slipped back perfectly into its planetary slot. When it was over, Sally kissed his scarred knee.

"It looks like buffalo hide that's been bow-and-arrowed by an Indian who couldn't hit a barn door with a sledge-hammer," he said, and they both laughed, confident again of themselves, confident again of each other.

That had been in late October, just before Kim left for Paris to cover the expected announcement of the Armistice. Now, in early December, everything had changed for Kim and nothing had changed for Sally. She made him close his eyes and led him into the Wilson parlor.

"You can open your eyes now!" she instructed. Long tables draped with white cloths ran around the room in a U shape. Wedding presents sent to New York rather than Saint Louis, at the bride's request, covered the cloth-draped tables. "My Aunt Christine from Boston sent the silver gravy boat and your cousin and his wife sent a dozen dinner dishes in our pattern! And, look, my father's partner gave us silver candelabra all the way from Sheffield, England . . ." Sally continued, her face glowing with happiness. "The three-tiered epergne is from a second cousin I never met and the flatware is monogrammed." Sally picked up a fork and showed it to Kim, pointing out the engraving. "*McKH!* Your mono-gram! *Our* monogram!"

"It's like a branch of Tiffany's," Kim said, and his sentence trailed off in a peculiar way that made Sally turn her attention from the impressive display of gifts.

56

"Kim?"

His knees had buckled slightly and he was clutching the edge of a table to hold himself up, pulling the cloth askew, threatening to pull it off and, with it, the mass of gifts that covered it. He didn't answer her. His shoulders were hunched painfully and his head was slumped over so that Sally couldn't see his face.

"Kim! Are you all right?"

Again he didn't answer. He began to shiver, his teeth chattering, his breath coming in convulsive heaves. He felt trapped by the wedding gifts, trapped into a marriage, a future, that seemed safe and dull to him after the piercing emotions he had discovered with Nicole Redon in Paris. He was trapped and he didn't know how to find a way out. He observed from an infinitely calm, detached vantage point at a great distance as the floor floated up to meet his face and a crystal glass bounced three times in slow motion on the flowered carpet.

2.

"The doctor says it's something you picked up in Europe. The food or the water, most likely," said Sally. "You ran a high fever for three days and all you kept saying was, 'the gifts make it real . . . the gifts make it real.' What did you mean?"

"The gifts make the wedding real," Kim said. He remembered very clearly what had been in his mind when he had fainted.

"*The* wedding?" Sally teased, feeling relieved now that the fever had broken and Kim was on his way to recovery. "Don't you mean *our* wedding?"

"Our wedding," Kim repeated obediently. He had been delirious for two days—two days he couldn't remember, vanished forever from his life. He was in his room, the room he'd had since he'd been a boy. There was a blue-and-white Yale pennant on the wall, along with photographs of Kim's idols: Captain Eddie Rickenbacker, Carl Sandburg, Theodore Dreiser and Vernon and Irene Castle. Kim could remember fainting, the flowered carpet floating upward. When he had been wounded in the Saint-Gobain Forest there had been blood and panic and the floor had been French earth, but the feeling had been the same, an odd combination of terrifying helplessness and swooning pleasure. He would have to remember it exactly. One day he would use it in a book.

"You have to eat well and rest to regain your strength," Sally said. She had been with Kim constantly, holding cool cloths to his forehead, helping change the damp, sweaty sheets, bringing extra blankets when he was chilled and taking them away again when the fever burned him again. She had looked fresh and lovely the whole time, and even in his fever Kim had been aware of her cool hands and soft voice. "The doctor said that it takes a little while to recover from these influenzas. You'll have to be a good patient and follow orders. You want to be in splendid health for our wedding. You want to enjoy every moment of it."

"I'll try," said Kim, feeling weak and woozy, and when his lids, unbearably heavy, fell shut, he did not try to resist but let himself fall into a warm, pleasant state that was half sleep, half waking.

He loved Nicole . . . he loved Sally too, but in a different way. If only he had time . . . if only he could postpone the wedding. . . . He needed time to think, to sort things out . . . he'd ask his father . . . he wondered if there was any mail . . . letters from Nicole, and he realized he hadn't mailed the ones he'd written on the

White Star. They must still be in his trench coat pocket. He'd have to mail them . . . he was so tired . . . so sleepy . . .

"How are you feeling?" The voice was his father's.

"Better," said Kim.

"You gave us quite a scare," Lansing Hendricks said. He did not have to say that influenza killed and that Kim's mother had been one of its victims.

"I'm sorry," Kim said. "You know I didn't mean to. Has there been any mail for me?"

"No mail," said his father. "But every newspaper in New York called again while you were sick. S. I. Brace has been calling twice a day."

"I can't go through with the wedding," Kim blurted. "It's too soon! Everything happened so fast! I need more time—"

"What you mean is that you're scared," said Lansing. His smile was understanding. "So is every man. It's a big decision and it scares everyone. If it will make you feel better, there's a name for your condition: 'bridegroom's nerves.' "

"It's not 'bridegroom's nerves,' Dad," Kim said. He was very pale but his voice quivered with intensity.

"Two weeks before I married your mother I told her I wanted my ring back. I told her that I didn't love her and that I couldn't marry her. Three days before the wedding I calmed down again. We had a happy wedding and a happy life, Kim. So will you and Sally."

"Dad, it's more complicated than that. I met someone else," Kim said. "I'm in love with someone else."

"Someone else?" His father blinked, taken by surprise. "Who? I didn't know you were seeing anyone but Sally."

"It happened in Paris. I met someone and we fell in love," Kim said. "Until I met Nicole I didn't really know what love was. It's rapture! It's ecstasy! She's more than I thought I had the right to expect in a woman. I didn't think she even existed except in my imagination." Lansing listened in silence. Kim, exuberant, sounded so much like his mother it was painful for Lansing to hear. "You don't believe me, do you? You think I'm crazy, don't you?"

"Kim, use your head! Sally loves you and you love her. Sally's from the same background you are, she's American, we've known the Wilson family for years. You've known this Nicole for two weeks. You don't know a thing about her. Kim, don't let infatuation turn your head."

"Nicole is *not* an infatuation!" Kim was furious at the way his father had trivialized his feelings. "You don't understand what happened to me in Paris. I can't go through with this circus!"

"Kim, I don't want to hear another word of this." Now Lansing, who was more moderate in his emotions than his son, showed his own anger and impatience. "Your wedding is not a circus. You've been ill and feverish. It's upset your thinking. Put this Nicole out of your mind. It was a last fling. Many men have them. They're not important," his father said. "Your Nicole is not important!"

"You mean you're not going to help me?" Kim was shocked. It was one of the very rare disagreements he had had with his father.

Few men would have sacrificed their own lives the way Lansing Hendricks had sacrificed his. He had had little personal life since Kim's mother had died; he had turned away the advances of attractive widows, had devoted the weeks to his law practice and weekends and holidays to his son, seeing to it that Kim had what other boys of his age had: birthday parties and dancing lessons and riding lessons, good private schools and summer camps. He had helped Kim with his homework, listened to his troubles, and encouraged his dreams. He had seen to it, as far as it was in his power, that Kim grew up as a normal boy even though he had so tragically lost his mother. Lansing had devoted his life to Kim. Kim knew it and appreciated it. But it also gave his father a very powerful hold over him. Defying his father, who had done everything for him, was inconceivable to Kim.

"No, Kim. I'm not going to help you get out of a marriage that's right for you. Marry Sally. You will never regret it. I promise you."

Kim felt that he had lost the battle. Part of him also knew that he hadn't fought as hard as he could have, and he thought his own confusion was the reason. Suddenly a thought came to him, new and shocking: "Dad, did you ever have a fling?"

"No, son," his father said, smiling softly and perhaps a bit sadly. "I never had a fling. Your mother was the only woman I loved."

"Why can't my life be simple?" Kim asked. "Why did I have to meet Nicole? Everything would have been so easy if I hadn't. Dad, I wish my life were as simple as yours."

"No one's life is simple, Kim," his father said, recognizing youthful arrogance and excusing it. "It only looks that way from the outside. Now try to rest. You still look very pale."

For Sally, the week before the wedding passed with parties and gifts and the arrival of her wedding gown. For Kim, it was filled with the compliments and the admiration of friends and relatives and strangers who had only read about him in the newspaper. The two stories he'd written in Paris "leaving out everything everyone else insists on" were bought immediately by

The Saturday Evening Post, which not only had a circulation of over two million but also published high-quality fiction by writers like Edith Wharton and Ring Lardner. The *Post* added a request to see "everything else you ever write." Kim was offered five newspaper jobs that same week, and all the compliments and success were heady indeed. All the attention, all the flattery, smoothed the edges off Kim's confusion and longing for Nicole and, in a egotistical haze of excitement, Kim allowed himself to drift toward his wedding day.

On the day before he and Sally and his father were leaving for Saint Louis, Kim went to call on S. I. Brace.

"Now that I've made you a celebrity, I guess you've gotten very expensive," the editor said in a tone that was a good two degrees less gruff than usual. The newspaper world was a small one, and S. I. was well aware that Kim's Paris articles had every paper in New York after him. "How much have your valuable services gone up since you returned from Paris?"

"This summer you said you'd pay me twenty dollars a week," Kim said. An S. I. Brace on the defensive was a novel pleasure, and Kim did not intend to let any pleasure pass unsavored to the hilt. "I've had a lot of calls," he continued. *"The Journal, The Times . . ."*

"The Herald, The Chronicle, The Trib and *The News*. I know, I know!" S. I. broke in, holding up his hands in a gesture of surrender. "Please! Consider my ulcer and just tell me how much *The Sun* has to pay you to keep you."

It was hard to believe that this was the same man who had called Kim in May right after *The Sun* had run the photograph and interview. "I'll pay you a hundred dollars for the exclusive story of the raid on the Paris Guns." S. I. had been gruff and curt on the phone and had not even wasted time with conventional hellos to former copyboys. "Provided it's good enough to print."

"I'll write it and you'll like it," Kim had answered. "When do you want it?"

"The same time I want everything! Yesterday! Yesterday!" S. I. had yelled, and slammed down the phone.

Kim's summer jobs had been at *The Sun*, fetching copy and cigars and coffee, absorbing the smell of newsprint, the raucous atmosphere of the newsroom, and hero-worshiping the City Editor, S. I. Brace—gruff, alcoholic, violent (it was a *Sun* legend that S. I. had run his mistress over when she accepted a car from another admirer and had left her bleeding on the sidewalk and begging for forgiveness). Although Kim's ultimate goal was to be a famous novelist, his immediate aim was to be a newspaperman. He had mentioned his ambition to S. I., who had laughed at him, taken a swig of whisky out of the bottle he kept in plain sight on top of his desk, and told him that society boys didn't belong in the uncouth world of newspapermen. But S. I. admired Kim's persistence, took him to lunch occasionally—lunch consisting of six shots of whisky and a ham sandwich in the dark bar on the corner opposite the *Sun* offices—and introduced him to the pressmen, deliverers, reporters and advertising salesmen who worked at *The Sun*. S. I. got to like Kim; would never have admitted in a hundred years that he was impressed by Kim's social background; and was not in the least surprised when Kim returned from the war as one of the heroes of the daylight raid on the Paris Guns. Kim wrote the story, headlining it: THEY TOLD ME I WAS A HERO. Kim thought his story was moving, exciting and yet properly modest.

"Not too bad," said S. I. after he had read it and sent it to be set in type.

"*Now* will you give me a job?" Kim asked. He had been begging S. I. for a job since the first summer he'd worked at *The Sun*.

"The salary for beginning reporters is twenty dollars a

week," S. I. said. "I'll make a deal with you. If you can get yourself back to Paris for the Armistice and if you can write me the best goddamn stories to come out of Europe, you've got a job. I want stories that will make 'em laugh, make 'em cry. I want stories that will make 'em *beg* for their copy of *The Sun*. Do you think you can do that?" As Kim was about to answer, S. I. stopped him with a gesture. "I know you *think* you can do it. Prove it! And remember the salary is twenty dollars a week. Not a penny more. Is it a deal?"

"It's a deal," Kim had said, and they shook on it.

Kim, exhilarated by his love affair with Nicole, feeling a sense of power he'd never felt, sent stories from Paris that were filled with emotion, with the telling details that got readers involved. The facts were always correct and the dispatches were written like stories, with a beginning, a middle and an end, rather than in the rigid who-what-when-where-why format of conventional journalism. They had been a sensation and S. I. had ordered them run on the front page.

"I wanted you to do well," S. I. told Kim now in December, Kim still slightly pale from his bout with influenza, "but I didn't want you to do *this* well! Now, look, don't get too big for your britches, but you're good. You're damn good. And you're worth whatever you can force *The Sun* to pay you," said S. I., his blue eyes level behind his wire-framed eyeglasses. "Tell me the bad news." He sat back, resigned, waiting for an astronomical figure.

"Well, sir, we had a deal. The deal was that if you liked the stories I filed from Paris, I'd have a job starting the new year and the salary would be twenty dollars a week," Kim said, pausing, watching S. I. nervously wait to hear how much of an increase he was going to demand. "Sir, as far as I'm concerned, I'll start work on January the first, 1919, and I'll expect my pay to be twenty dollars a week."

"That's it?" S. I. was astounded. "That's it? That's all?"

"That's it as far as I'm concerned," Kim said. "We had a deal. A deal's a deal."

Kim got up and shook hands with S. I. across the copy-littered desk, and excused himself, wishing his new boss a Merry Christmas and a Happy New Year.

Within the hour, the story was being repeated everywhere in newspaper circles in Manhattan. The phrase "A deal's a deal" was repeated over and over with awe and astonishment and was to become part of the Kim Hendricks legend of unshakable personal integrity.

By the time Kim arrived in Saint Louis he had made up his mind that marrying Sally was the right thing to do. He had no doubt that Sally would do everything to make him happy, and what with the excitement surrounding the wedding and the year-end holidays, the sale of his stories to the *Post*, and his new job at *The Sun*, Paris seemed very far away. Sometimes he wondered if he had simply imagined Nicole and the way they had been with each other. But then he remembered champagne and carnations, a twig broom and an apartment overlooking the Seine, and he knew it had all been real. A bittersweet love story with the ending written in at the beginning. He just hadn't known it would hurt this much.

On Christmas Eve Kim's father gave him a midnight bachelor party. It was a lavish affair with many toasts and a great deal of champagne. By the time the party was over, Kim was very, very drunk. His father helped him to his hotel room, helped him undress, and got him into bed.

"You're going to have a terrible headache on your wedding day," Lansing said. "Although I don't approve of it, I understand many young men nowadays go to the altar in that condition." Then he quietly closed Kim's door behind him and went to his own room down the hall.

In the dark hotel room, in a strange bed, his inhibitions obliterated by alcohol, Kim let the tears cascade down his cheeks, wetting the pillow. Sally would be a good wife to him and he would be a good husband to her. But he was cheating them both. He should get up now, should leave for Paris, should go to Nicole . . .

He did not remember going to sleep that night, and on his wedding day he had a gargantuan hangover and no memory of the tears he had shed in the night or the thoughts he had had while he shed them.

3.

In January Kim and Sally moved into a small apartment on Greenwich Village's Carmine Street and Kim went to work at *The Sun*. S. I. assigned him to the Times Square area. He covered fires and murders, scandals and larcenies; he hung around the police station, getting to know cops and robbers, and discovered a natural rapport with other reporters, sharing their jokes though not their cynicism. Kim had a romantic feeling about print and type and the written word, and was smart enough not to show it to men who could, with a bottle of whisky in one hand and a telephone in the other, call in a story, getting every name, date and address right the first time. He got to know the small-time thieves, the big-time Broadway gamblers, the shopkeepers, and he got to know the girls who plied their trade at the Andrew Hamilton Hotel, nicknamed the

Woodrow Wilson Hotel by his fellow reporters, whose punch line went: "A piece at any price."

On his own time, Kim wrote extras. In January he wrote a piece describing the reactions at a Greenwich Village bar to the ratification of the Eighteenth Amendment, which outlawed the sale of whisky and began Prohibition. He paid a visit to Father Divine's Mission in Sayville, Long Island. In July he covered the inauguration of daily air mail service between New York and Chicago, and wondered if his life would have been any different if there had been air mail service between New York and Paris. When he returned from his honeymoon there had been three letters from Nicole waiting for him. It took all his willpower not to open them, and when he didn't and tore them to shreds he felt it was the hardest test his marriage would ever have to undergo. On July 4th he wrote his first sports piece—Jack Dempsey had TKO'ed Jess Willard in the third round of a scheduled twelve-round fight. In August he wrote about the actors' strike that closed New York's theaters; in November, another sports piece: about the 6–0 Navy defeat of Army at the Polo Grounds.

For Sally, life was an exciting whirl, with Kim at its center. She never knew what to expect; no two days were ever the same. Sometimes Kim came home for dinner. She never knew in advance when he would arrive or with whom; usually, he brought unannounced guests—anywhere from one to a dozen; anyone from a judge to a bookie to a Ziegfeld girl. Sally was proud of the series of cheap, almost infinitely expandable menus she had invented to serve her husband's free-floating circle of friends and acquaintances. Other nights he'd call, at any time from five to midnight, and ask her to meet him in a Third Avenue bar, a Harlem Bar-B-Que palace, a Chinese dumpling parlor on Mott Street, a dairy restaurant on Essex Street. Life with Kim was hectic and exciting, and whenever things threatened to become routine, Kim stirred them up again. Life was a constant flow of people, ideas and adventures.

Kim's wife adored him; his boss thought he was the best young reporter he'd ever encountered. Kim's year was filled with love and success. Everything came easily to him and the only thing that troubled him was that it all had fallen into place so effortlessly. He had always been taught that success had to be earned by hard work. He was looking for a challenge. He decided the time had come to write the novel he had been thinking about.

Then there was the bad weather.
—Ernest Hemingway

CHAPTER THREE

1.

IN THE BEGINNING there was a torrent of letters from Kim. Dozens of pages long, they were just like him: exuberant, passionate, irresistible, filled with energy and longing. Kim's letters were fantasies and realities, dreams and promises. They were dramatic, heroic, romantic, idealistic. Kim's handwriting was a bold half-printed, half-cursive script that ran off the pages, up and down the margins, across the tops of pages, running out of space but never out of energy. His letters made him tangible, they were the outpouring of his very soul. All of them had been written on board the *White Star* and mailed in New York. They arrived the first week of 1919, in bunches of six and seven, three days in a row. Then, suddenly and inexplicably, they stopped.

At first Nicole blamed it on the vagaries of the transatlantic mails. Then she thought that perhaps Kim—and it would be just like him!—had gotten on board another ship going in the opposite direction and was already on his way back to her. But as the weeks went by and he did not appear in Paris and not one single additional letter of explanation arrived, Nicole didn't know what to think.

Sometimes she thought he had met someone else and didn't have the courage to tell her. Other times she thought he was mortally ill and unable to write. She even imagined he was dead. Then she changed her mind and decided he *was* on his way to her. Mentally, she called him a liar and a cad. She thought that his letters had been lost in the mails or that her letters, for some unimaginable reason, had never reached *him* and he thought *she* didn't care. She exhausted herself inventing possibilities and she got nowhere.

A torrent of passion and then silence. Nicole was by turns hurt, angry, confused and euphoric, thinking that the next day, the next moment, he would suddenly appear in front of her. She could not imagine what had happened and she had no one to ask. Her own letters went unanswered.

2.

Cyril returned to Paris in February of 1919 and in March he opened a small shop under the arcades of the rue de Rivoli, where he sold jewelry. Not rare and precious gems but stylish costume jewelry made of paste, the designs inspired by the jewels Fabergé had made for the Czar's court. Paris, starved for opulence after the austerities of the war, was drunk with Russia. Diaghilev's lavishly mounted Ballets Russes, with great stars like Nijinsky and Pavlova and romantic music by Rimsky-

Korsakov and Tchaikovsky, was all the rage, sold out to cheering throngs night after night! Cyril and Nicole were not the only ones who thought his shop would be a great success, and in a confident frame of mind, Cyril resumed his courtship of Nicole.

Cyril, now matured, was even more attractive than he had been when Nicole had first met him in Biarritz in 1917. Biarritz, near the neutral Spanish border, was far from the fighting of the Western Front. It was a fashionable resort devoted to flirtation, gambling and other lighthearted pleasures. Nicole was working at the milliner's shop, attaching egret plumes and great swaths of veiling and ribbon to hat forms while thinking, privately, how ridiculous these confections were and how absurd women looked in them. Leo Severin, a soap and essence manufacturer from Grasse, had come into the shop one day with his mistress to pay for several hats. The milliner, a former *horizontale* who had opened her shop with money saved out of the gifts of her lovers, was out at the time and Nicole waited on him, presenting the bill and rechecking the addition when he questioned it. In the ensuing discussion, Leo noticed something fresh and charming about Nicole and, soon enough, she had become his occasional friend.

It was during that time that Nicole made her little chemise, based on the linen dusters she wore over her street clothes to protect them while she worked. The waistless, untrimmed duster with neatly set-in sleeves which was perfectly comfortable, allowed her to move freely and easily and, for that reason, she soon came to see it as beautiful. She no longer wore the tight, binding frocks that required uncomfortable and restricting undergarments and made herself a dress that followed the lines of the duster. When she wore her little chemise at the shop with a string of pearls and a perfectly plain boater of untrimmed straw, tilted at a rakishly becoming angle, the clients, thinking that Nicole looked very stylish, soon asked her to make them a dress like the one she wore. In her spare time, Nicole made several but soon, even if she sat up all night long, she did not have enough time to make as many as the women were ordering.

"I've already made twenty dresses and I have orders for thirty-seven more," she told Leo. "I think I would be a success if I had my own little shop. I have the design and the orders—all I need is money. If you would lend it to me, I would set up my own shop. That way I would be less dependent on you," she said. Leo was prudent with money and Nicole knew that the thought of her being less financially dependent on him would appeal to him.

"It would be quite expensive," he said. "It would cost me . . . let's see . . . how many francs?" He did mental calculations. He gave Nicole gifts of money now and then, enough to help her out, but not enough to make work unnecessary. To set her up in a shop would cost him more than he presently gave her in gifts, and Leo saw no advantage to himself. He liked her well enough but he was very attached to his present mistress and had no interest in upgrading Nicole's importance in his life or increasing his investment in her.

Nicole heard the "no" in Leo's voice before he actually said the word. While he was explaining and justifying his refusal to lend her the money needed to rent a shop, to buy the fabrics, and to pay the salary of an assistant, Nicole was already deciding who might lend her the money Leo wouldn't.

That night Nicole went—alone—to the casino. Not to gamble. She never gambled so much as a sou; she was very, very careful with money because she didn't have very much and because all her memories were memories of poverty and deprivation and making do and doing without. She knew many of the people there—actresses and dancehall girls, glamorous airmen, rich businessmen and their conservative wives, aristocratic layabouts, handsome gigolos with the rich ladies-of-a-certain-age and beautiful courtesans elaborately dressed and bejeweled to show off the wealth of their benefactors. The rattle of dice, the laughter of lovely women, the baritone of men's voices, excited and intimate, the music of a band—the air in the casino was festive and gay. Grand Duke Cyril, an elegant and handsome White Russian émigré, stood at the chemin de fer table playing with the tremendous zest which had buoyed his life since the first auguries of the revolution and his escape from a stifling Saint Petersburg palace. Nicole had noticed him often, thinking him very attractive, with his brown eyes and tender, smiling mouth.

"Mademoiselle, come here," Cyril said. "You will certainly bring me the luck I need to make this point." Cyril spoke in English, the language in which he was most fluent because his parents had insisted on a fashionable education for the small Grand Duke. English tutors and English nursemaids were installed in the third floor, the nursery floor, of the Italianate palace fronting on the gray Neva and it was absolutely forbidden that any language save English be spoken to the child. The result was complete isolation, not only from other children his own age, but from every Russian on the face of the earth. Cyril was a lonely and therefore sad and listless young man when the revolution began to threaten. He did not understand the revolution nor did he have any particular interest in it until he realized that it would be his personal salvation. *Escape, escape, escape*, were the words he heard most. With his aunt, who traveled with a servant into whose garments were sewn precious jewels, they fled to Switzerland, where sums of rubles had

been fortuitously sent ahead. Once out of the mint–
green palace, which had really been a prison, Cyril
found heaven on earth. He was free to come and go as
he chose; he could, with his English, speak with almost
anyone. The sad and listless young man was transformed
into an outgoing and happy man. He cast the dice and
won his point. He scooped the pile of plaques toward
him. "You see, you've brought me luck!" he said, handing Nicole a handful of the winning chips.

"Thank you," she said, speaking in English. Nicole
knew the language fairly well from the English and
American officers on leave who had filled the streets and
cafés and dancehalls, and from the English clients of the
milliner's shop. "But I couldn't possibly accept."

"But you will accept champagne," said Cyril, "because
I will give you no choice." He ordered a bottle of champagne from one of the waiters who hovered nearby.
Nicole watched while Cyril gambled, then they drank
their champagne and danced until early in the morning.
Over scrambled eggs, which Cyril consumed with the
delight he brought to everything, he asked Nicole, "Why
didn't you ever speak to me before? I saw you almost
every day at the milliner's and on weekends I saw you at
the beach. Why wouldn't you speak to me? Was it because of your lover?"

"I don't really know why," Nicole said. Leo had been
part of the reason—she felt an obligation of loyalty toward him. And then part of the reason was that outside
of the shop she was very shy, always afraid that the
smallest slip would reveal what she was, beneath her
stylish clothes and behind her smiles—a nobody from
nowhere. The words were her mother's; the feeling of
inferiority, of having nothing and being nothing, was
Nicole's. "Perhaps it was Leo a little," she admitted. "I
am also shy."

74

"You mustn't be shy," Cyril said. "Although I completely understand." He told Nicole about the terrible shyness he had felt as a child, inhibited by others' uncomfortable consciousness of his rank and by his inability to speak the language of his countrymen. "A wall stood between me and other people. That wall has been torn down and I consider myself a free man. You must learn from my unhappy childhood and free yourself from your shyness."

"Of course, you're right. And I will try, although I know it will be difficult for me," Nicole said. It would in fact be years before Nicole felt any real social confidence outside the shop, where, certain of her taste, certain of her skill, she was also certain of herself. As Cyril spoke, Nicole thought of her own unhappiness and exclusion as a child. It was a situation identical to Cyril's—except that the barriers of status were the exact opposite. He had suffered from exalted rank; she from an absence of any rank at all. He had a history of ancestors; she had never even had a father. Odd, she thought, that the result of high station and no station should be so much the same.

"You are young. You will be able to change," said Cyril. "There will come a time when you will not even remember what it was like to be held back by shyness."

Nicole hoped Cyril was right; but just now she couldn't imagine it. Cyril was, Nicole would learn, a sensitive and emotional man, quite different from Leo, who had a businessman's approach, calculating and value-conscious even in affairs of the heart. Having been deprived in his childhood of normal love and ordinary contact, Cyril sensed in Nicole someone who had also been severely wounded in childhood.

A man who had been trained for leisure, Cyril admired Nicole's attachment to her work and her concern, which she took pains to hide, over money. When she mentioned her idea of having a shop, Cyril was impressed with her ambition. Without telling her, he took a diamond clip, one of the ones that had left Russia in the hem of the servant's skirts, and instead of giving it to Nicole as a gift, sold it and made her a present of the francs it brought. Nicole refused the gift but accepted the money as a loan. She rented a small shop on the rue Gardères, across the street from the casino. She had her name put in square black letters on a white awning and opened for business. Women loved the unpretentious little chemise. It was comfortable, it revealed their figures becomingly, it made them feel free and modern and they thought they looked young in it. Their friends admired it and asked where they might buy one, and soon friends of friends did the same. At the end of the second month, Nicole began to repay Cyril out of her profits.

Leo seemed chagrined, more because he had failed to get in on a good investment, perhaps, than that he had lost a mistress, but after a few jealous spats over her new attachment to the Grand Duke, Leo gave up his claims, such as they were, on Nicole. And Nicole, who could be aggressive and argumentative, was not the least bit vindictive and never carried a grudge, so that, after the tempests accompanying their breakup, Nicole and Leo maintained a friendly relationship, greeting each other pleasantly when they met, although it was now well known in Biarritz that the young dressmaker and the Grand Duke were lovers and spent much of their time together.

Cyril lived in a large, fine suite in the Hotel Miramar. Glass doors, reaching from floor to high, Third Empire ceiling, opened onto the dazzling white terrazzo terraces, and beyond, the blue of the Atlantic sparkled. But it was not the spectacular view or the healthful sea air that mesmerized Nicole. It was Cyril's dressing rooms. Bottles of scent, jasmine and patchouly, fern and tabac, lined the tops of his dressing tables. Cyril had brought with him to exile the luxuries and extravagances of the Russian court, the lavish use of scent among them. Nicole tried them all and began, this way and that, to combine them. That summer in Biarritz she moved in a constant cloud of scent, making it a trademark so that people said to her, as a compliment, that they knew whenever she was nearby, announced as she was by the scent in which she enveloped herself.

The other irresistible magnet to Nicole, besides the jars of scent, were Cyril's closets. They ran from floor to ceiling along all four walls of his dressing room. Muslin bags filled with lavender were suspended from the clothes poles, a custom which had the dual function of protecting against moths while at the same time faintly scenting the air and the clothing. And such clothing! Ceremonial uniforms with gold braid and buttons, shiny leather belts and high Oriental collars. Sumptuously braided dressing gowns in rich, glowing colors, with self-sashes and loose sleeves. Tunic shirts that closed on the side of the neck with braided frogs, their hems and sleeves banded with gorgeous embroideries. Nicole would spend hours trying them on, and little by little decorations of braid, gold buttons and a tunic shirt *à la Russe* appeared in her shop on the rue Gardères.

When the season was over, Cyril prepared to go to New York in response to the repeated invitation of the White Russians who had settled there. But first he accompanied Nicole to Paris. Nervous but determined, she wanted to open a shop in the capital. She had in mind a re-creation in Paris of what she had in Biarritz: a fashionable shop in a fashionable neighborhood. She had saved the profits she had made that summer, and Cyril had offered to lend her the difference between what she had and the Paris rents.

As careful of others' money as she was with her own, she did not allow Cyril to help her take the first opportunity that presented itself. Instead, she went out every day with real estate agents, looking at shops until she found what she wanted at a price which, although expensive, was not outrageous.

The rue Montaigne, a small street in the Eighth Arondissement, ran between the elegant rue Faubourg St.-Honoré and the fashionable Champs-Elysées, a central and chic location. Nicole negotiated the lease on the first floor for a two-year period and had written into the lease eventual options on the other three floors, at the time rented to a wig maker and a trousseau shop. Cyril, who had little experience with business, was impressed at the attention Nicole paid to the details of the lease and was immensely proud when her lawyer said to him after the meeting at which the contract was signed, "That one, she has a nose for business!"

It was, from a French lawyer, a compliment of the highest order.

3.

By September 1918, her shop mirrored and decorated, Nicole opened for business while Cyril went on to New York. Nicole, nervous at the audacity of her undertaking, had no way of knowing that she was absolutely in the right place at the right time.

In Paris in the closing year of the war all the rules were broken. Victorian pruderies had crumbled in the vast changes wrought by the war; social life was exceedingly

78

gay and active; morals were at their most relaxed. Paris was filled with soldiers on leave—French, English, American, Australian, Dutch, Canadian, Belgian, North African—with diplomats, with businessmen whose goods supplied the armies, with journalists and adventurers, war profiteers and politicians, and women, women attracted by men, women who had volunteered to serve the Red Cross or to drive ambulances, women who worked at jobs that had formerly belonged to men, and women who, quite simply, made a career of men. Paris under the nightly threat of the Big Berthas, filled with refugees with harrowing stories, with widows and the wounded, throbbed with an awareness of how short and how fragile life was. People treasured life and wanted to enjoy it to the hilt, and to enjoy it women naturally wanted new clothes.

Poiret, the king of Paris fashion, had patriotically turned his talents to outfitting the army and, without him, the competitive field of Paris fashion seemed a little bit less formidable. Seamstresses, cutters and fitters—the wonderfully skilled "hands" of France—were out of their usual jobs and Nicole benefited from the pool of available talent. Rules were being broken and that included rules of dress. With her two specialties, her chemise—it was not even considered a dress by the standards of the time—and her evening pajamas, Nicole's little shop, with its showroom, two fitting rooms and one workroom, continued the promise begun in Biarritz.

Some of Nicole's clients from Biarritz continued to buy from her in Paris and Nicole, an interesting woman, attracted the interesting women of the city—actresses, authors, artists and the newly independent working women. In the beginning, unconventional women were drawn to Nicole's unconventional clothes. Clothes whose buttons actually buttoned (other designers used buttons as decoration, the real fastening done with rows of tiny hooks which required the assistance of a ladies' maid); clothes that daringly showed the whole calf of the leg; clothes that were actually comfortable. Clothes, Nicole insisted, that were "logical" even though none of the reigning arbiters of fashion paid the slightest attention to them.

Margaret Berryman, who was unconventional and logical and a correspondent for the American magazine *Harper's Bazaar*, inevitably heard of Nicole's revolutionary clothes, came to see them, and ordered some—a kasha chemise and evening pajamas in violet—for herself.

Margaret, who was ten years older than Nicole, was a good example of what the French call *jolie laide*. She was unusually tall for a woman, just under six feet. She had no discernible figure: no bust, no waist, no hips. She was as elongated as a giraffe and, to keep comparisons within the animal kingdom, had a beaky nose rather like a hawk's. Her slate-blue eyes were deep and surmounted by dark, assertive eyebrows which she did not pluck or attempt to tame in any way. Her husband, Royce, a banker, was attached to the military branch of the Department of the Treasury. Margaret, childless but refusing to sit home and brood about it, went along with her husband when he was sent to Paris and volunteered to work for the Red Cross headquartered in the Hotel Crillon. Possessing an unusual sense of style as well as claiming relationship on her father's side with the editor of *Harper's Bazaar*, Margaret volunteered to send back to New York reports on Paris fashion.

"Can you give me a sketch of your chemise dress?" Margaret asked Nicole after she'd become a client. "I'll send it to *Harper's Bazaar.*"

"*Harper's Bazaar?*" Nicole had never heard of it.

"It's an American fashion magazine," Margaret explained. "If they like it, they'll publish it."

"I'll be happy to get you a sketch," said Nicole, who liked to work directly with fabric and rarely sketched. "I know a young man who does wonderful sketches. Stanislas Rackowski, a Pole. I'll ask him to draw one."

"Wonderful!" said Margaret with her usual exuberance when she discovered something new and stylish. "You're on to something with these clothes of yours! You'll be a tremendous success! You just need the right publicity, and I'll do everything I can to see that you get it."

Nicole thanked her, got Stash to draw the sketch, and three days later dropped it off personally at the Berrymans' apartment and promptly forgot about it until October 1918, when it appeared in the magazine, a month before Kim Hendricks came into her life and turned it upside down.

4.

By February 1919, when Cyril came back to Paris, Nicole had given up hope that Kim would return. Bruised by his unexplained and abrupt disappearance, Nicole found more and more to cherish in Cyril: his tenderness, his dependability, his way of enjoying every moment of life, his frank and obvious admiration of her. In the early summer when the weather began to turn hot, Nicole on the spur of the moment decided to crop her hair short to match her short skirts, and it was Cyril who cut the back for her. And when clients wanted the same short, liberating, easy-to-wear bob, Cyril wasn't the least bit surprised. "What woman wouldn't want to look like you?" he said. And when Nicole had the idea of hiring a live model to show her clothes, Cyril not only encouraged her but even suggested a girl who would be perfect. In 1919 women ordered their clothes from sketches or from samples shown on dolls.

"It doesn't make sense," Nicole said. "A woman can't tell anything about a dress from a sketch. They need to see clothes on a real person. I notice that clients often order whatever I'm wearing. They say to me, 'Make me a dress like the one you have on.' That's because they can see how it is going to look. But I can only wear one dress at a time. I don't have the time to keep changing clothes all day long. If I had a live mannequin she could do nothing all day but keep changing and model different outfits for the clients."

"You're logical as always," Cyril said. "Did you know that Stash has a sister? She just came from Poland and she's looking for work . . ."

"Can you introduce me to her?"

Cyril took Nicole to Stash's apartment on the Left Bank. It was unlike any apartment Nicole had ever seen: there were no chairs, only very low sofas, all covered in a neutral color similar to the kasha of Nicole's first chemise. There was a cocktail cabinet of blond wood and harmonious geometric lines and, the only color in the room, a Persian rug in faded shades of blue and beige. Nicole thought that if she ever had money to spend on an apartment of her own she would ask Stash to help her decorate it.

"This is my sister, Helena," Stash said, making the introduction. "Everyone calls her Lala."

"You've just come from Poland?" asked Nicole. Cyril had told her Lala's story: her parents killed before her eyes by the Germans, their property appropriated, their money seized. Lala had escaped, alone, fleeing in a sailboat, then by horseback and in farmers' carts, pretending to be mute whenever she saw soldiers, terrified of them, the images of her parents' torn bodies haunting her. "It's a terrible story. A terrible time to live in . . ."

"Yes," said Lala, whose French was made exotically attractive by her Polish accent. "I'm lucky to be alive."

"I understand you're looking for work," said Nicole. "I have an idea . . . perhaps you'd be interested."

Lala, who loved clothes ever since she was a little girl, thought Nicole's idea was brilliant and said she couldn't wait to come to work. Lala, slender and tall, with tawny hair, high cheekbones and green eyes set at a slant, became not only Nicole's model but, soon, the person on whom she created her designs. Nicole had always preferred working with her hands, taking her inspiration from the fabric and how it fell and moved. She had always worked using herself to pin and drape on; having another person to work on was not only much easier but also, Nicole thought, improved her designs, since working on another person gave her more objectivity.

Lala and Nicole spent hours a day together in Nicole's workroom. Nicole pinned and ripped, got down on her knees to mark a hem, reached up to fit a shoulder, hunched over to make a waist fit as well in the back as it did in the front. Nicole was a study in perpetual motion while Lala stood motionless for exhausting hours. As they worked they talked about everything under the sun and soon became good friends. Nicole told Lala of her growing attachment to Cyril and Lala was the first person she told when she and Cyril decided to announce their engagement.

5.

Nicole and Cyril planned to spend the 1920 year-end holidays at a borrowed villa in the hills

83

above Cannes. They would announce their engagement from there. Cyril went on ahead, closing for the holidays his rue de Rivoli shop, which wasn't doing very well and had hardly become the overwhelming success everyone had predicted. Almost no one wanted to wear paste jewelry; it was considered quite vulgar. Nicole was to meet Cyril in Cannes on December 24. Holiday orders were coming into the rue Montaigne shop at a better rate than she had anticipated and there was no question of her shutting down early, a circumstance Cyril understood and was terribly proud of.

On the evening of December 23, Nicole went to a dinner party at Margaret and Royce Berryman's. Margaret, who had taken a great interest in Nicole, wanted to introduce her to everyone who was anyone. The Berrymans' beautiful drawing room, lit with candles and decorated with a huge fir tree which scented the air, was filled with glamorous and glittering friends. Nicole was awed to find herself chatting with a Rothschild baroness, a favorite Poiret client; with the deposed Queen Marie of Rumania, who dressed at Lanvin; and with a maharanee in a Molyneux gown who dripped everyday diamonds from ears, throat, wrists and fingers, and who, for the festive holiday occasion, had added a belt encrusted with sapphires, rubies, diamonds and emeralds that reached from her ribcage to the top of her hipbones. Not one of these rich aristocrats dressed at Redon. They preferred the grand and elaborate creations of the established couturiers. Nicole couldn't help but wonder whether they would find their way to the rue Montaigne when she became a grand duchess. She was quite sure that sooner or later they would.

It was a pleasant thought and put Nicole in a delicious mood of anticipation—both of future success and of the romantic holidays in store for her in Cannes. She and

Cyril would be very, very happy together—of that she was sure. Nicole chatted and smiled, young enough and new enough to Paris to be thrilled with the realization that in a little black dinner dress of her own design, adorned with "jewels" from Cyril's shop, she was as attractive as any millionaire or aristocrat in the room. She treasured the compliments she received more than diamonds.

Dinner was interrupted by the arrival of a messenger. He had called first at Nicole's apartment on the Ile St.-Louis and had been sent by the concierge to the Berrymans' house. The messenger refused to give the message to the Berrymans' butler and so Nicole went personally to the door. Standing there, the cold drafts of December raising gooseflesh under her thin dinner dress, she opened the message and felt an inward chill. She hardly had to read the words to know that her sudden premonition was true: Cyril was dead.

The details of the accident were published in the French newspapers two days later. A tire had blown out on the Grand Corniche and the automobile had gone off the road into a deep gully. Cyril was dead, having died, according to the Cannes police, instantly. He had been on his way from the village of Cannes, his auto filled with cases of champagne for the party he planned to give to announce his engagement to the Paris dress designer, Nicole Redon. He was on his way to the villa in the hills when the accident occurred, the news story went on, even including the detail that, although the car was completely smashed, the bottles of champagne in their wooden crates had survived intact. Not one drop of the precious liquid had been lost.

As far as Nicole was concerned, *everything* had been lost. In Cyril she had found someone who wanted to belong to her and to whom she wanted to belong. She had been so close to touching happiness and it had been snatched away from her. It was unfair and it was cruel, and she wondered bitterly why *her?* What had she done to deserve such grief? To earn loss and reap pain?

She was bereft, in despair and shock, barely able to function, when a month after Cyril's death she received another shock. The executors of Cyril's will sent Nicole a copy of the document, since she was named in it. Cyril had left her five thousand English pounds as well as the inventory of his almost-bankrupt rue de Rivoli shop. Leadenly going through the necessary motions, Nicole closed the forlorn shop and wrapped the paste jewels in small gray flannel bags. Unable to look at the jewelry, afraid of the smashed dreams and shattered memories it evoked, she put the gray flannel bags into big Redon dress boxes and set them on the highest shelf, out of sight, at the very top of her clothes closet.

The money amounted to a small fortune. It was the first capital Nicole had ever had in her life and she, ever prudent with money, invested it wisely. She invested it in herself. Using the five thousand pounds she had inherited from Cyril together with a loan from Tissus Xavier, Nicole firmly pushed aside her fears and bought a building on the place Vendôme opposite the Ritz Hotel. The agent had shown her the building when she had first come to Paris from Biarritz and she had wanted it then but decided that she could not begin to afford it. The place Vendôme, a superb example of the perfect proportion and style of seventeenth-century architecture, centered on a column garlanded with bronze from the 1200 cannon captured at Austerlitz and topped by a statue of Napoleon as Caesar, was, with the rue de la Paix, *the* place for the great names among jewelers, perfumers and bankers. It was the best address in Paris and Nicole, crushed by Cyril's death, decided bitterly to abandon any thought of marriage and personal happiness; she would bury herself in her business: it was all she had; it was all she would allow herself to count on.

Nicole's new building had six floors. She planned to turn the ground floor into a showroom and a half-dozen fitting rooms. The next floor would be made into a big workroom and an office for herself—her quarters at the rue Montaigne had already become impossibly crowded with clients having to wait in line for one of the two fitting rooms. She would continue to rent out the remaining floors to the tenants who already occupied them, using the income to reduce her monthly payments.

Nicole had lost in love: she would succeed in business. She would follow her original dream—the dream Kim had encouraged her not to fear—of being the first woman to head her own grand house of couture, and in buying the building on the place Vendôme she had taken the first step. Roland Xavier had already helped; he promised more help in the future. Not only had he lent her enough money to complete the down payment for the building, but he would create fabrics especially for her, to her requirements; he would advance further capital if necessary; he would extend generous credit so that the two large seasonal—spring and fall—collections could be properly made and presented. Nicole had come a long way since 1917; Roland was sure that she would go much, much farther.

In the year following Cyril's death, Nicole threw herself into her work, using it as a narcotic. Each collection required two hundred new designs. Nicole would work out a design in fabric; a toile of muslin would then be cut and the toile would be refitted on Lala and either rejected or further refined. Then, when Nicole was satisfied, she would hand over the toile to the head of her workroom, where the toile would be marked for seams, insets, gussets, trimmings, fastenings. Once made, each step done painstakingly by hand, the toile would be taken apart and used as a pattern for the cutting of actual garments ordered by the clients. The work was slow and arduous; by the end of the day arms and shoulders and backs ached, but Nicole welcomed the physical pain, preferring it to the inner pain that had tormented her since Cyril's death. Nicole's ferocious concentration on her work helped her get through the days. But at night, exhausted, she had not the strength to crush down the tears that burned at her eyes and demanded to be shed. She cried alone, her only solace the sad pride that she was managing to endure.

She thought of Kim constantly during this period, always imagining that he was watching her and approving of what she did. She had endless imaginary conversations with him, discussing every detail of her day, every nuance of her grieving nights. She thought of him so constantly, he was such a constant invisible companion, that she wondered if she were quite all right. It seemed to her that their three weeks had been a dream, a fantasy conceived in euphoria. Only the packet of letters and the tweed jacket that still hung in her closet proved to her that the three weeks had been real. She wondered what had happened to him but she was too proud when she saw the Fitzgeralds—Mrs. Fitzgerald was now a client—to ask if they knew an American writer named Kim Hendricks.

Turned-up nose, turned-down hose,
Flapper, yessir, one of those—
Has anybody seen my girl?
                    —"Five Foot Two, Eyes of Blue"

CHAPTER FOUR

1.

Western Front had turned out to be very
long and it had taken Kim all of 1920 and half of 1921 to
write it, working nights and weekends. In June of 1921
he sent the manuscript to Maxwell Perkins at Scribner's
because Perkins was the editor of the book Kim had admired most in 1920, *This Side of Paradise*, which, although it was totally different from Western Front, had
two things in common with it: one, it was contemporary
and, two, it was also by an exceptionally young writer.
Three weeks later, Kim got a letter from Perkins saying
that Scribner's was interested in publishing the novel and
asking him to come to the office for a meeting followed
by lunch.

The Scribner's office was above the Scribner's Bookstore on Forty-eighth Street and Fifth Avenue, and the offices, Kim realized instantly, were nothing short of Dickensian. As the elevators opened on the third floor, Kim glimpsed men wearing green eyeshades, perched on high wooden stools and hunched over big ledger books. He would not have been surprised by quill pens, and he wondered whether the language he had used in the battle scenes might not be too far advanced into the twentieth century for Scribner's. Perkins' office was on the fifth floor and, unlike the raucous newspaper offices Kim was accustomed to, the offices of Charles Scribner's were positively genteel. For one thing, they were completely free of tobacco fumes and the telltale odor of strong drink; for another, the rough joking and casual cursing were noticeably absent. All Kim could hear was the clacking of typewriters—at least Scribner's had come that far into the twentieth century—and the soft, delicate voices of the young and exceptionally pretty ladies who were hired to operate them.

Maxwell Perkins himself was a young man, close to Kim's age; he had a long, expressive face, blue eyes and thick hair firmly brushed back from a vee at the center of his forehead. A gray fedora was slung on a wooden hat rack, the only piece of furniture in the office save for Perkins' desk and two chairs. Spartan was the word.

"*Western Front* is good. Very good," said Perkins, who was intrigued by Kim's masculine but sensitive looks. After reading *Western Front*, he had expected a big strapping fellow with a ferocious expression. "First of all, the story is dramatic—no reader will be able to put it down once he's into it. Second, the characters are people the reader can care about. And third, from a literary point of view, the economy of language is most impressive."

"Thank you," Kim said. Perkins' observation was astute; Kim had spent hours searching for the clearest, most direct way to express what he wanted to say. He was still working under the theorem Nicole Redon had supplied him in Paris.

"There's not one unnecessary word in the entire manuscript," Perkins went on. "It's a long, multi-charactered book but, still, you haven't padded or even overwritten. It's quite an achievement."

"I always thought the Victorians ruined a perfectly good language with their flowery descriptions," Kim said. "Not to mention their 'polite' evasions of the basic facts of life." It was an oblique way of getting into the problems he anticipated with some of the rougher language.

Perkins smiled a shy and appealing smile. Kim couldn't quite interpret its meaning. "A prissy bunch, the Victorians," said the editor.

Kim nodded. It was his turn to smile. He took Perkins' comment to mean that there would be no censorship problems after all.

"How do you feel about revisions? I hesitate to impose on a writer's intentions," Perkins said tentatively.

"I welcome suggestions. Constructive ones. I'd like to hear them," Kim said. Above all, he considered himself a professional and he could not imagine a professional writer who would not welcome suggestions about how to improve a piece of work. "Of course, I can't promise I'll change a thing. But I'll certainly listen."

"I think—and the other editors here agree with me— that the long flashback about the hero's bird hunting with his father stops the flow of narrative. It's good but it comes right at the beginning of the book. If you place it later it will help the reader understand the hero's love/ hate of guns but it won't stop the pull of the story," said Perkins. "The second problem—and, again, all of us here agree—is the transitions. Time transitions in particular . . ."

"They're clumsy and they go on too long," Kim interrupted, anticipating Perkins' comment. Perkins nodded. "I was aware that they were long and cumbersome but I couldn't figure out how else to let the reader know that there was a change in place or time."

"You could borrow an idea from yourself and do what you do with adjectives." Perkins' tone was diffident.

"Leave out the transitions?" The idea had never occurred to Kim in all the hours he had spent trying to find an acceptable way to deal with the boring yet apparently essential passages.

"Why not?"

"I never thought of that!" Kim said, excited. "What I'll do is leave a few blank lines of space. It will indicate a transition to the reader. What a brilliant idea! Thank you!"

"Well, it was *your* idea," Perkins pointed out.

"But I would never have had it without you!" said Kim. "You don't know how I struggled with those damn transitions and I still never did get them to satisfy me. I can't wait to cross every one of them out."

"I want to make it clear, though, that Scribner's wants to publish *Western Front* whether or not you make any of the changes," said Perkins. "Don't feel compelled."

"It's very gentlemanly of you to make that clear," Kim said. "But I agree with you one hundred per cent about the transitions. About the hunting flashback, I'll have to reread it to see what I think now that I have your reaction. If I agree, I'll be happy to place it later in the book. What I want is the best book I can write. I'm not interested in winning arguments with my publisher."

"Then Scribner's is going to be your publisher?"

"Definitely," said Kim. The suggestion about the transitions had sold him—not, he reminded himself, that he needed a lot of selling.

"I took the liberty of preparing a contract," Perkins said. "It has the usual terms plus an advance of five hundred dollars. We don't usually pay advances but we feel that it will show how highly we think of *Western Front*. If you'll sign the contract I can get a check ready for you by the time we return from lunch." He handed Kim the contract, stapled together and bound with the blue sheets so familiar to Kim from his father's law office. To Perkins' surprise, Kim leaned back in his chair and pulled out a pair of steel-rimmed eyeglasses that looked like military issue and began to read the contract. Perkins sat silently until he finished.

"It's wise of you to read it," Perkins said when Kim looked up. "You'd be surprised how many writers don't."

"My father is a lawyer," Kim said. "I was brought up not to sign anything without reading it." Kim signed two copies of the contract, one for Scribner's and one for himself, and the two men left for the nearby Algonquin, where Perkins had a reservation.

Perkins, a shy man, nevertheless seemed to know everyone. He was greeted by Alexander Woollcott, tubby, witty, powerful; by Heywood Broun, a hypochondriac who carried his electrocardiograms around with him; Dorothy Parker, slim, dark, with a fast mouth and sad eyes. At another table he greeted Ilona Vanderpoel, a well-known authors' agent, sitting alone, waiting to be joined by her lunch partner. He introduced her to Kim who had never met her before. She had ash-blond hair and was, even sitting, tall and straight. When she smiled at Kim, her smile reminded him suddenly, piercingly, of Nicole Redon. Nicole! His heart stopped at the thought of her. Strangely, in repose there was little resemblance between the two women; when they smiled, though, they might have been taken for sisters.

"How's Scott's new book coming?" Perkins asked.

"Very well, I understand," said the agent. "He left last month for Europe. Actually"—she looked at Kim—"I'm surprised there's an author left in New York. They're all living in Paris. They seem to find inspiration there."

"I'm no different," Kim responded. "My novel is set mostly in France."

"See?" said Ilona to Perkins. "What have I been telling you?"

At that moment her lunch partner arrived and Perkins and Kim made their way to a table in the very back, Perkins' usual table, and, drinks ordered, Kim told Perkins newspaper stories, Paris stories, and S. I. Brace stories. He told how he had come to have the experiences he had written about in *Western Front* and of the notes he already had made for another novel, which he was planning to title *A Matter of Honor*. The lunch was a great success: Kim talked and Perkins listened, each man doing what he enjoyed most. By the time they returned to the office the check was ready and Kim and Perkins had established a good rapport. In Perkins, Kim saw a sensitive editor who appreciated his work and his intention: to be both a popular entertainer and a literary artist. Perkins, for his part, thought that Kim had what the movies called "It"—an expansive, larger-than-life personality. Kim was that rare creature, a man's man and woman's man at the same time. It was a quality that would sell a lot of books.

"That word you've used—" Perkins said as Kim was about to leave his office. "We're not going to be able to print it."

"What word?"

"Kim, you're a sophisticated man and you have sophisticated friends but the people who are going to read your book aren't as worldly as you are. We're going to have to delete it."

94

"It? What?" Kim's blue eyes glinted with mischievous pleasure. "Delete what?"

"Well, you know," Perkins was a New Englander and he almost literally blushed crimson. "This is the United States. We can't print . . . words . . . like . . ."

"Like what? What are you talking about?"

"Four letters," said Perkins uncomfortably. "Begins with the sixth letter."

"A,B,C,D,E,F . . ." Kim counted out, using the fingers of both hands. "F! F? Four letters? Let's see . . . *from. Four. Fine. Foul. Farm. Fern. Furl. Fort . . .*" He let his voice run down. He gave his editor a look of mystified perplexity.

"You know," said Perkins soberly. "*Everyone* knows. It's just that no one uses it."

"Honestly, I'd tell you if I knew," said Kim innocently. "I don't have the faintest idea of what you're talking about."

Perkins drew his desk calendar toward him and wrote one word on it and pushed it across the desk to Kim.

"Oh," said Kim, the light seeming to dawn. "*Fuck!*" Perkins cringed as Kim's voice boomed out across the office. "*Fuck!*"

"Not on company time!" boomed another editor, who happened to pass Perkins office at that moment and stuck his head in the door. "Charlie Scribner has very strict rules against it."

Several weeks of negotiations, which embarrassed Perkins but entertained Kim, passed before an agreement was finally reached. The word would appear upon Kim's insistence. Upon the insistence of Charles Scribner's and Sons it would receive a new spelling. *Phug.*

"The negotiations were as complex as the one that led up to the Treaty of Versailles," Kim liked to say, and the anecdote of "that word" joined the "A deal's a deal" story to become part of the legend that was already growing up around Kim Hendricks.

2.

It was almost five when Kim arrived home, carrying his check and his contract and waving a bottle of real French champagne that he'd bought from a society bootlegger who worked out of a suite in the Waldorf-Astoria. He had Gus Leggett in tow—he'd run into him in the lobby of the Waldorf. Gus told Kim he was in New York on business, and Kim told Gus his good news and invited him to come along for the celebration.

"Look what I've got!" Kim was ebullient as he let himself into the apartment. Sally had just come in from marketing and was in the sunny kitchen, unloading bags of fresh produce from the nearby Italian greengrocer.

"The check, the contract, the champagne, or the friend?" Sally asked as Kim smothered her in a huge bear hug, kissed her as passionately as if they'd been alone, and then introduced Gus.

"All! Any! Take your pick!" Kim said. "Sally, Perkins is a genius! And so is your husband! Boy, do we have plenty to celebrate! They even gave me an advance! We're going to go on a five-hundred-dollar spree!"

As Kim went on, Sally thought happily that Kim had been even more to celebrate than he realized. While Kim had been at the Algonquin, Sally had gone to her gynecologist, Dr. Arden, who had told her that what she suspected was true: she was going to have a baby. She couldn't wait to tell Kim, but now—with Gus here, with Kim in seventh heaven over his new editor and the wildly optimistic prospects for *Western Front*—wasn't the time.

Kim opened the champagne—it fizzed over the neck

of the bottle from being waved around—and the first toast to *Western Front* was drunk standing up in the kitchen. It took less than an hour for the three of them to finish the bottle. Kim and Gus switched to gin that had literally been brewed in a bathtub, while Sally went to change clothes for a night-long celebration. Kim vowed that he would not return home until every penny of the five hundred dollars had been spent.

They started off at the dingy bar near *The Sun*, where Kim knew everyone and bought drinks for the room. Next they visited a Fifty-second Street speakeasy, where Kim ran into an up-and-coming gangster he knew, by the name of Legs Diamond, who joined the party at Kim's insistence. By then it was eight and they walked up to the Plaza, where Kim ordered huge dinners for everyone and a bottle of champagne apiece.

"At the rate you're going, that five hundred dollars isn't going to last very long," said Sally, who reveled in Kim's extravagance.

"It's not supposed to last," Kim said. "Money is to spend."

"New York is swell," Gus said when the food came and they had settled down to eat. "But now that you're a writer, you really ought to chuck New York and come to Paris. Living is cheap and good. They never heard of Prohibition. The girls are gorgeous—excuse me, Sally— and if you're a literary man it's nothing less than the center of the universe."

"Oh, would I love that!" Kim said. "I'll tell you, S. I. was right about reporting. Once you've done it long enough it's the same story over and over. Only the dates and names change. What do you think, Sal? Paris?" His words rushed out excitedly, thoughtlessly. The moment he uttered the impulsive invitation he thought of Nicole and nervously pushed the thought aside.

"It would be a dream come true," said Sally. She had a vision of walking their baby—their *baby!*—in the Bois. "It sounds like heaven."

"We have enough money to *get* there," Kim said, and he tried hard to shut out the glowing image of Nicole Redon that kept forcing its way into his mind. "I don't know if we'll have enough to *stay* there. If we go, I won't want to get another job."

"If you need money, you know you can count on me," Diamond said. He was very well-dressed—from Brooks Brothers—and very well spoken. He could have passed for a college man. He liked and admired Kim. He thought Kim Hendricks was a real gentleman. Kim always paid for alternate rounds of drinks, he never got sloppy drunk, he never used curse words of any kind, and he was a married man who kept himself clean. He kept his hands off the bimbos—both the two-dollar-a-night hookers and the society broads who gave it away for nothing. "Interest free. Just name the amount."

Kim nodded his thanks. He knew Diamond meant it. He was a man of his word.

"We can use my trust fund, too," Sally said. She had a small trust fund, left by her grandfather, that paid her an income of twenty-five hundred dollars a year—enough, carefully managed, to support two in Paris modestly.

"I don't know about being supported by my wife," Kim said. "Room and board, that's the husband's job. At least the way I was brought up."

"It doesn't bother Ernie Hemingway. They're living off Hadley's trust fund. But I don't think Kim's going to have much of a problem," Gus said. "In fact, I'll start you off on the right foot. I'll buy the French rights to *Western Front* for two hundred and fifty dollars in advance plus the usual royalties. How about it, Kim?"

Everyone turned to Kim. Advances were rare; on foreign rights, they were unheard-of.

98

"How can I refuse?" Kim asked, stunned. He had never had any interest in money except to spend it, and now it seemed to be pouring down on his head. He found he loved the feeling.

"Then it's a deal?" Gus held out his hand.

"It's a deal," Kim said, and the two shook on it.

"Waiter, more champagne!" Kim ordered.

The celebration moved on. There was a writers' bar on MacDougal where everyone knew Kim and had already heard the news about *Western Front*, and where the envy was more potent than the bootleg hootch; a speakeasy on Eighth Avenue where the girls were boys; an Irish bar on Third Avenue, under the El, where a fistfight broke out over who had reached for a hard-boiled egg first. At some point they went back to the Plaza, where Kim gleefully spent the last of the five hundred dollars. He announced that he was now broke and starving: "A real writer, at last," he said. Diamond insisted on taking a turn as host and took them to a place he knew in Little Italy, where he ordered big plates of pasta loaded with garlic and olive oil.

"It absolutely guarantees you won't have a hangover," he said, topping the pasta with pungent, freshly grated cheese and big flakes of black pepper from a wooden mill. The owner produced bottles of a heavy, delicious red wine that his father had made from the grapes he grew in his garden, behind his Mulberry Street apartment. Everyone ate and drank and talked about Paris and writers, about how the loan sharks worked, about the incredibly short skirts the flappers were wearing with rolled stockings and bobbed hair; about Negro jazz, the hip flasks college boys were wearing out in the open, and the big, tough bouncer at a speak on lower Fifth Avenue who belonged to some strict fundamentalist sect and, when he wasn't reading his Bible, used its heft to subdue unruly patrons. Sally listened to it all, taking it all in,

99

fascinated. With Kim she always felt she was right in the middle of everything, and she still had the biggest surprise of all! She had decided that as soon as she had the baby they'd go to Paris. Life was more perfect than she could have imagined when she was only just a bride. It seemed so long ago!

"You're not the only one in the family with exciting news," Sally told Kim the next day. They'd slept until two in the afternoon and were having eggs and bacon before Kim left for *The Sun*. "I saw Dr. Arden yesterday. Kim, we're going to have a baby!"

"A baby?" Kim was thunderstruck. It took him a moment to realize that he felt both thrilled and trapped. It was strange, he thought, feeling two conflicting emotions at the same time. It reminded him of the times he had fainted, once in the St. Gobain Forest and the second time in the Wilsons' Washington Square house. Feeling two feelings at once stopped a man from thinking straight. Numbly, Kim asked, "Are you sure?"

"Of course I'm sure. I suspected it anyway, and Dr. Arden confirmed it. Aren't you happy?" Sally's eyes glowed with her own excitement. "Aren't you just thrilled?"

"I thought you were using a diaphragm," Kim said, not yet recovered from his shock. When they had first gotten married, Sally wanted to make sure she didn't get pregnant. Their life together was so free, so untied-down, so exciting and unpredictable that Sally wanted to enjoy it for a while before she took on the responsibilities of a baby. Kim had been violently opposed to the diaphragm. He called anything that interfered with nature not only · unnatural but perverse. He told Sally that she would be playing with fate and that no one had a right to do that. But Sally, uncharacteristically, had been insistent and had gone to Dr. Arden for a fitting. Kim was still violently opposed, and after several days of argument they finally reached an agreement: Sally could use her diaphragm as long as she inserted it secretly and Kim did not know about it. But Kim's vehement objections and impassioned arguments had had their effect on Sally. Sometimes she used her diaphragm; sometimes she didn't. Sometimes she hoped she'd get pregnant; sometimes she hoped she wouldn't. Now that she was pregnant, she was overjoyed.

"I didn't always," she told Kim. "Now, tell me, aren't you just thrilled?"

"Half of me is . . ."

"And the other half?"

"Scared," admitted Kim. He could not bring himself to tell her that now that he was embarked on his career as a writer, now that he could begin to think about quitting his job and living the really freewheeling life he'd dreamed of, a baby was the last impediment he needed. He hadn't known it until right now, but he had changed his mind about the diaphragm. He had begun to depend on it, fully realizing that his hectic, impulsive life, the life he loved, the life he shared with Sally, depended on that disc of rubber. "How do you feel? Physically, I mean?"

"Wonderful! I've never felt better!"

"You've never looked better!" Despite their late night, Sally's eyes and skin glowed and her corn-blond hair reflected back the rays of sunshine that came in through the south-facing window. "And you're as slim as ever. There's no way to tell from looking at you that there's a baby in there." He touched her belly. The absence of an apparent physical change in Sally made Kim feel better. He knew he would need time to get used to the whole idea.

"I'm a little scared, too. I think everyone is," said Sally thoughtfully. "But now tell me about the other half. The happy half . . ."

"I'm ridiculously happy!" Kim said, his eyes beginning to light up. "I'm going to be a father! Imagine that! Yesterday an honest-to-goodness writer! Today a father! Now I'll really have to get to work."

"Why?" Sally knew that Kim always felt he wasn't working hard enough, and yet he worked harder than anyone she'd ever known.

"I've got to get rich and famous. The baby will need a father he can be proud of."

"And what if *he's* a she?"

"Girls need fathers to be proud of, too," Kim said. It had not occurred to him that their child might be a girl. Not that he cared one way or the other once he thought about it. "You always told me how proud you were of your father. Of the way people came to him with all their problems, not just their medical problems."

"You don't have to do one thing more for our baby—"—Sally felt a thrill when she said the words out loud—"to be proud of its father."

"Well, I'm going to be so rich and so famous that the Hendricks heir will be the proudest kid on two continents," said Kim, his ambitions refueled by Sally's news but his doubts, which resided next to his ambitions, refueled also. Now more than ever, everything—the kind of life he wanted and now the future of an unborn baby—depended on *Western Front*.

Kim kissed Sally a tender goodby and left for *The Sun*. By the time he reached the office, he felt on top of the world. He didn't know whether it was due to his meeting with Maxwell Perkins the day before or to Sally's surprising news, or whether it was simply his natural exuberance and the fact that Legs Diamond knew what he was talking about when he said that pasta and garlic absolutely prevented a hangover.

3.

"We're having circulation problems," S. I. was saying in late August. He had invited Kim to lunch at the next-door saloon and they were dining on their by-now usual large amount of whisky and small amount of food.

"We're being squeezed on two sides. The sob sisters on the tabloids are grabbing more readers every day. *The News* is going great guns. Hearst is planning a new rag called *The Mirror*. That's one side of the problem. On the other are the magazines. They're eating into our readership, too. *Collier's* and *The Saturday Evening Post* are topping their circulation figures every issue. The official line is that *The Sun*'s figures are stabilized, but that's a lot of bull. I've been telling the big bosses we have to get aggressive and compete, but I might as well tell Valentino to stop slicking down his hair. I was wasting my breath. Until this morning. There was a big powwow in the boss's office upstairs." S. I. was speaking intently and ignoring the chipped teacup of bootleg in front of him. "I went to that meeting armed. I had a list of our biggest-drawing stories. Do you know what was right there on the top of the list?"

"No," said Kim. It was the answer S. I. wanted. It also happened to be the truth.

"Your 1919 Paris articles," S. I. said. "And do you know what I want now?"

Kim shook his head.

"More! More! More!" S. I. said, suddenly sounding like his usual self. "I want you to go to Paris—this time

The Sun will pay for the trip—and do a series of updates. I want to read about the sexy mademoiselles, the *bon vin*, the Left Bank cafés, the artsy-craftsy bunch, the fairy clothes designers, the chestnut trees in blossom . . . you know, the kind of stuff that will make the average Joe's tongue hang out." S. I. stopped long enough to pick up the teacup and take a long satisfying pull. "Did I forget to mention the sexy mademoiselles?"

"You didn't forget." Kim grinned. "You know, that's the second time this summer someone told me Paris is practically the center of the world."

"Is the other guy paying?"

"Are you kidding?" Kim asked. "He's independently rich and he's a publisher besides. Need I say more?"

"Hell, no! Rich men and publishers—they're the cheapest bastards in the world," said S. I. "By the way, I hear Scribner's is going to publish a novel you wrote."

"That's right," Kim said. It was about time S. I. mentioned it, and Kim waited for the congratulations.

"How the hell did you get the time to write a novel? You're supposed to be working for me."

"It wasn't easy," Kim said. "I worked nights and weekends. I practically killed myself."

"That's good," said S. I., mollified. "Now when are you going to Paris?"

"Sally's pregnant," Kim said.

"So what does that have to do with anything? She doesn't need you any more. You've already done your part," S. I. said. "I want you to go the same time I want everything . . ."

"I know," Kim said. "Yesterday! Yesterday! Give me a little time to get ready."

"You can take all the time you want," said S. I. "As long as you leave the day after tomorrow."

Kim nodded. He would do the best job anyone ever

did on Paris. He would see everything. Meet everyone. Go everywhere. Except to the rue Montaigne.

"Dr. Arden says I shouldn't travel," said Sally.

"Is something wrong?" Kim asked anxiously. Now that he'd had the summer to get used to the idea, he was looking forward to the baby. The same day Kim had told Sally about the Paris assignment, Sally had returned to Dr. Arden and asked if she could make the trip. Secretly, she was pleased when he told her it wouldn't be a very good idea. She hadn't been feeling as well as she pretended to Kim, and she knew how impatient he was with illness, which he took for weakness. Earlier, Dr. Arden had quashed Sally's desire to take a trip to Saint Louis to visit her parents.

"Nothing's the matter. Except that occasionally I stain slightly. It's nothing to worry about, Dr. Arden says, as long as I take it easy."

Kim looked crestfallen. "I don't want you to feel tied down," Sally said. "The baby isn't due until December and you'll be back before then . . ."

"But I don't want to go alone," Kim said. He was afraid to go alone. No, that wasn't exactly true. He was afraid of the rue Montaigne. "I want you to come with me."

"How can I?" Sally asked. "Dr. Arden—"

"We've never been separated. Not for a single night since we've been married. I *need* you, Sal." The look on Kim's face was so bereft, so tragically downcast that at the moment Sally would have walked through the pits of Hell for him.

"I'll go to Paris, Kimbee, if you really want me to."

"I want you to," Kim said, and his eyes lit up again. With Sally by his side, the temptation of the rue Montaigne would be much easier to resist. Sally would be his protection against his own feelings. He expressed his passion ardently. "I couldn't bear to be without you. I wouldn't even be half alive without you. You *know* that."

"Then it's settled. I'll ask Dr. Arden to recommend a French doctor," Sally said, but she wondered if she was doing the right thing. What if something did go wrong? What if something terrible happened and she didn't know the words in French to explain what was happening to her? And what was a French hospital like? Hadn't she once heard that the French used midwives instead of doctors? Hadn't Dr. Arden told her that, although he saw no imminent danger, there was always a possibility that the staining might increase and cause a problem?

"Oh, that's wonderful! Sal, you're wonderful! We'll go to Paris together. The kid may even be born bilingual!"

When Sally asked Dr. Arden to recommend a French doctor, he asked to see Kim and in the end it was Kim who, after listening to what the doctor had to say, changed his mind.

"It really is better for you to stay here," he said. "I realize it was selfish of me to try to talk you into going to Paris. But it will almost kill me not to have you there with me." There were tears in his eyes when he said goodby, and he held Sally as if he would never let her go.

4.

Paris was every man's dream of Paris and Kim saw it all and wrote it all. Sylvia Beach's lending library and bookstore at 12 rue de l'Odéon, its shelves crammed with books and walls covered with photographs of famous writers. And Miss Beach herself, who had pretty legs, loved to joke and gossip, and knew all the writers in Paris and, it was said, supported half of them. The apartment at 27 rue de Fleurus, where Gertrude Stein gave advice and encouragement while Miss Toklas did needlepoint and served mirabelle, and the pictures—by Miró and Picasso, Modigliani and Matisse—changed the way people thought about painting. He visited Hadley and Ernest on the rue de Cardinal Lemoine and lounged on the huge gilded mahogany bed while Ernest read a story he couldn't sell called "Up in Michigan." He dined with James Joyce at Michaud's and was happy to pick up the check for the Irish author whose shocking work was already causing scandalized comments from the few who had read it. Kim met old friends and made new ones at the Anglo-American Press Club, went to the track at Auteuil, ate warm chestnuts from the street vendors' carts, drank café au lait at the Café des Amateurs, Martinique rum at the Deux Magots, old Cahors at the Closerie de Lilas. He wrote an ode to all the bridges that cross the Seine; wrote about the Hole in the Wall Bar, where dope peddlers sold opium in cold cream jars; about a White Russian prince who lived in a Pigalle cellar and drove a taxi; about the licentious *boîtes* on the Boulevard Montparnasse and the elegant *clubs de nuit* on the Champs-Elysées; and he filed a story on Edith Wharton's famous all-white garden. He was proud of himself for never setting foot on the rue Montaigne and ashamed of himself for being eternally tempted. He kept hoping that he would accidentally run into Nicole, surely a possibility, since she was one of the young, exciting people other people were talking about. He was sure—his heart pounding and his pulse racing—that he would bump into her just around the next corner, or that he would turn slightly in his chair at a bistro and see her at a nearby table, or casually walk into a party and there she would be across the room! He endlessly imagined their surprised smiles, their excited greetings, their rush to tell each other everything. He wrote words for them and gave them expressions and feelings. He confident, she speechless; he crushing her in his arms, she tender in response; he bold, she shy; he serious, she smiling. He constantly anticipated the happy accident, the surprised moment, the lucky encounter coming when he least expected it, when he was most off-guard. That way, whatever happened would not be his fault. Or it would be *less* his fault. But he never did bump into her, not once.

He also discovered, to his pleased surprise, that in a modest way he and his work were known in Paris, or at least that his journalism was. Hemingway complimented him on the Armistice stories and told him that he had never thought of trying to do anything nearly as interesting in the stuff he sent to the Toronto *Star*. Even Ezra Pound, determinedly aesthetic with his little beard and tantalizing Chinese quotations, complimented him, and Miss Stein, who always seemed to know everything and furthermore had an opinion about it, told him that she admired his journalism enough to allow him the privilege of reading her own experimental writing, which he did and found stupefyingly boring—although, of course, he did not tell her that. Flattered and curious that his columns from 1919 had been clipped and saved and passed around for so many years, Kim asked her how she had happened to get hold of them.

"The same way as everyone else," she said, a mystified expression on her face. "From the collection."

"What collection?"

She reached for a volume from her bookshelves and handed it to Kim. *Paris on the Way to Peace* was the title and when Kim opened it he saw that it was a collection of the articles he'd written for *The Sun*. The volume had been published in Paris by the Cyclops Press and the publisher's address was given as 3 rue du Dragon. Kim had never heard of the Cyclops Press and this was the first time he had known his articles had been reprinted. Reprinted, hell! Actually, they'd been stolen. Someone had published them without Kim's permission and he was furious. Someone owed him not only money but an apology!

He borrowed the book from Miss Stein and took a taxi to the address, which was on the Left Bank just off the place St.-Germain-des-Prés. The first floor of the building was occupied by a *confiseur*; the Cyclops Press was listed on the second floor and Kim walked up the steep staircase, only dimly lit by the old-fashioned gas lamps. Kim opened the door marked Cyclops Press, and an assistant, very young and very pretty, looked up from the paste pot and manuscript she was cutting up and gluing back together. She gazed at him, intrigued. This young man was very attractive and not French. Danish? American? German?

"I want to see the boss." American.

"In there," she said, and watched the good-looking American walk into Mr. Leggett's office without knocking. Without having exchanged another word with him, she knew two things: he was angry and he was, therefore, an author. The two conditions went hand-in-hand. She had never seen a contented author. She wondered if such a strange creature existed.

"Kim! How wonderful to see you!" said Gus. "How the hell are you? Haven't laid eyes on you since the famous five-hundred-dollar spree!"

"Never mind that! What the hell is *this*?" Kim held up *Paris on the Way to Peace*.

"Beautiful job of production, isn't it?" asked Gus, proudly. "Look at that. A genuine leather cover, hand-sewn binding. It's a real collector's item."

"Don't you have any shame? Any ethics?" Kim demanded. "You paid me for *Western Front*, not a collection of *Sun* articles!"

"Calm down, Kim. Calm down!" said Gus. "And *sit* down." Kim was still standing, looming over Gus's desk. "You want a contract and I've got a contract. It's right here just waiting for you. We've just been so busy we haven't gotten around to sending out the contracts." Gus opened a desk drawer and fumbled around, finally withdrawing a one-page printed form. He handed it over the desk to Kim, along with a pen.

"For Christ's sake, Gus, what kind of crook are you? You're supposed to ask the writer *first!*"

"Just an oversight, old boy," said Gus, not the least bit discomfited. "Look here, just sign it and we're in business." Kim glanced at the contract. It was blank.

"I thought all the gangsters were back in your home town with Al Capone peddling lousy hootch," said Kim. "I'm not signing a blank contract. What kind of fool do you think I am?"

"So I'll have it filled in," Gus said nonchalantly. "Sophie!" The girl, thin the way French girls who live on café au lait and Gaoloises will be, entered the small office. Gus started to give her Kim's name, spelling it out for her in French, and his address.

"Gus!"

"Yes?" Gus paused in his dictation.

"Money," said Kim. Gus gave him a blank look. "M-O-N-E-Y" Kim spelled it out for him in English. "I'll spell it in French too, in case you still don't understand me. I want two hundred and fifty dollars. The same as you paid me for *Western Front*."

Gus Leggett looked as if he'd been stabbed.

"I'm not kidding, Gus."

Gus recovered his blank look in record time. Kim admired the old crook. He was fast on his feet.

"Good God, Kim, you didn't think I wasn't going to pay you, did you?" Gus was a master of outraged innocence. Kim wondered if it was a trait genetically handed out to bankers and publishers.

"I'm not leaving this office until you do." He thought of Maxwell Perkins—the difference was night and day, black and white.

Gus pulled out a checkbook, scribbled in it with an 18-karat-gold pen, ripped out the check, and handed it to Kim. "Now let's go across to the Lipp. I'll buy you some lunch. How about some of their good *choucroute* and a bottle of sancerre?"

That afternoon Kim took the check to the bank. It bounced.

"Oh, my lord, this is terribly embarrassing," said Gus the next morning. "Look here, Kim, just put it through again. It was a bookkeeping mix-up. This time I *absolutely guarantee* it."

It bounced again.

The next day was rainy, cats-and-dogs rainy, and Kim planted himself in the *bar-tabac* opposite the offices of the Cyclops Press, waiting for Gus Leggett to show his face. At four in the afternoon Leggett stepped out the door of 3 rue du Dragon and stood on the sidewalk, the gutters running with rain, and in frustration hailed taxi after taxi. They were all taken and Gus got wetter and wetter, his trousers clinging to the backs of his legs, the water running down the brim of his hat into his collar, his raincoat getting so soaked that it stuck to the suit jacket underneath. Now that he had really suffered, now that his face was beet-red in a tantrum of frustration, Kim got up and ducked across the street to where Gus stood fuming and cursing.

"Gus," said Kim quietly.

"Kim!" said Gus, looking up, startled. "How the hell are you?"

Kim took his time and settled himself into a classic boxer's pose, left foot forward, right foot back, swung with his right, and landed a blow on Gus's face, knocking out two teeth and taking his feet right out from under him. Gus landed in the gutter, the blood from his mouth mixing with the Parisian rain, and there in the gutter Kim left him to the mercy of strangers.

The story spread rapidly through the cafés of Montmartre and Kim became something of a hero. It turned out, not unexpectedly, that Kim was not the only writer to whom Gus Leggett owed money, and there was no café into which Kim could go where fellow writers, gleeful at the thought of Gus Leggett lying bleeding in a gutter, did not buy Kim as many drinks as he could hold.

When Hemingway heard about it, he invited Kim to the Ritz. "I wish I'd beat you to it," Hem said. "That bastard's been running around saying that I'm living off my wife. A shot like yours deserves nothing but the best. Let's go have a *coup* at the Ritz."

Despite the fact that Ernie said he was having a rough time financially, unable to sell his fiction and having to depend on the stories he was sending back to Toronto, he was well-known at the Ritz. The barman knew him and they talked a little handicapping, and the waiter, a Berliner, asked after Hadley and bemoaned the recent depreciation of the German mark before bringing them their *fines*.

"I learned more about writing from Cézanne than from any writer, dead or alive. I want to do with words what Cézanne does with paint . . ." Hem was saying when the couple who had just entered the room called a greeting.

"Ernie! Back for the second time today?" The man, almost unreally handsome, nodded at Kim and so did the beautiful woman with him. Kim had noticed them at the doorway of the Ritz bar as soon as they had entered.

112

It was impossible not to notice them. They were extraordinarily good-looking. Both had dark-blondish wavy hair, sapphire-blue eyes and smooth, very rosy, very healthy skin. They resembled each other to an uncanny degree. A pair of almost-twins reflecting their golden gorgeousness back and forth, the reflection multiplying their physical beauty. The man wore what had to be a Savile Row suit, of fine dark wool, with a white, perfectly ironed shirt and a conservative but not somber navy-blue tie with a discreet dark-red figure. The woman wore a luxurious sable coat of a darker brownish-blond shade than her hair, over a dress of black silk cut in a particularly deep vee. Three strands of pearls, a paler creamy-rose than her skin, hung from her throat, luminescent against the naked skin exposed by the low-cut neckline. The two moved in their own golden aura.

"Scott, Zelda," Ernie said, indicating chairs and introducing the couple to Kim.

"You had a tremendous influence on my life," Kim said as they seated themselves. *"This Side of Paradise* is my favorite book and so I decided I wanted the same editor you have."*

Scott smiled, accepting the compliment graciously.

"Champagne, *s'il vous plaît.* Veuve Cliquot '92," Scott ordered. Zelda Fitzgerald moved into her chair as gracefully as a dancer. She turned her body so that it was angled slightly toward Kim, and she held herself so that the tops of her breasts were exposed. With the fingers of her left hand she played with the ends of her lovely hair, and in her right she held a long black cigarette holder banded with gold.

"Scott's in love with Maxwell Perkins," said Ernie.

"So am I," said Kim. "Anyway, I want to tell you again how much I think of *This Side of Paradise.* No one who reads it will ever forget it."

Scott smiled as if he'd just been handed a bouquet.

"See?" he said, turning to Zelda. "My reputation is spreading!"

Zelda didn't answer with words but sipped her champagne and smiled at her husband. The smile was seductive, and there was something strange in that smile, too. Scott responded to the seductiveness of it but, Kim thought, he did not seem to see the strangeness. There was something very touching about the way Scott paraded the compliment before his wife. As if it would make him bigger in her eyes.

"I know who you are!" Scott said in sudden recognition. "You wrote *Western Front*, didn't you? Max wrote me about it. He's not only the best editor. He's the best press agent."

"It's coming out in the spring," Kim said. "Everyone expects it to be a big success. I hope they're right."

"I'm sure they are," said Zelda, speaking for the first time. She had a slightly husky voice; it may have been from the Russian cigarettes she was smoking in her long holder. Hem looked at her, disapproval all over his face. He said nothing. Kim noticed the interplay and it was an uncomfortable moment.

"Are you writing a new book?" he asked Scott.

"I just finished one and I'm going over the proofs right now. I'm calling it *The Beautiful and the Damned*. What do you think of the title?"

"I'm surprised Scribner's will print such a naughty word. And in a title too!" Kim said. Everybody laughed.

"To *Western Front!*" Scott said, and raised his glass. Kim noticed that Hem did not drink; it occurred to Kim that he was envious. Scott drained his own glass in one swallow and leaned back in his chair to allow the waiter to pour another.

"I wonder if war books are going to sell," Hemingway said. "It's so soon after the war it's hard to tell if people are sick of it or if they're still interested in reading even more."

"Hem's planning a war book, in case you didn't know," said Scott. "It's going to be a good one, too. Hem never sells out. That's my fatal flaw, you know."

"Hem doesn't *need* to sell out, as you put it," Zelda said in her husky voice. She was defending her husband and Kim realized that all kinds of undercurrents were swirling about. Ernie and Zelda very obviously disliked each other. Zelda consulted a tiny diamond wristwatch. "Darling, we must go. You know how the French are about time."

Scott stood and helped his wife up, touching her tenderly. They exchanged an intimate glance. They were obviously deeply in love.

"Bye, Ernie. Bye, Kim," said Scott. "I hope Zelda and I will see you again, Kim. The truth is that except for Hem we hardly know any writers in Paris. Only aristocrats." Scott laughed self-consciously. He was simultaneously bragging and poking fun at himself for being impressed.

Just before Zelda left, she took the rosebud from the silver bud vase in the center of the marble-topped table and thrust it into the vee neckline of her dress. As she did, a thorn pricked her skin near the pulse point at the base of her throat. It must have hurt but Zelda did not seem to notice. A drop of blood beaded on her skin and clung there like a tiny, mortal jewel.

"He seems very nice," said Kim. "I like him."

"He's weak," said Ernie, "and Zelda's going to ruin him."

5.

Kim and Ernie stayed until eight. Ernie had a date to meet Hadley and he left the Ritz on the rue Cambon side, the same way he and Kim had entered. It was Kim's last night in Paris and he decided to stroll through the elegant lobby and out the main entrance on the place Vendôme. He stood there for a moment under the arcades of the famous hotel and enjoyed the cool, early-winter air after the warmth of the bar. He gazed absently across the place Vendôme and at first he couldn't read the lettering on the awning of the shop just opposite. Then it came into focus: *Nicole Redon*. Nicole! Then, as if directed by the very hand of destiny itself, she came out of the front door of the shop. She stood on the sidewalk for a moment, looking for a taxi. Without thinking, without even knowing when or how he had begun to move, Kim found himself running across the broad square, dodging traffic, causing drivers to slam on their brakes and blare their horns in warning. He almost got himself killed and drivers leaned out their windows to curse him. He did not stop; he did not even slow down.

"Nicole! Nicole!" he shouted.

He was too far away and with the noise of traffic, the sound of horns and shouted curses, she did not hear him. She glanced up for a second to see what the commotion was, but just then a taxi pulled up and she got in, closing the door after her.

"Nicole! Nicole!"

He was running, running, out of breath now, his heart pounding. He could see her clearly, illuminated by the soft interior light of the cab, leaning forward, giving an

116

address to the driver. Her hair was shiny and alive, shot with gold. Her lips moved silently. He could remember their warmth and their texture and their taste. He lunged forward, trying to rap on the window to get her attention. He was just a millimeter short. The taxi, already moving, picked up speed, changed gear, and turned out of the place Vendôme and into the rue Castiglione. Kim stood alone in the traffic-choked square. Did he really smell a trace of her perfume or did he just imagine it?

All at once, the square seemed to empty. Everyone had already gone wherever they were going. Home. To a restaurant. To some warm, well-lit place, anticipating dinner and the evening ahead. Kim shivered suddenly, feeling the cold, and he could no longer battle down the feelings he had barricaded himself against from the moment he had returned to Paris. All the times he had imagined running into Nicole, what he would say to her, what she would say to him, how they would be with each other, how it would feel the first moment they touched again. He was overcome with a horribly forlorn sense of loss and longing, and the tears that ran down his face mingled with the Parisian mist which closed over him like a soft, gray cloak.

The next day, as planned, he returned to New York. He thought it was just as well.

Nineteen twenty-two was the year of the new baby and new success. All the good things about success, he had imagined; all of the bad ones came as a surprise.

*Every day was different. There was a tension
and an excitement in the air that was almost
physical. Always a new exhibition, or a recital
of the new music of Les Six, or a Dadaist man-
ifestation, or a costume ball in Montparnasse,
or a première of a new play or ballet, or one of
Étienne de Beaumont's fantastic "Soirées de
Paris" in Montmartre—and you'd go to each
one and find everybody else there, too. There
was such a passionate interest in everything
that was going on, and it seemed to engender
activity.*

—Gerald Murphy

CHAPTER FIVE

1.

"THERE'S A CERTAIN CHEMIST at Coty
who's unhappy . . . very unhappy," Leon Severin was
saying in April of 1923. He had come to Paris on business
and had invited Nicole to lunch. Leo, who had missed
out on investing in Nicole in Biarritz and had never

stopped kicking himself, had an idea. "He's threatening to quit, to find another employer, to go into business for himself, He says Coty doesn't appreciate him. Well, naturally, I thought of you. I remember you in Biarritz, always in a cloud of perfume, raiding Cyril's scent jars, not to mention the samples I brought from my own factories. You're getting a name for yourself and it's time to think about marketing your own perfume."

"It's a good idea," said Nicole, who had also been thinking about it. "No one's done it really well yet. Poiret tried but it was only a halfhearted attempt. Worth has *Je Reviens* but he concentrates on his clothes and the perfume is just an afterthought. No one's really made a splash. You could advertise a perfume, you know."

"You sound like an American," Leo laughed. "They think advertising can sell anything."

"I like the Americans! They have everything anyone wants—jazz, automobiles, Coca-Cola, colored nail polish, movies and cocktails. No one was born wanting these things. The Americans know that if they advertise them they can create the desire for them," said Nicole, who subscribed to all the American magazines and found the advertisements at least as interesting as the editorial content. "I think there's no reason you couldn't sell perfume exactly the way the Americans sell soap and shirt collars. Just because no one's tried it, yet . . ."

"Then it would be a good idea for you to meet him," Leo said. "His name is Edouard Noiret. I'll make the arrangements."

Nicole thought the entire venture seemed like one of the Mata Hari spy stories that had emerged during the war. There was an intermediary: Leo. A clandestine meeting set up in a neighborhood where no one would be recognized. A would-be defector with a secret formula.

Edouard Noiret turned out to be a short, slender man

with the colorless skin of a person who never went outdoors, his blue eyes warily watchful behind thick wire-rimmed glasses. He sat at a back table in a shabby café on the rue La Fayette, in the Ninth Arondissement diamond district. The rest of the tables were occupied by bearded Hasidim sipping tea from glasses set in metal filigree holders and conducting business in Hebrew. They looked at the floor as Nicole entered, their religion forbidding them even to look at a woman they did not know. Noiret looked, thought Nicole, like a jailer, and only his hands, immaculately clean, tightly knotted into fists, one balanced on top of the other, betrayed emotion: a combination of anger and suspicion.

"You didn't tell me it would be a woman," was the first thing Noiret said to Leo. He spoke as if Nicole did not exist. Between Noiret, who would not talk to her, and the Hasidim, who would not look at her, Nicole had the same painful sense of isolation and exclusion that had poisoned her childhood. Edouard Noiret was descended on his maternal side from a family of Prussian warriors who despised women and everything about them. It was therefore, one of the ironies of his life that he spent it in laboratories creating perfumes and cosmetics for their adornment. "I thought we were here to talk business."

"Nicole's money is as good as any man's," Leo said. "She's here on my recommendation."

"What business did you have in mind?" asked Nicole, cutting through Noiret's attack and Leo's defense. "I've seen nothing yet. I don't even know what you're offering."

"A new perfume," said Leo.

"New!" exclaimed Noiret. His expression concealed emotion; his voice trembled with it. "I developed it in 1919—the formula sits in Coty's safe. They refuse to produce it because they say it's too expensive to make."

"Do you have a sample?" asked Nicole. She was not afraid of Noiret's anger. It was the kind of anger, the result of unfair treatment and frustration, that she had so often felt as a child.

Edouard Noiret shook his head in the negative.

Nicole realized he wanted her to beg. "I can't do a thing until I smell it, wear it," she said. "It's up to you if you want me to."

Noiret looked at Leo. He was torn between wanting to hoard his discovery for himself and the wish to have the world acknowledge his genius. "She's right," said Leo. "Nothing can happen until she has the scent."

Finally, speaking softly and deliberately, Noiret said, "I'll bring you a sample the day after tomorrow. Here, at this café. At the same time of day."

"Good," said Nicole. Ironic, she thought, negotiating for a new perfume in this dingy café, the smell of urine from the *pissoir* in the courtyard perfectly apparent.

"He doesn't inspire trust," said Nicole and she and Leo returned to the place Vendôme. "Is his formula really so good? There are many chemists in Paris, you know. We can surely find someone less prickly."

"Noiret's developed nothing but best-sellers," said Leo. "He's brilliant."

Nicole allowed herself to be persuaded to continue with Edouard Noiret. She had arrived at the point in her success when she felt that having a perfume would add to her prestige and increase the value of her label. When Leo mentioned that he had had the same idea and that he wanted to help, Nicole jumped at the chance. Whether or not the scent would be Edouard Noiret's was another question.

On the appointed day, Nicole and Leo went again to the rue La Fayette, where Edouard Noiret, checking his watch to make certain that they were precisely on time, handed over a chemist's vial stoppered with hard rubber. Nicole sniffed it from the vial, then rubbed some on her inner wrist, smelling it again for the top note as soon as she had rubbed it in.

"I'll wear it for the next twenty-four hours," she said. "Then I'll let you know what I think."

Nicole was intrigued by Noiret's scent for the very reasons Coty had refused over and over to market it. It was radical; it smelled like no other perfume available. All other perfumes smelled like the flowers from which they were formulated: rose, hyacinth, lily, jasmine, carnation. Scents had one dimension only, distinctive but unsurprising. Noiret's scent was elusive. It smelled like many flowers combined but like no one flower in particular. Like the paintings now revolutionizing the world of art, Noiret's perfume was an abstraction from nature. Nicole was intrigued. But one half-hour after she had applied it, Nicole noticed that the elusive, abstract quality had gone and that all she could smell was jasmine. The "radical" scent now smelled like other jasmine perfumes. The next day, when Nicole met Noiret for the third time on the rue La Fayette, she told him that although she thought the scent interesting at first, the complexity of it had disappeared almost immediately and it smelled like a jasmine one could purchase anywhere.

"I'm only interested in a scent that is like no other," Nicole said. "Do you understand? I want something no one else has. If you can make your scent last, if you can make it so that the second and third notes are *identical* to the first, then I will be interested."

"That will be difficult," Noiret said. "It's never been done."

But he seemed pleased at Nicole's astuteness and now the tables had turned: he suddenly seemed anxious to satisfy her and said that he would go back to his laboratory to see if he could revise the formula to meet her specifications. Over the summer and fall of 1923, Noiret brought Nicole three samples, each in a chemist's glass vial, each identified only by the number of the sample. Not one of them pleased Nicole and each time she sent Noiret back to his laboratory to try again. She was beginning to give up hope but Leo counseled her to be patient.

"The manufacture of a perfume is a very complex process and you, Nicole, are asking for something that's not been done before. Be patient."

"I'm not good at being patient," she said.

"Then this is a good opportunity to get some practice," said Leo. "It will be good for your character."

Nicole shrugged and returned to her atelier, where she knew what she was doing and could control it. Since the first "charming chemise," the dresses Nicole made had hardly changed. Unlike other designers, who raised and lowered hemlines, moved the waist up or down, and this year, influenced by the discovery of King Tut's tomb, were selling the "Egyptian look," Nicole evolved her designs along one strong, clean line. Like the work being done at the Bauhaus, Nicole's clothes were all line, all function, absolutely different from everyone else's clothes and immediately identifiable. By 1923, Nicole's clients included some of the most interesting women in Paris—the new group of successful working women: actresses, authors, intellectuals, artists. While other designers created exclusive models for society women who considered meeting a friend in the same design a social disaster, Nicole made twenty of the same dress and never thought about it twice. Nicole's little dresses were almost uniforms, and their wearers formed a select brigade of avant-garde chic. As her business grew and she became more successful, success brought her money and a degree of freedom, but it did not make her happy. She had not expected it to; she expected love to make her happy.

2.

OEDIPUS REX
By Jean Cocteau
Scenery by Picasso
Music by Honegger
Costumes by Redon

The billboard stood outside the Théâtre de Montmartre, a rickety old theater provocatively located just between the Sacré-Coeur and the honky-tonk nightclubs of Pigalle. The production was billed as a free adaptation, and since the avant-garde was young and uncelebrated at the time, the creators worked free of commercial restraints. The wings of the theater were visited by everyone attached to the arts. Man Ray made portraits of the actors. Frank Crowninshield of *Vanity Fair* and French *Vogue* published descriptions and sketches of the masks designed by Picasso and the costumes, in earth colors, designed by Redon. Journalists, artists and the mistresses of artists, musicians and aspiring directors wandered in and out during rehearsals. In future years many of them would become celebrated, but in 1923 their departures from convention offended people. Cubists made paintings that shocked, experimental writers wrote books without plots, poets created under the influence of their opium-induced dreams, composers wrote atonal, unmelodic scores. It was a stimulating experience for Nicole, who had never designed stage costumes, and she had been invited to do the job by Cocteau himself, who told her that her dresses were the only modern clothes in Paris.

Nicole went to the Louvre to study the arts and artifacts of ancient Greece and designed robes and tunics and mantles and classic draperies. The only similarity between the costumes she made for Cocteau and the dresses she made for her clients was that they moved, that they were clothes to work in, to be active in, to be *alive* in. Evenings, after work, Nicole went to the small theater, which was heated inadequately by an iron stove in one corner, and stood behind the rail behind the last row of seats to watch rehearsals and study how well or how badly her costumes worked.

Her mind was preoccupied by flow, drape and line when she was suddenly aware of someone standing next to her. He was tall and blond and exquisitely elegant. Then Nicole remembered meeting him at a party on the night of the Armistice. She'd been with Kim and Kim had been jealous later.

"My mistress likes your dresses so much she is threatening to buy dozens," he said. Boy Mellany had happened to pass the Théâtre de Montmartre on his way to the Pigalle nightclub where his Brazilian mistress was dancing in the Josephine Baker revue. He saw the name Redon on the billboard and, on a chance, had come in. "But this is not exactly the place I'd expect to find you," he said. He gestured at the shabby, not-very-warm theater. As Nicole turned slightly to face him, Boy became aware of her perfume. "I imagined you in your atelier, designing elegant gowns."

"If I had any sense, that's where I'd be," said Nicole. "Actors complain, complain, complain. 'This makes me look too thin. This makes me look too fat. And this one makes me look too short,' " she mimicked.

"Then I take it you won't be working in the theater again?" His delivery was astringently dry.

"This is the first time," said Nicole. "And I suppose, now that you mention it, the last. Actors are really impossible! Much vainer than private clients. You wouldn't believe it," she said, remembering backstage tantrums unheard-of in a house of couture. "Tell me, what are *you* doing in this neighborhood?" She was aware of the fine cut of his suit and the way it fit. She wondered about the body it covered. "I wouldn't expect to see a duke anywhere except in Maxim's or at the Opera."

"Dukes are people, too," he said. "My mistress dances in a Pigalle nightclub. I'm going to watch her perform tonight. She will not, by the way, be wearing a creation of Nicole Redon."

Nicole smiled, picturing spangles, sequins and feathers.

"When does *Oedipus* open?"

"In eight days," said Nicole.

"Until then," Boy said mysteriously. He left as silently as he had entered.

3.

The House of Mellany traced its origins to Arthur Lyon, who in 1066 was named Earl of Mellany by his uncle, William the Conqueror. In every century since then, through marriage, investment, inheritance, gifts made by the kings and queens of England, the House of Mellany had increased its holdings until in 1923 Mellany Estates owned, in addition to its mines in Wales, its mineral holdings in South Africa, its cattle stations in Australia, and its industrial developments in British Columbia, 200 acres in the center of London, including the entirety of Mayfair and three-fourths of Belgravia.

Hugh Edward George, the current Duke of Mellany —called "Boy," a fashionable nickname of the time—

had inherited every bit of it and had dedicated his life to two principles: enjoying it and increasing it. He was, at twenty-eight, once divorced, a renowned ladies' man, and when he took the time from sweet dalliance, a capable businessman. Boy was a perfect English gentleman, slightly taller than average, with a slender but strong physique hardened by an addiction to outdoor exercise. His hair was the color of taffy and his skin an advertisement for English complexions. His manners were so good they weren't noticeable and he was, as Oscar Wilde once said, rude only intentionally. He was extravagantly generous, bored with details yet able to read and understand the finest print of a contract, terribly fickle in his affections although he searched for the one woman he could love forever. He had a dry sense of humor and a sound intelligence, and was intolerant of the British tendency toward casualness about important things; he ate well and slept badly and was used to doing exactly as he pleased. He hunted at the Pytchley Hunt with the Prince of Wales, owned a yacht so splendid that Noel Coward made a joke about it in *Private Lives*, and in his private galleries hung paintings by Rubens, Rembrandt and Gainsborough that had attracted the acquisitive eye of Lord Duveen, who schemed to have them for his own. All in all, Boy was an intriguing man and, to Nicole, irresistible.

The opening night of *Oedipus* was like a family party. The general public, shocked at the aesthetic philosophy of the avant-garde—which was, namely, to shock—stayed far away. Boy had no trouble at all buying up the entire fifth row. He arrived in top hat and tails just as the curtain went up and seated himself in the middle of the row, empty seats stretching away to the aisles on both sides of him. Nicole, with Cocteau, was in the second row on the right side. There was no way she could not notice Boy. As the performance went on, Boy did not once look at the stage; instead, for two hours, he looked straight at Nicole. When the curtain fell to enthusiastic applause from the tiny audience—all of whom were friends and allies of the creators—Boy crossed the aisle and, leaning over Cocteau, addressed Nicole: "I have reservations for supper at Maxim's. Can you come with me?"

Nicole glanced at Cocteau, who had invited her to the cast party. He nodded his assent. "Go on. You'll have a better time."

"I hope your wife was pleased with the pajamas," Nicole said. They were at Maxim's number-one table: it allowed them to see and be seen; it also allowed them conversational privacy. The Duke had ordered whisky, neat. Nicole, who usually took hers on ice, asked for hers "neat" too. "I don't think she could have been. She never came back to Redon again."

"It isn't that the Duchess of Mellany wasn't pleased with the pajamas; she was," said Boy. "The point is that there is no longer a Duchess of Mellany. We were divorced last year."

"Oh." Nicole sipped her whisky. It seemed both smoother and stronger without the ice. "I didn't know," she said. She wondered why. "I'm sorry."

"Don't be," said Boy. "I'm not."

"It must have been . . ." Nicole searched for a word ". . . sad."

"It was necessary," said Boy. Then he smiled. "It was also, as you say, sad. But it's in the past now. I hardly think about it. Now, tell me, how are you? And whatever happened to that American? The 'freshwater biologist'?"

Nicole smiled at Boy's audible quotation marks. "I don't know. I haven't seen him in several years."

128

"I thought you and he . . ." Boy paused. "I thought there was something . . . special between the two of you."

"I thought so, too," said Nicole. "But I was wrong. It turned out there wasn't anything . . . special." She was unable to keep the wistfulness out of her voice.

"I don't understand why the French can cook fish and the English can't. The English assassinate it," said Boy, abruptly and without transition changing the subject, directing their attention to the Dover sole that had just been served. He sensed that Nicole's American was a sensitive subject with her. "The Channel is narrow. You'd think the French and the English would have the same talents, but they don't. The English are good at horses and gardening and the French are good with upholstery and wine. You need all of it to have a happy life."

"Then to have a happy life you'd need to spend half your time in England and half in France," said Nicole idly. She thought Boy had a most interesting cast of mind. She'd never heard anyone express himself quite the way he did.

"What do *you* think of that idea?" asked Boy. He looked squarely at Nicole. "Do you think you could be happy living partly in England, partly in France?"

"Well, I have my business," said Nicole. "It's very demanding, very time-consuming . . ." Boy was being very direct about his interest in her; she was flattered and alarmed.

"The actors should have complained about the script. Not Redon's clothes," Boy said, in another of his abrupt shifts of topic. He continued to talk about the play he had heard but not seen, and Nicole realized that he had sensed he had alarmed her and was retreating in deference to her feelings.

Boy took Nicole home to the Isle St.-Louis and invited

her out to dinner the next evening. Nicole accepted. Boy asked her if she owned the building she lived in.

"No. I rent my apartment."

"It's better to own than rent," Boy said, standing on the doorstep, his Rolls Royce waiting at the curb.

"I own the building my shop is in," said Nicole. "I can't afford two buildings, but of course you're right."

"Yes," said Boy. "Real estate is something I know about."

With that, he was gone.

Nicole saw Boy every night for the next week, and at the end of the week he canceled his plans to return to London. He ended by staying on in Paris for a month. During that month he bought a house, a Norman-style château just outside Paris, so they would have a place to go on weekends. He introduced Nicole to Cole and Linda Porter, and Linda, one of Europe's most beautiful women, became Nicole's first society client; he took Nicole to a scavenger hunt organized by Elsa Maxwell and escorted her to a Rothschild ball; he took a permanent suite at the Ritz and put it at Nicole's disposal. At the end of the month he told her that he would do anything he could for her.

"Anything," he had said. "Either personally or as the Duke of Mellany."

It was the first time that Nicole realized that Boy thought of himself as two different people. It would be a long time before she realized what it meant and even longer before she realized that the consequences would have a permanent effect on her life. Meantime, it was clear to everyone who knew them that Nicole and Boy had fallen deeply in love with each other.

4.

In January of 1924, Edouard Noiret brought a sixth sample to Nicole. It was perfect. The perfume smelled like a garden but like no one flower in it. It was unique; it was complex, and unlike other perfumes, which were very strong when first applied and then faded quickly, stable. The wearer could be assured of being ravishingly perfumed for an entire evening rather than just the first third of it. It was, above all, modern, abstract. Nicole gave a sample to Cocteau, who wore it at home with an embroidered Chinese robe, and she gave a sample to Linda Porter, who asked if she could buy the entire supply so that no one else could wear it. Nicole loved her new perfume. She was thrilled and excited. What she told Noiret was "It will do."

"I'll take a chance on it," she told Noiret. "Coty is right, you know. It will be very expensive to make." Noiret had told her that the difference between his perfume and all the others was that he used synthetic stabilizers: they were what gave the perfume its abstract scent and enduring qualities. Unfortunately, the synthetic compounds were far more expensive than the essences extracted from the flowers that grew in the fields outside Grasse. "It will be a big gamble but I'll do it," said Nicole.

"First we have to make a deal," said the chemist, who saw an end to his frustrated employment. "I want fifty per cent of gross receipt from your sale of the perfume . . . *my* perfume."

"That's impossible," said Nicole. "I must finance the manufacture, the bottling, the advertising, the distribution, the promotion, the design of the labels and boxes.

It will cost me a fortune. If you get half, there will be nothing left for me."

"Fifty per cent," insisted Noiret.

"It will be fifty per cent of nothing," said Nicole. "I will not agree to sell the perfume—which, by the way, is not yours—I told you exactly what I wanted. It took you six attempts to make it. Without me, you'd have nothing. No one else would take a chance on your perfume. It's too radical. It's too expensive to make. No wonder it collected dust at Coty for years until I came along. I'll let you have five per cent of the net profits."

"Do you think I'm a fool?" asked Noiret, white with anger, his pallid skin turning frosty.

"No," said Nicole. "I think you're a mechanic. I imagine. I create. You mix formulas. Why don't you go and try to sell your formula to someone else? Or have you already done that and failed? After all, you've had it since 1919."

"Bitch!" hissed Noiret, his frigid fury telling Nicole that her shrewd guess had been correct. He got up, almost upsetting the table in his rage. He hated women. All women. This woman in particular.

"Go back to Coty," said Nicole, in a tone that combined irritation and indifference. "Maybe you can persuade them to take a chance on your formula. Your *original* formula! Not the new one you developed under my direction! If you give Coty *my* perfume, I'll sue you and Coty so that you'll be lucky to have eyelashes left."

Fourteen months of bitter negotiations—longer than it had taken to perfect the scent—were required before Nicole and Edouard Noiret agreed to terms: he would receive twenty-one per cent of the net profits; he would leave Coty and would never formulate another perfume for anyone without Nicole Redon's express, written permission. He, in return, had the right to examine Nicole's

132

account books once a year and would be named in publicity as the chemist who had developed the formula—although, of course, he was forbidden ever to reveal its contents. When the negotiations were over and the contracts signed, Nicole and Edouard Noiret shook hands gingerly, filled with suspicion and grudging mutual respect.

Nicole had her perfume now. But she had nothing else—no financing, no distribution, no bottle to put it in, no advertisements, no publicity, no name and, strangely for Nicole, no ideas. All of her energy was focused on Boy.

5.

From the beginning, Nicole was not able to resist Boy for even a moment. His wishes became her wishes, his whims became her whims, his tastes became her tastes. When he rode, she rode; when he ate, she ate; when he drank, she drank; when he slept, she slept; she abandoned her own apartment and moved into his suite in the Ritz. She willingly surrendered her entire personality to him and only in her atelier did she express anything of her own. Her friends worried but they did not dare tell her that in finding Boy she seemed to have lost herself.

It was Nicole who invented the game of twins.

"We're twins, that's what," she said once, six months after they'd met, when for the fourth time in an evening they had been about to say precisely the same thing at precisely the same moment. "You and I are twins."

"But I'm three years older than you," said Boy, who tended to be literal. "And I'm British and you're French . . ."

133

"And you're a duke and I'm a designer," said Nicole, continuing his list. "But don't you see that we're exactly the same? We think the same. We feel the same."

"That's certainly true," said Boy. "We always have the same opinions. Most of the time, we can even read each other's minds."

"So then, we're twins!"

And it was Nicole who turned the game of twins, at first a private amusement, into high fashion. It would be the first time that people outside her private group of clients began to imitate her. Nicole had been among the very first to bob her hair. Now, in her game of twins, she went to further extremes and had the back of her neck razored every morning the way Boy did. On weekends at his country house she began to wear his cotton shirts and his soft flannel trousers, his plus fours and his belted Norfolk jackets, his golfing caps and his V-necked sweaters—all reproduced for her in her size, in her own ateliers, from samples borrowed from Boy's closet.

At first when Nicole wore clothes exactly like Boy's the other guests were slightly shocked and did not know what to say. Soon, though, they began to see that Nicole seemed more delicate, more feminine in her *garçonne* clothing. On her, the effect was charming, and she and Boy seemed happiest when, dressed in identical habits, they set off for a morning's hack; or, dressed in matching white flannels, they played tennis; or, in tweed plus fours and belted jackets, they went off to the links.

It wasn't long before Nicole's friends and clients asked if they could have the same things, and soon Nicole's seamstresses, using garments borrowed from Boy's closets, were making trousers and jackets in women's sizes. The fashion press, by now used to paying attention to the original and singularly modern designs of Mlle. Redon, called it the *"Garçonne* Look," the "Haberdashery Look," the "Tailored Look." Women in men's clothing became a fashion that never went out of fashion, and Nicole—raiding her lover's closets—had started it.

Nicole's style in dress was not the only thing that changed during her liaison with Boy. Her body changed, too. The tennis, the riding, the shooting, the hiking, the golfing, made her physically strong. Her energy increased and the color in her cheeks bloomed. The feminine ideal had already begun to shift away from the wasp-waisted belle who could barely alight from her carriage without the assistance of a muscular coachman, and was coming to favor instead the sportive woman—healthy, strong, with a natural waist and natural breasts and slim, strong hips—and Nicole, following her lover's addiction to outdoor sport, personified the new feminine ideal.

Boy was enthralled with this feminine version of himself. Nicole was special. She was a brilliant success as a designer. She was both an inspired creator and a shrewd businesswoman. Personally, she was unmatchable: intelligent, witty, vivacious. Nicole gave off sparks! Other women tried to copy her; other men desired her. The fact that she had chosen Boy made him feel far more able to measure up to his formidable grandfather, the Seventh Duke of Mellany, nicknamed "The Invincible Duke." Though a good businessman, Boy was not a brilliant businessman who amassed mines and factories and timberlands the way the Invincible Duke had done; Boy, at twenty-eight, had no offspring, no future Duke to carry on the Mellany line, whereas at twenty-six the Invincible Duke had already sired four boys and two girls; and, although Boy knew King George, he was not the King's advisor and the King did not solicit Boy's opinions on matters of state as Victoria and Albert had solicited his grandfather's advice on matters of Empire.

135

Boy's own father, the Eighth Duke of Mellany, had thought of himself as a cipher, his only purpose in life to enshrine the legend of *his* father. Boy did not often think of himself, finding introspection painful, but he had been given only one standard by which to measure himself: the standard set by his grandfather and magnified and embellished by his own father. By that standard Boy was a nobody, and Nicole's gift to him, made unawares, was her attempt to become his double. She found him worthy—worthy enough to imitate—and that incredible fact caused Boy to find himself worthy. Since he had met her, Boy felt more like Hugh Edward George and less like an inadequate successor to the Invincible Duke. Nicole Redon was the best thing that had ever happened to him!

And Boy's gift to Nicole was not who he was or what he did or what he said or what he had accomplished. It was, simply, that Boy treated her as an equal. And if she was the equal of anyone in the whole world! At twenty-four, Nicole finally began to acquire self-confidence outside the narrow walls of her shop, and for that, she loved Boy and wanted to marry him. Once married, she would be the Duchess of Mellany: she would acquire love and a name at the same time. Redon was not a real name. It was only borrowed and Nicole had always thought of it as temporary.

Once before, with Cyril, she had found love and a name, and she had been cheated out of it with Cyril's death. She had almost reconciled herself to never marrying when, in that one chance in a million, she met Boy Mellany. Her obsession to marry him was based on the fact that two opportunities were twice what she had a reasonable right to expect in life. She had lost once, because of fate. She did not see how she could be cheated twice.

She thought, therefore, that there was hope for her hopes when, one morning several months after they had met in the Théâtre de Montmartre, she woke to see, first thing upon opening her eyes, an enormous diamond ring that Boy had put on her pillow. It was the first important piece of jewelry she had ever owned. She slipped the ring on and dressed and waited for him to come to her with his proposal.

6.

In the summer of 1924 only two groups went to the South of France in the summer: those who were unaware of fashion and uninterested in it, and those who were secure enough to be above it. Nicole went there because Boy went there. He was taking delivery of a new yacht, The *White Cloud*. He would pick it up in Monte Carlo, sail along the southern coast of France, and then around Spain and North to the port of London. Nicole had spent the winter and spring in Paris as usual, abstractedly working, her mind and heart occupied by Boy, who was dividing his time between England and France. She wore Boy's diamond on her right hand and kept expecting him to propose so that she could move it to her left.

"I love you," he would say. "But I'm not man enough for you."

"But you *are*," Nicole would say. "You shouldn't keep comparing yourself to your grandfather. "You're everything I want and more . . ."

"I'm not as strong as you are," Boy would say.

"I'm not as strong as you think," Nicole would answer, and she wondered why people always thought of her as strong when she was just aggressive and that only from necessity. If people only knew how insecure and inferior she felt! And with good reason! "Besides, you're much stronger than you think."

"No, I'm not," Boy would say, and when Nicole would contradict him, he would tell her that she ought to believe what he said. "It would save us a lot of unhappiness."

"How can you make us unhappy?" Nicole wanted to know, but Boy never answered, just as he had never proposed. Nicole could not understand it. After all, he swore he loved her and always would. He told her there was no other woman like her and never would be. He offered her everything: jewels, money, business advice, attention, interest, compliments. Everything except a proposal, and Nicole could not understand why. Nothing stood in the way. As always, she turned to her friends for comfort and advice: to Margaret Berryman, who had returned to New York to replace her aunt as editor of *Harper's Bazaar*; to Cocteau, surrealistic in his art, dreaming his opium dreams, and sensible in his advice to his friends; to Lala Rackowska, who had been promoted from model to directrice and managed the day-to-day details of the House of Redon. Nicole's friends all counseled what Leo had once counseled: patience. Leo had been right. Perhaps her friends were right.

Nicole went to Monte Carlo, to the yacht basin, and greeted Boy with a kiss. She had been patient. More than patient. She was sure her patience would be rewarded and that she would leave the *White Cloud* wearing her diamond ring on her left hand. Cap D'Ail, Beaulieu, Villefranche . . . the cruise was leisurely, luxurious. Every night they stopped at a different port; every night they ate in a different restaurant; every night they made love in Boy's stateroom, a room of mahogany paneling and leather club chairs, curved hunt tables and

138

tattered copies of *Country Life*, all so English that Nicole had to remind herself that they were on a yacht on the coastline of France. She and Boy had never gotten along better. Nicole was sure his proposal was just a matter of time. Cap D'Antibes was next. Perhaps in Cap D'Antibes . . .

When the *White Cloud* arrived in the *vieux port* of Antibes, Nicole recognized the Murphys at the Garoupe Beach. She had met them through Cocteau when Gerald was painting scenery for Diaghilev.

"Our villa has finally been finished," Sara said. "We're calling it the Villa America. Cap D'Antibes is filled with Americans this summer. Scott and Zelda Fitzgerald have rented a house nearby in St. Raphaël. Ernie and Hadley Hemingway were here. They left yesterday. For Spain, I think. Kim Hendricks is here with his wife and son . . ."

Wife! And son! Nicole's hands and knees began to shake uncontrollably at the mention of Kim Hendricks' name, and she could not believe that Sara didn't notice the trembling of her entire body.

"Picasso has been summering here, too," Gerald was saying while Nicole's heart pounded and her hands trembled more than before. "He has a new pastime. He follows famous people as they walk along the beach and when they bend over to pick up a shell he takes their pictures."

"Yes! He has a big collection of photographs of famous backsides," said Sara. "He's very proud of it, too."

Nicole smiled mechanically. She hadn't heard a word. A wife! After all, it was five years since she'd met Kim. Could that be? Five years—time to get married. Time to have a son. She wondered how old the boy was. She wondered what it would have been like if she and Kim had had a child . . .

"We're giving a dinner party tonight. Will you and Boy be able to come?" asked Sara. "We'd love to have you."

"We'd love to. Boy is bored eating at restaurants every night," said Nicole, realizing she'd been ungracious. But she was distracted, preoccupied with thoughts of Kim, and she couldn't think straight. She wanted desperately to know if Kim Hendricks would be there but she didn't have the courage to ask. By eight, when it was time to leave the *White Cloud* for the Villa America, Nicole's knees still had not stopped trembling. She hoped Kim wouldn't be there. She hoped he would. She didn't know what she hoped. If only her knees would stop shaking!

The Villa America was located on a hill just below the Antibes lighthouse. Cocktails were being served on the terrace and dinner was to be served under a huge silver linden tree. Candles in hurricane glass flickered, dotting the terrace with specks of incandescence, and the pleated paper globes of Japanese lanterns delineated the boundaries of the terrace. Oleander, heliotrope, roses and camellias from Sara's gardens formed a long, low centerpiece. Jazz—the record, a new one by Louis Armstrong, was a gift from Cole, who shared Gerald's enthusiasm for Negro music—was playing on a Victrola.

Except for Nicole and Boy, all the guests were American. Theodore Ingraham, a literary critic said to be powerful, a corpulent man with a beard and a thin wife who wore exotic silver and turquoise jewelry from an American Indian tribe. Cole and Linda Porter—Linda, small-boned, with blue eyes and blond hair, in high heels just very slightly taller than her dark and exotically handsome husband. Scott Fitzgerald, seeming somewhat subdued, and Zelda, unusually vivacious. Zelda and Linda, in honor of Nicole's presence, each wore a Redon dress. Linda's was black, a color she frequently wore, set off by exquisite precious jewelry. Zelda's was a brilliant apricot color that seemed to shimmer. Kim and

140

Sally Hendricks. Kim was having an animated conversation with the critic, and Nicole observed that his wife listened to Kim's every word and stood very close to him. Kim's wife, Nicole thought with a clutch of envy, was very pretty in a soft, delicate way, with whitish-blond, baby-fine hair and Dresden-blue eyes. Her expression was filled with adoration as she looked up at her husband. And Kim—his even, refined features had acquired an authoritative strength since Nicole had last seen him. All the awkward but endearing traces of boyishness had disappeared, replaced with a self-confident animal grace that was the essence of manliness. Kim—with his elegant, lean body, his tanned, aristocratic facial features, his dark blond hair lightened by the summer sun—was, Nicole decided, the handsomest man she had ever seen in her life.

"There's your freshwater biologist," Boy said to Nicole as Kim, followed closely by Sally, walked toward them. Kim, like the other men, was in white linen, but only on his lean, long-boned body did the inevitable wrinkling seem truly elegant. Boy seemed oblivious to Nicole's shaking knees and pounding heart and trembling hands.

"I'm Kim Hendricks. I met you once in Paris," Kim said to Boy, reminding him. "On Armistice Day."

"Nice to see you," Boy said in his beautifully modulated voice.

"And Nicole, how are you?" Kim said, proud of how casual he managed to sound, of how socially suave he could be.

Nicole nodded in response to his question because nerves had stolen her voice.

"Sally, this is Nicole Redon and Boy Mellany," Kim plunged on, speaking slightly too fast, his own barely concealed nervousness preventing him from noticing that Nicole hadn't said a word.

Boy took Sally's hand to kiss it, overwhelming her with his continental *savoir-faire* and, while Nicole searched frantically for something to say and the voice with which to say it, Cole Porter, led by Sara, came up and introduced himself to Kim as a fellow Yale graduate. Cole, slightly older, had graduated before Kim had entered. Kim knew Cole by reputation as the composer of the Eli and Bull Dog fight songs, Yale football classics. As the two recalled college days, Nicole finally calmed herself enough to acknowledge Sally's flattering compliments on her dress.

Just then, cocktails over, Sara called everyone to the table. Nicole was seated diagonally opposite Kim at an impossible distance for conversation and Nicole, despite her agitation and her awareness that Kim seemed unable to keep his eyes off her, managed to follow the conversation. Everyone was talking about the incredible pomp and ceremony of Anatole France's funeral earlier that summer.

"Remember the time we sat on Anatole France's doorstep?" Scott asked Zelda, then turned to the rest of the table. "I just wanted to get a glimpse of him," Scott continued, "but I never did."

"In a year no one will read Anatole France," said Ingraham. "In ten years no one will remember the name. They'll remember you, Scott, and you, Kim."

"That's not what you said in your review of *Western Front*," said Kim.

"I want to keep you humble. It's part of my duty as a critic," Ingraham said. Everyone laughed. It was obvious that writer and critic liked each other, no matter who wrote what. Scott said nothing. Ingraham, like all the critics, had praised and praised *The Beautiful and the Damned*.

There was a discussion of the recent Republican convention in America, which had nominated Calvin Coolidge and Charles G. Dawes, people of whom Nicole had never heard; and tattle about a notorious and very fashionable New York speakeasy run by a boisterous blonde named Texas Guinan, who addressed her customers as "sucker," and how, amazingly, people lined up to be insulted. The talk moved to the spiraling inflation in Germany and a rabble-rouser named Hitler.

"Isn't it beautiful? My dress . . ." asked Zelda of no one in particular during a pause in the conversation. "It's beautiful, isn't it?"

No one answered her. Distracted by a new morsel of gossip, mentally composing a dazzling witticism, wondering what a man named Hitler could mean to far-off America, everyone more or less ignored Zelda's question. "Well, I think it's beautiful."

Nicole smiled across the table at her, acknowledging the compliment, and turned her attention to a conversation between Gerald and Linda.

"We really owe all of this to you and Cole," Gerald was saying, waving his hand at the terrace and the view of the Mediterranean, dark and glossy like satin, beyond the terraces of pine, mimosa and silvery olive trees. "You were the first people to come to the Riviera in the summer. It was 1921 wasn't it?"

"We rented a villa that summer," said Linda. "Everyone told us we were crazy. It was too hot, there was nothing to do, we'd be bored. But we loved it. It was so quiet and so peaceful and the flowers were so beautiful. There was only a little dirt road around the Cap and we had the beach all to ourselves. And the little cinema with the piano player whose cigarette dangled from the corner of his mouth! Leger loved that cinema!"

"He said it smelled like feet," said Cole, who was fully aware of the way his penchant for the earthy contrasted with the extreme elegance of his person and dress. He loved to shock. It amused him.

"The French are allergic to fresh air, that's why," said the critic's wife.

"Not all of them," said Boy, speaking for the first time. "Not this one here." He indicated Nicole. "She can't get the windows opened fast enough."

Everyone looked at Nicole, who shrugged and laughed. "He's right," she said. "My governess used to say the same thing. She was convinced that the night air was unhealthy. My father was on my side." She talked, trying to make her voice sound normal. Kim had been glancing at her and she had been glancing at him. She had seen him notice her diamond ring and it made her uncomfortable. She turned the big stone so that it faced inward toward her palm.

"Well, it *is* beautiful, isn't it?" Zelda suddenly got up and began to walk around the table, twirling and spinning like a model. Stopping every now and then as she made her way around the table, she'd repeat with increasing emphasis: "Well, tell me it's beautiful!"

"Zelda, your dress is beautiful," said Sara in her lovely, calm voice. "And you look especially beautiful in it."

"See!" said Zelda, continuing her promenade. "Sara agrees. Darling, tell me it's beautiful," she said, speaking to Scott.

"It's beautiful," he said. "A beautiful dress."

"But you didn't say *I'm* beautiful!" Zelda pouted, suddenly changing tack.

"You're beautiful, exquisite, ravishing, alluring . . ." Scott said. He meant it, every word, and he knew that people thought he was a fool, thought he didn't know about Zelda and her aviator. He put on a bright smile. "See, Kim. I've just used all the adjectives you're famous for leaving out."

144

Everyone laughed but Zelda.

"Gerald, you think I'm beautiful, don't you?" Zelda stopped at Gerald's chair.

"Yes, I do, Zelda. All your beauty is in your eyes. You have the most extraordinary eyes," he said. "And you have the best sense of personal style of anyone I know."

Satisfied, Zelda moved on and stopped behind Boy.

"And the Duke thinks I'm beautiful," she said. "Don't you, Duke?"

"You're an ass," said Boy in a languid, purposely insulting tone.

"Boy!" said Nicole. Mrs. Ingraham was seated between them. "Stop it!" Nicole then leaned forward across the critic's wife and lowered her voice. "Can't you see she's upset about something? Be kind."

"I'll do no such thing. She's drunk and she's a nuisance," said Boy, who had located a focus for his resentment at finding himself at this party. He was bored; he thought all writers were pansies, critics ridiculous, the creamed corn the Murphys served barbaric; American accents grated on his ears and intellectual talk seemed phony and pretentious to him. Linda and Cole were the only people there he could tolerate.

"She's not drunk! That's my wife you're talking about!" said Scott. He got up and went to Boy's place and stood over him menacingly.

"Don't, Scott!" begged Sally. "Don't spoil the evening."

"Who the hell do you think you are, talking that way to my wife?" Scott demanded. Boy sat imperturbably. Quite deliberately, he picked up a piece of lettuce with his fingertips and ate it delicately.

"You rich people think you can get away with anything!" Scott fairly shouted.

"Scott! For God's sake!" said Kim, getting up and

heading toward him. Scott stood over Boy, making up his mind whether or not to take a swing at him. That's how Ernie would handle it.

"I'm the Duke of Mellany," said Boy, drawling out his words exaggeratedly. "Who in hell are you? And who in the hell is your slut of a wife?"

With that, Scott took a wild swing at Boy; Boy ducked, avoiding Scott easily. Kim, arriving at Scott's side, used the fingers of his right hand as a prod and pushed Scott backward several steps and then, with another hard nudge, pushed him down into his chair.

"Scott, behave yourself," said Gerald in a mild but censorious voice.

Scott's anger collapsed. "I'm sorry," he said. "I'm so sorry. Please, I apologize."

Boy leaned back and lit a cigarette. "You needn't apologize," he finally said. It was impossible to tell from his tone if his words constituted an acceptance of Scott's apology or a total dismissal of his very existence. There was a pause, a dead, embarrassed silence, while the group tried to reimpose a sense of gaiety on the party.

"But Kim hasn't told me I'm beautiful," said Zelda, in a wistful voice.

"Zelda, you're beautiful," said Kim. With great kindness, he put his arm around her and led her back to her place at the table, murmuring to her as he did. She returned docilely to her place and, although she did not touch the raspberries that were served for dessert, she seemed completely calmed down. She behaved as if the entire episode had never taken place.

When coffee was finished, Scott and Zelda decided to drive into Cannes and look for a nightclub that had jazz. They made a general invitation to the rest of the party but no one wanted to go with them. After issuing their invitation three times and having it refused three times, Scott and Zelda went off into the night hand in hand, he white-pale because he loathed sunbathing, she gypsy-dark because she adored it. They seemed as if they had only each other in the whole world.

7.

Gradually the party broke up. Juan Gris and his wife had dropped by, and Gerald and Sara were giving them a tour of the brand-new villa. Boy went with Cole and Linda to the little casino in Juan-les-Pins. Sally was anxious to go home to the Hendricks' rented villa; she didn't want to leave the baby alone with the maid any longer than necessary. Nicole and Kim were left alone. "Come," he said, speaking to her privately for the first time that evening. "Let's take a walk in the garden." Wordlessly, she followed him down the stone steps.

It was quiet and still in the garden. From a distance came the faint tinkle of crystal and china as the servants cleared the table. The nightingales sang in the hills. The thick groves of cypress and cedar were dense, protective shapes in the moonlight. Kim and Nicole walked along the narrow dirt path that led down to the rocks from which, in the daytime, people swam. Nicole did not know what to say. So much ran through her mind: her letters which had never been answered; his letters which had stopped so suddenly; Sally; their baby; the success he'd had with *Western Front*. The questions raced through her mind. Her emotions—anger, awkwardness, shyness, tenderness and, above all, electric attraction— obliterated any words she might have used, and it was Kim who spoke first.

"He must not be easy to be with," Kim said. "Your duke."

"He was annoyed with Zelda," said Nicole, conscious that she and Kim had managed not to touch even though the path had been very, very narrow. Now that they had reached the flat rocks, they stood slightly apart, shaken by their awareness of each other.

"Even so," said Kim, "he seems awfully spoiled."

"You must remember he is the product of nine hundred years of Mellany heirs—men who are used to having everything their way. Everything. At any moment. Men who are used to doing and saying exactly as they please."

"You don't have to defend him so heatedly," said Kim. He could smell her perfume and he could remember the trace of it in the place Vendôme. He wanted to kiss her, to smother himself in her. His desire for her overwhelmed him exactly as it had the first moment he'd laid eyes on her in the rue Montaigne. It was as if moments had passed, not years.

"We once picked strawberries from one of his greenhouses," Nicole said, happy to have something outside themselves to talk about. "There were hundreds and hundreds of strawberries in long, long beds. We could not have picked more than a score. The next morning the housekeeper and the head gardener came to Boy. They were very upset. Someone had been in the greenhouse, they said; someone had picked the strawberries. The servants had all been questioned; all the delivery people. The entire household had been turned upside down to find out who had picked the strawberries. They had finally fired two undergardeners, thinking they'd taken them and then lied about it.

"Not one person thought Boy might have picked them," Nicole continued. "And Boy is so used to being waited on hand and foot that it didn't occur to him that it was strange no one would imagine that he'd picked his own strawberries. And furthermore he didn't think it at all strange that two people had been fired over twenty missing strawberries out of hundreds. He is so used to having his slightest whim, his slightest action, produce the most incredible consequences! Tonight he felt bored and left out. He is used to being the center of everything. The world is different for him than it is for you, for me."

"It's too unreal for me," said Kim. "I prefer something more down to earth."

Nicole didn't answer. There was a moment of silence, each waiting for the other to say something. Then Kim picked up her hand and turned the big diamond around. His touch was like fire. "It's his, isn't it?"

Nicole nodded. The moonlight gave enough illumination so that he could see the pale skin of her face, the darker outline of her lips. He remembered the taste of her mouth, the texture of her skin, the curve of her breast.

"You want to marry him, don't you?"

"Yes," she said. The awareness of his fingers on her hand blotted out every other sensation. She felt her entire being concentrated in the places where their skin touched. She was helpless to move her hand. She felt as if a spell had been cast on her. "How did you know?"

"I know about you. Everything about you. I always have, from the first moment I saw you." Nicole finally was able to take her hand from his grasp. She took a step backward. She had a sudden premonition of what he was going to say. "I know something else too," he said.

"No," she whispered.

He continued despite her. "You're not in love with him."

"That's a lie!" Her voice seemed loud in the quiet night.

"It's the truth," Kim said. "Isn't it? I'm right, aren't I?"

She said nothing. Kim took a step toward her and put his hand on the back of her head, caressing her hair, fine and silky and vibrant with life. He gently moved her head toward him and she didn't resist. He lifted her chin with his other hand and, leaning down slightly, kissed her, first gently, then yearningly. He was surprised to feel her tears on his face. He remembered his own.

"I saw you last year in Paris," he said a little later, when he could talk again. "I went there for *The Sun* and I promised myself that I wouldn't set foot on the rue Montaigne, and I kept my promise. But I didn't know you had moved. One night I came out of the Ritz on the place Vendôme side. I saw the awning with your name on it. Then I saw you. You were getting into a taxi. I ran. I called you. But you didn't hear. The taxi was gone," he said. "The next day I left Paris."

"Why?" she asked, although she knew.

"I was afraid," he said. "Sally was pregnant then. I was afraid if I saw you, talked to you, I'd . . ."

"Shhh," said Nicole, and putting her finger to his mouth, she silenced him. "Don't say it. It'll hurt you to say it. It'll hurt me to hear it."

"Then I'm right about you and your duke," Kim said. "You *don't* love him . . ."

"No," Nicole cautioned. "Don't continue. You don't know anything about it. You really don't."

"If you say so . . ." Then he was silent for a moment. "Will you meet me at the Garoupe Beach tomorrow? At one o'clock? I'll bring lunch."

"That would be nice," Nicole said, choosing bland words to disguise the exhilaration she felt, the heart-racing, breathless exhilaration she had always felt with this one man and no other.

Kim brought pâté and cheese and bread and fruit and wine in a straw hamper and settled down by his favorite rocks. He waited on the Garoupe Beach from twelve-thirty until seven o'clock. Nicole never came.

I want to be happy,
But I won't be happy,
Till I've made you happy, too.
—"I Want to Be Happy"

CHAPTER SIX

1.

THE MANUSCRIPT of *Gatsby* went to Scribner's at the end of October and the Fitzgeralds went to Rome. The Hemingways went to Paris with Bumby and settled down in an apartment with a view of a sawmill. Kim went to Italy to report on Mussolini and the Blackshirts for *Collier's*. Sally and Kimjy went to Paris.

Sally boarded the train for Paris at Nice, Kimjy in her left arm, the briefcase containing the manuscript of *A Matter of Honor* in her right hand. She had the compartment to herself. She put Kimjy on the plush seat next to her and the briefcase on her lap, where it would stay for the entire journey. She was to look for an apartment in

Paris—Hadley had said she would help—and when Kim returned from Italy he would have November and December to polish A *Matter of Honor* and be able to deliver it to Perkins at the end of December, right on deadline. The train lurched and moved. Sally leaned back. The motion of the train soon lulled Kimjy to sleep, and Sally relaxed, reveling in the solitude. Everything had changed since 1922. Not that Sally loved Kim less; she loved him more. The trouble was that a new baby, a new house and a suddenly famous husband were exhausting. On the first day that *Western Front* appeared on the best-seller lists, Kim had come home with a magnum of champagne and two pieces of news: he had quit his full-time job at *The Sun* and he had bought them their first house, an abandoned glass factory on Charlton Street in Greenwich Village. He wanted to move in as soon as possible, since from now on he would be working at home.

The transformation of the primitively heated factory to a habitable living and working space had taken over a year. New plumbing, residential heating and a kitchen had to be installed. Each one of the fifty-six windows turned out to have different dimensions and required months of custom work by a team of glaziers. Concrete floors had to be replaced with wood, and the brick walls Kim wanted exposed required extensive patching and plastering. The entire top floor was to be his office: seventy-one beams, each twenty-five feet long, were exposed and sanded. While Sally took care of the baby and cajoled, threatened and pleaded with plasterers, painters and plumbers, Kim, now in great demand, accepted free-lance assignments from all the major magazines as well as *The Sun* and, when he wasn't writing articles, wrote the rough draft of A *Matter of Honor*. When Kim wasn't working, he liked company. He continued his extravagantly extroverted social life and he wanted Sally to share it with him. Then, as soon as the work on the house was done, he had wanted to keep their promise to themselves to move to Paris for a while. Kim was exciting, exhilarating, fascinating and exhausting. Sally would never have believed it, but when Kim kissed her goodby and left for Italy she was actually happy to see him go. She looked forward to a calm and peaceful stretch of time.

When the train pulled into the Gare de l'Est, Sally got off—the baby in her left arm, the briefcase in her right hand. She waited outside the baggage compartment for their trunks and valises and counted them to make sure they were all there. Then she signaled a porter and watched him load all the luggage on a dolly. She followed him to the street, carrying Kimjy and the briefcase, which Kim had told her not to let out of her sight. Outside the station the porter hailed a taxi and, as he loaded the luggage into the trunk and into the front next to the driver, Sally searched for a tip. Her handbag was slung from her shoulder and she put the briefcase down on the sidewalk while she opened the bag to get the money. Kimjy, an active two-year-old, began to kick, but she managed to extract the money from her bag and give the porter his tip. She turned to pick up the briefcase. It was gone.

At first Sally did not believe her eyes. She turned her head away from the empty space on the pavement where the briefcase had been, blinked very hard, then turned back as if she were doing it for the first time. The briefcase had to be there. It had to be!

"The briefcase!" Sally shouted to the porter. "Where is the briefcase?"

"You carried it yourself, madame," he said, eager to leave and find his next customer.

"It was right here!" Sally pointed to the sidewalk. "Right here next to me!"

"Madame, please don't accuse me," said the porter, offended. "I never touched the briefcase."

"I'm not accusing you," Sally said. "Someone must have taken it while I was getting the tip. Didn't you see anyone? You were standing right here."

"I saw no one." The porter began to roll the dolly back and forth, preparing to leave.

"But you must have! You were right here!" Sally said, refusing to let him go.

"So, madame, were you," the porter said and, moving his luggage truck decisively, he disappeared into the station.

Sally made the taxi driver reopen the trunk and take out every piece of baggage. Perhaps the small briefcase had somehow gotten misplaced at the bottom of the pile of baggage. When every suitcase and footlocker had been removed, the briefcase was still not to be found. Sally then insisted on searching the front seat and the back seat and even the floor of the taxi. The driver, to whom she had promised a substantial tip, helped her search. They found nothing and, as Sally became more and more panicky, Kimjy began to cry. He set up a howl, his legs pumping back and forth against Sally's hips and stomach. His arms waved in the air, his face turned red and finally almost fuschia.

"*Shhh! Shhh!* Poor Kimjy, poor Sally," Sally tried to soothe her baby and herself. "Are you *sure* you didn't see anyone take the small case?" Sally asked the driver for the third time.

"Yes, madame. I was holding the trunk open for the porter. I saw no one. You ought to report your loss to the gendarme at the station."

The driver, who had taken Sally's cause as his own, accompanied her inside to the office of the gendarmerie. The policeman there listened to Sally's story, taking notes with a thick, stubby pencil. He gave her absolutely no hope that the briefcase would ever be recovered.

"Madame, it happens all the time in big, busy stations, especially with small, easy-to-carry cases. You must pay strict attention to all your belongings."

"But I did!" Sally protested. She was panicked, shocked at the swiftness of the theft. It had happened so quickly, in such a flash, that she had not yet had time to think of tears or of what she would say to Kim. How on earth could she tell him!

"What was in the case?" asked the policeman. "Your jewelry?" The pretty American was so upset that he could only assume it was something of extraordinary value. Jewelry. Money, perhaps.

"A manuscript," said Sally. "My husband's new book."

"Oh," said the gendarme his disappointment obvious. If there had been valuables there would have been a big reward for him in it—not, to be realistic, that there was much hope of finding the thief and the briefcase. But a manuscript . . . there were thousands of scribblers in Paris. "A manuscript . . . ah . . ." he said, and shrugged, turning his swivel chair to face once again the peephole that allowed him to overlook the vast central hall of the station. "A manuscript . . . you're lucky that's all it was."

"There'll be a reward!" Sally said. "One hundred American dollars."

"All right," said the gendarme, stirring himself at the mention of money. "I'll put the word out."

"Oh, thank you. Thank you!"

"Just don't get your hopes up."

2.

Italy was strikes, chaos, hysteria. The Fascists fought the Moderates; the Communists fought the

Democrats, and the Socialists fought each other. The food was delicious, Rome eternal, Venice a fantasy, and no one paid his taxes. Italy was, in the throes of oncoming dictatorship, more or less normal. With his *Collier's* piece researched and written, Kim returned to Paris toward the end of November.

Sally had found an apartment near Ernie and Hadley's on the rue Notre-Dame-des-Champs. The street was pleasant; the apartment wasn't particularly. Thick walls held in the damp and the cold. A narrow hall led into a kitchen with a stone sink. There was a small dining room with a large table practically filling it. The living room held an iron stove, and the master bedroom had a huge gilt *lit de mariage* and a small alcove for Kimjy. It was very similar to the Hemingways' apartment, the main difference being that the Hemingways' was very noisy, since the sawmill was an active sawmill. The Hendrickses' apartment had the advantage of quiet: it faced a courtyard.

Kim returned from his far-flung travels in Italy pleased with the article he'd written and looking forward to giving A *Matter of Honor* its final polishing. The minute he walked into the apartment, before he'd taken off his coat, kissed his wife, or even had a chance to say hello, Sally blurted it out: "The manuscript was stolen." All she had been thinking about all month was how on earth she was going to find the words to tell him, having failed to reach him by wire in Rome. Now it was out. She waited for the explosion.

"Don't joke around," Kim said, his attention drawn by the stack of mail on the hall table. There were letters from his father, Perkins, Mencken, S. I. Brace . . .

"I'm not joking, Kim. I wish I were. I had to put down the briefcase at the Gare de l'Est to get a tip for the porter. It took a few seconds. When I turned back to pick it up, it was gone." There was silence. Kim ignored the letters and stared at her. "Aren't you going to say anything?"

"I hope you're not joking, Sally," he said finally. The skin around his eyes had turned white.

"I told you. It's not a joke." It was worse than she had feared. Kim's anger was short-lived but explosive. His grim, rigid silence scared her. Kimjy began to cry from the alcove.

"Shut that kid up," said Kim. His eyes glinted black.

"'That kid' is your baby, too . . ." said Sally. The crying got louder, more insistent.

"Just shut him up," said Kim. Afraid to make him any angrier, Sally left the foyer and went into the bedroom to comfort the screaming child.

Kim methodically opened every drawer and every cabinet in the apartment. He left every one of them open and askew. He took every book from the mahogany glass-front bookcase in the living room and threw them on the floor. He removed the cushions from the sofa, upended the tables, tore down the curtains, removed all the linens from the armoire and scattered them on the floor.

"What on earth did you do?" asked Sally in horror when she had finally soothed Kimjy in the distant alcove beyond the bedroom. Busy with Kimjy's sobbing, she had not heard Kim. He was still wearing his trench coat.

"I was looking for my manuscript," he said. "I didn't find it."

"I told you what happened," Sally said. "It was stolen. It wasn't my fault! It wasn't anyone's fault!"

"It didn't happen! It couldn't have happened!" Kim's expression had turned wild. "You were supposed to watch it! It was the one thing you were supposed to do! I told you not to let it out of your sight!"

"Kim, don't you think this is hard enough for me? Don't make it any harder!"

"Hard for you? What about me? For Christ's sake, it's *my* book!"

"You'll reconstruct it. You still have all your notes," said Sally, trying not to cry.

"The notes are in New York." Kim's voice was now tight, his fury evident but under rigid control.

"Your father will send them to you," Sally pleaded.

"And what if they get lost in the mail?"

"You can reconstruct it! I know you can. You can do anything! Please, Kim! Tell me it's all going to be all right . . ."

"I'm going out," he said, turning toward the door. "I might not be back."

He went straight to the place Vendôme. He asked for Nicole. The receptionist told him that she was in Scotland. She didn't know how long Mlle. Redon would be gone. Was there a message?

"No. No message," said Kim. The small, elegant reception room carried a faint trace of Nicole's perfume.

Kim started at the Ritz. He ended at the Closerie de Lilas. In between, he got dead drunk. Somehow he made his way back to the apartment on the rue Notre-Dame-des-Champs, although the next day he could not remember coming home.

He couldn't write there. The noise of the children playing in the courtyard disturbed him. Kimjy's prattle drove him crazy. Kimjy had a perpetual cold and his sniffling distracted him. The apartment was damp and cold and Kim couldn't concentrate.

"Let's get out of this dump," Kim told Sally. "I don't understand why you rented it in the first place."

"Apartments are scarce in Paris now. It's near Hadley and Hem. You said you wanted to live near them. It's inexpensive too."

"I don't care. We have money. We're not broke."

"Do you want to move to a hotel?" asked Sally, trying to mollify him. He had not made love to her once since he had returned from Italy. He had not even kissed her. "I could ask people to recommend—"

"I don't care where. Just get us out of here."

The Hemingways recommended a hotel called the Angleterre on the rue Jacob. Kim couldn't write there either. The room was small and too hot and stuffy. The desk was too dainty on its spindly French legs. Gus Leggett, with whom Kim had made up after the success of *Western Front*, offered an empty room in the Cyclops Press offices. Kim couldn't write there either.

Paris in the winter of 1924 was jazz, champagne, white fox and dashing Bugattis, and Kim and Sally missed almost all of it. Kim went days without speaking to Sally. He never picked up his son or played with him.

"You act like you hate us," said Sally.

Kim didn't answer.

In December he told her that Paris was driving him crazy. He couldn't work there. His notes for *A Matter of Honor* were in New York. He wanted to go home.

On the day before the *Berengaria* sailed, Kim went back to the place Vendôme. The receptionist, who remembered him, told him that Mlle. Redon was still in Scotland.

3.

"Now is the time to buy stock," Lansing told Kim in early January, one night after dinner. Sally had cooked a roast beef, and while Kimjy played on a wooden rocking horse that was taller than he was and Sally cleaned up in the kitchen, father and son sat over coffee and brandy. "Coolidge is a businessman's president and I think we're headed for a bull market. Right now Steel is paying a five-dollar dividend and Telephone is paying nine dollars. All the indications on the Street are that the dividends will increase and that the underlying prices will go up, too. I've even begun to put my estate portfolios into common stocks."

"That's quite a switch. You were always such a staunch believer in bonds for your widows and orphans," said Kim. "Although I've noticed that now that the Teapot Dome scandals have died down people talk about four things: Knute Rockne, Greta Garbo, Charlie Chaplin and the stock market. Even taxi drivers give you tips. When you say you've gotten on the bandwagon, I'm impressed."

"It's not a bandwagon," Lansing said. "It's just sensible."

"Last week Perkins told me that Scribner's owes me eight thousand in royalties on *Western Front*," Kim said. "The house is all paid for and Sally and I can live easily on what I make from the magazines. Suppose I give you the eight thousand? Will you invest it for me?"

"I'll be happy to," said Lansing. "I'm glad you asked. I was hoping you would. You know I think you're much too wild with your money. I always have."

"I know! I know!" Kim laughed. His father had been appalled at Kim's extravagance from the days when Kim was seven years old and spent his entire nickel allowance the same afternoon he got it. The $500 champagne evenings and the Charlton Street house had not changed his father's opinion, only confirmed it. "The president says the business of America is business," Kim said. "I guess it's high time I got patriotic."

"You shouldn't really joke about it," said Lansing. "Financial security is a serious matter and you know how conservative I am. Believe me, I'm not going to put your money or anyone else's money into Florida real estate or

Peruvian uranium mines. You'll have nothing but solid blue chips."

"Personally, I'd prefer the real estate and the uranium mines," Kim said, "but I have a son now." Both men glanced over at Kimjy, who was urging his horse to an even faster gallop. "I have to think of the future."

"Radio's the future," S. I. said. He and Kim were having their usual liquid lunch at the saloon opposite *The Sun* and S. I. was telling him about his new job in the new field of radio. "Did you know radio sales rose from less than two million dollars in 1920 to over three hundred and fifty million in 1924?"

"But aren't you going to miss newspapers?" asked Kim, thinking that he and Sally were among the Americans who had acquired their first radio in 1924. A table model Westinghouse had been Sally's Christmas present to Kim. "Won't you miss the city room?"

"I don't know. Maybe," said S. I., his corned beef sandwich going untouched. "WEAF gave me what the kids would call a hotsy-totsy deal. They're setting up a news department and I'm going to be the head of it. The Al Smith nomination gave them the idea. Literally millions of people tuned in to the convention. It made them feel they were right there in Madison Square Garden. WEAF thinks the news could be a big thing for radio."

"Maybe they're right," said Kim. "But suppose people turn you off for Barney Google?"

S. I. balled up a paper napkin and threw it at Kim. "It's my job to make sure they don't."

"So you're definitely taking it?"

"Definitely," said S. I. "The money is sensational and the challenge is irresistible."

"I wonder if it will feel funny not to be an ink-stained wretch any more."

"Frankly, I was getting sick of it," S. I. said. "I'm

almost forty years old. It's time for a change. Tell me, Kim, how would like a change? How would you feel about being on the radio?"

"And compete with Rudy Vallee?"

"I'm serious, Kim."

"What would I do? I can't sing. I don't have a megaphone. I don't play jazz. I can't act and there's no way I'm going to read advertisements for cold cream."

"The news," said S. I. "You could read the news. You have a solid reputation not only as a novelist but as a fine journalist. People would trust you."

"Read the news? Are you kidding? That sounds like the world's most boring job."

"You could write your own scripts," offered S. I.

"Oh, hell! Look, S. I., it's nice of you to want me. But I'm a writer. A real writer. Newspapers, magazines, books. I'm not a reader. Not an actor. Not a news deliverer. I'm really not interested."

S. I. sighed. "To tell you the truth, I was afraid you'd say that. But I'm not going to give up on you. Remember how you pestered me until I gave you a job?"

Kim smiled and nodded. He well remembered his summers as a copyboy and the *Yale Daily News* articles he'd bombarded S. I. with. Not to mention all the pleading and begging and the deal that sent him to Paris to cover the Armistice. "I sure do."

"I'm going to be just that persistent with you."

"As long as you throw in a free lunch now and then," Kim said, and the two of them laughed.

The dinners and the lunches were exceptions to Kim's routine. Every morning he went up to his huge top-floor study, with its bank of windows overlooking the Hudson River, and using the notes he'd made, reconstructed *A Matter of Honor*. It was slow, frustrating work. It came to him painfully, not paragraph by paragraph, not sentence by sentence, but word by word.

A Matter of Honor was set in the winter of 1922–1923. Kim had written the outline and notes in the summer of 1923 and the novel itself through the end of that year and the beginning of the next. It was triply, quadruply hard now, two full years later, to recapture the texture of that winter of 1922–1923. The sights and sounds and the way people felt. They were fed up with Wilson's idealism. They had just won the war but were wondering just what it was they'd won. They were bold with victory, drunk with expectation, reckless with hopes, and yet, underneath, they knew that America had gotten off almost scot-free. People were afraid that the next time it wouldn't get off so easily. It was a period when the undercurrents were at odds with the surfaces of life. It was tricky to capture, and there were weeks when not one word Kim put on paper satisfied him. He threw pencils, ripped up papers, and devoured by frustration, would run along the piers on the Hudson River until physical exhaustion washed away the fury of frustration.

He blamed Sally. If she hadn't lost the manuscript, he would already have had his second novel in Perkins' hands and be under way on a third. Instead, he'd had to tell Perkins that he would miss his deadline. It was the first time in his life he'd ever missed a deadline.

"Someone stole the briefcase with the manuscript outside the Gare de l'Est. Right out from under Sally's nose," Kim told Perkins over martinis followed by creamed chicken at Cherio's, on Fifty-third Street. "I still have the notes, luckily. But I have to start all over."

"That's terrible! Sally must have been awfully upset!" Perkins shook his head sadly in commiseration.

"She was. But it was nothing compared to how upset I was. And am. I'm making progress but it's slow," said

Kim, feeling mellower than had been usual lately. The gin in Cherio's martinis was pre-Prohibition.

"Do you have any idea when you'll be finished?" asked Perkins. "I don't want to put pressure on you but . . ."

"I'm used to pressure. I like it," said Kim. "Remember, I started out as a newspaperman."

"We need a big book for the fall. We were planning on A *Matter of Honor*." Perkins spoke cautiously. Some writers panicked and blocked when pressured.

"I'm sorry. I'm terribly sorry," said Kim. "The best I can do is to get it to you by early summer. June. Will that give you time for fall publication?"

"It'll be an awful rush," said Perkins, "but let me talk to the production department."

"I'm letting you down," Kim said. "I'm letting you and Scribner's down . . ."

"Kim, don't torture yourself." Perkins looked at him earnestly. "You'll make it even harder for yourself. Just don't worry about it, and let me know if I can do anything to help. Anything."

Writer and editor parted. Perkins gave Kim an advance copy of *The Great Gatsby*, which was scheduled for spring publication. "You'll be impressed," said Perkins. "It's splendid. Scott wants people to stop thinking of him as the author of *This Side of Paradise*. I think he'll get his wish with the publication of *Gatsby*."

Perkins' words and reassurances weren't magic but they did help. Kim, by working hard, harder than he had ever worked, made progress, first slowly, then with increasing speed as the book's own momentum took over. Writing had always been easy for Kim. It had come as naturally as breathing. Doing the reconstruction of A *Matter of Honor* was not easy. It was the first time Kim had found writing hard work, and he knew that the reason was the constant ugly resentment he felt toward

Sally for losing the original draft. The resentment got in the way of the creativity, the flow.

Kim did not, as he had with *Western Front*, give Sally his daily output to type up for him. Instead, recalling Perkins' offer to be of assistance, he asked Perkins if he could recommend a typist. Perkins sent a girl who worked in the Scribner's pool. Cornelia Post arrived at the Charlton Street house every morning at nine and went to work with Kim. She sat on one side of an immense mahogany table Kim had rescued from a Wall Street law firm's conference room. The table had been made to seat all fourteen partners, and it had had to be hoisted by a crane to be moved into Kim's study, after the entire bank of windows had been removed. The floor had had to be braced to support its tremendous weight.

Kim sat opposite Cornelia and she typed the pages of *A Matter of Honor* as he handed them across the table to her. After three weeks Kim stopped resisting. Cornelia was young, intelligent and awestruck at the thrill of working with Kim Hendricks. They began to make love every afternoon on the comfortable couch that took up the wall facing the windows. It was the only time Kim had been unfaithful to Sally except for that episode in Paris with Sophie, who worked in Gus Leggett's office.

But sex was only a diversion. Most of the time he and Cornelia worked, and by April Kim was more than half finished with his reconstruction and in the mood for a break. The offer from *Collier's* "to do for London what you did for Italy" came at just the right time.

4.

Lady Miranda Towles-Falconer was one of London's Dream Girls. She attended the same house parties as Noel Coward, was photographed by Cecil Bea-

165

ton, danced with the Prince of Wales, talked clothes with Diana Cooper, dined at formal dinner parties with Winston Churchill. She had come out, at a party at her parents' house, at the reckless cost of 750 pounds. She also played tennis at Frinton-on-Sea, Essex, recommended a face cream in a well-known advertisement, went to *thé dansants* on Sunday afternoons, stayed up until dawn, and as dawn broke, drank milky, highly sugared coffee out of thick mugs at the Hyde Park Corner coffee shop and wondered whether the young man she was with would try to kiss her and, if he tried, what she would do.

Miranda had fair hair, conservatively bobbed so that it fluffed becomingly over her ears; she had large eyes whose color the Fleet Street press called Devon violet, and the kind of complexion for which English beauties are famous. Innocent, curious, suspended between the Edwardian influences of her upbringing and the blaze of publicity generated by flappers, by Negro jazz bands, by the romantic escapades of American bootleggers, by Margaret Sanger's crusade for birth control, Miranda had turned down six proposals of marriage in the first eighteen months after her coming-out. Her parents expected her to be married by the age of twenty-two and they promised her a wedding at St. Margaret's, Westminster, with white lilacs and white doves by the hundred. All that was up to her was to find an appropriate husband.

Miranda's family had known the Mellany family for four generations and Miranda had known Boy as long as she had been alive—Boy was almost eleven years older than she. When he was twenty and she was nine, the difference in age was the distance between galaxies. And when he was twenty-five and she was fourteen, it was the difference between planets. But now that he was thirty and she was nineteen, the difference suddenly disappeared.

Boy and Miranda moved in the same circles and saw each other constantly. Boy had been married and divorced; he was known as a blade and he was admired for his sophistication and elegance. Excepting the Prince of Wales himself, he was considered the best catch in London. Miranda, not immune to his glamour, would secretly watch him. He was usually with a slightly older group that included HRH, Mrs. Dudley Ward and Thelma Morgan, one of the celebrated Morgan twins. Miranda thought Boy the handsomest man she had ever seen. One night in February their paths crossed two times: first at the Berkeley and then, later, at Rector's, a wildly fashionable after-hours dive in Tottenham Court Road. Miranda danced three dances in a row with the Prince of Wales, who was due to leave on a royal tour to India. He seemed most comfortable with women who talked a lot and Miranda chattered on, amusing him with snippets of gossip. He had a charming smile which, charming as it was, never completely chased a trace of sadness in his eyes, as if he were waiting for something or someone to make him happy. Whenever she made him laugh, Miranda always had the most satisfied feeling that she had done something not only for the Prince but for England itself.

Then Boy asked for the next dance. Unlike HRH, Boy did not like to talk while he danced and his silence increased the romantic fantasies Miranda had about him. They Charlestoned energetically, keeping the beat, not touching each other yet matching each other's steps.

"Come," Boy said when the dance was over, and taking her hand, he led Miranda to the cloakroom, where he bought himself a gin and Miranda a ginger beer. "Let's waltz," he said when they had finished their

167

drinks. From the main room, Miranda could hear the brass band as it started up again.

"Waltz?" Miranda was confused. There was no way to waltz to the syncopated beat of a jazz band.

"I'm in the mood to waltz with you," said Boy and, collecting his coat and Miranda's wrap, he led her outdoors to where his Rolls waited, the chauffeur half-asleep in the open front seat.

"The Berkeley," Boy instructed the chauffeur.

"But the Berkeley closed at two," said Miranda. She had been there earlier when the band played "God Save the King."

"*Shhh*," said Boy, making the gesture of shushing, placing his forefinger vertically in front of his lips. Then, deliberately touching his lips with his forefinger, he moved his hand and placed the finger on Miranda's lips. His touch thrilled something in her she had never been aware of before and could not possibly have described. Boy helped her into the spacious back seat. A silver bucket of ice in which a bottle of champagne was placed stood on a rosewood bar, and two glasses floated in another bucket of ice. With a linen cloth, Boy dried the glasses, now as cold as the wine, and poured the pale, bubbling wine into them.

"To the next waltz," he said, raising his glass.

Miranda raised her glass and sipped the wine, wondering what he was talking about.

When they arrived at the Berkeley, Boy got out of the automobile first and exchanged a few words with the night doorman, a tall, burly Welshman in a braided and gold-buttoned uniform. Miranda waited inside the car, surreptitiously touching up the powder on her nose. As Boy returned to the car the chauffeur held the door, and Boy helped Miranda out. He led her to the doors of the hotel and directly to the ballroom, which, when Miranda had left it two hours before, was already dark, the tables stacked with chairs.

Now the crystal chandeliers blazed, their light reflecting off the polished parquet dance floor, the gilded paneling and the silver champagne bucket with two glasses centered on the one table set up with fresh, stiff linen cloths. The full band was in the bandstand and, as Boy and Miranda entered, it struck up a waltz.

"Dance?" Boy asked and, turning to her, he held his arms out to her. Miranda moved into his arms and they twirled into the waltz, the tails of Boy's coat whirling out like the wings of a bird and the skirts of Miranda's dress, caught in the rhythm and the movement of the dance, spinning out and moving with the same grace that she did. She became dizzy with the dance and with the thought that now, finally, she knew what it was like to be rich: you could waltz alone at four o'clock in the morning in a splendid ballroom that existed for your pleasure alone. They danced the night away and Boy escorted Miranda home at dawn.

The next morning when the maid brought tea, she was followed by three footmen wearing the dark-green Mellany livery. Each carried a hamper of flowers: peonies, roses, iris, tulips, narcissus and daffodils. On Miranda's tea tray was a small envelope containing a stiff, crested board inscribed with the single word *"Tonight"* . . .

Every morning bouquets arrived, borne by liveried footmen. Every night Miranda saw Boy: at the Savoy, at the Berkeley, at Rector's; at the Café de Paris, the Regent palace and once at the Piccadilly Hotel, which was considered rather fast. Everyone in London noticed, everyone in London talked, and Miranda spent the next two months in an agony of suspense.

Her suspense came almost to an end at a *thé dansant*

at Sir Ernest Cassel's Park Lane mansion, a monument to the Edwardian style which the financier had decorated with eight tons of Tuscany marble shipped in from Italy, along with the crews of Italian workmen who installed it. In the vaulted ballroom which occupied the entire fourth floor of the mansion—which itself took up almost an entire square block—Boy asked Miranda to waltz. Added to the dizziness of being in his arms was the dizziness produced by his question: "Will you lunch with me Sunday at Claridge's?"

Sunday lunch at Claridge's was a sign and a symbol. All of fashionable London gathered there, and to be seen there with Boy made Miranda's heart race. She told her parents the exciting news: "Boy has asked me to lunch at Claridge's this Sunday."

Miranda's parents exchanged glances. The glances spoke volumes. Beryl Towles-Falconer, like all mothers, wanted her daughter to have everything: a happy marriage and a good match. Hugh Towles-Falconer, whose daughter was the center of his existence, had hopes for Miranda that surpassed his wife's: to be happy, first of all, but also to be unimaginably rich and to be a duchess! Their daughter, their beautiful, sweet, unspoiled Miranda, to make a brilliant, brilliant match . . . well, there were really no words in the language to express their emotions.

"Darling, have a wonderful time," said her mother.

"I wish there were time to buy you a new dress," said her father. "I want you to be the most splendid woman there."

"It doesn't *have* to mean anything," Miranda cautioned, trying to shield herself and her parents from disappointment. What if Boy was simply amusing himself?

"He's been divorced, you know," Beryl said to her husband when they were alone in their bedroom that night.

"Everybody knows that," said Hugh. "His wife couldn't give him an heir. You can't hold it against the man."

"No, I suppose you can't," said Beryl. "After all, every man, and most especially the Duke of Mellany, has an obligation to leave an heir."

"I wonder if this Boy is of good character," said Miranda's father, wanting every fatherly assurance of the man he had already begun to imagine as his son-in-law.

"I've never heard a word whispered against him," said Beryl, "except that he's quite a ladies' man." She paused. "Of course they say the same thing about HRH."

"Oh, well, they're young men. They all settle down when they marry."

"As long as Miranda's not hurt."

"Who would want to hurt Miranda?" asked her father, posing a question which both he and his wife knew needed no answer.

Implicitly and explicitly, Boy Mellany had been brought up to know that there was One Most Important Purpose to his life: that purpose was not God, money, honor, or even Empire. That one purpose was to produce sons, to carry the Mellany name forward, eternally, into history.

Boy's first marriage had ended because the first Duchess had been unable to maintain a pregnancy past the third month. The divorce was a lineal necessity and the first Duchess understood this, having realized even before her marriage that her one and only obligation was to bear sons. When she had been unable to do so, lawyers, discreet and versed in such matters, arranged a divorce and a generous settlement. Boy was free to find another Duchess.

Boy was a man of strong passions but not of strong emotions. Since the divorce was a matter of necessity, he carried neither scar nor stigma because of it. His only regret was that at twenty-eight he still did not have a son, and he blamed that fact entirely on the first Duchess. His family ignored his affairs and tolerated his long liaison with Nicole because they understood that never, ever would he marry her. Whatever else he was, Boy was the Duke of Mellany, and he would marry one of his own kind. In 1925, the year Miranda Towles-Falconer was London's Dream Girl, the match seemed to Boy's family and to Boy himself inevitable. She was from the right background, she had the right accent, the right manners, knew the right people. She was, in addition, delightful, adorable and good-hearted, and Boy had in fact fallen for her like a ton of bricks.

Lunch at Claridge's was sumptuous, fashionable, served by waiters in knee breeches. The food was the best in England, the beef the most perfectly marbled, the fish the freshest, the vegetables the greenest, the berries the sweetest, the wines the finest, but no one went there to eat. They went there to see and be seen. As Boy swept Miranda into the dining room, Miranda was pleasantly and unegotistically aware that they were the handsomest couple in a room that was filled, that Sunday, with equerries to His Majesty and ladies in waiting to the Queen. Syrie Maugham, the decorator, was lunching with Diana Cooper in one corner, and in another Mikhail Essayan, an orange orchid in his buttonhole lunched with three Arabs wearing white robes and headdresses. Noel Coward sat with Tallulah Bankhead, and Kim—who had just come back from the Midlands, where he had been interviewing factory workers, and was acutely aware of the gulf between the rich and the poor and wondering how long the rich could continue in their splendid oblivion—was lunching with Stash Rackowski, who was making quite a name for himself as an illustrator. When Boy and Miranda entered, Kim told Stash about the incident the summer before on the Murphys' terrace, when Boy had been rudely insulting to Scott.

"Nicole and Boy had a big fight about that," Stash said. "He insisted they leave Antibes. He apparently hated it and she never refuses to do what he wants." "Did they leave that same night?" Kim asked. "I had a lunch date with her the next day. She never came."

"I guess so," said Stash. "I know she returned to Paris ahead of schedule."

Kim and Stash, like everyone else in the room, kept glancing at the Duke and the Dream Girl. Kim saw Miranda, at a few words from Boy, pick up a champagne glass, and he noted the surprised expression on her face. He saw Boy take the glass, turn it upside down, empty the wine into the bowl of roses on the table, and extract something from the glass. Then he saw that the something was a diamond ring as big as an ice cube, and he saw Boy slip it on Miranda's third finger, left hand.

"I wonder if Nicole knows," he said to Stash, who did Nicole's fashion illustrations for her.

"I don't know." he said. Stash was an unusually short man, of slight build. His face, though, was strong, with well-modeled bones, arresting grayish-green eyes and a pointed chin which gave him the look of an intelligent pixie. "I just know I don't want to be the one who tells her."

"The Duke himself is going to have that honor," Kim said.

The next day Kim returned to New York. Before he did, he wrote a note to Nicole and mailed it in London.

5

Everything in England seemed slow, even the traffic. The speed limit was 20 miles per hour, and in the month Kim was there he collected half a dozen speeding tickets. He was happy to be back in New York, where he was free to proceed at full speed. Sally thought the trip had been good for him because he seemed to her like the old Kim. He brought her a suitcase full of tartans and Kimjy a cricket bat. He kissed her hello, picked up Kimjy and threw him into a big overhead cartwheel, and that night he made love to her. Sally smiled as she slept. Kim's anger at the lost manuscript had finally been forgotten.

He sent his article on England to *Collier's* and in May and June he finished *A Matter of Honor*. The day before they left for Cap d'Antibes, where they had rented the same villa as the summer before, Kim had lunch with Perkins and personally delivered the manuscript.

There was no one at Antibes this summer except me, Zelda, the Valentinos, the Murphys, Mistinguet, Rex Ingram, Dos Passos, Alice Terry, the MacLeishes, Charlie Brackett, Maude Kahn, Esther Murphy, Marguerite Namara, E. Phillips Oppenheim, Mannes the violinist, Floyd Dell, Max, and Crystal Eastman, ex-Premier Orlando, Étienne de Beaumont—just a real place to rough it, an escape from all the world. But we had a great time. I don't know when we're coming home . . .

—F. Scott Fitzgerald

CHAPTER SEVEN

1.

BOY, A PRODUCT of centuries of tradition, liked the year to pass in ceremonially repeated events. He was most comfortable when something he did was something he'd done before. Leaving Miranda in London to order her wedding dress, oversee the redecoration of his Belgravia house, and do all the thousands of things women do when they are about to get married, he invited Nicole to join him in Monte Carlo for a cruise. Nicole, who never could resist Boy, could not resist him now, even though she had reached a new plateau of success. Her ateliers—there were now three of them—were busier than they had ever been. Each new season had brought more clients than the season before, and the orders for the summer collection of 1925 set a brand-new record. On top of that, Nicole received the first official recognition of her existence: the committee of the forthcoming Exposition des Arts Décoratifs had invited her to show her designs at the exhibition scheduled for that autumn. Although the exhibition was to be devoted primarily to furniture and architecture, a very few dress designers had been invited to exhibit their work and Nicole was one of them. Redon, a new house, less than a dozen years old, would now be classed along with Worth, Lanvin, Patou and Poiret. Nicole's first dream of having her own house of couture was coming true. But despite her success, despite her honors, Nicole dropped everything and went to Monte Carlo. Boy welcomed her with a kiss and a gift, a jeweled cigarette case. Nicole thought the cruise would begin right away, but the *White Cloud* stayed in its moorings.

Every day for three days the yacht stayed in its slip, tethered to the landing, and every night Boy went to the casino, where he changed large amounts of pounds into vast piles of chips. If he lost, he bought more, enough to last until morning. If he won, he doubled his bets and gambled until he lost. Nicole did not gamble, not even with the money Boy gave her for that purpose. She had no moral objections to gambling, but she could not forget poverty and torn dresses, and she could not bring herself to play with money, to risk it on the throw of dice, on the turn of a card. Money was too valuable to her, and even though Boy reminded her she was becoming a rich woman, she did not feel rich. And so she stayed in the casino, watching Boy, by turns bored and indifferent, later irritated and finally angry. She had not left Paris, where she was admired and in demand, to share her lover with the gaming tables. She kept asking him when they would start their cruise; his answer was that he didn't feel like leaving Monte Carlo yet. He expected Nicole to bring up the subject of Miranda and his engagement, and he was angry at her because she never did.

On the morning of the fourth day, Boy arrived for coffee and croissants on the afterdeck in the top hat and tails he had worn the previous evening. Nicole could smell the tuberose of another woman's perfume. It was not the first time Boy had been unfaithful to her, but it was the first time he had dared her to accuse him. He expected tears and screams and threats, abuse and insults. He expected an angry scene ending in violence, a slap, perhaps, followed by a tender and passionate reconciliation. He did not expect Nicole's response: she was logical; she was calm.

"We're twins, don't you remember? Always in our matching things . . ." she began, gesturing at the yachting whites she was wearing, copied from Boy's own. "What we have is unique. Irreplaceable. We've healed each other's loneliness. Why do you want to destroy it?" Her voice was calm but her hands shook, Boy noticed, as she picked up her café au lait.

Boy had been taken off guard. He was surprised; he was confused. Why *did* he want to destroy what he had with Nicole? A marriage didn't have to change things . . . he didn't know. "I don't know," he finally said. He could not meet her eyes.

"Don't you care?" asked Nicole.

"No," he said. "I don't care." He *did* care; he didn't know how to admit it.

"I *do* care," said Nicole. "We have a past. A history. I don't intend to throw it away."

"What do you want to do?" Boy asked.

Nicole thought for a moment and decided to take his question literally. "I want to enjoy this vacation," she said. "I've been working hard and I've been looking forward to the cruise. I think we should raise anchor and set sail this morning."

"Is that what you'd like?" Boy asked. He was relieved and angry. He was let down by Nicole's refusal to make a scene. He was angry because Miranda's name had not yet been mentioned. He wondered what kind of game Nicole was playing with him.

"Yes, that's what I'd like," said Nicole.

Boy went to give the captain the order and Nicole thought she had saved her love affair and her future. Boy, who did not know how to show his feelings, was furious at Nicole but he didn't understand why. She'd done nothing to give him the right to feel so angry. He felt cheated of something but he didn't know what.

2.

For Kim, July had been an unendurably long month. He had counted out the minutes on a clock that was invisible to everyone else: the clock that governed the arrival of mail by train from Paris or by ship from New York; the clock that dictated the opening and closing hours of the cable office. He was in an agony of suspense because he had not heard from Perkins. His pride would not allow him to contact Perkins to ask, like an amateur, what he had thought of A *Matter of Honor*. For the first time in his professional life, Kim was tormented by doubts.

He haunted the post office and the cable office and told Sally only the good news: the reports from his father

178

about how rich they were getting in the great bull market; the requests from *Collier's* and the *Saturday Evening Post* for articles; the fan mail for *Western Front*, which Scribner's was still forwarding in large packets. Sally watched while Kim taught Kimjy how to swim. Kimjy laughed and chortled and imitated his father by propelling his chubby arms like windmills. Kim was fatherly and protective toward Sally, talking about the future and financial security and giving her money now and then and telling her it was hers and that she should put it aside for herself. To Sally, life seemed to have settled down. She hoped she would become pregnant again that summer.

Then Kim got a long letter from Scott, who was spending the summer in a rented house in Oyster Bay. The letter was about wild drinking, wild parties, and about the people he met at them: debutantes and young matrons, elegant gangsters, stock market manipulators, movie producers, rumrunners, gamblers, Eastern-seaboard aristocrats, all mingled together in a mad, dazzling society. People whose paths would never have crossed had it not been for the great shower of money that blurred, like a golden haze, roots and pasts, and cast the population of Long Island's North Shore, its polo fields and swimming pools and great white yachts moored to private docks, in a glamorous halo. Scott wrote that he felt he and Zelda were characters in one of his own novels. The letter was long and affectionate. The postscript was all that interested Kim: it advised him "not to worry" about *A Matter of Honor*. "A lot of people, including me, are fighting for it."

3.

A series of big rocks, boulders really, stood at the far eastern end of the Garoupe Beach. They formed a secluded niche where one could sunbathe nude. In the morning the sun, trapped in the sand and reflecting off the surfaces of the rocks, magnified the heat and the sense of languor. In the afternoon, when the sun had passed its zenith, the rocks cast welcome, cool shade. The rocks of the Garoupe Beach were Kim's favorite spot and every day, while Kimjy and Sally followed the southern custom of lunch and a siesta, Kim went there with a loaf of bread and a piece of the local chalky-white cheese, some apricots and a bottle of white wine. He had written Nicole from London saying that he would be in Cap d'Antibes that summer and that his invitation for lunch still stood. He would wait for her every day.

On the morning he received Scott's letter he took it with him. Scott's ominous postscript filled Kim with a terrible sense of apprehension and a feeling of impotence, of being left out of his own destiny. He sat there in the shade of the Garoupe rocks, sipping white wine, the letter anchored by a stone, its thin airmail paper whispery in the puffs of breeze that came in off the sea. He was wondering what to do when he became aware of the scent of Nicole's perfume.

"I'm only a year late," she said in a quiet voice, standing close behind him but not touching him. He turned around and looked up at her. Her expression was serious, tentative. "Am I still welcome?"

"Well, as they say, better late then never," Kim replied lightly. He smiled at her and wanted to touch her. His heart pounded at the sight of her and he hoped she couldn't see it race. She looked so beautiful, so golden of hair and eyes that she seemed to challenge the sun. "Come, sit down," he said, gesturing at the sand, almost overcome by the exhilaration he always felt in her presence. He wondered how long he could sit next to her and bear not to kiss her, not to embrace her, not to caress her. Her perfume invaded his nostrils and his longing overwhelmed him.

"You looked very distracted just now, gazing at the sailboats," she said. Ever since she had received Kim's invitation, postmarked London, Nicole had debated with herself over whether she would or wouldn't accept. Memories of her too-brief, inconclusive meeting with Kim the summer before had haunted her with thoughts of what might have been and although she deluded herself that her inner debate was an honest one, there had never really been any doubt that she would come to the Garoupe Beach to keep their rendezvous. And now, here she was in Antibes with one lover, running off to meet another. It was something she had never done and she did not admire herself for it. And yet her knees shook and she was breathless at the very sight of him, and she prayed he would not notice the effect he had on her. "Are you sure you want company?"

"I *was* distracted and I do want company," he said. "*Your* company. And I can even provide the lunch I promised. You see, my famous integrity isn't just publicity," he said, hoping his voice was steady. He poured her wine from the bottle he kept cool in the wet sand. "Now, tell me: why did you stand me up last year?"

"Boy and I had a terrible fight the night of the Murphys' party," said Nicole. "The *White Cloud* left Antibes the next morning at dawn. "I stood you up because I wasn't here."

"What did you fight about?"

"Boy was bored. He hates being bored and he blamed it on me. He doesn't like my friends."

"Oh," said Kim. "What does he think is wrong with your friends?"

"He doesn't like 'artistic' people. It's a good thing the

181

Porters were there or things would have been even worse."

"Cole is 'artistic.' "

"Boy said Cole is an exception." Nicole shrugged. "Don't ask me to explain it logically. It's not logical."

Nicole sat on the sand, her knees drawn up, her arms around them. She wore a loose navy-blue cotton shirt with white cotton pants. Kim noticed she still wore the huge diamond on her right hand and he wondered why she would still want to wear it now that Boy was engaged. She also wore a man's wristwatch. It intrigued him, as everything about her intrigued him.

"I've never seen a woman wearing a man's watch," he said.

"It's Boy's," said Nicole. She held out her wrist. The watch, of Swiss manufacture, was extremely thin, with a gold case and a strap of black crocodile. "Boy has a big collection of timepieces. I'm allowed to borrow."

"You're still seeing him?" Kim was surprised despite himself.

"Of course. How do you think I got to Antibes? We're on the *White Cloud*. the same as last summer. Boy likes everything to become a tradition, and as soon as possible too! We've visited the same ports, the same restaurants . . ." She smiled, amused at her thought. "I suppose we'll be taking this cruise ten years from now—the same ports, the same restaurants."

"What's the Duchess going to have to say about that?" Kim realized he was much more provincial than he liked to imagine.

"Boy's been divorced for several years. There's no duchess to say anything," Nicole said. "Didn't you know?" She was nibbling cheese and sipping wine in a perfectly tranquil way.

"Don't *you* know?" Kim could not believe that Boy had not told Nicole about his engagement. And if Boy hadn't, wouldn't someone have told her? A friend? An enemy? *Someone?*

"Don't I know what?" Nicole calmly put a piece of cheese on a nugget of bread.

"No one's told you?" Kim knew he had blundered, but there was no going back. He remembered his words to Stash. How could he have imagined that he would be the one to tell Nicole? It was inconceivable.

"Told me what?" Nicole put the bread down. She looked alarmed. "Told me *what?*" she insisted. When Kim was silent, she insisted again, this time urgently. "Don't do this to me! Whatever it is, I want to know! Tell me!"

Kim was quiet. Nicole grasped him by the arm and shook him. "Tell me!"

"Boy is engaged," Kim said finally.

"That can't be true," Nicole said in a matter-of-fact tone. And then a gradual pallor drained the color from her face. This time her tone was questioning: "How can that be true?"

"It's public knowledge," Kim said. "All of London knows. I was there this spring when it happened."

"In April?" Nicole asked. Kim's note telling her that he would be in Cap d'Antibes again this summer and that he hoped to see her there had been postmarked April. Boy had been spending his weeks in London at that time, and most of his weekends in Paris.

"Yes. April," Kim confirmed.

"I don't believe this," said Nicole. "I've never heard one word of this. It simply can't be true."

"Ask Boy," Kim said. He was in a terrible position—one lover telling a woman that her other lover was marrying another woman.

"It isn't true. It just can't be true," she said. She began to shake. Her shoulders seemed particularly small and delicate in the oversized shirt. She seemed fragile and vulnerable, and Kim had never seen the vulnerability in her before, only the strength and the confidence. "It just can't be true."

Kim said nothing. What was there to say? Obviously no one had told her; everyone had been afraid to. He waited quietly until her shaking stopped.

"I guess I still have to eat," Nicole finally said in a peculiar tone. She took the piece of bread and put it into her mouth. She tried to eat. "I can't," she said. "I can't swallow." She removed the bread into a napkin. "I don't know what to do with this," she said, looking around for a place to deposit it. "I don't know what to do with anything." At that trivial frustration, she began to cry without a sound. Kim took the napkin-wrapped bread from her and tucked it into his picnic basket. He wanted to comfort her. It was time to touch her. For a moment she stiffened in his embrace as if to reject him and his comfort, and then she allowed him to hold her and the tears to flow. After a long time there were no more tears and she dried her face on his handkerchief. The mascara and the powder left their traces. "I'll wash it out for you" was the first thing she said once she could speak again. "I must look a terrible sight! Red eyes and all . . ."

"No. Not you," Kim said. Without the armor of makeup, her naked vulnerability was even more affecting. Boy had trifled with her; Kim promised himself he never would. She was a proud woman; to strip her of her pride was unforgivable. "Are you feeling better?"

"Better?" she repeated his intonation. "Better than what?"

There was again no answer. They sat silently, side by side. After a while Nicole straightened herself and gently removed Kim's arm from around her shoulder.

"Tell me how you are, Kim," she said. Her voice was under control although she was still pale. Her thoughts were still far, far away. She felt numb and ravaged at the

184

same time. "I hope you're getting along better than I seem to be."

"Not really," Kim said. "The difference is that my problem is professional, not personal. I just got a letter from Scott. I seem to be in big trouble on my new book."

"But you're famous now," said Nicole, anxious to talk about Kim, about anything except herself and Boy. "I read *Western Front* in the French translation. It was a best-seller in all of Europe as well as America. How can you say you have a problem?"

"I'll tell you the whole horrible story," Kim said, and as he sipped his wine he told Nicole about the manuscript being stolen outside the Gare de l'Est, about the difficulties of reconstructing it, about handing it to Perkins at lunch, about the limbo of not hearing from his editor, and about the unsettling postscript Scott had added to his letter. He showed it to Nicole. "All I can say is that this book has been doomed from the very beginning."

"Doomed? You're as superstitious as a French peasant!" Nicole said.

"What would *you* know about French peasants?" Kim said, and laughed.

"What are you going to do about this book?" Nicole asked, and Kim did not notice that she had not joined him in his laughter.

"That's what I was trying to decide when you came along," Kim said. "If only there were transatlantic phones! I'd call Perkins and have it out with him. Damn phone company! They've been promising service every year for years! What's the matter with them?"

Nicole smiled for the first time since Kim had told her about Boy's engagement. "You're so American, Kim. So impatient!"

"I'm not impatient with you," Kim looked at her and returned the smile. He took Nicole's left wrist in his hand

and turned it toward him so that he could read the time on Boy's elegant watch. "It's almost two o'clock in the afternoon. July. The year 1925. I've only waited for this lunch for one year—you have to admit that with you I've been patient."

"Yes," said Nicole. "That's true."

She did not pull away her hand, soothed by his touch. She was suddenly aware that Boy never touched her except when he was about to make love to her. She was, she realized then, starved for moments of affection without passion but even as she thought it, the affection turned to a spark of electric emotion between them that left them both breathless and speechless. It was as if no time had passed since they had first laid eyes on each other in the rue Montaigne and they were both shaken by the power of the attraction that neither time nor circumstance seemed to alter.

Finally, to break the tension of the moment, they agreed, when they found words again, to go for a swim. Kim got to his feet and gave Nicole his hand to help her up. As she rose to her feet, Kim suddenly pulled her to him. They abandoned themselves to a kiss that had haunted them for as long as they had known of each other's existence. The kiss warmed and deepened, they had a sense of melting and fusing into each other. They forgot the rest of the world, and it was inevitable, there behind the sheltering rocks of the Garoupe Beach, deserted now that everyone had gone home for the long French lunch and the afternoon siesta, that they would make love.

He was strong and passionate, kissing her and loving her and her body, never for an instant separating them. He made love to *her*, to all of her, her body and her soul, with an extreme of emotion. She was responsive and tender, hungry for completion, finding in Kim's intensity

186

a match for her own. They made love a second and then a third time within what seemed to them the space of a moment.

They were both people who talked a lot. Now for a long while neither said a word. At first both were overwhelmed with feelings that were beyond words. Slowly their thoughts began to form. Thoughts colored by emotion, thoughts dominated by emotion.

"This . . . us . . . isn't casual," Kim said finally, unconsciously using the old words, the safe euphemisms. "It never was. Not from the very beginning."

"I know," said Nicole. "I always wondered . . . why didn't you come back to me, to Paris, in the very beginning . . . the way you promised you would?"

"Because I was weak. There were too many pressures. Too much flattery. Too many compliments," said Kim. "It was very easy to stay . . ."

"And it would have been hard to leave?"

"It would have been hard," Kim admitted. "To me, at the time, it was impossible."

"And so you thought you'd forget all about me?" Nicole asked, remembering all the time she had waited for Kim, waited for mail, waited for him, waited and waited until she had finally given up.

"Yes. I told myself that what we had was an adventure. A last fling. I thought I'd get over it. I thought I'd get over you. I didn't. I know that now. I didn't know it then," Kim said. There was quite a long silence. Neither knew what to say; neither knew what would—or should —happen next. Finally Kim asked, "Will you still be here in Antibes tomorrow?"

"Yes," she said.

"And will you meet me here again?"

"Yes."

4.

"I got an answer to my cable this morn-
ing," Kim said the next day. They were picnicking in the
shelter of the Garoupe rocks. "Perkins says that Charles
Scribner himself refuses to publish *A Matter of Honor*.
He objects 'violently' to the language."

"Can't you change the language?" Nicole asked. She
was in white from head to toe—white shirt, white trousers, white espadrilles. She dazzled in the pure sunlight.
Kim noticed she still wore Boy's diamond ring. He wondered whether she had confronted him with his engagement to Miranda.

"I've been through this battle with Perkins before.
Certain language in *Western Front* caused a problem.
Apparently it's even more of a problem in *A Matter of
Honor*. Charles Scribner doesn't seem to understand that
I can't—and won't—write about twentieth-century people and have them talk like Victorians. It destroys the
whole point of the book," said Kim. "I thought we had
resolved the problem for good with the last book. Apparently I was wrong."

"Scribner's can't be the only publisher in America,"
said Nicole.

"Scribner's is the only publisher that has Maxwell Perkins as an editor," said Kim. "I'm disgusted with this
book. It's been doomed from the beginning. I wish I
could forget that it ever existed. If I had any sense, I'd go
back to full-time journalism. I could make enough
money and I wouldn't have to fight with these damn
publishers. They think they're the guardian of public
morals."

"You writers!" said Nicole. "Always complaining. Cocteau complains about his publisher. So does Joyce, I

188

hear. Somerset Maugham swears his is trying to cheat him! I think you're worse than dress designers!" Poiret, as far as Nicole knew, spent more time with lawyers, suing and being sued, than he did in his atelier designing, and he wasn't the only one.

"Maybe we are," said Kim. "Unfortunately, that doesn't solve my problem. And, Nicole, it's not my only problem. I didn't sleep last night. Not at all. I've been thinking about us. About the future, our future."

Nicole listened, wanting to believe in a future but afraid to. She had been wounded too often. By Kim a long time ago. By destiny itself when Cyril's automobile had gone off the Corniche. By Boy . . . She still couldn't bring herself to think about Boy and what he had done. She still hadn't had the courage to confront Boy.

"I have a wife and a son. I love them both and I owe them something." Kim said. He had one arm under Nicole, cradling her to him. He had covered them with a white towel and he felt that they were united against the world under the protection of that mantle. Her fragrance surrounded him, entranced him. He could remember how she smelled on cold days in Paris, and now in the heat of the *midi* . . . "I made a terrible mistake when I didn't come back to you that first time. I was weak. I let myself be pressured, flattered . . ."

"And this time? Will it really be different?" Nicole was wary. She would never believe anyone any more.

"Would you have me?" Kim asked.

"I don't know. You'd have to come to Paris," said Nicole. She heard her own words in astonishment. She had never set conditions for a man, and now she was . . . she was worried, apprehensive. "I can't leave Paris, you know. My business—"

"I can write anywhere," Kim said. "Geography isn't the problem. Sally is. Kimjy is. A *Matter of Honor* is."

189

"You have a complicated life," Nicole said.

"And so do you," Kim answered. "There's your business, your duke . . ."

Nicole did not contradict him.

5.

"I spoke to Boy last night," Nicole said the next day, their third noon together in the shelter of the rocks. "He admitted that it was true. That he was engaged. It was odd but he seemed relieved when I brought up the subject. He admitted it right away. When I asked him why he hadn't told me, he said it was because he didn't want to hurt me."

"And he didn't think it would hurt you more to find out from someone else?"

"He admitted he hadn't thought of that," Nicole said. During her conversation with Boy, he had asked her if she remembered the time he'd told her he would do anything he could for her, either as Hugh Edward David or as the Duke of Mellany. She remembered; she hadn't understood what he meant at the time, but now she did. It was as the Duke of Mellany that he had a duty to marry someone of his own kind, and produce thoroughbred heirs. But it was as Hugh Edward David that he loved her, only her, and had loved her in the past and loved her still. Nicole was torn, devastated. She was in love with one man who was really two, and now Kim, with a wife, had come back with his talk about a future . . .

"He's very selfish," Kim said.

"I know," said Nicole. "But isn't everyone?"

"No." Kim thought of Sally. Sally wasn't selfish. "Are you going to leave him now? Your duke?"

"So that I can wait for you?"

"That isn't fair," Kim said.

"But it's what you mean, isn't it?" asked Nicole.

"I don't understand how you can stay with him," Kim said, evading her question. Of course, she was right—he wanted her and he wanted her to wait for him. "You're much too good to let anyone treat you the way he's treated you."

"Then I'm too good for a married man. Please, Kim, I don't want to talk about it," Nicole said. "I'm free. If I want to be with him . . ."

"But why? Why? What is his fatal attraction?" Kim asked. He could not believe that Nicole was such a snob and social climber that Boy's title would make her accept any kind of treatment from him. But what else could it be? "Is it because he's a duke?"

"No. You know better than that."

"Then why?"

"I told you I don't want to talk about it," Nicole said. "It makes me unhappy to talk about it." Then she added, "Some things can't be explained."

And Kim wondered what she meant and what it was that made her so unhappy she couldn't talk about it.

6.

"Doesn't your duke wonder where you go every day?" Kim asked on the fourth noon at the Garoupe Beach.

"He knows," answered Nicole. "I've told him."

"And he's not jealous?"

"Well . . ." Nicole blushed.

"Well, what?"

"Boy thinks all writers are pansies," she finally said.

"Oh, my God," Kim said. He didn't know how to react at first, and then finally he laughed. He and Nicole had been unable to keep their hands off each other, making love for hours every day with a passionate greed that surprised them both and slightly shocked them. Afterward they lay in the sun, naked. In the beginning Nicole had covered herself, not out of modesty but to protect herself from the sun.

"You'd look good with a tan," Kim had said.

"It's not at all fashionable," she said.

"It looks so healthy. I can't understand why you want to stay so pale."

"Only Americans get tan," Nicole said. She was meticulously careful to protect herself, even her hands, from the sun. To her, a suntan was a sign of humble labor. The peasants who worked the fields near Laronel were deeply tanned, the backs of their hands leathery, the lines in their necks and faces sharply etched by the burning sun. Better class people made a point of their freedom from the chains of the fields by keeping themselves pale and unburned.

"You'd look very nice," Kim insisted, "in your white clothes with a tan. You wouldn't have to get broiled, you know. Just enough to add a touch of color."

"Perhaps you're right. Sara Murphy looks lovely," she said. "I'll try," and so, carefully, a little bit at a time every day, and using a formula Sara had told her about, of iodine and baby oil, to protect your skin, Nicole allowed herself to become lightly tanned. She gradually turned a rosy biscuit color and was pleased at being able to go without makeup. By the fourth day she was a convert to the American fashion of suntans.

"I got a very interesting cable this morning," Kim said. He was in the most cheerful mood he'd been in all summer. "From a man named Jay Berlin. We went to the same college. He's a publisher now and he's heard of the difficulties at Scribner's with A *Matter of Honor*. He says he's interested in publishing it the way I wrote it."

"That's certainly good news!" Nicole said. "There's nothing like a little competition. I found that out with Roland Xavier. Every time we have an argument, I have to threaten to go to another mill. Once I actually did it —the time he told me it was impossible, absolutely impossible, to print jersey. The other mill managed it. Roland came around with his hat in his hand."

"The problem is Perkins . . ."

"Ummm, I see. Supposing Perkins worked for this Jay Berlin?"

"Maxwell would never leave Scribner's," Kim said. "He's identified with the firm, with all its best-sellers."

"Never say never! After all, if Perkins worked for Jay Berlin, then you'd have the editor you want plus a publisher who would publish your books the way you write them."

"Yes, but . . ." Kim began. Nicole cut him off.

"If I were you, I'd get on the next boat and go right to New York. I'd confront Scribner's. I'd have a talk with Jay Berlin. I'd take Perkins to lunch—" Nicole's expression was very determined as she sat on the sand in her characteristic position, knees drawn up to her chest, arms around them. She had tied her sea-wet hair in one of Kim's big white handkerchiefs, pulling it low on her forehead, just over her eyebrows. The effect was to throw her broad cheekbones into high relief and emphasize the strong planes of her face. She looked pugnacious, and Kim could see in her determined expression the reason for her success. In a way, he had never seen her look more appealing. He realized she was used to obstacles, used to struggling for what she wanted. For him, everything had come easily. Now, facing his first obstacle, he had been ready to give up right away. His first reaction had been to quit. But Nicole was showing him how to resist. He thought he was not at all reluctant to fight, he just wasn't practiced. As he listened to Nicole, he realized he was even looking forward to it.

"If I go, will you come with me?"

Nicole was startled. "How can I?" Nicole answered his

question with one of her own. "Apart from the fact that you have a wife, I have a big show to get ready for the fall, on top of the regular collection for my clients. Two hundred designs! Did you know that I'm even going to have a stage at the Exhibition? I'm going to design it myself, too, with props and backdrops! It's time I left Antibes and returned to Paris anyway. I didn't plan on staying this long." She looked at Kim shyly. "I didn't plan on seeing you, on spending this much time with you."

"And where do I stand with you now?" Kim asked. He took Nicole's right hand and held it flat on top of his. The diamond glittered red and blue and yellow and green in the brilliant daylight. "You're still wearing his ring."

"It's a complicated situation," Nicole said. "In my business I see everything very clearly. In my own life—" She broke off and shrugged her shoulders slightly in discomfort and confusion.

"What's going to happen now? To us?" Kim asked. "Now that we've come this far, what are we going to do?"

"I wish it were easy," said Nicole. "Everything's so complicated."

"It doesn't have to be," Kim said. "I'll give up everything for you. It's up to you. Tell me what you want. I'll do whatever you say."

"I remember a long time ago," Nicole said, "in my apartment. You were in the chaise and I was taking a bath. You were talking about all the 'competition' and I told you that there didn't have to be any if you didn't want it. You never really answered me then, and in the end you left me. I don't want to be the one who makes the decisions all alone," she said. She was wary of men now, of their promises so easily made, so easily broken. "Tell me, Kim, what do *you* want?"

194

"I want you."

"And?"

"And I'll find a way to be with you," he said fiercely. He would fight for his book; he would fight for her. "I don't know how I'll do it but I will. I lost you once. I won't make the same mistake twice."

"I wish . . ." she began and now tears almost glistened in her wide, intelligent eyes. Where moments before in discussing business, there had been determination and resoluteness, there was now, when it came to her personal life, vulnerability and uncertainty. "I wish . . ." she began again and abandoned her sentence. What she wished was that he would tell her how he felt about her. She wanted to know where she stood with him. She wanted to know if, this time, she dared to believe him. But her pride would not allow her to ask and so she let the sentence trail off, unspoken.

While Kim waited for her to finish her sentence, he thought, *I love you. I've loved you from the moment I first saw you on the rue Montaigne. I loved you then*, he thought, *and I love you now*. He almost said it but didn't.

"What are you thinking?" Nicole suddenly asked.

"Oh, nothing," he said, afraid to say the words, afraid of their power.

Nicole got up and kissed him gently. She walked away from him along the water's edge, forcing herself not to look back. Kim watched her until he could no longer see her and he was afraid it would be a long time before he saw her again.

The writer in him wanted to go to New York. The lover in him wanted to follow Nicole. The husband in him wanted to think that nothing had happened, although the man in him knew that he had gone past a point of no return. From now on, everything would be different.

To be twenty-one, fresh out of Iowa, alone,
utterly free, and with a job in Paris in the
mid-Twenties! In the ensuing weeks, months
and years I felt I was getting as near to paradise
on this earth as any man could ever get. They
were the happiest and the most wondrous, if
not the most important and eventful, years of
my life. Few setbacks, disappointments or sor-
rows marred those radiant days. These, as they
were bound to, would come—but later, and
mostly in other places.
                                        —William L. Shirer

CHAPTER EIGHT

1.

BY THE TIME Kim got back to New York, the fight was over and he had lost. Perkins believed in literature; Charles Scribner believed in morality; Charles Scribner owned the company.

"Mr. Scribner said he has no objection to printing the

word so long as it refers to a female dog," Perkins told Kim at lunch. "In *A Matter of Honor* you use it to refer to the heroine, and he absolutely refuses to publish the book. He was never really happy over the compromise we reached over the word . . . the one beginning with f . . . in *Western Front*. He had to defend it to the board, to the publishers' association; there was pressure from religious groups—and now he's drawn the line. Scott wrote in your behalf, so did Theodore Ingraham, so did S. I. Brace, but Mr. Scribner refuses to be budged," Perkins said. "I'm sorry, Kim. I fought as hard as I could with every weapon I could think of . . . and I lost."

Kim shook his head. "It's hard to believe one word could make that much difference," he said. They were in the Algonquin and the scene had barely changed since Kim had last been there. Dorothy Parker, petite, dark-haired and good-looking, caused Alexander Woollcott's triple chins to quiver with laughter. George S. Kaufman sat quietly, his usual gloomy expression unchanging, and when Woollcott stopped laughing Robert Benchley topped Miss Parker's wisecrack with one of his own. The round table was now internationally famous and Kim had the distinct impression that what had once been fun for the participants was now work.

"I'm afraid Scribner's is going to lose you," Perkins said, speaking passionately. "The thought almost kills me. *A Matter of Honor* is even better than *Western Front*. Kim, you're a good writer who's getting better." The stress of the past eight weeks of argument showed in Perkins' face—he seemed a smaller man, a tired man.

"Would you mind if I called you at home tonight?" Kim asked. "I have an idea."

"Of course you can call me at home," said Perkins, slightly mystified, because Kim, like all his authors, had his home number. Perkins prided himself on being available to his authors twenty-four hours a day. He signed the lunch check, charging it to Scribner's, thinking it was the least he could do for Kim, afraid it would be the last time he'd lunch with him.

2.

Jay Berlin was from an upper-middle-class New York Jewish family. For three generations the Berlins had owned a chain of retail stores that sold better-quality ladies' clothing. For as long as he could remember, Jay had wanted to be a publisher. He had gotten the idea from one of his family's best friends, a music publisher who made a fortune in sheet music. But Jay's aspiration was to be a publisher of books. At Yale he had written skits for student theatricals, had written for and been an editor of the *Yale Daily News*, and summers he had worked in the raffish offices of Reed & Christie. His summers in the famous publishing company had put the seal on his ambition. He adored the lively, bohemian quality of life in that office. All the smartest, prettiest girls in New York worked there, and every night when "work"—it hardly seemed like work, with the amount of gossiping, visiting and joking that went on—was over, Horace Reed pulled out a bottle of pre-Prohibition hootch and poured drinks for the staff, who, after a few, felt even more animated than usual. Then they went to dinner at a small Italian dive on West 46th Street, where the spaghetti with tomato sauce was plentiful and cheap, and the red wine was served in thick, chipped teacups. As soon as he graduated from Yale, in 1922, Jay Berlin went to work full-time for Reed & Christie.

Jay had known of Kim, although not at Yale. Kim had already volunteered and left for Europe when Jay was about to enter as a freshman. But despite the difference in age and the difference in religion—the Hendrickses were part of an old-line gentile society that rarely mixed with either Jewish or Catholic groups—the two young men were aware of each other and well-disposed to each other. Jay remembered Kim's name from the early *Sun* articles and Kim had met Jay when Jay was working at Reed & Christie and attending a lot of literary parties. Both Yale men, both literary men, they moved in the same New York circles.

After two years of working for Reed & Christie, two things happened all at once to Jay: first, he developed a sense, at the age of twenty-five, of going nowhere in life while his friends from dancing class and prep school had already begun to rise in the world; and, second, his grandmother died and left him ten thousand dollars.

Jay knew that Horace was in debt because Horace complained about it constantly. Horace owned everybody—printers, paper suppliers, advertising agencies, cover artists, authors—and kept Reed & Christie going with mirrors. Jay now had something Horace wanted—money—and Horace had something Jay wanted: the rights to fifteen books, all of them considered literary classics. The books lay unpublished and undistributed in Reed & Christie's inventory. Whenever Jay mentioned publishing new editions of them, Horace always promised to "do something with them," but he never quite got around to it.

"I'll buy the rights from you," Jay offered the next time Horace complained about his financial difficulties. It seemed that his father-in-law, who had put up the money for the firm, had the annoying habit of asking about his money and inquiring why there were no profits. This habit irritated Horace, who blamed his drinking on the meddlesome interference of his father-in-law. Despite his amateurish womanizing, his inability to keep a treasurer, and his lack of luck at making money, Horace was not unintelligent. The second Jay expressed interest in the dormant list of books, Horace became suspicious.

"Why do you want them?"

"I thought I'd like to try to publish them," Jay said.

"You can sell them for me. For Reed and Christie," offered Horace.

"I'm an editor. Not a salesman."

"Well, change jobs. I'll let you," Horace offered magnanimously.

"No, I'd like to buy the rights to them outright," Jay persisted. "I'm not interested in becoming a salesman for Reed and Christie."

"How much are you offering?" Horace knew when he was defeated.

"Five thousand dollars," Jay said.

"It's not enough. They're worth more than that." Horace may not have been a brilliant businessman or a profit-making publisher, but neither was he an idiot. He knew the rituals of buying and selling as well as anyone. "It's nowhere near enough."

After a few drinks, a few discussions, a few weeks, Jay arranged to buy the fifteen titles for nine thousand five hundred dollars. Using them as a base, he quit his job at Reed & Christie and set up his own company. He called it Twentieth Century Books.

Four years later, when Kim Hendricks called in response to the cable he'd received in Cap d'Antibes, Jay Berlin's Twentieth Century Books had survived its growing pains and was coming along satisfactorily. But Jay Berlin was infected, like the rest of the world, by the gold rush of the twenties. The stock market was going through the ceiling, breaking new records every day; athletes like Red Grange and Babe Ruth were being paid record sums, and Jack Dempsey, the Manassa Mauler, gave boxing its first million dollar gate; Constance Talmadge, it was said, was being paid the huge sum of five thousand dollars to advertise Lucky Strike cigarettes; movie stars who had been soda jerks six months before were driving Duesenbergs and dripping diamonds. Jay, happy with his accomplishments at Twentieth Century Books, yearned to get into the big time. He craved the excitement of the big author, the big best-seller, dreamed of movie deals and magazine sales, of big bucks and big excitement. He was more than ready for Kim Hendricks. He suggested lunch at a popular speakeasy called Jack and Charlie's, on West 49th Street and, over decent pre-Prohibition whisky, Kim told Jay the story of his problems with *A Matter of Honor.*

"I'll tell you what, Kim. Twentieth Century will publish it," said Jay, expansive, optimistic, in an expansive, optimistic era. Jay had read *Western Front*, had liked it and appreciated its commercial success.

"Sight unseen?"

"Sight unseen," said Jay. "If Maxwell Perkins is going to bat for you, who am I to disagree?"

"And what about *bitch?*"

"What about it? My company is called Twentieth Century," said Jay. "Charles Scribner's and Sons ought to be called Fourteenth Century. Fifteenth, at the latest."

"You'll publish it the way I wrote it?" Kim said, wanting to be sure there was absolutely no chance of a misunderstanding. "Word for word?"

"Word for word," said Jay.

"There's one problem," said Kim.

"Yes?"

"Perkins. He's the editor I want," said Kim, who had ordered a fourth whisky. Jay was impressed by Kim's ability to drink and show no effects at all. "I'd like to be associated with Twentieth Century. With you, Jay. But I don't see how I could leave Perkins."

"But if I hired Perkins you'd have no problem in coming over to us?" Jay wondered what other conditions Kim had in mind. As Kim's demands escalated, Jay's respect for him grew. Kim, Jay realized, was a good businessman. A very good businessman.

"I can't say there'd be no problem," Kim said. "You haven't mentioned money."

"How much was Charles Scribner's paying you for A *Matter of Honor?*"

"Three thousand dollars."

"I'll double it," said Jay.

"And add five hundred dollars for advertising?"

"And add five hundred dollars for advertising," Jay agreed, amazed and awed by Kim's demands. After all, Kim, a well-known journalist and magazine writer, had published only one novel. *Western Front* had been a solid success but it hadn't exactly stopped the world in its orbit. But Jay wanted, needed, lusted for a star, and sensed that Kim had that star quality. The mood of the times was to gamble and Jay was ready to gamble.

"That doesn't sound too bad," Kim admitted. "Let me think it over."

"No, you have to decide immediately." It was Jay's turn to exert pressure. It was time to put a limit on Kim's demands. If he didn't establish limits now, he knew that this would go on and on, Kim demanding and Jay giving and no end in sight. It would be a bottomless pit of demands, requests, concessions. "You have to give me an answer now," Jay said, and waited quietly.

Kim picked up his glass and stared into it as if it held the answer to his questions. The fact was that Twentieth Century was the one publisher in New York he wanted. He and Nicole had gone over the reasons at the Garoupe Beach: one was that Kim knew of Jay and knew him to be extremely smart and totally honorable; the second was that Twentieth Century, although doing well, needed a star—the minute Kim put his name on the contract, he would be the star, with all the benefits of publicity and advertising that that entailed; and three, Kim knew that Jay had solid money behind him and that, in business, money made all the difference—money bought the most and the best advertising; money bought the best artists to design the best covers; money produced the most books to be distributed in the bookstores; and, quite simply, money generated money. Twentieth Century had a combination of assets that made it the ideal publisher from Kim's point of view. Kim was not interested in money for its own sake, but he respected what money could mean to his career, to his self-esteem, to his confidence. He was not one to sneer from literary heights at money.

"The deal is that you'll publish A *Matter of Honor* exactly the way I wrote it, that you'll try to hire Perkins, who will be my editor, that you'll pay me six thousand dollars in advance and add an advertising budget of five hundred dollars?" Kim asked, to confirm the terms.

"That's the deal," said Jay.

"Well, shake," said Kim. He extended his hand across the table and the two men shook on their agreement.

Jay ordered a bottle of champagne, which he would learn over the years was Kim's favorite drink to celebrate. When they left the restaurant at four-thirty in the afternoon, Jay, who drank very little, was amazed that Kim, who had drunk most of the champagne in addition to the whisky as well as a few brandies after, was as steady and as solid as a rock. He commented on it to his new author.

"Lucky genes is all," Kim said. "I've been drinking since I was eighteen. I started on *le bon vin* and old *fine* in France and never stopped since."

"And what about hangovers?" asked Jay, who already

felt the beginnings of a headache from the modest amount he'd consumed.

"Never had one." Kim said, conveniently forgetting his wedding day.

"Never?"

"Never," said Kim.

Two days later the contract was signed. Twentieth Century was going to rush A *Matter of Honor* for publication in the spring of 1926. Jay Berlin's attitude, like the attitude of the whole country, was full speed ahead!

Kim cabled Nicole the good news and told her that the first thing he'd bought with the check from Twentieth Century was a ticket to Le Havre on board the *Lusitania*. This time he was keeping his promise. This time he was returning . . .

3.

Nineteen twenty-five was the year people would think of when they thought of the twenties. It was the year of Josephine Baker and the *Revue Negre*; of Fred and Adele Astaire dancing to the music of Gershwin; of Barrymore's *Hamlet*. It was the year of spats and white satin, of full-length raccoon coats, fraternity parties, Stutz Bearcats and hip flasks; of champagne and midnight sailings and orchid corsages. It was the year of Diaghilev and King Tut and the Bauhaus; of Tallulah Bankhead. Sophie Tucker, Billie Burke, Ina Claire, Paul Whiteman, Red Grange and Rudolph Valentino. There were nightclubs with glass dance floors and maharajahs in turbans doing the Charleston. And more than anything else, it was the year of Nicole Redon.

When she had walked off the *White Cloud* into the Carlton Hotel in Cannes that summer, with her new suntan, wearing a white jersey suit trimmed with navy, she had launched an immediate worldwide fashion. That fall she was photographed by Hoyningen-Huene and sketched by Cecil Beaton, interviewed by *Vogue* and *Vanity Fair*, was the model for the heroine of a new novel, *La Garçonne*, which was a best-seller throughout Europe. No fashion magazine on either side of the Atlantic was complete without several pages devoted to the newest creations from the ateliers of the House of Redon. Buyers from American department stores bought original Redon dresses and coats for the express purpose of copying them, line for line, for their customers. Samuel Goldwyn of Hollywood offered Nicole a staggering sum to design the clothes for his movies, an offer which, to the amazement of the former Samuel Goldfish, born in Poland, Nicole turned down.

A simple Redon day dress cost as much as a beaded creation from another designer and still the clients— now including the wife of the president of France as well as a covey of duchesses, princesses and Rothschilds— lined up to order. Women liked the way they looked in Redon clothes and men liked the way women looked in them. Nicole's style, a style which she had barely changed since her earliest days in Biarritz, was now the style that swept the world. The Exposition des Arts Décoratifs, visited by millions of people and officially dedicated to the arts of architecture and furniture design, was in fact a tribute to Nicole and the Redon style. The women who thronged through the pavilions that stretched from the Concorde to the place d'Alma had a certain style—slim bodies, short skirts, easy dresses of soft fabric, cropped hair, healthy skin—and that style was Nicole's own. Without her having planned it, without her having sought it, without her having expected it, time had caught up with Nicole and by 1925 her "look" had spread through all of Paris. There was one look now for fashion-conscious women and that look was Nicole's.

Her professional life was one triumph after another; her personal life was chaos.

"Everyone wants to copy me," Nicole told Lala late one evening, after the atelier had closed. "But no one would want to *be* me. It's ironic: what I do automatically, without thinking, for my business, turns out to be just right; in my personal life I ponder and ponder and *nothing* turns out right."

"Boy or Kim?" asked Lala.

"Both," said Nicole. "Boy's coming to Paris in November—not one month before his wedding—and he asked to see me. I should have told him no, that I never want to see him again. But I can't resist him. I have no character at all when it comes to Boy. I told him he could come . . . that I would see him. I shouldn't have."

"You shouldn't be so harsh on yourself," Lala said. "There's no rule that says love has to be logical. Every woman in Europe can understand why you find Boy so irresistible. He's divinely handsome, he's exceedingly charming, he's intelligent, he's rich, and he's a duke. A woman would have to be made of iron not to find him irresistible."

"He's also a cad," said Nicole. "He led me to think he would marry me at the same time he was courting his Miranda in London."

"Men . . ." said Lala, who was having trouble herself with a French businessman who couldn't seem to decide whether or not he loved her. "And Kim? I thought he was coming to Paris this winter."

"He is, he says," said Nicole. "At least I think he is. I got a letter from him this morning with two pieces of news: he's got a new publisher and his wife is pregnant again! He feels responsible and guilty and he loves me and he's coming to Paris, only he doesn't say when." Nicole shrugged, bewildered.

Lala smiled ruefully and shook her head. "I suppose

some people lead simple lives in rose-covered cottages, but not us. I'd really like to marry and have a lot of babies. But no one seems to want to settle down these days. All anyone thinks of is jazz."

"And business," said Nicole, suddenly practical and down-to-earth. "Leo's been after me. I'm having lunch with him tomorrow."

4.

Leo Severin had grown with the twenties. His perfume factories were now among the most important in France, and he personally had become a connoisseur of art and wine and the owner of a stable whose horses regularly ran—and won—at Auteuil, Longchamps and Epsom Downs. He was still, after all these years, a little bit in love with Nicole. He took her for lunch to Fouquet's on the Champs-Elysées.

"Nicole, you are at the top now," Leo said over poached turbot. "You have to capitalize on your fame. You have to launch your perfume and I, for one, can not understand what you are waiting for. Guerlain is having a fabulous success with its new Shalimar. You could have even greater success." Leo had a contract with Nicole to manufacture and market the scent formulated by Edouard Noiret. Noiret was threatening to sue because his creation was still gathering dust, and every week Leo had communications from Noiret and from his lawyers. It was costing him money to fend them off. "What are you waiting for, Nicole? All you need is a bottle."

"I'm stuck, Leo," said Nicole. "I always have a million ideas about everything and I don't have the first idea about this perfume of mine. I've seen a thousand samples for bottles and there isn't one I like. Unfortunately, I can't think of an idea myself. I don't even know how to tell the glass designers what I have in mind. All I know is I want something no one else has."

"Surely there must be *one* design that appeals to you," Leo said. He had gained a certain amount of weight since Nicole had first known him in Biarritz and it was intensely becoming to him, adding a certain authority and a certain presence to his personality. "I have to talk about money, Nicole. It's been costing my company money to have all these samples made up for you. It's been costing me money to keep Noiret more or less quiet. So far, I haven't had one sou in return. All that stands in the way, my dear Nicole, is you."

"Leo, can I help it if I don't know what I want?"

"But that's your job! You're the designer, the creator! You knew what you wanted sure enough when you had Noiret make the formula. That, you knew!"

"Leo, I can't even think of a name. Do you know how many lists of names I've made up? Not one of them is right. Not one! My perfume is radical, abstract, modern! Every name I think of just seems ordinary to me. Just another variation of cupids, romance, or pseudo-Oriental gibberish!"

"Good God, Nicole, what difference does the name make? You could call it practically anything. Heart's Desire. Or Love's Dream. Or Enchanted Garden. Look, Nicole, for all I care, you don't even have to give it a name. Give it a number! Because it's yours—because it's Nicole Redon's—it would sell!"

"I can't do that, Leo," Nicole said. "You know what a perfectionist I am. My clothes are the best-fitting clothes in Paris. That's why they cost so much. Hour after hour of labor goes into the simplest skirt. I work and work until every seam, every pleat, every sleeve is perfect! I'm not going to market a perfume that isn't *exactly* perfect!"

"Nicole, I'm losing money on you as long as that

208

perfume sits on a shelf." Leo was completely exasperated with her.

"And I'm not budging until I think of something perfect."

"Now I know why Roland Xavier's hair is turning white! Dealing with you! You're impossible!" Leo, a man who liked food, ignored the pear tart sitting in front of him. He tried to stay calm, but dealing with Nicole was aggravating, causing him to lose his appetite.

"Why don't you ask Roland how much money he's made off me? Not only selling to the House of Redon, but copying the fabrics I design and selling them to every other designer in Paris as well as shipping them to every country in Europe and even the United States. Ask him for the figures on the printed jersey alone! The printed jersey he swore couldn't be made!"

"Nicole, it's been two years since Noiret made the perfume for you. It's cost me thousands in samples, thousand in lawyer's fees. I'm going to have to sue you for my costs if your perfume isn't marketed by 1926. And that isn't a threat, Nicole," said Leo. "It's a promise."

"You'll never collect," said Nicole. She had a way of being stubborn and determined that only added to her charm, because she always spoke in her pleasant, low-pitched voice no matter how antagonistic her words were. "I'm the creator and my contract with the Severin Perfumes Company says: you have to please me. Well, Leo, so far you haven't shown me one bottle that I like."

"Any court is going to see that you've been totally unreasonable, Nicole." Leo's stomach was in a hard knot. He pushed the pear tart away, indicating that the waiter should remove it from the table. Looking at it was giving him indigestion.

"Well, we'll see about that!" said Nicole. "This autumn the French government gave me an award and a citation for my contributions to the French fashion industry. I think a court will see my side very sympathetically."

"Nicole, look, a lawsuit isn't going to help either of us," Leo said, taking her hand and trying to speak reason. "Our interests in this are mutual. Will you do just one thing?"

"If it's reasonable," answered Nicole. She was, even when angry, logical. It was one of the characteristics that made her successful in business.

"Will you spend a little time thinking about the kind of bottle you want?" he asked, and then added: "And a name, too!"

"All right, Leo," said Nicole. "I will."

"Let's have lunch in one month," said Leo. "We'll talk again. Is that a deal?"

"You sound just like an American." Nicole laughed. "But all right. It's a deal," she said, and she thought of Kim.

5.

The end of 1925 was a roller coaster of ups and downs for Nicole. Her accountant told her that never before had the House of Redon made such a large profit. In the past, Nicole had taken only enough money to live on and had put all the rest back into her business. This year there was enough left over so that her accountant advised her to begin investing some of her profits personally. It confirmed what Boy had been telling her all along: she was in the process of becoming a rich woman.

"What should I do with the money?" Nicole asked her accountant. It had never occurred to her to put her money into anything except the House of Redon.

"If I were you, I would invest it in shares in the New York Stock Exchange," the accountant said. "Everyone is making money hand over fist there, and there's no reason you shouldn't join them."

"You've always given me good advice," Nicole said. "I'll look for an American broker." She was sure that Kim could give her the name of someone good.

"It would be a good idea to do it as soon as possible," said the accountant. "The American stock market is the thing right now. The idea is to get in on it before the bubble bursts, as I think it will—but not for a while yet. Not for a couple of years at least."

Every afternoon at six Nicole walked across the place Vendôme to the Ritz, where she had asked the concierge to save the London newspapers for her, and every day she tortured herself reading the gossip and society columns, which were filled with stories about the forthcoming wedding of the Duke of Mellany. Guest lists were printed, descriptions of wedding gifts, descriptions of the bride's gown, an itinerary of the couple's honeymoon safari in Africa. When Nicole had seen Boy in November he had been more attentive than usual, and more tender. He had told her that the obligations of being the Duke of Mellany had caused him more unhappiness than any other single fact of his life. He felt constantly inferior to his illustrious predecessor, the Invincible Duke, advisor to kings and upholder of Empire. He felt undeserving of the vast fortune he had inherited. He felt that his life was not entirely his own to do with as he pleased. There was the constant anxiety that the weight of centuries to come would judge him and find him wanting. He had been sad, his usual gay charm replaced by a touching vulnerability, and by the time he left, to return to London and his marriage to another woman, Nicole had never felt more attached to him. And so she read the newspapers and wept.

The great family holidays—Christmas, Revillion, Easter—had always been miserable for Nicole. Christmas of 1925 was no exception. Boy was marrying someone else. Kim was far away in New York with a pregnant wife. As always, Nicole invited her mother to come to Paris for the holidays; as always, her mother refused the invitation but kept the check Nicole had enclosed with her invitation.

On Christmas Eve Nicole, who believed in God but was not a good Catholic, went to a midnight Mass alone. On Christmas Day she woke up alone and went to bed alone. In between, she went to the empty House of Redon and sat alone in her office and wrote a long list of names for her perfume, not one of which she liked. She folded the sheet of paper and put it in the top drawer of her desk. Perhaps something would come to her . . .

She then went to a reception at Linda and Cole Porter's at 13, rue Monsieur. Linda and Cole had created a life for themselves that Nicole admired. It was a rich life: rich in money, to be sure, but rich in other ways that were even more important than money: socially rich; intellectually rich; creatively rich. If she had ever wanted to emulate anyone, she wanted to emulate Linda and Cole.

The guests were a mixture of all the most interesting, attractive people in Paris. Artists, dancers, musicians, writers, aristocrats, millionaires. Elsie de Wolfe and Charles Mendl, rumored to be about to marry despite their advanced ages and the differences in their sexual inclinations, were there. Diaghilev and a dozen of his Russian dancers; Elsa Maxwell; the usual kings, Carol of Rumania and Paul of Yugoslavia; Mikhail Essayan, the legendary oilman; an assortment of White Russians, pretty girls and handsome men. Nicole knew almost everyone and stopped to exchange a word, a holiday greeting. An overheard phrase stuck in her mind with an insistence that took her by surprise. Picasso, his dark eyes glittering, his voice animated, was talking to a dealer about some paintings: "Cubism is the painter's way of painting what can't be seen." He went on to say that cubism was an abstraction; a way to paint the profile as well as the full face of a portrait, for example; or a way to show different sides of a building at the same time. Nicole did not attempt to join the conversation, but something in Picasso's words, about showing what can't be seen, struck a deep chord in her. What, she did not know.

As she left the reception and wished Cole and Linda a happy holiday season, Nicole caught sight of herself in a mirror. She looked lovely, she thought, and she was very pleased by the thought. Many of the women at the reception were wearing Redon dresses, but no one looked as good in them as their creator. It was strange, thought Nicole, to feel so sad and so lonely on a festive holiday—one lover at this very moment marrying someone else; another across an ocean—and yet to look so beautiful. It was odd how the inside and the outside did not seem to match. Of course, she reflected, she could remember a time when she was sad and lonely and did not even have the consolation of thinking she was beautiful.

At a Revillion party the next week, a gypsy fortune-teller read Nicole's cards and told her that there was an ocean voyage in her future. Nicole laughed and said that the gypsy was reading the wrong person's cards.

*I loved her and I loved no one else and we had
a lovely magic time while we were alone. I
worked well and we made great trips, and I
thought we were invulnerable, and it wasn't
until we were out of the mountains in late
spring, and back in Paris that the other thing
started again.*

—Ernest Hemingway

CHAPTER NINE

1.

RETURNING TO PARIS was like returning
home. Kim left the boat train at the Gare St.-Lazare,
and while all the other American tourists went to the
plush hotels on the Right Bank, he went directly to the
boulevard St.-Germain and, in a lengthy and loving negotiation, bought out the entire stock of the flower seller
who set up every morning in front of the Deux Magots.
For an additional sum, also lovingly negotiated, he arranged to rent her barrow too, and pushing it in front of

him, he set off for the place Vendôme. He crossed the pont Alexandre III, the wheelbarrow filled to overflowing with iris and anemones, baby's breath and peonies, mimosa and lilies, roses and carnations, violets and daffodils.

Here, indeed, was a man madly in love! He turned left on the rue de Rivoli, maneuvering the barrow under its arched arcades, right into the elegant rue Castiglione and into the broad place Vendôme. It seemed that Napoleon himself smiled down! It was just eleven in the morning and the day for the fashionable citizens of Paris was just beginning. Yellow Isotta touring cars, white Duesenbergs, drop-head Rolls Royces with basketwork bodies, bottle-green Cadillacs and canary Packards were lined up in front of the Ritz, and opposite, in front of the House of Redon, a reflecting brigade of rakish and luxurious automobiles also waited. The sidewalk was freshly washed, the windows gleamed, the white awning with the black block letters flapped in the crisp January wind.

"Monsieur Hendricks!" The pretty receptionist greeted Kim with a kiss and then with laughter as she glimpsed the mountain of flowers. "Oh, la la!" she exclaimed as the doorman held the door open and Kim pushed the barrow of flowers up the two stone steps and into the pale-gray entrance foyer. It was going to be a glorious day! Kim put his finger against his lips to silence the receptionist. Nicole, who seemed to know everything that happened in the House of Redon, must not have the slightest warning. Silent conspirators, Kim and the doorman wedged the barrow into the small elevator and with a push of the button sent it up to the second floor and Nicole's office. The black-and-gilt lift was so minute that Kim and the barrow could not fit into it at the same time. Kim left the barrow in the elevator and paced it up

215

the curved, carpeted staircase which the models descended to show off the new collections. He arrived at Nicole's office floor just as the elevator did. He opened the grillwork door of the elevator cage, extracted the flower-bedecked barrow, and threw open the door to Nicole's office.

She was working, pinning a sleeve, clear plastic glasses sliding down on her shiny nose, her honey-golden hair mussed. She looked up, amazed, as Kim pushed the barrow, its flowers by now spilling all over the floor, into her office.

"I brought you some flowers," Kim said with a giddy smile.

Nicole stared, hardly believing her eyes. For a second she was stunned, for a second she was speechless, for a second there were tears, and then the two stepped through the brightly colored petals into each other's arms. They kissed and it was as if they had never spent a moment apart.

"We deserve the Ritz and the Ritz deserves us!" Kim finally said. "We'll have the best lunch in Paris."

2.

"You still live in the same place!" Kim was surprised. Nicole, who was now a full-fledged celebrity in Paris, had been treated like royalty at the Ritz, but Kim noticed that she had not been able to eat or even to drink the champagne he ordered. She said that she was overwhelmed and that when she was emotional she lost her appetite. She was excited, she said, almost literally delirious with joy. This time Kim had come back! This time there *was* going to be a future! She decided to take the rest of the day off in a rare self-declared holiday, and they walked back, by their old route along the Seine, to Nicole's apartment on the rue de Bretonvilliers on the Ile St.-Louis.

"Of course," said Nicole. "What made you think I'd move?"

"Success! More money! Why not? You moved your shop," Kim said. "I was sure you'd moved your apartment too. I expected something very grand with central heating. On the avenue Foch, at least!"

"Oh, no," said Nicole, holding up the key as they stood on the doorstep where they'd first kissed. "It suits me here. See? I even have the same key!"

They let themselves into her apartment and fell onto and into each other, merging and separating only to merge again. They were in a state of joy, of ecstasy, in a suspension of moments no one could ever take away from them and when they finally found words, it was Kim who spoke first:

"I will never, never leave you again!" he said, almost at the brink of tears, thinking of all the time he had wasted without Nicole nearby, without her scent and her voice and her calm, intelligent presence. "Never!"

"Never?" she wanted him to repeat it. Her feelings for him went beyond love, beyond wanting, beyond needing. He was a part of herself. "Never?"

"Never! I was a fool to go," he said. "I was half a man without you."

"And I half a woman."

They kissed and touched and tasted, losing themselves in each other and finding themselves in each other. They were tremulous and strong, yielding and demanding, splintered and whole. They both realized it: when they had found each other, they had found themselves.

As the breathless newness of their rediscovery of each other wore off, as their comfort and certainty of each other grew, they began to talk of other things: of Kim's good luck in finding a new publisher—good luck he attributed to their conversations at the Garoupe Beach that past summer.

"I could never have done it without you," he told Nicole. "You inspired me to fight back . . ."

They talked about Nicole's enormous success and its official confirmation by the Art Déco Exposition.

"I notice that all the prettiest girls in Paris try to look like you," Kim said. "It's a pleasure to walk through the streets of this city because everywhere I look I see you."

"People tell me that, but it's unbelievable to me. I never planned it. I never imagined . . ." Nicole shrugged, unable to find words to express what had been happening to her. "Do you know that they copy my shoes now? My handbag! My haircut, even! I could never plan anything like it!" Nicole said, flattered yet astounded by the way women emulated her. "Leo says if I give my perfume a number he could sell it."

"Are you?" asked Kim. "Going to give it a number? It's not a bad idea, you know."

"They say Chanel has already thought of that and is planning to go ahead with it. Anyway, I don't like the idea of a number. It's too impersonal," said Nicole. "Perfume is something a woman puts directly on her skin. Perfume is so personal; a number is so *im*personal. I want a name—a real name for my perfume. It's just that I can't seem to think of one that I really like."

"I can," said Kim. They were in big fluffy white robes made of toweling, sitting in Nicole's living room. It was night now, and the lights of the boats on the Seine and the lights of the quais reflected in the water and back up against the shiny cream ceiling of the apartment. The furniture—the big oak table, the gilt-framed sofa, the undistinguished chairs—didn't look as shabby as it had

218

the afternoon when Kim had first come home with Nicole. But the whole apartment gave the distinct feeling that no one really lived there, that no one really cared about it. It was strange that Nicole, who was so personally fastidious, should live in such indifferent surroundings. Kim wondered why. "I can think of a first-class name."

"You can?"

"You ought to name it after yourself," Kim said. "You ought to call it *Redon*."

"Absolutely not," she said in a cold, flat tone Kim had never heard her use before. "I would never do that."

"Why not? The press refers to you as Redon," he argued, not catching the warning in her tone. "The American magazines write about the 'Redon Look.' Everyone would know immediately whose perfume it was. It would be a sensation!"

"It would be a lie!" said Nicole, the expression on her face hardening against Kim. "It would be a disaster!"

"But it's logical, Nicole," Kim said, carried away by his own idea and wanting Nicole to see how good it was. "And you said you wanted something different, something that's never been done. No one has ever named a perfume after himself. It's perfect! Easy to pronounce! Everyone has heard of it!"

"I'm not going to be the first! It's too egotistical! It's in terrible taste. Horrible! Never, never, never!"

"Nicole, I've never known you to be so stubborn. So illogical! I don't understand."

"It doesn't matter if you don't understand," she said. "I understand. It's not a name! It's not a real name!"

"What are you talking about, not a real name?"

"It doesn't make any difference! I refuse to talk about it another second!" And this time Nicole spoke with a violence that made Kim drop the subject. She was so obviously upset, almost furious. He didn't want her anger to turn against him.

They went out to dinner at a small nearby bistro and, pointedly not mentioning Nicole's perfume, talked as if they would never run out of things to say. That night they fell asleep in each other's arms, intertwined as they were destined to be.

Nicole dreamed. In her dream, her father had come home. She and her mother and her father had had dinner together. Her mother looked young and pretty in the dream; her father looked handsome and was elegantly dressed, as he always had been. He promised Nicole that the next morning he would let her look through all his samples and that he would give her all the material and all the trimmings she wanted and that when they were done and she had made her choices he would take her out to lunch. Just the two of them. Just father and daughter. But the next morning when she woke up in her dream, her father was gone. She knew, without knowing how, that her mother and her father had had another fight. She went to the door and looked out. She saw her father walking away down the street, tall and handsome and elegant. She called after him and then ran out into the street chasing after him. "Father! Father!" she called in the dream, but he did not look back and he did not answer. He stayed impenetrably out of reach and refused to acknowledge her presence.

Nicole woke up in a frustrated rage, feeling even angrier than she felt when Kim tried to talk her into naming her perfume *Redon*. She had never been angrier, and her rage was both frightening and liberating. All day long the dream kept coming back to her at odd moments, catching her off guard. For the next three weeks she kept dreaming the same dream and it kept coming back to her in the daylight hours with the same intensity, the same

220

frustrated anger. The night before she was to have her lunch with Leo Severin she dreamed her dream again, only this time the ending was different: "Father! Father!" she called out in her dream, and as usual her father continued to walk away from her, ignoring her existence. Only this time the dream didn't end. She continued to call out, and when her father still didn't turn, she began to cry and then, suddenly and shockingly, she began to scream curses at him, accusing him of ignoring her and hurting her; of humiliating and debasing her by treating her like a nobody. As she screamed and cursed and as the tears poured down her face in her dream, she woke up. At first she couldn't distinguish dream from waking, but then as she awoke fully she realized that she felt a sense of great release and serenity after the dream's startling violence. She felt as if she had resolved something that had been troubling her for a long time. An old score had been settled.

"Your idea gave me an idea," Nicole told Kim that morning over café au lait and croissants.

"Yes?" Kim asked curiously, recalling Nicole's peculiar vehement rejection of his suggestion. He had been on dangerous ground with her. He was cautious now.

"I've got a name for my perfume. It came to me in the middle of the night," she said. "I'm going to call it *Nicole*."

"*Nicole!* Well, good for you! That's even better than *Redon!*" said Kim. "More feminine. More personal. Congratulations!"

Nicole smiled and said nothing. She spread marmalade on a croissant and felt content. The irony! The sweet triumph of being a nobody who had something named after her! She savored her feeling as fully as she savored the flavor of the marmalade.

Leo was thrilled. *"Un coup!"* he said. "A real stroke of genius. I'll tell you, Nicole, you're difficult but you're worth waiting for. You have a knack for what the Americans call good publicity!"

"So it's settled? We'll definitely call it *Nicole?*" she said, still inordinately pleased with herself.

"Definitely."

"And if it doesn't sell we can always change the name," Nicole said, and they both laughed because they both knew that calling the perfume *Nicole* was exactly what Leo had said—a stroke of genius.

"Now all we need is a bottle to put it in," said Leo, "and we're in business."

"I know exactly what I want there too," said Nicole. "I got the idea from Picasso."

Leo looked at her, raised an eyebrow. He kept thinking he should stop being amazed at Nicole Redon, but then she'd do something else amazing. "An idea for a perfume bottle from Picasso?" Part of Leo, the businessman part, had to wonder how much *this* was going to cost him. Picasso, rare among painters, was known for getting good money for his work.

"I want the bottle to be a plain glass cube," Nicole said. "My perfume is abstract. At a party I overheard Picasso describe cubism as an abstraction, as a way of painting something that can't be seen," she went on. Leo did not understand what she was talking about or what it had to do with bottling perfume, but he let her continue. "Cubism is modern, Leo, and it's radical. Just like the perfume I told Noiret to make for me. I remember. I told him I wanted a modern, abstract scent; the scent of a garden that can't be seen, of an imaginary garden that can only be smelled but never seen. Picasso's words stuck in my head and the moment I had the idea for the name, I had the idea for the bottle. A cube, Leo! A plain modern cube!"

"Do you really think women will buy a perfume in a plain modern cube?" asked Leo, appalled. "Women like etched and frosted glass. And a cube has square edges, Nicole. Women liked curved edges. A cube is so sharp, so plain, so unromantic . . ."

"I'm selling perfume, Leo. Not romance."

"If you say so."

"And I want the stopper to be a plain cube, too. Of Lucite." Nicole had seen a new material called Lucite at the Art Déco Exhibition. Avant-garde designers had made Lucite stair railings and Lucite cocktail cabinets. "I want a Lucite stopper, Leo. It's modern."

Nicole spoke with her usual intensity when excited, and Leo stopped her with a gesture of his hand. "Whatever you want, Nicole, you will get," he said, "Even if it involves throwing away the past."

"That's what I want," Nicole said. "To throw away the past." She smiled at Leo, still a little bit in love with him, too, but she thought of Kim, thought of her strange, violent, liberating dream.

3.

Parisians complained that the winter of 1925–1926 was horrible. *Affreux!* It rained and it rained, and when it finally stopped raining it snowed. It was dark and cold and gloomy, so it was said, but Kim and Nicole didn't notice. They were wrapped up in each other and in Paris. The atmosphere in Paris was rich and relaxed. The Locarno Pact, which had been signed the previous fall, had brought a defeated Germany back into the European community and even into the League of Nations. The borders between France and Germany, which armies had savaged for a generation, were now guaranteed by the Big Four, and the strongest French Army in history stood watch over the Rhine. Now, in 1926, peace at last seemed a reality.

While the temperature that winter fell to new lows, so did the franc, and Kim's dollars were so valuable that he felt like a multimillionaire, and he spent with a lavishness that alarmed Nicole but which she also admired. They quickly settled down to a pleasant routine: Nicole went to the House of Redon every day, while Kim, between books, hung around the Select and the Deux Magots and visited his old friends on the *Paris Tribune*. They reverted to his former habit of picking her up at eight o'clock every night, and the evening would begin with an aperitif and the delightful Parisian ritual of deciding where to eat: at the Knam near the Panthéon, run by Russian émigrés, where the *prix fixe* dinner was six francs, or thirty cents, and where, from the more expensive à la carte menu, Kim would always order caviar and vodka to share with the White Russian refugees from the Bolsheviks and the flamboyant, always amusing Hungarians who had fled the Hungarian Fascists; or perhaps at the Café de la Paix, where they would watch, feeling sophisticated and superior, while the American tourists threw their dollars around. Or to Prunier, with its superb oyster bar and selection of dry-as-a-bone white wines, near the Madeleine. Or to Chez Francis, on the place d'Alma, with its view of the Eiffel Tower and the golden dome of the Invalides in the distance. Or to Pharamond's, in the middle of les Halles, for an earthy dish of *tripes à la mode de Caen*. Or to Flo's, an Alsatian brasserie deep in a small court off the Faubourg St.-Denis, which no tourist could ever find.

They walked all the crooked little streets in Paris and Nicole was not really surprised to find that Kim knew Paris better than she did: she had been on a straight track between her apartment and her shop. He was showing her the place where she lived and she loved it. On weekends they shopped in the markets and stayed in all day Sunday, never leaving bed except to make something delicious to eat. They abandoned themselves to a festival of the senses. They resisted nothing. They did what they wanted to do: they let themselves fall in love.

"This time," Kim told her, "we're not going to have a brief affair with a bittersweet ending."

4.

"It's a year of endings," Ernie said in February. He had just returned from New York, where he had seen Perkins and Sally. He and Kim were washing down orders of *choucroute* with carafes of cold white wine, at the Lipp. "I'm finishing the revisions on *The Sun Also Rises*. I took Scott's advice and went to Perkins with it. Glad I did, too. Perkins's not a phony."

"I hope I didn't make a mistake," Kim said. "Leaving Perkins. Jay Berlin tried to hire him for Twentieth Century. Offered him all kinds of money. But Perkins is loyal to Scribner's. He refused to leave. I just couldn't stay. Not and write the way I want to write." Ernie nodded. He anticipated problems with his own language, but he knew that Kim went further than any of the other good young writers. "So now I'm committed to Twentieth Century. It's a good enough publisher although, unfortunately, there's no real editor there. But Jay promised me the moon, the earth, the sun and the stars for *A Matter of Honor*. I wasn't man enough to turn him down."

"Just as long as you don't go the route Scott did. Changing endings for the *Saturday Evening Post*. Selling out. You do that, you can't buy yourself back," said

Ernie. Selling out was one of his favorite subjects and his second favorite was how he would never do it, would resist to the bitter end.

"I needed the money," said Kim matter-of-factly. "The house cost me double what I planned. Plus I can't sit still. I need traveling money. When I'm in New York, I wish I were in Paris . . ."

"And when you're in Paris you wish you were in New York?" Ernie finished the sentence for him.

"No. Not any more," said Kim. "I could spend the rest of my life here."

"Is your 'thing' with Nicole serious?"

"It always was," said Kim, "from the very beginning."

"Don't do anything you'll regret," said Hem. There was a strange expression in his eyes.

"Are you giving me adivce?" asked Kim. "Or are you addressing it to yourself?"

"Both," admitted Hem. "Hadley's in Schruns with Bumby. My thing with Pauline goes on here in Paris. She goes to the fashion openings during the day and we spend the nights . . ." Ernie shrugged his massive shoulders. "I know I ought to cut it off with Pauline. But I can't. I'm in love with two women at once and it's hell. It was wonderful in the beginning but not any more. It's against everything I believe in and it's tearing me into little pieces."

"Does Hadley know about Pauline?"

"No," said Ernie. "Pauline is very careful to maintain their friendship. She writes to Hadley, buys presents for Bumby. Hadley doesn't suspect. I don't think."

"What's going to happen?"

"I don't know," said Ernie, signaling for another carafe. It was their fourth. It was almost five o'clock and the afternoon crowd was beginning to drift in. "And what about you? Jesus, Sally's pregnant. She suspects something, you know."

Kim blanched. "No, she doesn't. She's never said a word. Not one syllable."

"She has to me," said Hem. "She asked me what the attraction was in Paris. I didn't know anything at the time, so I said the usual: freedom, life, liberty, an artistic atmosphere, no bourgeois restraints. Said you were restless as usual. Book done. Needed to roam a little."

"If only she weren't pregnant it wouldn't be so difficult," said Kim. "I'd take good care of her and cut it off clean. We'd stay friends."

"You're a dreamer, Kim," said Ernie. "Women can't forgive you for being unfaithful to them. They don't have any emotional generosity." Hem drained off a glass in one swallow. "Do you ever think about suicide?"

Kim shook his head.

"If you could arrange to go in your sleep," Ernie mused. "That would be best. Second best would be to go off a liner at night. You'd just jump and that would be it." He went on, talking about death. Sweet death in an avalanche, heroic death in the bullring, valiant death on the battlefield . . .

"On and on about death," Kim told Nicole that night. "Ernie has death on the brain. He got awfully tight at lunch. He's a mess. He loves Pauline and he loves Hadley and he hates himself."

And you? And me? And Sally? thought Nicole. She wanted to ask but didn't. Kim kept talking about their "future," but he was never specific. In fact, he had never, in so many words, told her that he loved her.

"He's too self-important for my taste," Nicole said out loud. "Ernie's a cruel man."

"Hem? You're kidding. Hem's a prince. Generous, honest. He's bigger than almost anyone I know. If I have any hero, it's Hem," said Kim. "And I'm not the only one who feels that way, either."

"You only see what he wants you to see," said Nicole,

who did not understand the need of Americans to hero-worship. "Hem likes rich women. First Hadley. Now Pauline. I know her. She covers the collections for *Vogue*. She's very pretty and very rich. Richer than Hadley. Hem has his precious honor because he can afford it—on women's money."

"Oh, come on!" Kim said, but he remembered what Gus Leggett had said a long time ago about Hem living off Hadley's trust fund, and he wondered about Hem and money. Hem always said he despised it, despised the rich. But now that Kim thought about it, he realized that Hem was always where the rich were.

"Speaking of money," Kim said, "if I had the money I'd buy you a present. A great big present. And I know exactly what I'd buy you: I'd buy you this whole house. Nicole, you deserve a house of your own."

"But this apartment is enough for me. I'm almost never here except to change and to sleep."

"You deserve more," Kim insisted. "And now that we're together, we spend quite a lot of time here."

"Sometimes I don't think I deserve what I've got," Nicole said. "Never mind more."

"How can you say that? You know the first thing I did when I made some serious money? I bought myself the kind of house I wanted. A huge elephant of a place, an old glass factory, and I had it fixed up exactly the way I wanted. For me, for my work, for my pleasure. Now if they take everything else away from me, I still have my house."

"I have the shop. I own that whole building on the place Vendôme! It's the first thing *I* bought when I had some money," said Nicole, a little defensive. She remembered how scared she had been when she had signed the contract, not sure that she wasn't biting off more than she could chew. "So we're not really very different at all!"

228

"Oh, yes, we are. Your building is an investment. It's your business, Nicole. My house is personal. It's *me*." Kim motioned about the room. "Nicole, you don't even have your own furniture."

"I make do with this very well," she said, but Kim's words were beginning to upset her. She thought of her friends' veiled comments when she had dropped everything to live wherever Boy lived—in his country house outside Paris, in his suite at the Ritz. For months she had used her own apartment as storage space, as a closet.

"What's this 'make do'? Why should you of all people 'make do'?"

"It's the way I was brought up," Nicole began, and then stopped immediately, conspicuously. She had been about to say more than she intended.

"Go on," Kim said. "It's the way you were brought up? I thought you were brought up with all kinds of comfort —governesses and a pony and closets of clothes," he quoted Nicole back to herself.

"I was," said Nicole.

"That contradicts what you just said." Kim looked at her carefully. "Nicole, I think you're lying to me."

She began to object. Violently. He cut her off.

"It doesn't matter if you lie to me. It doesn't matter if you lie to the world. But I think you also lie to yourself," he said.

Nicole looked at him. It was a brand-new idea to her. "I never thought of that," she finally said, her anger gone, replaced by reflectiveness. "One day, maybe, I'll . . ." She didn't finish her sentence and Kim didn't press her. "It's very difficult for me, Kim. Painful."

He remembered what she had told him in Cap d'Antibes: some things were too painful for her to talk about. They'd been talking about Boy then. Now they were talking about her past. Kim wondered if the two were linked. And if they were, how.

Nicole had always fought to moderate her feelings and to contain them. She was suspicious of feelings. She did not trust them. She had no wish to be carried away. She saw what being carried away by feeling had done to her mother, and Nicole had promised herself she would not fall into the same trap. She had always succeeded in controlling her feelings when she was a little girl, then with Cyril, and even with Boy. She had loved them, but only enough, never too much.

Now, with Kim, she gave up measuring out her feelings. She allowed herself, gingerly at first and then with growing confidence, to follow her instincts, to explore her emotions, to see where they led, and she stopped holding back. She fell madly, passionately in love with Kim. She loved him for what he was: attractive, honorable, irresistibly charming, suddenly vulnerable, intelligent, generous. And she loved him for what he was giving her: a new way for her to define herself and a slowly emerging sense of personal freedom—even, possibly, freedom from her past. Her understanding of what he was giving her took time to develop, and her acceptance of it took time. Her ability to act upon her new freedom would also take time. But in the winter and spring of 1926, Nicole, already at ease with professional success, was just beginning to feel the first stirrings of personal success.

When Kim impetuously invited her to return to New York with him for the publication of A *Matter of Honor*, Nicole, who rarely did anything spontaneously, surprised herself by agreeing, on the spur of the moment, to go. She was amazed to find that she could be just as rash as he was.

5.

The *Berengaria* sailed from Le Havre at midnight, and as Nicole stood at the railing, leaving France for the first time, she remembered the words of the gypsy fortune-teller and smiled. Kim had been in her life for just a little over a month and already her world had turned upside down.

"You look happy," Kim said, his arm around her, holding her close to him.

"I feel happy," she said. "I'm almost thirty years old and it's taken me this long to learn what happiness feels like."

"You must have been very sad in your past."

"Once upon a time," she said. "But now I think only of the present."

"And the future too, I hope," said Kim. "Our future."

There it was again. Talk of the "future." Nicole wished he'd be plainer about what he had in mind. She turned to him, not quite sure how to say what she wanted to say, but just at that moment the great horn of the ocean liner sounded and the powerful engines pulled the most luxurious ship on the seven seas out into the Atlantic. Kim and Nicole threw their champagne glasses into the dark, glistening water and kissed, a kiss that sealed a promise for the future. A future that had not yet been put into words.

Kim had taken a lavish suite for the crossing, and kept it filled with champagne and caviar and every sort of luxury. Nicole spent all her time with him. She visited the much more modest room she had taken for herself only to change clothing. She and Kim had decided to observe all the proprieties, and that meant separate accommodations. Kim was, after all, married. Nicole wondered how Kim would handle things once they reached New York. In Paris there would be the *cinq à sept*. But New York was not Paris and Nicole did not know how these things were done in America.

6.

Nicole went to the Waldorf-Astoria, Kim went home to Charlton Street, and A *Matter of Honor* went to the top of the best-seller list. Jay Berlin did everything he promised and more to ensure its success: advertisements were placed in newspapers all over the country; critics were lunched and dinnered; booksellers were cocktail-partied; a press agent was even hired to ballyhoo book and author. By the time copies of the book arrived in the stores, everyone had heard about it and wanted to read it. The book's success—and Kim's— were stupendous.

The Charlton Street house was the center of the pandemonium. The phone rang constantly and the doorbell competed with it. Stacks of messages piled up for Kim. There were invitations from the Swopeses for a weekend, any weekend Kim chose; requests from Harold Ross to write for the brand-new magazine *The New Yorker*; almost countless requests for interviews and photo sessions; manuscripts and galley proofs from every publisher in New York, sent in hopes of a quote from Kim. Jay Berlin called constantly to ask if Kim was free to attend this dinner or that lunch or the other cocktail party; S. I. Brace offered Kim air time to talk about anything that interested him; editors of magazines and newspapers deluged Kim with requests for stories and articles. Kim thrived on the attention, and seemed endowed with a superhuman energy that allowed him to go everywhere and see everyone and to write a stream of articles and stories as well. He commuted between the Waldorf and Nicole, and Charlton Street and Sally. The frenzy of his success and his hectically unpredictable schedule made it easy to conceal his double life from Sally.

Sally, who was eight months pregnant, was thrilled by Kim's triumph. Kim himself seemed leaner, handsomer, more vibrant than ever, and she could hardly believe her luck in being married to a full-fledged celebrity. She noticed that people treated her differently now. She was an extension of Kim and as soon as people found out who she was they were impressed; they went out of their way to flatter her and court her. They treated her as if she were a somebody, too. But the attention was a double-edged sword. Sally had always been piercingly aware of the way Kim drew women. Women had always been attracted to his good looks, his vitality, his charm. Now that he was famous too, it seemed that women— beautiful, rich, accomplished, celebrated women— swarmed over him and he, quite obviously and under- standably, reveled in their attention. These women had a way of looking at Sally as if sizing her up to measure themselves against her. She felt their envy sometimes; at others, she could see in their eyes that they dismissed her and wondered to themselves what someone like Kim had seen in someone like her. Sally must have asked Kim a hundred times if he loved her. One of the times was after a champagne party at the Plaza, where Kim had been the center of attention.

"Do you still love me?" she asked when they had finally gotten home, sometime toward four o'clock in the morning.

"You know I do," answered Kim. Sally had been cling- ing possessively to him lately. Perhaps it was her preg-

233

nancy, but Kim felt stifled by her possessiveness and irritated at her for showing her insecurity. He tried his best to conceal it. He wanted to tell her about Nicole but he wanted them to stay friends.

"Those Morgan twins wouldn't let you alone for a second. They were all over you. It was shocking."

"Don't worry about them," Kim said. "They're only interested in rich husbands. I'm not nearly rich enough for them."

"They're beautiful, though, aren't they?"

"They're all right," Kim said, trying to discourage Sally. Nicole had been at the party; Kim had had her name added to all the lists, and she had come in—the most elegant woman there, in a black dress of severe cut —stayed for a glass of champagne, and left. Nicole's simple, dégagé elegance made the flappers, with their rouged knees and cropped hair and flimsy shift dresses that left nothing to the imagination, look brassy and pathetic, as false as the strings of pearls they knotted at their waists and let fall to their knees. "The Morgan twins are all right if you like the flashy type."

"They think they're the cat's meow but I'm glad you don't," Sally said. Kim could hear and feel her relief. "Everything's different now, isn't it?" she said wistfully. "Sometimes I wish things could go back to the way they were before you got so famous. We're hardly ever alone any more. Oh, Kim, won't it be nice when things go back to normal?"

"They will soon enough," Kim answered. He didn't want to disagree openly with Sally but he liked the attention, loved the excitement, the ringing phones, the invitations, the flattery. He just didn't want to say so. He knew it would make her unhappy. "Sally, let's go to sleep. I'm exhausted."

"But I never see you, Kim. I never have a chance to

234

talk to you," Sally said. "Even the secretary you hired to answer the phone and handle your mail sees more of you than I do." She paused, gathering her courage. "We don't even make love anymore," she said shyly. "I'd like it if you made love to me, Kim."

"Even with your pregnant stomach?"

"Even with my pregnant stomach," she said. She reached out her arms to him and kissed him, wanting to show him how much she loved him, adored him, how important, essential he was to her. Kim kissed her and held her and he began to make love to her the way he always had. He put his face against the side of hers and then, turning his head slightly, kissed her dozens of times all over her cheeks and forehead and hair and finally moved to her ear and then to her mouth, increasing the intimacy of his kisses.

"Oh, Kim, it's been so long," Sally said, opening her arms and her feelings to him. "Too long . . ."

"Sally . . ." Kim murmured, his breath warm on her. Sally felt a difference in his kisses at that moment, and then she realized that something had gone wrong. The passion and the desire were absent from his kisses; only the affection and the tenderness remained.

"Sally . . . I'm sorry," he said.

"Perhaps you're tired," she said. She was sad and terribly disappointed. She tried not to show it. "It's been exhausting ever since the book was published. You must be all worn out." She held him and stroked his hair tenderly the way she sometimes stroked Kimjy's. In a way, she had never loved him more.

"Oh, Sally . . ." he said, and that was all he said. He felt unutterably humiliated. He was angry at Sally and flooded with tenderness toward her at the same time. He remembered what Hem had told him at the Lipp, about being in love with two women at the same time. He wondered if this was what Hem had been talking about but hadn't spelled out in so many words.

"Everything will be fine the next time," Sally said.

It wasn't. The next two times were embarrassing and so horribly humiliating that neither she nor Kim was able to talk about it. Both times Kim was unable to be a man. The first time Sally had provided the same excuse: fatigue. The second time Kim provided one: he had drunk too much. The failures were never discussed, never referred to even obliquely, but after the third failure Kim never again attempted to make love to Sally, and Sally never again summoned the courage to make a passionate advance toward her husband. The prospect of another failure crippled her and paralyzed him.

Sally wondered what was wrong, but she had no one to talk to. The only explanation she could think of was that her pregnant condition was responsible. She tried to remember whether Kim had made love to her when she was pregnant with Kimjy, but she couldn't.

7.

"I didn't know you were from a rich family," said Nicole as Kim turned the car into the big iron gates that guarded his father's house and drove it up the curved, graveled driveway.

"I'm not. We were comfortable but not rich," said Kim. "My father has made a lot of money in the stock market. He moved to Scarsdale just two years ago."

"Still, it's not at all what I imagined," said Nicole. "Somehow I always had the idea of you growing up on a ranch or in a log cabin . . . or something," she concluded lamely.

"Good lord!" Kim said, and laughed. "I grew up in the

236

heart of New York City. On Eleventh Street, in a brownstone."

"But you always seemed so American. I thought all Americans grew up in the wide-open spaces," said Nicole, who was very impressed by the magnificent Tudor house, so large it almost counted as a mansion. "I never thought of you coming from such a . . . substantial family."

"Does it make you love me less?" Kim asked as he parked the car. He switched off the ignition. He turned to Nicole for her answer.

"More," she said. She was half joking, half serious. She also realized that she wasn't the only one who liked to misrepresent a childhood.

Lansing Hendricks had been prepared to dislike Nicole. He had been shocked and disapproving when Kim told him that Nicole was in New York and that he wanted to bring her to Scarsdale.

"I didn't want to like you, you know," Lansing said after lunch. "I don't approve of what Kim is doing. Married to one woman; having an affair with another. I'm very old-fashioned about these things," he said. "But now that I've met you I find to my amazement that I like you very much. That confuses me."

Nicole smiled. Lansing Hendricks was an older, distinguished version of Kim. If she could have chosen a father, she would have chosen someone like Lansing Hendricks.

"I'm not sure if I approve either," said Nicole. "Sometimes I don't approve of myself."

Her honesty took Lansing by surprise.

"I hope you two aren't ganging up against me," Kim said. He was pleased that his father so obviously liked Nicole, although it did not surprise him.

"No, but I have to be honest with you, Kim. I don't

237

think all this success is good for you. It seems to give you the idea that you can do no wrong. That you can get away with anything. Everyone tells you you're wonderful twenty-four hours a day; no one tells you that you're still the same man you've always been, with strong points and weak ones. No one is there to bring you down off your pink cloud," said Lansing. "I worry about you, Kim, but I know you didn't come here for a lecture from me. And I know you well enough to know it wouldn't change a thing."

"You're probably right, Dad. You usually are," Kim said, but that was all he said and then he changed the subject. "Actually I had a practical reason for bringing Nicole here. She wants to invest some money in the American stock market and I thought you might be able to help her."

"My accountant tells me I ought to invest some money in Wall Street," Nicole said, "and I don't know the first thing about it. Kim's told me that you handle his money for him, and very well too. Perhaps you'd do the same for me."

"I'm much more conservative than most. Too conservative, a lot of people say," Lansing warned. "I'm flattered that you asked for my help but I want to tell you that you will probably be able to make much more money with someone else. Many advisors put their clients' portfolios entirely on margin. It multiplies their profits tremendously. But I feel it's too risky. I will put only fifty per cent of my clients' holdings on margin. I insist they keep the rest for outright purchases. I've lost clients for that very reason. They know they can make more money elsewhere. But I prefer safety to fast profits," Lansing said. "I want you to understand my position . . ."

"I do," said Nicole, who understood the thrust of what

238

Lansing had told her though not the intricate details of margin accounts. "I prefer a conservative approach. I don't have so much money that I can risk it." She thought of how Boy had teased her about her refusal to gamble even with other people's money, and how impressed Cyril had been when she had insisted on the best rental value for her first Paris shop. "I've been criticized myself for being too conservative."

"As long as you understand my theory of investing," Lansing said. "I'll be happy to handle your American investments for you."

"Thank you," said Nicole. "I have confidence in you."

Lansing walked Kim and Nicole to their car as the spring dusk began to settle. Now, late in March, it was just beginning to turn warm, the world just beginning to turn green once again. Two weeks before, when Nicole had arrived in New York, it had been bitter cold and women were swathed in furs from morning to night; now, suddenly, it was almost balmy. The weather in New York seemed as explosively unpredictable as everything else in that city.

Lansing helped Nicole into the passenger side of the car and walked Kim around to the driver's side.

"What's going to happen now?" Lansing asked. "Sally just about to have a new baby . . . and Nicole . . ."

"I don't exactly know," Kim answered. "I'm sure everything will work out, though. I love her, you know."

It was perfectly clear that Kim meant Nicole. Lansing remembered talking Kim into marrying Sally. He had meant well at the time. All he wanted was Kim's happiness. But now he wondered if he had been right in insisting. Nicole *was* special, different, one in a million. He could see that even in an afternoon.

Lansing stood at the curve of the drive and waved goodby as the car passed the gates and turned into the

239

road. Kim was daring where he himself was conservative, bold where he was cautious. Lansing was now old enough to realize that his way was not the only way, and he wondered whether he shouldn't be a little less cautious. Perhaps he was missing a lot; perhaps he ought to try to get more in tune with the modern world.

8.

New York was an astonishment to Nicole. In Paris you could see the sky; in New York you could see the skyscrapers. New York was jammed with cars and their sounds: horns and brakes and engines. New York was fast and it was bright. In Paris, many sections were still lit by gaslight and every night the lamplighters came by with their torches. New York blazed at night. Electric lights shone from apartment buildings, from the bridges that radiated from the island of Manhattan, and most of all, from the signs. Every shop, even the smallest, seemed to have a lighted sign: restaurants, barbershops, theaters, parking garages, tobacconist's, tailor's and shoemaker's shops, banks, drugstores and even mortuaries. Nicole had read that there were over twenty thousand illuminated signs in New York City and that it took over a million lamps to make them glow. The city dazzled at night, and both day and night people thronged the streets. It was said that there were five million inhabitants of New York, and it seemed to Nicole that they were out all the time. Forty-second Street and Fifth Avenue thronged and swarmed with crowds even on an ordinary Tuesday morning. All the people seemed to be going somewhere, doing something; they gave off energy and sparkle.

Nicole was astonished at the way people welcomed her

into their homes. In Europe, you might know someone for twenty years and never see the inside of their home. Not in America. No one was concerned with who she was or where she came from. There was a total freedom from the past, a sense of complete abandon to the present. Park Avenue hostesses entertained actors and actresses, bootleggers rubbed elbows with bankers, debutantes with Negro jazzmen, Ivy League fraternity boys with girls who had nothing to offer but their youth and good looks. It was an open society, completely different from the Europe in which Nicole had grown up, where past and family determined your life from the moment of your birth. Here in America anybody could be anything.

"I love this sense of freedom," Nicole told Margaret Berryman. "This sense of possibility."

"And New York certainly loves you. Everywhere you go, women admire you and want to look like you." They were in Margaret's office at *Harper's Bazaar* and Nicole was approving some advance sketches of the 1926 fall collection that *Harper's* would publish in August and September. "Women look at you and they immediately feel overdressed."

"All that silk chiffon and all that beading," Nicole said. "And those hems that fall in points with rolled stockings! I've even seen women wearing diamonds at lunch! It's the fashion here, I suppose." She didn't want to insult Margaret, who was an American, and so she did not add that in Europe wearing precious jewels before nightfall was considered unspeakably vulgar.

"The diamonds show that they're rich, and clingy chiffon and rolled stockings are supposed to give a woman Sex Appeal," said Margaret. "Since Sex Appeal is what everyone wants, that's what they wear."

"This 'Sex Appeal' . . . it was started by the Hollywood

movies?" asked Nicole, who was absolutely mystified by the great importance Americans placed on it. She had never heard the term until she came to New York, but here it was practically all she heard. People talked constantly about Sex Appeal and held intense discussion about who did and did not have *It*.

"Sex Appeal is democratic," said Margaret. "Even people who have no brains, no talent, no family, no energy, can aspire to Sex Appeal. It's quite democratic, you see, because everyone has a chance at it."

Nicole shrugged and smiled.

"Nicole, I'm surprised you didn't bring your samples with you. We would have had a fashion show of the new Redon collection. American women will do anything for French clothes, and you would be a tremendous success here. You have the American spirit of ease and informality plus the French sense of style and French craftsmanship. You'd be—" Margaret paused, searching for a word "—fantastic!"

"Really?" asked Nicole.

"Really! You should have brought your collection. Or part of it anyway," Margaret said. Americans who could afford it went to Paris to order their clothes; it had never been done in reverse. The more Margaret thought about it, the more she thought the idea was a good one. "You could bring some of your mannequins to show the clothes just the way you show them on the place Vendôme. Nicole, it would be a sensation!"

"It *is* a good idea," Nicole said slowly. "Maybe next time. But this is a private trip, Margaret. I decided to come on the spur of the moment. I barely had time to pack my own clothes, let alone a collection! I came with a man, Margaret," Nicole added shyly.

"Do I know him?" Margaret had known Nicole a long time. Had met Cyril. Had met Boy. She wondered who Nicole's new lover was. "A Frenchman?"

"Kim Hendricks."

"Kim Hendricks! You've certainly kept it a secret!"

Margaret realized that all of Nicole's lovers had been foreigners. She wondered why Nicole had never fallen in love with a Frenchman. Perhaps it was just fate.

"I wanted to keep it a secret," said Nicole. "Perhaps if I keep it a secret my luck will change. You know, Margaret, I would really like to get married."

"What about Sally?"

"Kim says he can't say anything to her right now," said Nicole. "Because of the new baby . . ." Sally's baby had been a girl; Nicole was the first person Kim had called with the news. The little girl was named Christie.

"Sally is a very nice person," said Margaret, who thought that Nicole was also a very nice person.

"Yes, she is. Do you know that she invited me to a party at her house?"

"Does she know about you and Kim?"

"I guess not," said Nicole. "I love New York, and you know that I love the Americans, but I don't understand how things work here. In Europe a man would never invite his mistress to his house—the house he shares with his wife. Never! It just isn't done. And yet it was Kim who asked his wife to invite me. I felt very uncomfortable but Kim acted as if it were the most natural thing in the world. And he took me to meet his father. He acted as if I were his fiancée.'

"What's going to happen?" asked Margaret.

"That's what I'd like to know."

"Has Kim asked you to marry him?"

"No. But he talks about the future all the time. Our future," Nicole said. "I'm confused by Kim. He walks in any time of the day or night. I can't imagine what he tells his wife . . ." Nicole shrugged, uncomfortable, unhappy, ill-at-ease.

"Well, you know what they say now—anything goes!"

said Margaret. "As long as you and Kim are reasonably discreet . . . well, between the sob sisters, Prohibition and necking in the backseats of flivvers, nothing shocks anyone any more."

"I don't know where I fit in," said Nicole. "I love Kim but I miss my routine, too. I miss the House of Redon. I'm not used to not working. I'm going to go back soon."

"When you do, would you like to write a monthly column for *Harper's Bazaar?*" asked Margaret. The idea had come to her as she spoke with Nicole. Nicole was good with words; American women were starved for news from Paris, the center of the world of fashion. Margaret nostalgically recalled the articles she had sent back to her aunt. She had met Nicole because of those columns. "We could call it 'Dateline: Paris.' "

"What would I write about?"

"Anything you like. Fashion mostly. But society, gossip, art, personalities too, whatever interests you."

"But I don't really know much about fashion. I have only my own style," said Nicole. "Other designers make fashion. They change the waist, the hem, the shoulders. I hardly ever change anything."

"Sometimes I'd like to take you across my knee and spank you. It is one thing to be modest; it is another to be as totally self-effacing as you are. A column from Paris! Signed by Nicole Redon! Women would line up to read it!"

"I don't know," Nicole said hesitantly. "I'm really only a dressmaker, you know."

"You are too modest, Nicole," Margaret said. "I will never understand your shyness. All of Paris at your feet, every woman trying to look like you—and you say, 'I'm just a dressmaker.' " Margaret paused, seeing that her words were hurting Nicole. "Nicole, please think about it. You'd be very good."

"I'll think about it," Nicole said.

"Say yes," Margaret prompted. "Nicole, say yes . . . you're too good to deny yourself any opportunity."

Nicole left New York in mid-April. That summer she prepared her fall collection. That fall she introduced *Nicole*. Kim wrote and cabled constantly. When Gertrude Ederle swam the English Channel, Kim said that he missed Nicole so much that *he* was ready to swim the Atlantic Ocean.

9.

"Take the train and I'll pick you and Sally up at the station," Scott said in early November, and now he was at the Oyster Bay station in a canary-yellow Rolls Royce. The car needed to be washed, but a bottle of champagne stood open on the dashboard. Scott was standing by the car, and the moment Kim and Sally got off the train he poured a glass of champagne for each and served them as ceremoniously as a butler.

"To *A Matter of Honor*," said Scott. Seven months after publication, *A Matter of Honor* was still prominent on the best-seller lists.

"Thanks, Scott," said Kim. It was extraordinarily gracious of Scott to toast *A Matter of Honor*, since his own *All the Sad Young Men* had been published that same spring and was best forgotten. "How's everything with you?"

"Couldn't be better! I'm going to Hollywood in January. A screenplay beckons," said Scott. "And so does lots of Irving Thalberg's Beverly Hills gold."

"How's Zelda?" asked Sally.

"Oh, fine. She's sorry not to be at the station to meet

245

you, but she's home seeing that lunch gets on the table. She's really excited about going to Hollywood. You know how bored Zelda gets when I'm home working on a novel. We don't go out at all." He turned into a very long, curved driveway. "We love it here in Oyster Bay. And look at that mansion! It's a real bargain too, if you rent it in the off-season. The owner let us have it for a song. I think he was happy to have someone living in it."

Scott described the house while giving Sally and Kim what he called "the grand tour." The house, Scott told them, was on two thousand acres of land with three miles of beaches on Long Island Sound. Designed by John Russell Pope, the main house had sixty-seven rooms, and there were a number of outbuildings: a dairy barn, a three-story polo pony stable with a clock tower, half a dozen stone farmers' cottages. There was also, Scott said proudly, continuing the inventory of luxuries, a saltwater swimming pool, a boat dock, a croquet lawn, a polo field, two tennis courts and an indoor ice-skating rink so that the owner could offer his guests ice-skating in July.

Scott was enraptured with the house and did not seem to notice its uncared-for look, the dust on flat surfaces, the pillows that needed plumping, the ashtrays that needed emptying. Sally said nothing, thinking that it would take an army of servants to care for such a grand residence. When the tour was finished, Scott led them back down the curved flying staircase to a glassed-in room filled with plants also in need of care.

"Zelda!" he called. "Zelda!" There was no answer. "She must be in the kitchen," he said. "I'll go get her and let her know you're here."

Before he left the room, Scott tried to refill their glasses, but he spilled the champagne when he poured Sally's. He apologized effusively and tried to dry her hand with the sleeve of his blazer. As he turned to leave, he seemed to lurch slightly.

"Is he drunk?" Sally asked Kim in a soft voice.

"He hasn't had enough to drink. Maybe just a little high."

Sally dropped the subject and went to the windows to admire the view over the Sound. On this cold and blustery day, the sun shining through the windows of the conservatory made it seem deceptively summery. From a distance, Sally heard raised voices.

"I hope we haven't interrupted a domestic argument," Sally said.

Kim shrugged. "As long as they don't drag us into it."

Before Sally could answer, Scott returned, an unconvincing smile on his face. "They forgot to deliver the smoked salmon. Zelda's going into town to pick it up," he said. He opened another bottle of champagne. "Come, let's have another drink while we wait."

"I couldn't," Sally said. She had had two glasses of champagne since getting off the train. It had been a long time since breakfast and, hungry, she could feel the sparkling wine go to her head.

"I will," said Kim, holding out his glass for a refill.

"Are you working on a new book?" Scott asked.

"No," said Kim. "I'm written out. I need a rest. And you?"

Before Scott could answer, Zelda appeared. "I need the keys to the car if I'm going to get your goddamn lunch," she said.

"You have the keys," Scott said placatingly. "They're in your purse." Zelda had a Ford coupe she had insisted on buying in a fit of economy. She said she preferred it to Scott's "shiny toys."

"I want to take the Rolls. I'm not leaving this place unless I take the Rolls." Zelda stood with her hands on

247

her hips. It was the first time Sally had seen her since Cap d'Antibes. Zelda was startlingly thin and she looked terribly young. There was something vaguely and indefinably alarming about the look of artificial youth of Zelda's stick-thin body, and her eyes seemed enormous in her thin, oddly unlined face. "If I'm going to be the messenger service here, I'm going to do it in style."

Then she seemed to notice her guests for the first time. "Hello, Sally. Kim. How is fame? How is success?" she asked. "Are you controlling it? Is it controlling you? Be careful, Sally. I'm warning you."

Scott took the keys from his blazer pocket and gave them to Zelda, who took them without a word and left the room. Scott looked crushed.

"Things aren't very good for us," Scott said. "We had everything. Love, youth, success, money, fame, pleasure. Now everything's gone. I don't understand what happened. Or when it happened." He reached for the champagne.

"Don't," said Sally. "Drinking isn't going to help."

"Drinking is all I have," said Scott, pouring the wine.

"Zelda doesn't look well," said Kim. "Is she all right?"

"She's my wife and I love her," said Scott. "It's not easy for Zelda. We're having money problems. I'm not earning as much as I was. In 1922 I earned thirty-six thousand dollars. This year I've earned three thousand, and that was for an old story I rewrote for Hearst. We can't afford the servants to keep this place up and Zelda resents all the housekeeping. It's my fault. But once we move to Hollywood everything will be different." Scott brightened at the thought. "I know it! Ilona got Thalberg to pay me a fortune. She did a prizewinning job of negotiation. But Zelda can't imagine it until it's real. She thinks we'll be poor and unsuccessful forever."

"She's wrong," said Kim, who thought Scott was

among the most talented of the young writers then at work. "You'll have another hit in no time. Zelda will cheer up again!"

"When she comes back I'll help her get lunch," Sally said. She was starved and she knew Kim was, too.

"That would be nice of you," said Scott, and very suddenly his words were so slurred they were almost incomprehensible. He seemed dead-drunk all at once, his eyes glazing and his steps unsteady. As he got up to refill his glass, he staggered and almost fell. Altogether, he had had four glasses of champagne in an hour and a half. Quite enough, but not enough to produce such an exaggerated effect.

"Are you all right?" asked Sally. She was alarmed. She didn't know what to do.

"Drunk, that's all," said Scott. "Did you do anything special to get pregnant?"

His question came out of the blue and Sally was stunned.

"That's none of your goddamn business," Kim said. He was furious. He had not made love to Sally since Christie had been born. It was a subject they skirted like a minefield. Sally was afraid of Kim's anger and Scott was oblivious to everything except his own problems.

"Zelda's desperate to get pregnant," Scott went on. "It would solve a lot of problems if she did."

"Won't solve a thing," said Kim. "Children tie you down—complicate your life, not simplify it."

Scott looked at him, his eyes unfocused.

"I wonder where Zelda is," Sally said. She wanted to change the subject. Kim resented the new baby. She had sensed it from the beginning; now he was admitting it out loud. She could barely endure listening to him. "She's been gone almost an hour. How far is it to town?"

"Ten minutes each way," Scott said, sobering as suddenly as he had become drunk. "We better go look for her."

They squeezed into the front seat of Zelda's Ford. The key was in the ignition, and Sally drove. They did not even have to leave the driveway to find Zelda. The Rolls was half on the paved drive, half suspended over the drainage ditch that ran beside it. There, in the swimming pool, with the leaves of autumn on its surface, was Zelda, nude, floating face-down, a dead man's float.

"Zelda!" shouted Scott. "Zelda! What are you doing?"

"Get out of the water! It's freezing cold out!" Sally took her coat off and held it out. "Zelda! Here!"

"It's beautiful, isn't it?" Zelda cooed. Leaves were plastered to her arms as she held them out in front of her. One large maple leaf was plastered to her hair and down over her forehead like a rakish cocktail hat.

"Come out of the pool, Zelda," Scott said in a soothing voice, the kind of voice one would use to quiet a child who had awakened from a nightmare. "Sally's nice enough to lend you her coat." Scott leaned out over the pool and reached out his hand to help his wife out of the water. Deliberately, with a few strokes, Zelda swam farther away from him. "Zelda, Zelda," he pleaded. "Please come out."

"Oh, no," Zelda giggled. She acted as if she were in a cocktail lounge. "You'll have to come and get me," she teased.

"Please, Zelda," Scott said. "You'll get sick. Please?"

"Spoilsport!" taunted Zelda, and then she relented. "Oh, all right," she said with a heavy sigh, and paddled over to the side of the pool where Scott again held out a hand to her. She reached for it and then, suddenly and shockingly, began to pull him into the water with her. Kim, standing nearby, grabbed Scott by the waist and pulled him back with such force that Zelda's wet hand

250

slipped out of her husband's. Zelda laughed shrilly, the laugh echoing over the water from the tile sides of the pool. Finally her mad laughter died down and she said, very quietly, "I guess I'll come out now."

She emerged from the steps of the pool and wrapped herself in Sally's coat as if she were doing the most normal thing in the world.

Sally took Zelda, still wrapped in her coat, upstairs. Kim could not wait to leave and paced impatiently while Scott slumped into the big sofa in the conservatory. They agreed that something stronger than champagne was needed and so they were drinking scotch. Scott delivered a long, drunken speech about how Zelda's eccentric behavior was his fault. He blamed himself for everything and accused himself of being a failure as a man, as a husband, and as a writer. Kim said nothing, recoiling from Scott's squalid and self-indulgent monologue. He just wished he were someplace else, anyplace else.

Upstairs Sally ran a tub of hot water which Zelda, gratefully by now, got into.

"I'm so unhappy," she told Sally. "Everything's turned to shit." She paused, then continued. "We got everything we wanted and we threw it away. I don't know when and I don't know how. But we did. Sally, I don't know how you're coping with Kim's success, but try to learn from the mess we've made. Don't do the same thing."

Sally didn't know what to say. She and Kim were in a mess but it was a different kind of mess, and Sally didn't think Zelda could help. She was afraid no one could help.

"Scott thinks if we have a baby it will make everything better. It won't. It will make everything worse. I'm doing

251

everything I can not to get pregnant. Don't tell Scott. We can't afford a baby," Zelda said, stepping out of the tub. She was so thin that her ribs showed and her hipbones were two pointed knobs. "I don't mean only financially. I mean emotionally. We can hardly take care of ourselves. A baby would be . . . too much. Too much for me."

"Oh, Zelda, I'm sure this is all temporary. You'll see," said Sally, trying to comfort her. "Scott will write his screenplay and then he'll write a novel and one day you'll think back and you won't even be able to remember today."

"I hope so," said Zelda. She slipped into a flannel nightgown, so grandmotherly, so opposite to the flashy, seductive clothes she usually wore. "You're probably right, Sally. I tend to be dramatic."

Zelda thanked Sally for being so nice. Then she got into the big canopy bed—its rumpled sheets and blankets indicating that it had not been made that morning, Sally noticed—and she was asleep before Sally could cross the master bedroom and shut the door behind her.

10.

"There was seven hundred and fifty dollars in Scott's Rolls," Kim said the moment they had boarded the train back to New York.

"Seven hundred and fifty dollars?" Sally was nonplussed. Scott had talked obsessively about how poor they were. How they were so behind on their bills. How they couldn't afford this and couldn't afford that. How he had had to borrow from his agent, his publisher.

"It was in the side pocket on the door by the driver's side. I noticed it when I got into the car. I counted it."

"What was it doing there?"

"I don't know." Kim shrugged. "I gave it to Scott and he looked at it as if he'd never seen it before. The he said he must have put it there once when he'd cashed a check and forgotten all about it."

"No wonder they have money problems," Sally said.

"No wonder," said Kim. "I'm starved. They never fed us."

"Kim, you made it so obvious you couldn't wait to leave," Sally said gently.

"They upset me."

"Everything seems to be going wrong for them," she said.

"It's not going to happen to me," Kim said fiercely. "That, I can guarantee you."

"Maybe it's just a phase they're going through," Sally said.

"Shut up!" Kim's patience collapsed. "You don't know a goddamn thing about it."

They were silent for the rest of the trip, each wrapped in his own thoughts. They stopped for a large meal and it was five-thirty when they got back to Charlton Street. The usual stack of messages had piled up for Kim. He picked them up along with a bottle of white wine and went up to the bedroom. He got into the bed, which was cluttered, the way his beds inevitably were, with magazines, newspapers and books, and began to read the messages out loud.

"Jay wants us to have dinner with a bookstore owner from Chicago tonight," he said. "Hell, I just finished lunch, thanks to the Fitzgeralds. Sally, tell them we're busy or something. Think of some excuse."

"You're sure?" Sally asked. Usually Kim was the one who was anxious to go out while Sally looked for an excuse to stay home. He was always ready to go anywhere and do anything, and he often teased her—sometimes playfully, sometimes not so playfully—about being a spoilsport. "You always tell me how important it is to be nice to the people who sell the books."

"I'm sure," Kim snapped. "I'm sick and tired of being trotted out like Lady Astor's pet horse to amuse the gawpers."

He had had a bottle of red wine with his late lunch and now he sipped the white wine, refilling the glass as soon as he emptied it. Sally had noticed that since the success of A *Matter of Honor* Kim was drinking more than usual. He started earlier in the day and seemed unwilling or perhaps unable to stop once he began. He drank at lunch and continued until it was time for him to take a nap; then, when he woke, he would start again and drink until he went to sleep for the night. His drinking worried her and it was one more thing they couldn't talk about.

"Tell Jay we can't make it for dinner, okay?" Kim said in a softer tone. "Please."

"All right," said Sally. "You know people are trying to be nice to you, Kim."

"I know," he said. "But it's eating me up alive. This afternoon with Scott and Zelda really upset me. He's a writer. I'm a writer. He's a success. I'm a success. He's young—I'm young. He's ambitious. I'm ambitious. When I look at him, I can see myself. It scares me, Sally," he said. "I feel terrible. The last thing I can face is being a 'famous writer' over dinner. Please get me out of it."

"Of course. I'll call and tell them that you've come down with a touch of the grippe. I hear they're nice people. They'll understand."

They *were* nice and they *did* understand. They sent a big bouquet of red roses and a card wishing Kim a speedy

254

recovery. The man's kindness made Kim feel even shabbier about the small social lie.

Kim stayed in bed for three days. He lay there all day long, propped up on pillows, reading and drinking wine. Finally Sally could bear it no longer.

"Kim, can't we talk?"

"Sally, I'm so tired. I'm exhausted. Can't we talk later?"

"No. I want to talk now. Kim, what's wrong?"

"Nothing."

"Is it something I did?"

"No."

"Then what?"

"Sally, I want to leave you."

"Oh, my God," she said.

Kim was silent.

"Is there someone else?" Sally finally asked.

"Yes."

"Do I know her?"

Kim nodded. "Nicole."

"Do you love her?"

"Yes," Kim said. Then he added, "The problem is that I love you too."

"Oh, my God," Sally said, repeating herself. Then she said, "What's going to happen now?"

"I don't know," Kim said, and for the first time in months he took Sally in his arms. They both cried and they tried to comfort each other, but nothing helped.

Isn't it fine what the American embassy's doing for Lindbergh? It's as if they'd caught an angel that talks like Coolidge.

—Ernest Hemingway

CHAPTER TEN

1.

LINDBERGH'S FLIGHT and Babe Ruth's sixty home runs; Al Jolson in the first talkie, *The Jazz Singer*; Laurel and Hardy, Charlie Chaplin and Buster Keaton; Cannes, Antibes and the Lido; the stock market at its highest and skirts at their shortest; Noel Coward, the toast of London, with four plays running simultaneously in the West End; cocaine and champagne, the Kit Kat Club, the Prince of Wales, silver cocktail shakers, the Surrealist conference on sex, movie palaces and the Dempsey-Tunney fight; brilliantined hair, kohled eyes, spats and orchid corsages; Pola Negri and Tallulah Bankhead; the Morgan Twins, Gloria Vanderbilt and Lady Thelma Furness; Mrs. Reginald Fellowes in a sequined evening jacket with a green carnation; Oliver Messel and Cecil Beaton and Gertrude Lawrence in Molyneux's white satin—the twenties roared on and 1927 was called the year of a million parties.

It was a vintage year for Kim and Nicole. It began when they boarded a freighter, the SS *General Helbschmidt*, in Marseilles, settled into the mahogany-paneled owner's suite, and sailed South for Africa.

Two trips in one year for Nicole! First to New York and now to Africa. Skyscrapers and a safari! Kim had turned her life upside down! In between the trips, Nicole had worked. *Nicole* had finally been launched. Full-page advertisements had appeared in all the French magazines and Frenchwomen could now go into a perfumerie and buy a flacon. At Nicole's insistence, there had also been advertisements in German, English and American magazines even though the perfume was not yet being exported. Authorities in the perfume business said that Redon was throwing money away. Who had ever heard of advertising a perfume in places where it couldn't be bought? But Nicole had insisted. She wanted to establish *Nicole* right from the very beginning as a perfume of international importance. By the time Leo would be ready to export *Nicole*, women would already have heard of it, would already be eager to buy it.

The advertisements themselves attracted enormous attention—they were without precedent! No one had ever seen anything like them. The idea had come to Nicole during her stay in New York. Instead of the usual, misty pastel drawing, there was a bold photograph, by Man Ray, of the cube-shaped bottle seen from a perspective that made it look enormous—as big as a skyscraper! There were no promises of love or romance in the advertisement, either. Simply one word. *Nicole*. It would take at least six months, Leo told Nicole, to get an idea of how women were reacting to the brand-new scent with the brand-new bottle and the brand-new advertising campaign.

By November, the fall 1926 collections had been shown and sold and the toiles for spring 1927 were being made in the ateliers. Kim had cabled and said that he wanted to take Nicole on a trip. The destination was up to her. She had thought of Africa immediately. Boy had honeymooned there; Picasso had a collection of African masks which had, he had told Nicole, influenced his work tremendously; Madame Valery Lucien, wife of the French Resident General of Tunisia, was a client of Nicole's and during fittings she had spoken of the beauty and the splendor of Africa, which she had traveled north to south, east to west. Kim had loved the idea and suggested the safari. A man who grew up in the city, who loved cities, Kim had a passion and a nostalgia for the wilderness, inspired by the memories of his boyhood hunting trips with his uncle and his romantic ideas about men and nature.

Kim made the arrangements and left New York, the situation with Sally unresolved but now, at least, out in the open. Kim was no longer living a lie; the need for constant duplicity was gone and, with it, the depression that had undermined him since Nicole had left New York in April, reaching its devastating nadir after the visit to the Fitzgeralds. The trip would be a bridge between an old life and a new one.

The *General Helbschmidt*'s first stop was Port Said, where Kim and Nicole first set foot on African soil. It was not like being in a new country; it was like being on a new planet. Crowded, hot, smelling of freshly ground spices, earth, garbage, incense and oranges, colored azure and dun, terra-cotta and olive, it assaulted and bombarded Nicole's senses. In the crowded, ominous, enthralling maze of the souks, she abandoned her normal conservatism and moderation and bought strings and strings of colored beads, of amber and lapis and obsidian, rose quartz, aquamarine, topaz, garnet, coral and jade, and she wore them not one at a time but as Arab women did, in stacks of four and five.

They sailed south and Kim and Nicole stood for hours at the ship's rail as it passed through the Suez canal, gazing at the desert, at the endless miles of sand, marveling at the hills and valleys of sand, at the ripples of sand caused by the siroccos blowing east from the Atlas Mountains. They had never known how many colors sand could be: pink and tan in the early morning; mauve and violet and finally purple at sunset; gold when the sun struck it from above; olive and black when the sun, at a slant, caused hills of sand to shadow valleys of sand. That evening, just as the sun was setting, silently, from out of nowhere, an Arab draped in white from head to toe appeared on a camel and, urging the animal into a gallop, raced the ship and then, when he had won the race, disappeared into the desert, going into nowhere as suddenly and as silently as he had come from nowhere.

"It was magic. A vision," said Nicole, spellbound by the man, the camel, the sand, the silence, the richness she could see with her eyes and a new richness she was now beginning to feel within. "Everything is different now. I see things differently. I feel things differently. It's affecting my senses." She had heard Cocteau talk about the effect opium had on his senses but she had never been able to understand what he meant; now she did.

"I've never had a honeymoon," Kim said. He did not have to say "until now"; it was what he meant and they both knew it.

They stood at the rail, their arms around each other's waists, aware of the changing position of the sun as it

259

dropped below the horizon, of the sudden drop in temperature, the breeze that came up with evening. They shared a feeling of being beyond time and space, totally absorbed by and with each other.

From the Red Sea, they crossed the Gulf of Aden and continued along the east coast of Africa. They disembarked at Mombasa and took the train that climbed from the steamy tropical coast up through the bush to Nairobi, cool and sunny and sparkling, set in the rolling hills and broad plains of Kenya. They met their white hunter—recommended by Boy—for the first time at the bar of the New Stanley Hotel.

Nigel Storey was a rugged man of medium height, in tan safari jacket and shorts. He had the strongly muscled legs of a soccer player, and alert eyes of robin's-egg blue, startling in his permanently sunburned face. Nigel's father had owned a coffee plantation, and Nigel had been born in Africa and knew it and its animals as well as any man alive. He was one of the legendary white hunters, an interpreter between the white man and the African, between the city dweller and the plains and the game. He had learned—because his life literally depended on it—to size men up instantly: to know how they would handle a gun; how they would react to a scared elephant who decided to charge at the last second rather than run; whether they could handle their drink and their women.

Kim Hendricks talked a good shot—of his hand-tooled Purdys; of deer hunting in the State of Maine; of boar hunting in the forests of Northern Italy. He seemed strong and reliable. He would be no trouble as a client, Nigel decided, as long as he did not try to use the taking of game as a way of showing off. There was something of the show-off in Kim Hendricks, Nigel thought; he also thought that Kim knew it and was able to control it.

This dress designer, Nicole Redon, was beautiful and

she was competent. She was, according to Boy Mellany, a sound shot. She had the air of being both seductive and emotionally stable, and Nigel was attracted to her the first moment he laid eyes on her. Sexual complications were the last thing anyone needed on safari, and Nigel decided he would never show how he felt; he also knew it would be difficult to conceal.

After an hour and a half getting acquainted over gin and tonic, clients and hunter agreed to meet the next day. They spent two days in Nairobi getting outfitted. Then they left, heading due south on the Cape-to-Cairo road, for the vast game preserve of the Serengeti Plain.

Game was plenty; Africa had not yet been overhunted. In the first weeks they took eland, bushbuck and waterbuck. They shot gazelle, Grand and Robertsi for meat and Kongoni and impala for heads. Nicole was a solid shot—she took her time setting up and squeezed the trigger exactly at the right moment, always shooting slightly ahead of the target, never making the amateur's error of waiting the split second too long, till the target was exactly in the crosshairs, but always firing just the split-second before. She had, she said one night at dinner, learned to shoot with her father, a very elegant man and an excellent sportsman, in Sologne, about two hours outside Paris, where they hunted small game.

"I thought you said you hunted in Varengeville," Kim said.

"I did," answered Nicole, reverting to the automatic lie. "We hunted in several places. We had several homes."

"You don't have to pretend to me any more," Kim reminded her later, when they were alone.

"It was Boy who taught me to shoot," Nicole said quietly.

"I knew it wasn't your father," Kim said.

"How did you know?"

"I can tell when you're lying."

Nicole did not object or argue. She was beginning to get used to the idea that one day she would tell Kim the truth. Not now. But one day.

The truth would be something new for Nicole but just now in Africa she was experiencing something else new and overwhelming: she was discovering her sensual self. Linked to her emotional self, her sensual self was the side she had always controlled and moderated. But here in Africa with Kim, having him all to herself, with no time limit this time, with no sense of an ending written in at the beginning, she began to come fully alive physically. She had always been on good terms with her body, dressing it carefully and exercising it regularly, but now she began to value her body and to love it. At night, after a full day's shooting, Nicole was physically tired and relaxed and that made her physically responsive, aware of the infinities of desire and satisfaction her body could feel and express. She loved Kim. She had from the very beginning. But now, in a brand-new and overwhelming way, her body loved him, too.

"You've led me into a new world," she told him one night when they had finished making love, when they were warm and close. "A new world that was always inside me but that I never knew."

"I feel the same way," said Kim. "I thought love was loving someone else. I never knew it was also loving yourself."

It was the first time Kim had used the word "love." Nicole caught her breath. She waited for the next, logical words. She could almost hear them: *I love you*, he would say at any moment, any second now. But he held her close to him and said nothing more. He had come as close as he ever had to telling her in so many words that he loved her. She knew in her heart and her soul that he did—but for some reason he always shied away from the words, and Nicole was haunted by a vague feeling that until he uttered them, something between them would be incomplete.

Holding each other, wrapped in silence, they fell into the deep, refreshing sleep they would always associate with Africa and nowhere else.

Each day at sunrise a shooting brake custom-fitted to a Rolls Royce understructure took them to a drop-off point in the bush. The rugged vehicle, designed for high clearance and 360-degree vision, sat six. The driver, a Kikuyu, and Nigel, binoculars hanging from his neck, sat up front. Behind them sat Kim and Nicole, and behind them, the second guns, M'Baula and Kamutu. M'Baula, Kim's second, was a wiry black man with yellow eyes and tribal scars on his face and chest. Kamutu, Nicole's second, was a man who could have been twenty-eight or fifty, of powerful athletic build, with muscles sculpted in ebony. Kamutu wore, with dignity and even elegance, patched shorts and shirt, immaculately clean and perfectly starched and ironed, a khaki U.S. Army woolen skullcap and sandals made from automobile tires. He had a true bass voice, rare in a man, but he almost never spoke, expressing himself not in words but with his physical presence. He possessed in silence more capacity for expression than a man with a dictionary.

They came upon their first lion near sundown. The air, which seemed to turn colors in Africa, had begun to turn mauve. It still held the warmth of the sun but the coolness of evening could just be sensed. The very air in Africa seemed to have a life of its own.

The lion, a dark-maned male, first spotted against a thorn tree, was pure yellow. Its head was enormous, seeming almost too heavy for the sleek, lithe body, its great bulk increased even more by thick hair and heavy mane. The lion, the first of the safari, was to be Kim's.

Kim stepped from the shooting brake, M'Baula behind him. Nicole took up a position on his left, Nigel on the right. They froze, waited motionless. The lion lazily licked its flank, totally absorbed in grooming itself. The tableau was silent, time and distance and quest held in suspension. Then, a whispered word from Nigel. Kim dropped to one knee, raised the Purdy to his shoulder, and aimed. He squeezed the trigger steadily and firmly. The gun roared and bucked and the lion wheeled and suddenly turned toward Kim. Its padded feet were silent against the stubbly, pale grass. A small spot of blood stained its visible shoulder—the shot had gone high. Its mouth opened in a roar, its large vicious teeth exposed; ready to attack, the lion moved with incredible power and speed, paralyzing Kim into immobility. In that split-second, Nigel fired. The lion flipped over crookedly in mid-lunge. It fell to the side and backward. The whole incident had taken place with shocking speed, the two shots sounding almost as one.

M'Baula leapt up. "Papa hit!" he yelled. "Papa *piga simba!*" And he ran off shouting the news to the boys in camp. They dropped their ironing and laundry, left the cooking pots and the tent-making chores, and ran out to the scene of the kill. Babbling and shouting, they clustered around Kim and lifted him to their shoulders. Chanting the lion song, they paraded him back to camp and set him down in front of his tent as if he were a king. Champagne appeared and amid shouts and cheers, many toasts were drunk. To Kim, the taste was bitter. He knew for certain that Nigel had dropped "his" lion.

"Bwana Storey's lion," Kim kept saying, trying to set the record straight. He could not get his moment of

264

frozen horror, of cowardice, out of his mind. The memory seared, destroying his self-respect. At least he could tell the truth, get the record straight. "Bwana Storey's simba."

"Papa's simba!" M'Baula insisted, his large white teeth dazzling in a happy smile. "Papa's simba!" M'Baula was convinced, and he had convinced the boys at camp. Every safari had to have a hero, and Kim was this safari's hero.

"It's a lie," Kim said later that night, when he and Nicole were alone. "I feel like a fraud. It was Nigel's lion. Not mine." Not even to Nicole would he admit the extent of his devastating humiliation: the knowledge that he had panicked.

"It's not important who shot the lion," said Nicole, carefully.

"Yes, it is," Kim insisted. "Kamutu knows it's a lie. Did you see him? He refused to drink the toasts. He won't look at me."

"It's not your fault. M'Baula made a mistake, that's all," said Nicole.

"It matters to me," Kim said. "It's a lie. *I* can't live with a lie. I *won't* live with a lie." His words were a double-edged weapon—aimed at Nicole, accusing her of *her* lie. The one he had divined and that she had almost but not quite confessed. The lie—whatever it was—that she had chosen to live with.

"I'm going to shoot another lion and I'm going to do it cleanly and honestly. Kamutu will see that I'm a real man," Kim said.

Nicole said nothing. She sensed they were on dangerous ground and she would tread carefully.

By the rules, the next lion would be Nicole's, the one after, Kim's. It might be days or even weeks before an-

265

other two were sighted, and it was not only a question of finding a lion. The circumstances for the kill had to be right. There might be five lions and no chance for a clean shot. They were hunters, not butchers. Kim arranged with Nigel to extend the duration of the safari for as long as it took him to kill his lion. He didn't care how much money it cost. He wanted his lion, a clean kill.

He had to prove to Nicole that he was as good a man as Nigel. Nigel was in love with Nicole. Kim could see it. He needed to show Nicole that he was the equal of any man—in this instance, the legendary white hunter of Africa. Kim's permit allowed him two lions. The one Nigel had shot had already been chalked up to Kim. He had only one chance left.

Kim became a man obsessed, thinking and talking of nothing but the lion he would kill. For a week they trekked the dry bush, skirting the thick *donga*, taking the Land Rover along the dry riverbeds, early morning and evening, the times when lions were most likely to emerge and show themselves. The week dragged on, Kim obsessed with his kill, obsessed with his awareness that Nigel was passionately attracted to Nicole and having more and more trouble hiding it. He saw the way Nigel looked at Nicole; he saw the difficulty Nigel had in not touching her; saw the effort Nigel put into being as warm and attentive to Kim as he was to Nicole. At the end of the week they glimpsed lions—three of them, two adults and a cub—at dawn. But they were downwind; the lions caught their scent and disappeared instantly. Then for days there were no more, although at night they could hear them roar in the distance. Kim was indifferent to anything else. He took a bull buffalo cleanly, making a textbook kill, and felt merely a faint disappointment. The animal, immense and clumsy, was slow afoot, an easy hit.

266

"It was fixed," Kim told Nicole afterward. "The buffalo never had a chance. It was like shooting a truck. All you need is a big enough gun."

Nicole said nothing. Nothing she could have said would have swayed Kim from his obsession. She was frightened by the intensity of it. She felt there was something dangerous about it, but she didn't understand what. She hoped he would get his lion soon. She was ready to leave Africa.

On the tenth day after the first lion, Kim got his chance. It was at the same time of afternoon, late, the landscape just beginning to turn a pale violet, when from the Land Rover they spotted not one lion but two: a big-maned male accompanied by his smaller, sleeker lioness. They were profiled against the sky, the Kibo Peak of Kilimanjaro in the background. The lions were walking away from them, upwind, unaware of their presence.

"Take the male," Nigel whispered to Kim. "You take the female." Nicole nodded.

Kim stood up to shoot. The lion, disturbed by something, suddenly turned back to look, his giant tongue licking his upper lip, a puff of breeze rippling his mane. Kim, seeing it all as if it were in slow motion, aimed, fixing the lion in the crosshairs of the sight, matching his slight swing of the Purdy to the stride of the lion, and fired. The rifle cracked, and in a graceful motion the lion slumped as if the air had been let out of him and dropped, motionless, to the dry African ground. The female, understanding the threat, turned ninety degrees and with a silent, powerful lunge disappeared into the *donga.*

"Good shot!" said Nigel. "Damned good shot!"

They moved in on the kill. The lion, its body elongated and smoothly tawny, its head massive, seemed even bigger close up than it had through the sights of the

Purdy. This lion was much bigger than the first. Much, much bigger and finer. Kim felt a tremendous surge of pride as he stood over his kill.

"Kim! Hold still a moment!" Nicole cried. Kim turned toward her voice, the expression of triumph illuminating his features. He had never looked handsomer, more desirable. She snapped his photograph.

That night, holding her close, Kim spoke to her of marriage.

2.

Kim and Nicole had been gone almost two months when they returned to Paris in March of 1927. His face sunburned, his body leaner and more muscular from the hard physical exercise, Kim, in a tan safari jacket, disembarked looking like everyone's idea of a great white hunter, a figure of legend, romance and myth. Cameras clicked, flashbulbs popped, and the reporters waiting for him on the platform of the Gare de l'Est addressed him as "Papa."

"Where did you pick that up?" Kim asked. Nicole had come into the city on an earlier train and had escaped into Paris uninterviewed.

"Jungle drums," said Pete Asturias, a friend of Kim's from the *Paris Tribune*.

"Call me Kim, okay? The boys on safari call the white clients 'Papa.' I couldn't make them stop. But I'd hate it if the papers picked it up," he said. "It's so corny."

"Is your next book going to be about Africa?" someone asked. The interview had begun; notebooks and pencils appeared.

"You bet," said Kim. "Africa is where a man can discover whether he's a man or not."

"How does it feel to shoot a lion?"

"Tell us how you dropped the bull buffalo!"

"We hear you got three impala for heads!"

"What about the kudu and the gazelle?"

The shouted questions came one on top of the other. "How did you know about the buffalo? The kudu?" asked Kim, astounded.

"African drums," said Pete. "The jungle grapevine."

"And what about Nicole?" someone shouted. "We hear you and the Mademoiselle are going to tie the knot!"

"Where did you hear that?" Kim was taken off guard.

"Will you and Mademoiselle Redon live in Paris or in New York?"

"How did they hear about Nicole?" Kim asked Pete.

"The drums of Paris beat just as loud as the drums of the *veldt*."

"I'll tell you anything you want to know about Africa, but please don't print anything about Mademoiselle Redon," Kim bargained. He did not want Sally to be publicly embarrassed, and above all, he did not want Sally to get angry. In New York she had not ruled out the idea of a divorce. He did not want her to reconsider. "I want to spare Sally's feelings. Please don't print that Nicole was in Africa with me."

"It's too late," said Pete. "It's already been in the Paris papers. It's only a matter of time before the New York papers pick it up. You're both famous, you know."

"But we're entitled to a private life," said Kim, worried about Sally's reaction to reading about his romance in the newspapers. It would be a public humiliation for her.

"Don't be innocent!" said Pete. "You're a celebrity and people want to read about you."

"Damn it! I don't like it!" Kim protested, although not too convincingly. He loved being a celebrity and his obvious pleasure at being the center of attention took the teeth from his complaint. "Why don't you write about someone else?"

"But you and Mademoiselle Redon *do* plan to marry, don't you?" the reporters insisted.

"And what about your divorce? What does your wife say?"

"Have you and Mademoiselle Redon set the date yet?"

"All right! You've got me cornered," Kim finally said. "Mademoiselle Redon and I have talked about marriage but nothing has been decided."

"And about your divorce?"

"My wife has said she won't stand in my way."

"Did you propose in Africa?" someone yelled.

"During the day? Or was it under the stars?" someone else shouted.

"Or in your tent? Come on Kim, give us the juicy details!"

"Oh, no! No more! I've told you all I'm going to," Kim said. "Some things are private!"

His eyes twinkled. He loved the attention and could not resist the press but they had gotten all they were going to get from him. He wanted to keep things with Sally on an even keel. A newspaper story about his romance with Nicole might upset the applecart. Meanwhile, smiling, sunburned, vital, Kim looked like the happiest man in the world and it was with that observation that many of the reporters began their story about the planned marriage of the famous American writer and the famous French couturiere.

3.

Kim went to New York to ask Sally for a divorce. By the time he arrived the papers had printed pictures and stories about the glamorous romance between Kim and Nicole. One of the stories was headlined "HONEYMOON SAFARI."

Sally was bitter and vengeful, hurt and humiliated. She wept and cried, she begged Kim to come to his senses. She swore she would never give him his freedom. But she kept coming back to the point that they had a marriage. They had Kimjy and Christie, a shared past; a promising future. They knew each other and they loved each other. There were *promises* they had made to each other, promises sealed with a kiss, promises made in front of God and sealed with a ring. There was no reason to throw it away for an affair.

Kim pleaded, argued, threatened. Sally now refused even to consider divorce. Kim, who had always gotten everything he had ever wanted, was for the first time faced with the possibility of not getting what he wanted, and it made him a wild man. Tormented, he turned into a tormentor.

"Do you mean you want to stay married to a man who doesn't love you?" he demanded. "A man who *never* loved you?"

"Never?" Sally turned pale. She looked as if she had been struck. That had been Kim's intention.

"I met Nicole before I married you. I was in love with her when I stood at the altar with you! I've been living a lie for years! I don't love you now and I didn't love you then."

"I don't believe it," Sally finally said. Her voice was a hoarse croak. "You've gone crazy!"

"Believe it," Kim said. "Because it's true."

Sally looked shattered. Her face crumpled. Her body shrank within itself. Her eyes went dead and then suddenly blazed ferociously. "I hate you!" she screamed. "I hate you!"

"Good!" said Kim. "I'm glad. Now you have a perfect reason for a divorce." He turned to leave.

They had been arguing in the kitchen of the Charlton Street house. Sally suddenly picked up a bread knife, a lethal serrated blade, and rushed toward him. "I'll kill you!" she screamed. "I'll kill you for this. For discarding me like garbage!"

Kim moved away, terrified. Of himself. Of Sally. Of the situation he had created. "Don't!" he cried, trying to catch her arm but failing. "Don't!"

"I'll kill you!" Sally yelled, lunging at him again, driven by her fury—and then suddenly, as if she were another person, she looked at the knife in her hand and her hand was a stranger's hand. She stared at it a moment longer and then at the distorted reflection of herself in the curved top of the waffle iron. Her mouth was twisted in an ugly grimace, her hair wildly disheveled, her body contorted with rage, the weapon in her hand poised with murderous intention. She thought she looked like a crazy woman.

"Oh, my God," she said, appalled. She put down the knife. "Kim, leave. Just get out," she said, not trusting the volcano of emotion she had only barely managed to control. She did not trust herself to be in the same room with him.

He turned to leave, as afraid and horrified as she was at what they had come to.

"Only one thing," Sally added as he stood at the door. "Just remember: there will be no divorce. Never!"

Kim returned to Paris. He had everything—except his divorce—to make him happy: life, freedom, talent, success, Nicole. Maybe Sally would change her mind. Perhaps when enough time went by . . . He tried not to remember the way she had said "Never!"

4.

"I have a wedding present for you," Kim told Nicole on the tenth of May.

"For me? But it was Ernie and Pauline who just got married," Nicole said. She and Kim had gone to the wedding at the Paris Church in Passy and to Ada Mac-Leish's reception afterwards. Pauline had talked fashion to Nicole, and Ernie had pumped Kim about Africa, saying that he too had always dreamed of going on safari.

"For *you!*" Kim told Nicole. He leaned forward and directed the taxi driver to the rue de Bretonvilliers.

"Home?" asked Nicole. It was the middle of the day!

Kim's smile was devilish. His silence tantalizing.

"What's happening? Why on earth are we going home?" Nicole asked. "Don't keep me in suspense. You know how I hate surprises!"

"You'll like this one," Kim said, enjoying the mystery he had created and the suspense that piqued her.

"Please . . ." begged Nicole. "Tell me now! I can't stand suspense."

"Oh, no," said Kim. "You're going to have to wait."

"But I'm not good at waiting. I never was."

"Now's a good time to practice," said Kim, echoing Leo's long-ago words. He turned to Nicole and put his arm around her, sensually aroused by her perfume. "Let's pet," he suggested, with another devilish smile. They shared a lovers' secret smile and then they kissed as the taxi bumped over the cobbled streets of Paris.

Nicole's apartment was at its most beautiful now, at midafternoon, with the sun shining into the living room through the leaves of the trees and the reflected ripples of the Seine making a moving design across the ceiling and far wall. A bottle of champagne in a silver ice bucket stood on the cocktail table where Kim had left it that morning. He opened the wine and poured two glasses, handing one to Nicole. Kim drank more champagne than any human being Nicole had ever met or heard of. She sometimes wondered how he would have managed to live if the sparkling wine had never been invented.

"This isn't only a present," Nicole guessed, knowing Kim's habits almost as well as her own. "It's a celebration too."

Kim smiled. "Nothing's real until you toast it in champagne." He handed Nicole a large white envelope of stiff paper, sealed with blue wax and a red ribbon with a tassel. "Open it," he said.

Inside was a legal document. A deed. Nicole read for a moment.

"This house!" she exclaimed. "You bought this house!"

"I thought it was time you had a house of your own," Kim said.

"Well! I don't know what to say! I'm speechless! I'm . . . I can't believe it! A house! For me! I've never had . . . I've never thought! I don't know what to say. I'm so surprised. I never dreamed! Well, I never imagined anything like this!" Nicole was astounded and thrilled, reduced to babbling, overcome by excitement. "When did you think of it? How did you do it? I mean, what gave you the idea?"

Kim waited until she ran out of breath. "You've been living in rented rooms and I've been living in a hotel," he said. "We deserve more than that. I wish I could propose but I can't. Sally refuses to give me a divorce. But it's about time we made some solid plans for the future."

"A house!" Nicole said, still overcome. Kim's words had not yet registered on her.

"All yours," Kim said. "To do with as you wish." It had

274

taken his entire advance for the African novel plus some of the accrued royalties from his other books to buy the house and to buy out the leases of the other tenants. His lawyer had been negotiating since January, when they had left for Africa. He was anxious to make their future real; a house was the way to do it. Nicole had given him so much; he wanted to give her something spectacular, stupendous. He looked at her now and saw that he had succeeded.

"Will you let me live with you?" he asked. "And be your love?"

It took a moment for Nicole to hear his words, and then she nodded, so moved she could not speak. She had worried about Kim's vague mentions of the future, wondering what he could mean, knowing of Sally's adamant refusal to give him a divorce, and becoming, almost, resigned to never marrying him. But now he had given her a house and he wanted to give her himself. The future, Nicole realized, was now. The future was just about to begin. Happiness and gratitude washed over her.

"Well, will you?" Kim asked.

"Yes," Nicole whispered.

"Yes, what?" Kim pressed.

"I want you to live with me and be my love," Nicole said, her voice husky.

Now it was Kim's turn to be speechless, although only for a moment. "We have to seal the promise with a toast," he said, and they sipped their champagne. "And with a kiss too," he added.

"Darling," said Nicole several weeks later, "where are we going to live while this house is being renovated?"

"The Ritz, of course," said Kim. "You don't have to be a duke to live there, you know."

Nicole was touched by the way Kim had to measure

up to every other man in the world. When, she wondered, would he be convinced that she loved him and that he did not have to compete with phantoms?

5.

At the end of May Paris was in a delirium of excitement over Lindbergh's triumphant flight across the Atlantic, and Nicole was deep in plans for the renovation and decoration of her house on the rue de Bretonvilliers. She had asked Stash Rackowski to help her with the planning, the drawings and the execution. The first floor, they had decided, would contain a reception hall, a salon, a dining room and a kitchen. The second floor had only two rooms: a living room and a library, both comfortably overscale, with bookshelves running from floor to ceiling not only in the library but also in the pleasant, windowed corridor that separated rooms. On the third floor was a master suite with a dressing room and a marble bathroom, the only conventionally luxurious touch in the entire house. The fourth floor was to be given over entirely to Kim as a writing area. The fifth floor had guest rooms, and under the eaves were rooms for the staff. In June Kim and Nicole moved out so that construction could begin.

The house would have the modern luxuries, rare in Paris even in the most expensive *quartiers*, of central heating and a private bathroom for every bedroom. As Stash and Nicole worked, the house began to have Nicole's style—her unique blend of informality and elegance, of simplicity and luxury. In Europe, where luxury so often meant the discomfort of museum-quality eighteenth-century chairs and stiff, formal, gilt *canapés*, Nicole had the idea of basing luxury on comfort. All the

276

upholstered furniture was large enough in scale for the biggest man and stuffed with the softest, most inviting goosedown; every chair had a table nearby for a cigarette, a drink, a book. She and Stash designed the lighting so that it could be adjusted for comfortable reading as well as for more general illumination. The fabrics were not the fragile, formal damasks and taffetas usual in luxurious rooms, but cotton and linen, suede and leather and wool. It emerged as a house whose design was based on its use and whose beauty and sense of luxury depended on the care with which the details were thought out and executed rather than on showy and elaborate decorations installed with a thought to impress and intimidate.

By December the house was ready to move into and, tired of hotel living, Kim and Nicole spent Christmas Eve in their new home. They entertained a few friends, and when their guests had left they moved into the library and enjoyed the fire in the fireplace, the view through the large windows—the snow gently drifting down, sticking to the twigs and branches of trees and melting into the waters of the Seine.

"I have a special Christmas present for you," Kim said when they were alone. He had already given her an onyx and diamond clip from Cartier.

"Another?" Nicole was always amazed by Kim's extravagance. He spent his money with the same abandon he brought to everything he did. He had told her often enough, when she had been cautious with his money, that as far as he was concerned money was only good after he'd spent it. Until then, it was useless paper and coins.

"This isn't a diamond clip or a house or a barrow of flowers," he said, handing Nicole a letter. "I think you'll like it more."

277

Nicole read. The letter was from Sally.

After her first shock and anger, Sally wrote, she had gradually come to adjust herself to the reality of Kim's love affair and to the reality that, even before she had learned of the affair, their marriage had not been what it was in their earliest years together. Sally had become more mother than wife, more sister than lover to Kim; their marriage had become a comfortable habit rather than a passionate involvement.

Sally went on to say that she still loved Kim and always would but that she had reconsidered: she would no longer stand in the way of a divorce. She would, however, impose one condition: that Kim and Nicole agree to wait one year. If in 1929 Kim still wanted the divorce, it was his. Nicole finished reading and handed the letter back to Kim.

"I know I will still feel the same way in a year," he said, taking Nicole in his arms. "In ten years. Forever."

"And I," she said. "Always and always and forever."

"Will you marry me?" Kim asked formally. His voice was husky with emotion.

"Yes." Nicole's was a whisper. She closed her eyes and abandoned herself to the joy that flooded through her.

"Here," said Kim. "In this room. In front of this fire." He held her to him, his warmth and strength becoming part of her.

"Darling," she said. "Darling, darling . . ."

Dinners, soirées, poets, erratic millionaires, painters, translations, lobsters, absinthe, music, promenades, oysters, sherry, aspirin, pictures, Sapphic heiresses, editors, books, sailors. And how!

—Hart Crane

CHAPTER ELEVEN

1.

"WHAT WE NEED IS A COOK," Kim said as winter turned to spring. They had been in their new house almost three months and, except for a cook, it was already staffed and running smoothly. Kim had settled down to the writing of his African novel, now titled *Time and the Hills*. "I'm alone all day writing and I need to see people at night. We need someone to cook for us and our friends."

They had had an Irish cook who served everything— including dessert, Kim liked to joke—with potatoes; a Spanish cook who drowned everything in olive oil; a cook from Burgundy whose temper tantrums scared the dogs and children of the neighborhood; a Russian cook, a disciple of Gurdjieff, who burned everything; and a cook from Provence who was a culinary genius and would have been perfect except for the fact that she ate enough for six and stole more than she ate.

"I know where to get a cook," Nicole said finally.

"Where?"

"In Laronel," she said.

"I'll come with you," Kim said. "I'd like to see the place where you grew up."

"No," she said. "I'll be gone only a day or two."

She did not add that she felt that enough time had gone by so that, finally, she and her mother could be friends. She would invite her mother to Paris, to meet Kim, the man she loved, the man she would marry. At last, Nicole imagined, she would be part of a happy, loving family. At last, she would be just like everybody else.

2.

Laronel was a village where nothing happened. It was located 120 kilometers southeast of Clermont-Ferrand, in the middle of nowhere, a dull, provincial backwater. The wines from the surrounding vineyards weren't good enough to deserve their own labels and none were ever exported. They were the kind of wines that were sold in bulk to truckmen's restaurants, for sale, very cheap, by the *pichet*. The labor for making a cheap wine, the sheer backbreaking work in the fields, the planting, the tending, the harvesting, was just as much for a poor wine badly regarded as for the greatest vintages of Burgundy and Bordeaux. The men—and during harvest, the women—of Laronel worked in the hot sun, breathing dust in dry summers and wading in the heavy, damp soil of wet and cloudy summers. They became old before their time, stooped and defeated and bereft of pride, passing from youth straight through to old age with barely a moment's ripe maturity in between. Laronel was a place, Nicole had decided the year she turned twelve, to get away from.

Her mother worked in a poor café, serving stews and *frites* and full carafes of the rough local wine to the laborers who worked in the fields, to the warehousemen, to the barrelmakers, to the men who worked with tools, with hammers and chisels, saws and planes, and never thought of romance. Nicole did not remember her mother as a young woman; she had always, even in Nicole's earliest memories, seemed an old, angry woman who came to life only when Nicole's father came to Laronel. She and Nicole had never gotten along. Jeanne-Marie Redon accused her daughter of putting on airs, of trying to be something she wasn't and would never be, warning that she would try but fail to outwit the plan life had for her, a plan that was destined to repeat her own miserable experience: work and loneliness. Although mother and daughter did not get along, they had lived together and were deeply attached, perhaps because they were all that existed of their little family.

Nicole had no brothers or sisters and Jeanne-Marie had no husband. She never had had a husband, Nicole's father had refused to marry her. Everyone in Laronel knew it and in the small, Catholic town it was a stigma never to be erased. Mothers from respectable families warned their daughters not to be friendly toward Nicole, and when Nicole became a little older and showed the first signs of the personal attractiveness that would grow

281

as she grew, they warned their sons to have nothing to do with her. Knowing that they would reject her, Nicole rejected them first. It was one of the reasons that none of Nicole's lovers had been French. She was afraid that a Frenchman would be able to see through her lies, would see her for what she was: a bastard daughter of an absent father, himself a salesman of fabric and trimmings, who on one of his trips through Laronel had met and seduced and abandoned Jeanne-Marie.

The women of Laronel, though, had a talent: they were wonderful cooks in the way that poor people, having to make the poorest cuts of meat and the most sinewy of fowl tender and tasty, often are out of necessity. When Nicole, eager for her new life with Kim, needed a cook, she knew exactly where to go.

The inhabitants of Laronel still looked at her, now in her own dresses of elegant, Parisian design, as they had always looked at her—as if she were a freak and an outcast, as someone to be avoided at all costs. Jeanne-Marie looked at her daughter as the rest of Laronel looked at her, and after their first cautious greetings, Jeanne-Marie, who still carried dishes and glasses in the café, who still pretended to laugh when the customers pinched her bottom and made crude suggestions of a sexual nature, began to criticize Nicole before she could say a word about Kim, about Paris, about the future.

"It's indecent. You can see the shape of your breasts. No wonder they look at you as if you're a fallen woman," said Jeanne-Marie. Nicole noticed that her mother's hands were red, that the skin was dry and chapped and that her cuticles were raw and must sometimes have bled. She felt a terrible compassion when she looked at her mother's poor, worn hands. Nicole's hands were her mother's hands—square and capable and strong—but

282

Nicole had promised herself as a child that her hands would always be clean and freshly manicured, their skin soft and the cuticles invisible, the nails buffed to a rosy glow. "You may fool them in Paris," said Jeanne-Marie, "but here in Laronel people know you for what you are! An illegitimate whelp with no past! A nobody with no name!"

"I send you plenty of money! You don't have to work. You don't have to take the abuse of *routiers*. You don't have to have your nose stuck in your shame every day!" said Nicole, who had learned never to respond to her mother's criticism but to counterattack with criticism of her own. "You could move away from here. You could live comfortably. You could tell people you're a widow. They'd respect you. There's plenty of money now for that."

"I couldn't live a lie the way some people do!" her mother said accusingly. "And I wouldn't know how to live on charity," she added proudly. The fact was that every month Nicole sent her mother money and Jeanne-Marie accepted it but never spent it. She kept it in a strongbox hidden in her clothes closet because she did not trust banks.

"I've come to Laronel to find a cook," said Nicole, anxious to get off the subject of money, since her monthly checks were the closest she could come to expressing the love that, deep down, bound her to her mother. Although her mother cashed the checks, she never acknowledged them, and Nicole considered the fact that she didn't return them a triumph in itself. But now Nicole wanted to let her mother know that the tables were turned—that now Jeanne-Marie could help her, that Nicole respected her opinion and had sought it out. Nicole was starved for tenderness; her mother was, too. Nicole was not ashamed or too proud to offer hers first. "I'd like your opinion. You're a good judge of people and you know everybody. I want to hire someone who is willing to move to Paris."

"You always had fancy ideas. Now you need a cook!" said Jeanne-Marie scornfully. "Aren't there any restaurants in Paris? What do you need a cook for? To impress a bunch of people who don't know any better? Who don't know what you are and what you came from?"

"I want a cook," Nicole said firmly, "Because I'm going to get married!"

There! She had told her mother her good news. *Now* her mother could be happy! Now they could get along. Now they could be like a real mother and daughter, affectionate and warm and loving.

"*Married?* Who would want to marry *you?*"

Jeanne-Marie's voice scalded Nicole with its contempt. It took a moment for Nicole to be able to speak.

"Aren't you happy I'm getting married?" she asked. She so desperately wanted her mother to share her happiness, not to poison it.

"Marriage? Men always promise marriage. They do it to get their way with you. That's all. You'll see!"

"Maybe that was true with you and my . . . father," Nicole said. "But it's different with me."

"I'll believe it when I see the ring on your finger," said Jeanne-Marie. "And not before!"

"I want to invite you to my wedding," Nicole plunged on. "Will you come?"

"Absolutely not! You know I don't like Paris."

"You've never been to Paris!" said Nicole. "I will make you a whole wardrobe of clothes! You'll fit in everywhere. People will welcome you because you're my mother," said Nicole. "Don't you see that the rest of your life could be happy? Comfortable!"

"I wouldn't wear those clothes you make!" said

284

Jeanne-Marie. "And show my breasts like a hussy. I have my pride, you know."

"All right, *maman*," Nicole said, exhausted by the bitterness of the argument, the impossibility of getting through to her mother, the inevitability of the criticisms and the accusations. Nicole knew that, although it wasn't fair, her mother looked at her and blamed her for the years of pointed fingers and whispered remarks. When Jeanne-Marie looked at her daughter, what she saw was her own shame and her own failure to have found a man who valued her enough to cherish her and to marry her. After a silence which meant that neither woman had changed her attitude but which allowed the anger to subside, Nicole again asked her mother if she knew a good local cook. Someone who would be willing to move to Paris.

"Louisette, the baker's daughter."

Louisette was thirty-eight and looked fifty-eight. Nicole had known her all her life, just as she had known everyone in Laronel her whole life. Louisette had been married, but after two years of marriage her husband had left her, left Laronel, and never been heard from again. At first Louisette seemed relieved to be rid of him and a certain lightness had come into her personality. But this was temporary, and Louisette slowly settled into an attitude of sour resignation and, as the years went on, seemed more a spinster than a woman who had once been married and then, unfortunately, abandoned.

Louisette lived with her parents and kept house for them. She was rigidly clean in her habits, and whatever sensuousness there was in her was expressed in her handling of food. She produced the most flavorful fricassees, the tenderest roasts, the lightest potatoes, the greenest young vegetables, the most ravishing salads. When Nicole offered her a salary, a room of her own, the opportunity to leave Laronel and go to Paris—which seemed to her, as it did to everyone, the very capital of the world —it did not take her half an hour to agree to all of Nicole's terms.

When she left Laronel, Nicole swore, as she did every time she left, that she would never again return. And she thought, as she always did, that never once had her mother asked about her, her business, her life in Paris. She had not even asked about the man Nicole planned to marry. Her mother revealed no interest in her and no curiosity about her. Her mother's lack of expressed interest and her lack of curiosity about her were at the same time both liberating to Nicole and the source of a sense of profound abandonment. It left her with a feeling that she was free to do whatever she chose. It left her with a feeling that there was no one who truly cared what happened to her. She wondered if Kim would ever be able to fully realize what he meant to her.

Louisette, sitting in the passenger seat next to Nicole, studied her new employer carefully, sure that she was wearing powder and rouge, although, to be sure, so skillfully applied that even with minute study it was difficult to be absolutely certain.

Louisette wondered what she had gotten herself into, and she wondered how long she would stay in Paris. She would, as it turned out, stay with Nicole thirty-eight years, until the day she died, and she, unlike Nicole, would never again return to Laronel.

3.

"Why wouldn't you let me come to Laronel?" Kim asked when Nicole had returned to Paris. "What are you so ashamed of, Nicole?"

"I have no father," Nicole said. In those simple words she told the truth about herself for the first time in her life.

"Everyone has a father," said Kim, not comprehending.

"I don't. My father didn't want my mother. And he didn't want me."

"Then you knew him."

"A little," said Nicole. "I was telling the truth when I said he was elegant. He was. He always was so beautifully dressed. His linen so white and fresh. And he smelled so good. So clean," she said. "But he wasn't a father. He wouldn't marry my mother even though he knew the shame his actions caused her in a town like Laronel. He refused," said Nicole. Then slowly and painfully she added, "He even refused his name."

"What do you mean?"

"My mother petitioned the court to let me use his name legally. The one thing I wanted more than anything was a name. A real name of my own. My father refused. He hired a lawyer and fought the case my mother brought to the court, and he won," said Nicole.

"He admitted he was your father, didn't he?" Kim asked, not quite understanding the legal nicety.

"Yes."

"Then why did he object to letting you have his name?" In the social class in which Kim had grown up, such a thing was impossible.

"Money," said Nicole. "It was a question of the money. He was afraid that if I had his name my mother would ask for money for my support. He never gave a penny toward my support, you know. Sometimes he would come to visit. When he would leave he would promise to send some money for me, but he never did. The curious thing is that I never cared about the money.

We made do one way or another. It was the name I cared about. It was the name he refused to give."

"That's what you meant about the perfume! That's why you were so angry with me," Kim said, suddenly understanding many things about this proud woman he loved. "When you said Redon wasn't a real name and I didn't understand what you meant . . ." Nicole nodded. "Whose name is it?" Kim asked.

"My mother took it from the manufacturer's trademark printed on the bottom of the dishes used in the café where she works. She lied and told everyone that she had been married but that her husband had been killed in the trenches of the Western Front. The trouble was that in a small town like Laronel, where everyone knows everyone else, they all knew it was a lie," Nicole said. "Redon! A name from the bottom of a cheap plate!"

Kim saw in her expression the pain, the bitterness she must have felt as a girl. And the anger. All the anger! Against fate; against a father who refused to recognize her and legitimize her and who thus condemned her to the life of an eternal outcast; against a mother who, having no one to blame for her predicament but herself, instead blamed the blameless child.

"A name," said Kim, thinking out loud. "That's why Boy Mellany meant so much to you. The Duke of Mellany. A name that echoes in history. A name with a past. A name with legitimacy behind it, *centuries* of legitimacy . . ."

"Legitimacy," repeated Nicole, and Kim saw her begin to cry. She cried with abandon, giving herself to the emotions she had denied for as long as she could remember. Those pent-up emotions now poured out of her in a convulsion of resentment, bitterness, anger at the injustices she had had to endure and to struggle against when she was too young and too defenseless to have weapons.

No wonder she had dreamed of cursing her father! No wonder the dream had freed her! The dream had been the anger. The tears were the hurt and the pain and the humiliation.

Kim put his arms around her, thinking that there was nothing in the world he wouldn't do for her. Kim admired courage and Nicole had so much. What she had was moral courage, and Kim doubted that he possessed it in the measure she did. His head was so easily turned, he was so weak in the face of flattery, he was so unversed in facing obstacles. In the liberated artistic and social group in which they moved, no one blinked an eyelash at the fact that Nicole and Kim were living together without being married. It bothered Kim occasionally, but he knew that their "irregular" status was a source of constant pain to Nicole. She felt inferior, as if she were not quite as good as anyone else—and most cruelly of all, as if it were somehow her own fault, her own doing.

"You don't want me less?" Nicole asked when her tears finally dried. "Now that you know the truth?"

"I want you more," Kim said simply and sincerely, realizing that of all the things he could give her, his name would mean the most. "And when we get married, then you'll have a real name."

She looked at him with a smile that broke his heart.

4.

If 1927 had been the year in which Kim and Nicole had discovered and explored their love, 1928 was the year in which their love came to maturity and found expression in the way they led their lives and produced their work. Both were creative people, and never had they been more richly creative.

In his spacious study overlooking the Seine, Kim began *Time and the Hills*. He knew from the beginning that it would be his longest book, a rich, complicated novel that spanned three generations of two families who lived in Kenya, one white, one black. Kim had been moved by the vastness and beauty of the country, by the courage and the heroism of the people who coexisted, struggled and survived in it. He wrote of their physical courage but also, for the first time, inspired by his awareness of the invisible scars borne by Nicole, of their moral courage. Using as a basis the anecdotes Nigel had told every night after dinner, Kim created a fictional world in which he could lose himself. He worked every morning, enjoyed a long lunch with a friend, and in the afternoons, edited what he had written in the morning. After a bath and a nap, he picked up Nicole at the place Vendôme and they enjoyed, together, the excitements and stimulations of Paris, the most creatively inspiring city in the world and the easiest to live in.

Kim, who had always needed crowds of people around him, found that he was content with Nicole. The inner sense of emptiness, his half-conscious fear of being bored and going stale, totally disappeared with her. She could be stimulating and provocative; she could also be calming and soothing. Because she did not depend on him the way Sally had, he felt free with her, and because she did not abjectly adore him, he did not perceive her as a burden. And because her personality was constantly interesting to him, he did not become sexually bored with her. In 1928, for the first time, Kim would feel satisfied—personally and professionally. Only later would he come to value exactly how much that meant.

While Kim kept to his writing schedule, Nicole went to the House of Redon and there continued to pour forth from her ateliers the elegant, simple clothes that had come to represent the essence of modernity. In 1928 a brand-new element appeared in Nicole's work: for the first time there was a sense of out-and-out luxury in her designs. This new feeling of opulence was the result of two influences: one the mood of the times, and the other the new richness in Nicole's emotional life.

By 1928 the air of abandon, hedonism and creative freedom in Paris was intoxicating. Everyone had plenty of ideas and plenty of money. Nightclubs, ballets, theaters, entertainments were filled with people looking for pleasure, with people who were joyously giving themselves up to the indulgences of a dazzlingly liberated and plenteous time.

Privately, the sensual awakening that had begun in Africa continued for Nicole and she, who had always sought to moderate and control the emotional and sensual parts of herself, now abandoned herself, no longer afraid, to the luxury of feelings, both physical and emotional. The result was made tangible in the new opulence of her work. But, characteristically, Nicole expressed opulence as no other designer had. For the first time Nicole worked with furs, and she used the most precious of furs—as linings! A quilted crimson jacket lined in dark mink, with only a border of fur showing around the opening of the neck, down the edge of the front closing, and around the bottom of the jacket's hem. A black cloque evening coat sumptuously lined with white ermine, which showed only as a woman removed the coat and threw it casually against the back of her chair at the opera or at a restaurant. A trench coat, adapted from Kim's, with buckles and straps and practical deep pockets was lined with warm brown nutria. Redon's furs were nothing less than a sensation, no sooner sketched and produced than universally copied.

And jewelry! Nicole had made her dresses as simple

and as unadorned as possible, taking away and taking away. Now, suddenly, it seemed to her that it was time to add. She got the idea from the necklaces she had bought in Port Said. When she had cleaned out her closets for the renovation of her house she had come across the boxes of jewelry from Cyril's shop. Made of paste, Cyril's pieces added an effect of splendor and luxury at a price every woman could afford. Nicole, single-handedly, made "junk jewelry" acceptable and her next ambition, soon to be realized, was to make herself acceptable. Married: Nicole looked forward to it as a vindication and a confirmation. Married: no longer a freak, a misfit, an outcast. Married: at last she would be somebody.

Men have been swindled by other men on many occasions. The autumn of 1929 was, perhaps, the first occasion when men succeeded in swindling themselves.
— John Kenneth Galbraith

CHAPTER TWELVE

1.

NICOLE RETURNED HOME one snowy evening in January, just after 1928 had turned into 1929, to discover a party going on.

"Join the celebration!" invited someone she didn't know, as she let herself in the door. "The champagne is free!"

Nicole headed across the living room toward Kim. He was sitting on the floor in front of the fireplace with Pete Asturias from the *Tribune* and, just beyond, a man Nicole recognized as one of the waiters from the Lipp. The waiter was stretched out full-length on the floor, poised on the palms of his hands and the tips of his toes, doing

293

push-ups. Kim and Pete were counting out loud in unison: "Twenty-three! Twenty-four!"

Nicole smiled and knelt down to kiss Kim. "Hello, darling," she said. "I waited for you until quarter to nine . . ."

"*Shhh!*" cautioned Kim. "This is very important. I can't afford to lose count. Twenty-five!"

The waiter was red in the face and beads of sweat gathered on his hairline and trickled down his face. The tendons in his neck stood out, bunched with the effort of his exertions. As he tried to raise himself from the prone position the twenty-sixth time, his arms suddenly gave way and he sprawled on the floor.

"Now you've got to pay the penalty!" Kim gloated. He poured a wine glass full of red wine and gave it to the waiter, who drank it down in one gulp. "You have to earn the champagne around here!" Kim explained to Nicole. He was ebullient, agitated, his voice in a higher key than usual. "If you fail, you only get *vin ordinaire*."

"What do you have to do to earn the champagne?" Nicole asked, surprised at the noise, the people and this odd contest which seemed to have three participants and a circle of a dozen or so who watched, commented, bet and cheered. The elegant living room she and Stash had worked so hard to achieve was a smoky, crowded den, with glasses, bottles, ashtrays, trays of cheese and cigarette wrappers strewn messily around.

"Kim just did thirty push-ups," Pete Asturias explained. "That's the record. Anyone who wants to can try to beat the record. If they succeed they get a whole bottle of champagne. If they fail, it's back to the *ordinaire*."

A man Nicole knew as an unsuccessful Spanish poet who frequented the cafés of Montmartre pushed his way through the circle of spectators.

294

"I'll try," he said, loosening his shirt and getting down on the floor. "I can do it, I'm very *macho*."

As cheers went up and informal bets were placed, the wiry Spaniard started to do the push-ups. Nicole watched, somewhat amused and amazed. People always had such a good time around Kim.

"Eighteen! Nineteen!"

"I bet he doesn't make twenty."

"Betcha he does."

"It's a bet!" Franc notes were pulled out of pockets.

"Twenty!"

Cheers, whistles and shouts went up. By now the whole room was gathered around. The Spaniard continued, the tendons of his lean arms straining.

"Twenty-eight! Twenty-nine! Thirty! Thirty-one! Thirty-two!" There were forty people in the room, all watching the Spaniard and shouting out the count in unison. At forty-one, he stopped. With deliberate grace, he stood up.

"The champagne, please," he said in his courtly Castilian, not even out of breath.

Kim opened a bottle and handed it to the poet, who drank it down in one smooth draft.

"Now, sir, I challenge you to a duel," he said to Kim.

"What are the terms?" Kim asked.

"Push-ups. A marathon. The loser drinks a bottle of rum. The winner champagne. Is it agreed?"

"Agreed!" said Kim. Nicole was appalled. She watched. She said nothing.

"You be the referee," the poet said to Pete Asturias. "Do you agree? Señor Pete as the referee?"

"Agreed!" said Kim. "And Pete should take the bets, too. Now, move back everybody!" Kim directed. "Make way for the all-Paris championship!"

Kim loosened his shirt collar and rolled up his sleeves.

He and the Spaniard got to the floor, taking face-to-face positions so they could look each other in the eye, and they began, rhythmically, to do their push-ups to the chanted count of the onlookers.

Twenty-five went easily. Thirty went easily. The chanting turned to a shouted cadence. At forty Kim began to labor. The sweat beaded on his forehead and the blood vessels along his forearms bulged. The muscles of his upper arms began to tremble. Still he continued. At forty-two a cheer went up and the shouted cadence grew even louder.

"Forty-six! Forty-seven! Forty-eight! Forty-nine! Fifty!" A huge shout went up.

Nicole could see Kim's arms begin to waver, the muscles bulging and twitching. The Spaniard, a thin, sinewy man, continued to pump up and down, but now even he was laboring, breathing hard His muscles began to go into spasms. The counting continued.

"Fifty-one . . . fifty-two . . . fifty-three . . ."

"Why don't you stop now?" Nicole asked.

"Never!" Kim was breathless, hardly able to speak. "I can outdo any man on the continent of Europe."

"Fifty-four . . . fifty-five . . ." Suddenly the Spaniard collapsed. His arms seemed to lose all their strength and he fell to the floor, sweating and gasping for air.

"Kim's the champ!"

"The new record-holder!"

"See! I told you American men weren't sissies," a French girl Nicole had never seen said to one of the *Paris Tribune* contingent.

"Now you've got to drink the rum!" Kim said.

"I can do that. I'm very *macho*," said the Spaniard. He took the bottle of Martinique and downed it as he had the champagne, in one smooth draft. Nicole expected him to fall to the floor but he merely smiled and addressed Kim: "We must schedule a rematch."

296

"Anytime you say," Kim replied, and amid the popping of champagne corks someone upended a bottle of champagne over Kim's head and poured the bubbling wine through his hair. It ran down his face and Kim licked it off the corner of his mouth and got up, sweaty and soaked with champagne, and kissed Nicole to the applause of the guests. She tasted the champagne and the salt of his sweat and she smiled. She had begun to understand what was happening. By ten o'clock the party was over and Kim and Nicole were alone. By eleven-thirty the staff had almost cleaned up and in front of the newly lit fire, at midnight, Kim kissed Nicole and said, "I finished my book today."

"I know," she said, and smiled.

2.

The celebration continued nonstop for two weeks. Flocks of friends, acquaintances and café layabouts orbited around Kim, at his invitation, gossiping with him, drinking with him, joining him on his spur-of-the-moment whims to visit the flea market, the red-light district around the rue St.-Denis, or to les Halles for onion soup at dawn. Nicole kept up with Kim's raffish ways at night and continued to be the first to enter the House of Redon in the morning.

"Darling, I have to sleep," she told Kim on the second Sunday after he had finished *Time and the Hills*.

"But the entertainment editor of the *Trib* has gotten us tickets for a private midnight show at the Follies," Kim said. "I can't go anywhere without you. You know that."

"Can't we go another time?" Nicole asked. She had not had more than two hours' sleep for the past ten days. She was exhausted and she was beginning to make mistakes. An evening dress had gone out to an important client with the hem left unfinished, and Nicole, who personally checked the orders as they went out, blamed herself. She had snapped at the première of the atelier for tailoring over a piece of soutache braiding and discovered later that it was she who had been at fault, not the première. She had left Roland Xavier waiting alone at lunch for an hour because she had written the wrong date on her daily agenda. "I'm tired and it's having a bad effect on my work. I need to get some sleep."

Kim's face fell. "I don't want to go without you. I need you or it isn't the same. It's no fun without you."

"All right," Nicole finally relented. She knew Kim wanted to celebrate. He had received a cable from Jay Berlin that day, filled with praise and compliments and the-sky's-the-limit forecasts for *Time and the Hills*. "I don't want you to be unhappy. Jay's cable is definitely worth a special celebration. And you know I *do* want to be with you."

They went to the midnight party and at some point in the entertainment Nicole fell asleep. The next evening when she got home to the rue de Bretonvilliers Kim wasn't there. He didn't come home that night at all and finally showed up the next day for breakfast with three people Nicole didn't know. He had, he said, met them at a party. They were hungry and he wanted to feed them. They were Bolsheviks, Kim explained, and they would purge the world of all its evils. The three Ukrainians nodded solemnly during Kim's introduction. They turned out to be very serious and gloomy and definitely in need of baths.

"And this is Nicole," Kim said, speaking to the depressing-looking trio. "I'm going to marry her if she can stay awake."

Kim's silly dig stabbed at Nicole all day. She decided

298

to say nothing, though. She thought Kim was entitled to special consideration. He had just finished his book and she knew how writing drained and exhausted him and left his nerves raw, exposed. He had told her often enough that he always needed to "let off steam" when he finished a book. He did not come home for dinner that night, and late, after Nicole was in bed, she heard him come in with company. As she tossed and turned she could hear the clinking of glasses, the laughter and the friendly arguments. She wondered how long it would be before Kim returned to normal.

The next day a messenger delivered a package to Nicole at her office. It was a pastel drawing of a young girl, by Cézanne. The drawing was enchanting and the card said simply, *Love, Kim*. That night, as in their early days together, Kim was at the House of Redon at eight o'clock and he waited, chatting with her, while she refreshed her makeup for the evening. It was as if nothing at all had happened. He took her to dinner, just the two of them, and then home. By eleven thirty they were in bed and Kim, who had not made love to her since he had finished his book, made lovely love to her.

He had not said a word about it, but Nicole understood that Kim realized he had been childish and was sorry. The gift, the quiet evening were his way of apologizing.

"I'm so happy," Nicole said the next morning. "It's nice to have you back."

Kim smiled. "Now things will go back to normal. You were very patient and very nice to me and I appreciate it."

Nicole imagined that Kim's idea of "normal" and her own were identical. They had been when Kim was writing: a routine of healthy moderation, up early in the morning, to work, a relaxing evening, and in bed by midnight. However, when Kim was between books, Nicole soon found, his definition of "normal" was infinitely elastic. He might read twenty hours in a row, sleep six, sit in a café for eight. The clock meant nothing to him. Some days he wouldn't go to bed and other days he wouldn't get up. He might eat out or he might eat home or he might not eat at all. He never warned in advance what time he'd be home or with how many people.

His personal habits were the despair of a constantly changing stream of maids. He used six towels for every bath and left them strewn all over the house: in the bathroom, of course, but also in the bedroom, the library, the dining room and once, memorably and inexplicably, in the kitchen. His side of the bed was a jumble of eyeglasses, books left open, face-down to keep his place, crumpled pieces of paper with scrawled notes, matchbooks, Lifesavers, book contracts, mail, vitamin pills, aspirin, Evian bottles, pencils and pens and notebooks. If the maid tidied up, Kim would fly into a rage, accusing her of losing things or, even worse, of throwing them away. A parade of maids came and went, and in April Louisette threatened to quit. Nicole came home every evening to the complaints and threats of the household staff. Her stomach would begin to knot as she approached her own front door.

"I can't do my job and I won't take your money for not doing it," Louisette had said. "That man"—which was now how she referred to Kim—"comes home any hour of the day or night with God knows how many guests and he expects me to get a meal on the table. Then for days he doesn't come home at all. I never know what to do, how much to buy, what to prepare, or when to serve it. Mademoiselle, it's impossible. I'm making myself ill with migraines."

"Sally never complained," Kim said when Nicole

asked him if he couldn't be more considerate of the staff. "She'd throw it in the icebox if I didn't come home or she could feed ten. It didn't matter to *her*."

"You're divorcing Sally!" Nicole reminded him. "For me!"

"Maybe I should go back to her while there's still time," Kim said. Sally was still in Reno and the divorce wasn't yet final.

"What makes you so sure she'd take you?" Nicole snapped.

"After the way I treated her. . . ." Kim said, and he shook his head. He had gone into his marriage with doubts and into his divorce with certainty. Now he wondered—not about Sally, not about Nicole, but about himself. His divorce, he realized, was bothering him more than he wanted to admit.

"It's unfair of you to mention Sally," Nicole said. "You told me you would never do that. Besides, Louisette is not your wife. She's your cook. She wants very much to please you."

"But you're my wife. Or, you're going to be soon, and you know I already think of you as my wife."

"But I work all day long. Sally had nothing to do but plan her days to suit you. I can't do that."

"I don't see why Louisette can't cook the way Sally did."

"And how did Sally cook?" Nicole hated this conversation. She wanted to please Kim and to make him happy. But her nerves were on edge with the constant domestic upheaval, the unhappy staff, with never knowing what Kim would want to do or when. Her stomach was so upset most of the time that she could barely eat.

"She had some recipes. . . ." Kim said. "Hell, I don't know. That's the woman's department. She used to cook a lot of spaghetti, I think."

"Kim, you're living in France. I plan the menus with Louisette every other day. Every morning she goes out to market and she buys just enough for that day. We don't have the refrigeration you do in America. It's a different way of life. It's not going to change to adjust to you. And it's making me sick. To deal with problems at work all day long and then to walk in the door at night to more problems! I'm upset. I can't eat. I'm losing weight. It's taking all the happiness out of my life," said Nicole. "I can't be the woman I want to be for you in this . . . chaos."

Kim was silent for a moment. He had noticed that Nicole was looking thin and drawn. He hadn't realized it was his fault. He was ashamed of being so inconsiderate. "You're right. I know I'm spoiled. Sally spoiled me. She always told me that to be married to me meant giving up everything else," Kim said. "She used to tell me that I was a full-time job."

"She was right," Nicole said.

"Why don't you quit working? You could give up the House of Redon."

"Kim! Don't be ridiculous!"

Kim had the grace to be embarrassed. He blushed, his ears turning red.

"I'm sorry. I wasn't thinking," he said, still beet-red. "I'll try to behave," he promised, abashed. Then he smiled. "Are you mad at me?"

He was conscious of his boyish quality, and even though he was shamelessly manipulating her, Nicole melted. "I *was* mad at you," she said finally.

"Things will be different now," Kim promised.

But they weren't. Kim didn't see why he had to adjust his life to the demands of his cook, and Nicole could understand his point of view. She could also see Louisette's: how could Louisette do her job when she never knew when meals were to be served or for how many? Nicole was caught in the middle.

If the domestic problems niggled away at Nicole little by little, the conflicts between the full-time attention Kim demanded as his right as a creative person and the demands of running a large and complex business seemed to eat Nicole alive. She could not divide herself in two. She could not be there for Kim at any hour of the day or night, to talk to him, to play with him, to listen to him, or to applaud him, and at the same time create two large collections a year and attend to all the daily details of running her business.

Moreover, there was a serious problem they could not even discuss: Kim's drinking. Now that he wasn't working, Kim steeped himself in alcohol. He thought it virile, an essential part of the fully lived creative life. Nicole was offended, finding his fondness for wine, brandy and champagne, spirits of all kinds, excessive and irritating. Although Kim never became violently drunk, he drank enough that he slurred his words and became boringly repetitive, forgetting what he had said, losing the thread of his story or just long-windedly running on. It particularly upset Nicole when Kim would open a bottle of wine at nine o'clock in the morning. He would accuse her of a small-minded, bourgeois point of view.

"I left America to get away from that Babbittlike mentality. What is there supposed to be, some kind of timetable? If I want to drink at nine in the morning, why not? What difference does it make? *I* don't have a job I have to go to."

Nicole knew better than to argue, and Kim's drinking became a taboo subject. Nicole wished Kim would begin another book but he told her it was too soon.

"A book takes a lot out of me. I need time to regroup,"

303

he would say, and he continued his erratic, excessive, unpredictable ways, keeping the household and Nicole in a turmoil.

3.

Nicole, who had always been excellently healthy, got sick. One beautiful warm morning she woke up and was physically unable to get out of bed. A doctor was sent for, and after an examination and several tests he told Nicole that she was severely anemic and had a bad case of stomach ulcers, that she absolutely had to rest, to remove all the sources of stress from her life. If she didn't, the doctor warned, her ulcers would begin to bleed and she could expect to spend a lot of time in a hospital.

"Two weeks," the doctor said. "In bed."

Nicole was surprised to realize she had no impulse whatever to disobey him. She craved rest; her body and her soul demanded it. Nothing interested her except regaining her health.

"You're not sick," Kim said. "That doctor doesn't know what he's talking about. They're all a bunch of quacks." He wanted her to get out of bed and go to a Slavic party at a restaurant in the rue Mont Thabor that was run by Prince Yousoupoff, the Russian émigré who took credit for the murder of Rasputin. "I thought I'd do a story on the murder of Rasputin and have a good time in the bargain. You know what good parties the Russians give. They're the best hosts in the world! Would you wear your white dress? I want everyone to be sure to notice you . . ."

"I've been sleeping almost all day," said Nicole groggily. "What time is it?"

"Ten o'clock. Come on!"

"I'm exhausted. Why don't you go alone? Tomorrow you can tell me all about it. I need to sleep."

"Sleep? What is your fetish for sleep? Hell, you're my love. My woman. And I want you to go with me."

"Kim, my legs won't hold me up. I can hardly get across the room to the bathroom."

"You're coddling yourself, Nicole. You're giving in! What you need to do is resist," Kim said. "You have to fight back. You can't just lie there!"

"Kim, please. You go to the party. You'll have a good time and I'll look forward to hearing about it."

"I might as well be a bachelor!" Kim said, and he stormed out of the room.

The next day Kim moved to one of the guest rooms. He refused to see Nicole as long as she stayed in bed.

"I can't stand weakness, that's why," Kim told her when she was better. Nicole asked him why he hadn't come to see her, to talk to her, to cheer her up, to see how she was. "I can't stand being around sick people."

"But I'm not 'sick people'! I live with you. I'm going to be your wife." Nicole said.

"Not if you're going to be an invalid, you're not!"

"Kim! How can you be so cruel? Can't you understand how hurt I am that you wouldn't even look in on me? I was sick and you acted as if I were dead!"

"I don't believe you were sick," said Kim. "You're a healthy, strong woman. You just wanted an excuse to stay in bed. That's all."

"Oh, my," said Nicole, half despairingly. She still felt weak and shaky and she was on a bland, boring diet of soft white food. "Why are you so hard? So lacking in any compassion?"

"You leave me alone all the time!" accused Kim. "You don't care about me any more!" he said, and Nicole felt that now at last they were getting to the bottom of things. "I can tell and you won't admit it. That's why you got 'sick'!"

"How can you say that? How can you even think it?" Nicole was shocked and angry. "All you think about is yourself! You're the most self-centered man I've ever met!"

"You see! I'm right! You don't care about me. You don't even like me!"

"You're right. I don't like you when you're selfish and inconsiderate and cruel."

"So now what?" asked Kim in a suddenly different, softer tone of voice.

"Can't we be happy together?" asked Nicole. "That's all I want."

"And it's all I want, too."

Despite their argument, they still loved and always would love each other. Nothing could change that simple fact. They kissed and thought the arguments and tension were in the past. But after a few days Kim went back to his erratic schedule and self-indulgent drinking. He admitted to Nicole that he didn't know what to do with himself when he wasn't writing.

"The trouble is that I can't write all the time. It's too tiring. I just don't have that many ideas. I need time between books to recuperate and fill up again."

"I understand what you're saying," Nicole said. "But it's no way to live—to be healthy and satisfied when you're writing but to go a little crazy when you're not!"

"You're right," Kim said. "I just don't know what to do about it."

Kim continued his old ways, his drinking and meandering and café-sitting and doggedly competitive push-up contests, which had become a sudden fad among the artistic bohemian group of Montmartre and St.-Germain. Nicole tried to run her business and to please her lover. She had a relapse at the end of June. The Murphys called her from Antibes, telling her that they knew of a lovely villa for rent. Why didn't she spend the summer in the South of France and recuperate in the sun and fresh air?

"What do you think?" Nicole asked Kim. "Should I go?"

Both were conscious of her use of *I* and not *we*.

"I don't know," Kim answered. He knew he was the cause of their unhappiness and yet he didn't know how to change.

"All we do is fight," Nicole said. "I don't want to live this way. What's going wrong with us?"

"Nothing's going wrong," said Kim. He wanted to diminish the seriousness of what she was saying. "We're the same as we've always been, you and I. If anything's wrong, it's my fault. I always go a little crazy when I finish a book."

"But you finished it in January," Nicole said gently. "It's summer now."

Kim nodded. What could he say? She was right.

"I have an idea," Kim said finally. "Why don't you go to Antibes? It would be good for you. You'd really be able to rest and regain your strength. I have to go to New York. I've been putting it off, but I have to see Jay Berlin. I have to see my accountant. I want to see my father and my children, and there are the final details of the divorce to be worked out. Maybe if we have a little time apart. A vacation from each other. Then I'll come back and meet you in Antibes or here in Paris . . . depending."

"I think it's a good idea," Nicole said reluctantly. "A little perspective might do us good."

They did not want to admit it to each other or even to themselves, but each looked forward to being alone for a while.

"I have a going-away present for you," Nicole said the

day Kim was to leave for Le Havre and the boat that would take him to New York. She handed him a rectangular package wrapped in white paper and tied with a gray bow.

"Should I open it now?" He was moved. He really didn't want to leave her.

"Of course."

He ripped off the bow and tore the glossy paper. Inside the protective wrapping was a large photograph. It was the one Nicole had snapped as Kim stood over the lion he had shot. "That's the best photo anyone ever took of me!"

"I thought it would be good for your book jacket," Nicole said.

"You're a genius! You're beautiful and you're smart and you're nice and I'm crazy to leave you even for a second!"

"I wish you weren't going," Nicole said.

"I wish I wasn't too. I don't know what I'm doing," Kim admitted, "and that's the truth. I don't seem to be very good at making the people happy who make me happy. Will you forgive me?"

"I've already begun to wait for your return," said Nicole, who was already thinking about what kind of dress she would design for her wedding.

She had promised herself she wouldn't cry when they said goodby but she did anyway. She couldn't help herself; as usual, when it came to Kim, the intensity of her feelings swept all resolution aside. The next day Nicole took the *train bleu* to Nice. The Murphys met her at the station and drove her to the villa they had rented for her in the hills above Antibes. The house was an old stone farmhouse, what the French call a *mas*, terraced and heavily shuttered, situated on a hill that overlooked fields of lavender and strands of cypress and the blue Mediterranean below. Nicole fell in love with it on first sight and later that summer sold all her American stock to buy, renovate and redecorate it. She planned it as a surprise for Kim and imagined all the happy times they would share there as man and wife.

4.

Time and the Hills was published to excellent reviews on October 15. Kim was happy but restless; he had finished his business in New York and was anxious to return to Nicole. The divorce from Sally was now final; he and Nicole could marry at Christmas as they'd planned. The first thing he would do when he got to Paris would be to order wedding rings for them—he hadn't worn one when he was married to Sally; he wanted everything to be different with Nicole. The strains between them had been his fault entirely, and he was ready to settle down and put her happiness first. He was ready, at long last, to begin his real life—everything up until now had been waiting, wishing, wanting.

Kim asked Twentieth Century not to schedule any interviews or appointments for him after the first of November—the week he planned to sail for France. The third week of October was filled with press interviews, parties, autographing sessions and literary receptions. It was also the week Wall Street crashed.

The stock market had reached one glittering peak after another through the first nine months of 1929; now, appallingly, the bottom fell out. On October 22, over six million shares were sold; on the 24th almost thirteen million were sold and, in an increasing wave of panic, on the 29th almost sixteen and a half million shares were sold. There were half a million margin accounts and a

million and a half margin investors who were being carried by their brokers, who in turn had borrowed heavily
from banks in order to carry their margin customers. All
of them were wiped out.

Among them was Lansing Hendricks.

The day Kim and Nicole had visited him in Scarsdale,
in 1926, had made a vivid impression on him. He
thought of Kim's confident optimism and admired it.
Optimism, after all, was the very keynote of the times—
as people kept saying, misquoting the French psycho-
therapist Emile Coué, every day in every way, things
were getting better and better. Lansing had decided that
he was still being far too influenced by his memories of
May 31, 1919, when the stock market had been shut
down by financiers worried by the runaway bull market
of 1919 and the Federal Reserve was on the brink of
issuing a warning against speculation. After all, Lansing
thought, despite the worries, nothing had happened—
except that the market had continued its upward climb.
General Motors had gone from 130 to 191; International
Mercantile Marine had gone from 23 to 47⅝; Baldwin
Locomotive from 72 to 93; and a seat on the exchange
had risen from $60,000 to $110,000. And that was 1919!
By 1926, those figures seemed ridiculously low. Why,
even conservative people were saying that the day of the
$500,000 seat wasn't very far off!

Kim's optimism was suited to the times, not Lansing's
anxious caution; Kim's confidence was what was called
for, not Lansing's careful conservatism. It was important
to move with the times and so, gradually, Lansing had
begun to transfer additional moneys—his own at first,
and then Kim's, Nicole's, his other clients'—into margin
accounts, borrowing heavily and leveraging the funds
aggressively. Month after month, year after year, the
money had increased in a Midas dream of riches, and it

went on so long and so steadily that few thought it could ever end. A total of five million 1926 dollars increased to fifteen and a half million 1929, pre-Crash dollars in portfolios managed by Lansing. But, in less than a week in late October, dollars that had been in families for generations, dollars that had been earned by hard work, dollars that had been accumulated with thrift and self-denial, dollars, some of them, that had been earned by hook or by crook, dollars that belonged to Lansing and his family and his clients, dollars that others had entrusted to Lansing Hendricks to protect, conserve, invest and increase, had disappeared in an avalanche of panic.

On the thirtieth of October, Lansing Hendricks shaved carefully, splashed himself with bay rum, dressed in his habitual well-cut dark-gray vested suit, fastened his father's gold watch chain across the front, left the baronial fieldstone mansion he had recently bought for himself in Old Brookville, crossed its graveled drive, got into his silver Pierce-Arrow, had his driver take him to his office at 10 Broad Street, told the man to come back for him up at five-thirty to take him to Delmonico's, where he was meeting a business associate for drinks, took the elevator up to his twelfth-floor office, greeted the receptionist and his secretary, went into his private office, closed the door behind him, opened the window and jumped.

Kim, who had become used to having everything, now suddenly felt he had nothing. No father, no wife, no children, no money, and the woman he loved across an ocean. Although he had accepted the words that had informed him of his father's death, he could not accept the reality those words conveyed. A hundred times he began to dial his father's number on the telephone and was half done before he hung up, realizing that his father

311

wasn't there to take his call. He bought pairs of seats to the boxing matches at Madison Square Garden and then realized he'd have to decide whom to invite because his father wasn't there to go with him. When Kimjy asked him what they would do for Thanksgiving, Kim answered, without thinking, that they would do what they usually did. Then he realized they couldn't. The cranberry sauce with raw—not cooked—cranberries, which the cook had made for as long as Kim could remember and which, for as long as Kim could remember, Lansing had surreptitiously spiked with bourbon, wouldn't be. The smile on Lansing's face as he carved the turkey into fine, even slices with the bone-handled knife that had been one of his mother's wedding gifts wouldn't be. The ceremony Lansing always made of opening a fine claret to go with the bird—it wouldn't be. Lansing Hendricks was dead and a crucial part of Kim's world had died with him.

Sally, keeping the promise she had made with such pain, had gone ahead with the divorce. As part of its terms, Kim had moved out of the Charlton Street house and Sally was living there with the children. Kim was shocked at how much he missed them. His father's death made him treasure his children. He thought of his father constantly and of all the things his father had done for him. He himself had been an indifferent father; his father had been a loving one. Kim had been busy, away much of the time, preoccupied when he was with them. His father had been one of the most important people in his life; he wanted to be important in his children's lives. He called them frequently, wanting to see them, hating having to ask Sally's permission to do so. He had not anticipated the emotional repercussions of divorce and, now, with the added blow of his father's shocking death, and living in a single room in the Algonquin Hotel, Kim compared himself with Sally. After the first upheavals of

312

the separation and divorce Sally had settled down into a new life of her own. She had never looked better and she had never seemed more confident. She was a loving mother to her children; she did occasional free-lance work for magazine editors she had met when she was married to Kim; she even had, as Kimjy proudly informed Kim, "gentlemen callers." The early frigid bitterness with which she had treated Kim now had dissolved into casual indifference. It was a far worse insult than the bitterness had ever been, and coming home to his empty hotel room night after night, Kim wondered if he had made a mistake.

But the devastating blow, the crushing blow, perhaps because it was the one that could be measured and counted, had to do with money. Several days after his father's death, Kim met with his father's executor. Kim knew that his father's will left half of Lansing's money to Kim outright and that the remaining half was to be used to establish a trust fund for Kimjy and Christie. Kim did not know how much money his father had, although he did know that he had made a lot during the great bull market of the twenties. If Kim had been forced to guess, he would have said that his father was worth $750,000— almost but not quite a millionaire—before the Crash. Now, of course, the value of the estate would be considerably less, perhaps by as much as half.

"My sincere condolences . . . a tragedy . . . a fine man . . . terrible times . . ." said his father's lawyer, a thin, sere man who looked older than he was; who was the kind of man who had always looked older than he was.

Kim half-heard the murmured words of sympathy. Then, with a rustle of papers, the executor, who had gone to Yale with Lansing and had been his lawyer for thirty years, began to get to the specifics of Lansing Hendricks' last will and testament.

". . . large mortgage on the Old Brookville house . . . uncovered margins . . . $300,000 in paper profits wiped out . . . massive losses in the Chicago and Winnipeg commodities markets . . . worthless certificates . . . panic selling . . ."

Kim heard the words but, more than the words, he heard the tones in which they were spoken.

"How much, exactly, is left in the estate?" he asked. "Once all the debts are paid?"

There was total silence.

"I'm sorry, Kim," his father's lawyer said finally. "There will be nothing left except—"

"Except?" Kim repeated the word mechanically.

"Debts," said the lawyer after another long silence.

"I see," said Kim. He felt empty. He remembered his father on a hundred different occasions—smiling, generous, expansive. So pleased with the comfortable inheritance he would be able to leave Kim. So happy he was rich enough to be able to leave a trust fund for his adored grandchildren. So filled with joy at being able to give, to provide. Kim remembered how his father had told him, with such visible pride and pleasure, how he would leave everyone so well taken care of. Not ten times, not twenty times, but hundreds of times. His father's greatest pleasure had been his generosity. Now, nothing. His poor, poor father. Kim flinched as he imagined the pain and the humiliation that must have driven his father to . . . to do what he had done. Kim, wanting to get away from the pain, got up to leave the office, and then he thought of something. "How much are the debts? What do they add up to?"

"Just under half a million dollars," said the lawyer. He did not even have to consult the papers in front of him. "They total $486,731.24."

"I'll pay it back. Every penny," Kim said. "It's the least

314

I can do." He thought of how much his father had done for him; he had been mother and father both to Kim, and he had given up his own life to do it. Kim remembered evenings devoted by Lansing to a ten-year-old's nervous rehearsals for a school play. He remembered weekend afternoons of sailing toy boats on the pond in Central Park. He remembered a vacation to the Rocky Mountains when they had brought along a friend from school and Lansing had bought dozens of ice-cream pops and dozens of hot dogs, and had mercurochromed what seemed like dozens of scraped knees. Unselfish. That was the word for his father. And his father had never, never expected anything in return. Now it was Kim's turn. He could at least pay back the money. "I'll sell my own stock to do it."

The lawyer's expression was oblique, unfathomable. Kim wondered if there was some legal obstacle that would prevent him from repaying his father's debts.

"Why not?" asked Kim after a long silence. "Can't a son pay back his father's debts?"

"Of course," said the lawyer. "But your own portfolio had been eroded."

"Eroded?" It was a lawyer's bland word. An ominous euphemism. "It was worth almost two hundred thousand this summer."

"In today's market," the lawyer said, "it's worth fifteen thousand."

"I don't believe it," Kim said numbly. But he knew the lawyer was telling the truth.

"I'm sorry, Kim," the lawyer said.

Kim wondered how many other people the lawyer had had to inform of the same bleak news. He thought he ought to feel sorry for the man, but he had no pity left for anyone except himself.

"Brother, can you spare a dime?"
—"Brother, Can You Spare a Dime?"

CHAPTER THIRTEEN

1.

NICOLE WENT TO NEW YORK early in 1930. The Christmas date of the wedding she and Kim had dreamed of had come and gone, and Nicole was worried about Kim and anxious about their future. He had written to her often over the years and she had packets of his letters—exuberant, passionate, energetic. He was a man who put his soul on paper. The letters he'd written since the phone call when he'd told her, in an oddly unemotional voice, about his father's death were far different: flat, impersonal, dead. Nicole was afraid his feelings for her had changed. She remembered how strained they had been with each other; all the arguments over Kim's chaotic habits; his accusations that she wasn't understanding enough; how she had actually looked forward to being away from him for a while.

316

Perhaps he had felt the same way then. Perhaps he felt the same way now.

She was shocked when she saw him. Kim had moved from the Algonquin to a small and depressing hotel on a seedy street in the West Twenties. He looked like his letters. His color was wintry, his posture tired; his movements had a heavy, exhausted quality.

"I'm sorry about your father." It was the first thing Nicole said. The words were prim, almost proper, but the tidal wave of emotion she had felt for him from the beginning—by now familiar but no less breathtaking—swept over her.

"Yes," he answered in the same unemotional tone he had used on the telephone. "Sorry." Kim remembered that his father's executor had also used that inadequate word, and he let his tears come closer than he ever had before. They glistened dully in his eyes.

"Oh, Kim," Nicole said, moved by what his loss had done to him, and she embraced him, knowing that nothing she did would really help. Only time could help. But he responded to her warmth, to the familiar scent of her perfume, and he allowed her to cradle him and comfort him. For the only time in his life, Kim liked feeling like a baby. He rested in her arms while she stroked his hair and crooned to him in universal sounds that weren't French, weren't English. She stayed with him that night —and three more nights—in the small, chipped, white-enameled bed in the drab room. He wanted to talk and she listened. He talked about his father.

"It didn't have to happen. He didn't have to do it. I could have helped my father. All he had to do was tell me. We could have handled it together. I owed him so much . . .

"He cheated me by not letting me help him. It would have been a way for me to begin to repay all he did for me, and he cheated me out of it . . .

317

"He didn't even leave a note! He didn't even say goodby! Not to me. Not to Kimjy. Not to Christie. He didn't stop to think about us, about how we would feel . . .

"Why didn't my father tell me? Why did he have to take it out on himself? My poor, poor father. How he must have felt. Shamed, humiliated, defeated . . ."

Kim talked on and on. He spoke in anger, guilt, sorrow, submerging himself in grief, mourning with a flood of words, the tools that had always served him best. By the fourth day he seemed a little better. He said he did. And then he began to talk again, this time about himself.

"Everything's gone sour. My marriage. My children. Do you know I have to make an appointment to see them? I have to ask Sally if it's convenient for her. Kimjy didn't even want to see me last week. He wanted to go to a birthday party instead. I'm reduced to begging my children to see me, to bribing them with offers of movies and ice cream and circuses. My own father is dead and I'm an orphan. But by necessity. My children seem to want to be orphans by choice!

"My work! What work? I've lost interest. I've lost the touch. I'm sick of entertaining the masses. I have nothing left to say. I've already said it all. Jay said I ought to write a novel about the Crash. Who the hell wants to read about the Crash? Who the hell wants to write about it?

"I have nothing to live for. My father had the right idea. If I had any brains I'd jump, too, only this dump is on the second floor. The worst I could do is break a leg. Ha."

The torrent of words that had poured out of him for days ground to a defeated halt. He looked at Nicole, anticipating the sympathy she had shown him for almost a week.

318

"You're disgusting," she said, using French, the word somehow stronger in that language. *Dégoûtant*. "Your self-pity. Your self-indulgence. You've *chosen* this." She gestured at the drab room, the stained wallpaper, the sink in the corner, its faucet dripping into a rusted bowl, the venetian blinds with broken slats, the limp, dirty curtains. "You, who gave me all the speeches about *my* shabby apartment . . ."

"I can't afford more."

"Baloney!" she said, cutting him off. He looked at her, shocked. "*I've* been poor. *I* know what poor is. You're just playing at it, trying for drama and sympathy. *Time and the Hills* is on the best-seller lists. *The New York Times* reported that it broke a record, selling a hundred thousand copies in ninety days. You're not poor!"

"You don't understand! My father's debts—I have to pay them off," he said. "I couldn't live with myself if I didn't. I have my children to support. Sally . . . I lost everything in the Crash. Sally has the Charlton Street house. I have nothing. Nothing!" He paused for effect, letting his dramatic words sink in.

"Kim, do you want to talk about your problems like an adult or do you want to drown yourself in self-pity?" Nicole looked at him, waiting patiently for his answer.

"Can't I do both?" he asked. Then he smiled. His smile, for the first time since Nicole had arrived, was his old smile. Intelligent, mischievous, charming.

"No," she said, and her smile was her old smile. Intelligent, incandescent, alluring. "Absolutely not!"

"I was afraid of that," he said. "Okay. Let's talk. Like adults. But first let's get out of this dump."

"21" was crowded with prosperous, ebullient people. Nicole, who had read all the dire international headlines about the October Crash, was surprised that America

319

seemed to have recovered—and so completely!—so quickly. The big department stores—Altman's, Arnold Constable, Wanamaker, Lord & Taylor, Bloomingdale's and Gimbel's—had done huge holiday business, adding staff to take care of the volume and the president of Macy's was predicting new sales records. The marquees of the great movie palaces glittered with the names of stars—Lionel Barrymore, Charlie Chaplin, Wallace Beery, Norma Shearer, Mary Pickford and Marie Dressler—and crowds lined up patiently despite the record-breaking cold temperatures. The optimistic pronouncements of Secretary Mellon and President Hoover were reflected in what the financial pages were calling the Little Bull Market of the winter of 1930. Daily trading volume reached the levels of the golden summer of 1929, and prices of indicator stocks had regained more than half the value they had lost during the panic sell-off of October.

Yet subtle signs made Nicole wonder about the future. She had visited Margaret Berryman and they had talked about fashion. Skirt lengths had gone down with the market and were staying down. Bobbed hair was "out" and the "flaming mamies" of the twenties were long gone. The look now was polished and sophisticated, the ideal woman mature and knowingly glamorous. Historically, Margaret pointed out, skirts had been long during economically depressed times, short during prosperous times. And she added that it was her impression that the "woman" reigned during depressed times, when there was a yearning for comfort and stability, and that the "girl" emerged during good times, when the focus was on pleasure and hedonism.

At parties, Nicole noticed, people no longer talked incessantly about sex, trying to shock. She did not hear the term *It* or the phrase *Sex Appeal* once. Instead, people talked about politics—socialism, communism, the Russian Five-Year Plan—with cautious interest. On the surface New York looked much the same, with its busy crowds, electric activity and tall buildings. The President was optimistic, the stock market going up; it was as if the Crash was yesterday's news. Yet when Nicole looked around her and thought more deeply she saw reason for concern. Perhaps it was because she was European.

In France things had been different. There had been no "Crash," no sudden, dramatic period with doomsday headlines, followed by apparent, almost-immediate, scarless recovery. There was something about that particular cycle—instant disaster followed by immediate recovery with no discernible after-effects—that seemed uniquely American to Nicole. Perhaps it was the resilience of a young country, a country still unburdened by memories, by history.

In Paris the drama of the black-headlined days of the actual Crash was less vivid, but the consequences seemed more real. Jewelers in the rue de la Paix were said to have lost fortunes in suddenly canceled orders. Art and antiques glutted the market, unsold. The Americans went home, the only trace of their presence the columns of ads in the *Paris Tribune*, offering for sale "cheap" their houses in Neuilly and their châteaux just outside Paris. The impact on the business of fashion was personal to Nicole.

In that first season after the Crash not one single American department store buyer had come to Paris, and the crucial income they had provided totally disappeared. The coutures' long-standing custom of extending extremely long-term credit to customers cost the House of Redon and all the other great houses a lot of money. Scores and scores of clients who could in the past be counted on to pay—eventually—now could not pay at all for dresses which had been made and delivered and worn. They had simply been wiped out. In addition, gyrating currency values further undercut the profits now that couture had become an international business serving an international clientele.

The ripples spread from the top down: the seamstresses and small manufacturers in the Quartier de l'Europe who made their livings copying the designs of Nicole Redon and the other great couturiers went out of business, one after another. Buttons, braid, lace and other trimmings were made by small independent ateliers so the losses were spread—some survived, others didn't. The fact that Nicole had fortuitously cashed in her stock during the summer of 1929 to buy the house above Antibes had saved her personally and the cash reserves she had thriftily put aside during the highly profitable years of the twenties gave her a cushion. But the House of Redon had been wounded; Nicole did not know what the future would bring. Nevertheless, her worries about Kim and her personal happiness overrode her concerns about her business and brought her to New York.

"I don't want you to go back to Paris," Kim said. They had the best table at "21" and Kim had been welcomed like the celebrity he had become. He and Nicole talked about money during lunch. Nicole advised Kim to sell his stock right now that the prices had staged a recovery, and she encouraged him to pay back his father's debts but to do so on a payment schedule that was comfortable for him. There was no need, she pointed out, to pay it back all at once; no one expected that—in fact, no one expected that any of the losses would ever be paid back. Kim listened carefully and told Nicole that she was very

322

good about money. She replied, sardonically, that it was one of the benefits of being born poor. One of the *few* benefits.

"My problem is that I want to have my cake and eat it too," Kim said. "I want to be near my children. I want to be near you. Why don't you go into business here in New York? You'd be an enormous success, you know, and we can have a life together. We owe ourselves that."

"Yes, we do," said Nicole. She was piercingly aware that Kim had not mentioned marriage. She, in fact, had had the feeling that he blamed her for his divorce, his separation from his children. "It's an interesting idea. Going into business here."

"Good! Wonderful!" said Kim. "You're a good influence on me, you know. Before my father . . . this . . . all happened, I made up my mind that things would be different between us. That *I* would be different. It's time I put you first. I haven't always done that."

Nicole smiled, happy that at last Kim was talking about her, about *them*. He was divorced now, free. They could do what they wanted. They could be together. "And what about you? What will you do if I set up a business here?"

"Try to behave," he said.

"Seriously."

"Maybe look for a job. S. I.'s offer is still open," Kim said.

"And what about your writing?"

He looked at her. "I guess I'll write. When the inspiration strikes. *If* it strikes."

"Writing is what you do best," Nicole said. "You can earn the most money that way."

"Are you suggesting I write for money?" Kim was shocked.

"Why not?"

"It'll ruin my talent! I've discussed it with Ernie a million times. Look at what writing for money did to Scott. He hasn't published anything worth a damn since *Gatsby* in 1925. Zelda's had a breakdown. Scott's wandering around the world with a bottle in his hand."

"And you think writing for money caused all that?"

"That's what Ernie thinks."

"It's ridiculous."

"No self-respecting writer writes for money."

"Dickens did. So did Thackeray. And what about Balzac?" asked Nicole. "I design for money. I hardly consider designing dresses on the same creative plane as writing, but whatever talent I have has only improved through use."

"Well, I don't know. I'm very dubious."

"I know something about you, Kim, that you don't know."

"What's that?"

"Money means more to you than you like to admit." Kim tried to interrupt and object but Nicole silenced him with a gesture and continued. "I remember how gleefully you told me how you negotiated such a good deal with Jay Berlin. How you got exactly what you wanted, the money, the advertising budget, the terms. It gave you a lot of pleasure, Kim."

"Now that you mention it . . ." he said, and he remembered besting Jay. It had been right here, too, at this same table at "21". He smiled involuntarily at the memory.

"You don't have to write junk, you know, and you don't have to compromise yourself either."

"You're right!" said Kim. "In the first place, I couldn't write junk if I wanted to; my conscience wouldn't let me. And in the second place, my publishers wouldn't publish junk," he said, beginning to be carried away with excitement. It was so like his old self! Nicole thought, thrilled at having him—the real him—back. She smiled, sharing his excitement, and he returned her smile, thinking that she was the loveliest woman in the room, the loveliest woman in the city, the loveliest woman in the world. Lovely on the outside. Lovely on the inside. How lucky, how incredibly lucky, he'd been to find her! "Darling . . ." he began.

"Yes?"

"I've been very selfish. Preoccupied with my own problems. You've been incredible this week. But you always are." She tried to acknowledge his praise but he continued. "I know I haven't said a word about marriage." Involuntary tears flooded her eyes. He leaned forward in response, touching her golden hair with his hand. "It's not that I don't want to marry you. I *do* want to. Now more than ever." He paused, struggling with the emotion that rose in him. "But you were right when you said that money is important to me. I don't have any now. And it doesn't look like I will for quite a while. And I can't ask you to be my wife if I can't support you. I just can't. It isn't in me. What would it be like? If you supported me? I couldn't tolerate it. I'd feel like less than a man and I'd *be* less than a man." He stopped. This time his tone, Nicole noticed, was serious, not solemn. There was a difference. This time the self-pity was gone. He seemed restored. "I want to marry you if you'll still have me. If I have the money—" he began, and then stopped and began again, correcting himself, "*When* I have the money, will you marry me? Will you still?"

"Yes," she said. "Yes."

"I want you to be mine. More than ever."

"More than ever," Nicole said and, looking at him, she thought that the love she felt for him must have been visible to every person in the big, noisy, smoky room.

2.

Nicole went back to France, mulling over Kim's suggestion of opening a business in New York. Conditions in Paris were troublesome, New York seemed filled with opportunity. She wondered if she'd be able to hire such highly skilled needlewomen as were available in Paris and thought it would be worth trying to solve that problem. The idea was an exciting one and, of course, if she moved to New York she'd be with Kim. She talked over the pros and cons with Lala, with Leo, with Royce Berryman, who had helped her in the past with business problems. Word that Nicole Redon was seriously considering moving her business to New York inevitably got around, and ten days after Nicole returned to Paris Roland Xavier, now president of the Chambre Syndicale, came with the Minister of Economics of the government of France to pay a personal call on her.

"The House of Redon is now a large business," the Minister, a bald but extremely handsome man, said. Nicole nodded in acknowledgment. There were now five ateliers, two for *flou*, the soft work needed to make dresses and evening gowns, and three for the tailoring of the coats and very popular suits. Each atelier had a *patron* or *grand premier*, the person responsible for supervising *toiles*, patterns and finished garments. Each *grand premier* had two assistants, and each atelier had between twenty and thirty hands. Directly, the Minister pointed out, his topaz eyes sober, the House of Redon employed over six hundred people, including *vendeuses*, fitters, secretaries and bookkeepers, packers and wrappers, delivery men and receptionists, assistants and apprentices, janitors and maids. Indirectly, he continued,

326

there were several thousand people who owed their living to the House of Redon: they worked in the mills whose fabrics went into Redon dresses, in the independent ateliers that produced the thread, buttons, trimmings, braids, bindings and ribbons; and then there were the people who were employed directly and indirectly in the manufacture, production and sales of Nicole's perfume, now one of the best-selling perfumes in the world —from the agricultural workers in the fields outside Grasse who grew the flowers to provide the basic essences, to the chemists, the manufacturers of bottles and boxes, the printers who made the labels, the truckers who delivered it, and the saleswomen in the small perfumeries and the big department stores who urged customers to try just a drop of *Nicole*.

"The ripples of the Wall Street Crash are being felt all over the world," said the Minister. "Unemployment in our small country is rising dangerously. If you left, thousands of people would be affected."

"I understand," Nicole said. "But there are . . . other considerations."

"Nicole, the Minister is asking you to at least reconsider," Roland Xavier said, rudely interrupting her. She looked at him, startled.

"But I have other considerations . . ." she began again.

"Nicole, all the Minister is asking is that you think over your decision very carefully," Xavier said sharply. He turned to the Minister for confirmation.

"Yes, Mademoiselle Redon, Monsieur Xavier is correct," said the man, the strength of his will obvious despite his charming manner. "The government of France, at this time, is making a request."

"I understand . . ." Nicole began. "But . . ."

"Of course, Mademoiselle Redon will think over her

plans carefully," Xavier interrupted again. "Very carefully." He turned to Nicole and she did not mistake the warning in his glance.

"Of course," she said, responding to the seriousness in both men's voices. "I wasn't planning to make any . . . sudden moves."

"Good! Good!" said the Minister. "This is a crucial time for France. For Europe. I know you understand."

After a round of handshakes, the two visitors departed, leaving Nicole with an ominous feeling she did not totally comprehend.

That evening, Xavier returned, alone.

"I don't think you quite understood," he said. "*Monsieur le Ministre* is very delicate. But there is almost no doubt that the French government could step in and compel you to continue here. And do so quite legally."

"Behind the 'request' there was a threat?" asked Nicole. She hesitated, thinking of Kim, wanting Kim as she had always wanted him. Wasn't it time she thought of herself? Of her own happiness? Hadn't she at least earned that? "You're saying that the government could actually *force* me to stay?"

Xavier nodded. "You have to understand, Nicole, that you are no longer running a little shop in Biarritz with a local clientele. You are running a big business in an industry that is one of France's most important. Your responsibilities have increased in proportion to the size of the House of Redon. You, your wishes, your preferences, your happiness are no longer the only considerations."

"I see," said Nicole. She felt terribly unhappy, sharply aware of how unfair life was. Her personal happiness was face-to-face with her responsibilities. And Nicole was not only extraordinarily conscientious but also, to her very fingertips, a patriotic Frenchwoman. "Of course, I'll stay," she said. And then in a tone Xavier could not decipher, she added, "Moving to New York was really only a thought . . ."

3.

Time and the Hills started a mania for Africana: women wanted leopard skin coats; living rooms were decorated like trophy rooms; ivory jewelry found a huge market; schools offered courses in the wildlife of the African plains; youngsters entertained fantasies of growing up and becoming white hunters, noble African warriors, glamorous, wealthy sportsmen traveling on safari with beautiful, sophisticated women.

The photograph of Kim standing over the felled lion, the open-breached rifle cradled over his forearm, an expression of sheer triumph on his handsome, sunburned features, appeared on the back jacket of the book and was an immediate sensation. Bookstore owners, checking their stock at the end of the day, found that the photographs had been ripped off countless copies of *Time and the Hills*. Jay Berlin liked to joke that Twentieth Century could have made more money selling the photograph than the book. The photograph was to become another element in the building of the legend.

In the spring of 1930 Kim signed a contract with Twentieth Century for a second African novel, *The Plains of the Serengeti*. He would base it, again, on tales Nigel Storey had told, which he hadn't used in *Time and the Hills*. Kim was now writing for money. To his surprise, the writing came easily, was less exhausting, the quality high enough to satisfy even Kim's high standards.

He had thought when Nicole left for France that she would close the House of Redon and return to New York. He had thought that the separation would be both temporary and brief. He missed her as he would have missed a part of himself, an arm or a leg, and he veered from wild optimism that their separation would be over quickly to black despair that he would never see her again. In this first year of separation, Kim found that he had the same narcotic that Nicole had: work. He worked all day long in a room he rented in an office building on West Forty-fourth Street near the Algonquin, where he was now living. As he wrote he thought constantly of Nicole. He could picture here as she worked: pinning and ripping, standing back to see if the effect was the one she was after, her nose growing shiny, the clear Lucite glasses she wore while she worked slipping down, her hair becoming mussed, her entire being absorbed in her work. Kim never felt closer to Nicole than when he lost himself in his novel, writing and rewriting, reading and rereading to see if he had achieved the effect he was after.

While Kim's professional life in the early thirties went well, his private life was barren and empty. He was living in an anonymous hotel room because he kept telling himself that his separation from Nicole was only temporary and there was no point in looking for another permanent home in New York. But the more he missed and wanted Nicole, the more impossible having her became.

As the Depression deepened, she was more and more tied to the House of Redon, and as his children grew and his dependence on Twentieth Century increased, he was more and more tied to New York.

He and Nicole spent the 1930 year-end holidays in Cuba, a time out of time, romantic, sensuous, indulgent. They lost themselves in each other day after day and night after night, abandoning themselves to desire, to intimacy. But when it was over, it had the unreality of a dream. Nicole remained for him an unreachable ideal, and he remained for her an ungraspable illusion.

Over the next years, every time they made plans to

meet—in Switzerland in February, in Paris in April, in New York in autumn—something stopped them. Events conspired to keep them apart: Kim's continued money problems as the Depression worsened in America and bookstores closed and book sales faltered; threatened strikes against the House of Redon in increasingly strike-torn Europe; a publicity tour for Kim, a trip to the silk mills of Lyon for Nicole; the polio which threatened to cripple Kimjy, the serious fall in which Jeanne-Marie broke her hip.

Kim was bitterly lonely and the letters and phone calls he and Nicole exchanged only added a piercing bleakness to the loneliness he felt. Just as people depended on Nicole in Paris, people depended on Kim in New York, and as 1931 turned to 1932, relentlessly gloomy, the bread lines lengthening, Hoovervilles appearing on the outskirts of big cities, apple sellers on the sidewalks of Fifth Avenue, Kim's loneliness became an inner ache.

Whenever he gave in too much to his despair, he had only to remind himself that he enjoyed an income and growing fame while millions and millions had not even a job, not even a meal, not even a warm place to sleep. When he compared his lot with theirs, Kim felt guilty and selfish for ever giving in to his personal longings, and eventually the inner ache was replaced by a profound emotional numbness from which he thought he would never recover. It came as quite a surprise, therefore, when he found himself beginning to feel again.

4.

He met her accidentally one night in Manhattan's Stork Club.

Hoyningen-Huene was in New York en route to Arizona, where he was going to photograph the new fashions for *Harper's Bazaar*. He had had an offer from an American publisher who wanted to publish a collection of his striking photographs, and he had engaged Ilona Vanderpoel as his agent. Over drinks with Ilona late one afternoon the photographer had invited her to join him on the café-society rounds with a group of fashion editors who had been assigned to show him the town.

A little after ten, Kim Hendricks came into the Stork Club with Jay Berlin and Jay's wife and with Margaret Berryman and her husband, Royce, who was now working in Washington in FDR's government—Kim wasn't quite clear what the job was, but he thought it had something to do with the new economic policies and one of the alphabet agencies. S. I. Brace, who had just gone to work for CBS radio and was still trying to get Kim to agree to a newscasting job, was also with Kim's party. Sherman Billingsley placed the Twentieth Century table and the *Harper's Bazaar* table next to each other—good tables, satisfyingly far from Siberia.

Heads turned when Kim entered—thanks not only to the success of his books but also to the now-famous photograph Nicole had taken, he had become a celebrity's celebrity, recognizable on sight. Ilona smiled at him and said hello as he passed her on the way to his own table. Kim stopped dead in his tracks and gave her a startled look. She was surprised and flattered at the intensity of his reaction and waited for him to greet her. Then, as he looked at her more closely, a visible expression of disappointment crossed his face. Ilona realized that he had obviously mistaken her for someone else. She consoled herself by remembering that it had, after all, been several years since she'd last spoken to him at the Algonquin. Throughout the evening Ilona stole glances at him, unable to keep her eyes off him, as he drank champagne, chatted, laughed, danced with Jay's wife and Margaret Berryman. Ilona was acutely aware that Kim was alone. She knew, of course, that he had recently been divorced and she wished she could think of something to say to him; something that would remind him that he knew her; something that would make him want to know her better. Not a word, not a phrase came to her mind.

Suddenly, the noise, the laughter, the clink of ice in glasses stopped. A whisper ran through the room. Francesca La Monte had just arrived with Prince Abdul Saud.

Francesca La Monte was the original platinum blonde. When she refused Hollywood's every offer, every blandishment, every promise of eternal fame and adoration, Hollywood, never daunted by rejection, invented Jean Harlow. But it was Francesca who had done it first and done it all. Her hair was bleached a pale, pale platinum and her skin, which she told reporters she bathed in mother's milk, was as fine as the thinnest porcelain. Francesca wore only white, which she accessorized with diamonds, the gifts of her lovers. Her automobile was a white Rolls Royce cabriolet with an interior of white unborn kidskin fitted with platinum. A chauffeur in white livery with platinum buttons and braid attended the automobile. A white ermine lap robe was provided to keep Miss La Monte safe from drafts, and a white Borzoi seated imperially in the front seat completed the setting in which Miss La Monte transported herself from boudoir to nightclub to rendezvous.

Miss La Monte said that she was French and she intimated that her real father was none other than the pretender to the throne of France. There were those who said that she had come, in point of fact, from Brooklyn and others who said that she had started out as a sailor's girl in Marseilles. She was famous for the men who had loved her, Charles Chaplin and Rudolph Valentino among them, and whatever she was, Francesca was not the girl next door.

She was sultry, provocative, temperamental, demanding, spoiled, passionate. She had once clawed Valentino's face, stopping filming on his movie-in-progress at a cost to the studio of half a million dollars. She had once burned a priceless sable coat, given to her by a lover, when she discovered that he had given his wife an identical coat. Francesca loved with equal extravagance —she had had her mattress stuffed with fresh gardenia petals so that when she and a lover made love on it the crushed petals gave off their heavenly scent. After a fight, she had once crawled to a lover's house on her hands and knees and with bloody palms and bloody knees begged him for forgiveness.

At the time she swept into the Stork Club with Prince Abdul, Francesca had been having a torrid love affair with the young, macho Pepe Dominguín, one of the most famous of the Latin Lovers. Pepe was darkly, magnetically attractive to women, innately gracious, an excellent dancer, a man who seemed to hold a primitive danger just beneath the surface of his fine, custom-tailored wardrobe. Pepe adored speed, sensual experience and the fine things of life. Above all, it was said, he adored money, and his macho pride was not in the least offended by the fact that the women in his life were usually rich women used to picking up the bills for his extravagances. Pepe's talent was in the boudoir. He could, it was said by women who had been in the position to know, "go forever." In addition, the Negro blood that ran in his veins colored his member a startling hue of brownish-violet, an exotic extra that did nothing to diminish his attraction.

The indefatigable Pepe had occupied Francesca's time and attention for almost six weeks when she met the

334

Prince at a cocktail party. Prince Abdul, educated at Harrow and Oxford, was a swarthily handsome pasha—his darkness a perfect foil for Francesca's whiteness—who wore a turban, fastened with a ruby the size of a duck's egg, with his perfectly cut Savile Row suits. The attraction was instant—and mutual. Abdul and Francesca left together, Francesca thoughtlessly abandoning poor Pepe. Ivor Troubetskoy, who was writing the Cholly Knickerbocker column, knew a good story when he saw one. He got the front page when he followed Abdul and Francesca home and had a photographer snap them as they alighted from Francesca's white Rolls in front of her Park Avenue apartment building.

Pepe's reaction made a good story even better: Pepe donated a black eye to Francesca, spoiling her white-on-white color scheme and bringing her back to her senses. Francesca told Ivor (who told his readers) that although Abdul was a gentleman in every sense of the word, it was Pepe with whom the earth shook. However, several days later, when Abdul presented Francesca with a pair of diamond earrings that cascaded from her earlobes to her shoulders, Francesca seemed to forget about the movements of the earth and she and Abdul were, as the papers reported faithfully, "seen everywhere." Everywhere, at that time and in those circles, meaning the Stork Club and El Morocco.

Ilona watched, fascinated, as did the rest of the room, as Francesca and Abdul swept into the dark, smoky club and seated themselves at a prominent table for two, a bottle of champagne already chilling in a silver bucket, compliments of Sherman Billingsley, who appreciated what publicity meant to his business. Francesca, happily aware of being the center of attention, began to nip at Abdul's ear, whispering to him between delicate nibbles. Despite the show Francesca put on, the room eventually returned to its own gossip, and everything was back to normal in the Stork Club when another *frisson* of whispering caused the entire room to shiver with anticipation.

Dominguín had arrived!

He pushed past the head waiter and jumped the red velvet rope that barred entrance to the room. He called Abdul and Francesca a few choice names in French and Spanish, languages he spoke better than English, and, taking the Moët et Chandon from the cooler and helping himself first to a drink right from the bottle, he reared back, somewhat unsteadily—for the champagne wasn't the first alcohol to have passed his lips that evening—and finding his balance, prepared to take a swing at Abdul.

Kim was on his feet instantly. Inserting himself between Pepe and the Prince, Kim held Pepe's arm and warned Abdul to move back. Women screamed with the thrill of it all; Francesca, who had looked genuinely frightened for a moment, recovered as soon as she realized that, thanks to Pepe's torrid Latin temperament and the intervention of a celebrity like Kim Hendricks, she would again be the star of the morning newspapers (for the *Mirror*, the *News*, the *Journal-American* and the *Herald-Tribune* were all breathlessly following the Francesca-Abdul-Pepe love triangle). She arranged her luscious mouth into an expression of surprised shock for the benefit of the photographers who had materialized from nowhere.

"Calm down!" Kim told Pepe, still holding on to him, surprised at how strong the Dominican was.

"Darling!" exclaimed Francesca. No one—most particularly none of the principals—was certain to whom she referred.

"Bitch!" shouted Pepe, making it exquisitely clear to

whom he referred, having just remembered the word he searched for in English. "Bitch!"

"Please, let's be gentlemen about this," said Abdul, embarrassed, not yet entirely accustomed to having his love affairs made public.

"Pepe, be a good boy and go home," said Kim, speaking to him in Spanish. "I told him to leave," Kim told Francesca in English. "Is that all right with you?"

"I never want to see him again!" Francesca swore. "Never!"

Kim escorted Pepe to the door, waited until the doorman flagged down a cab, and, almost tenderly, put him into it, making sure that Pepe was coherent enough to give the driver his address. "Take good care of my friend," Kim told the driver, and handed him a five-dollar bill. "He's had a rough night."

By the time Kim returned to his table, the nightclub was still buzzing about the incident. Billingsley had sent over another bottle of Moët by way of thanks, and Kim offered a glass to everyone at the adjacent tables. The first words Ilona spoke to him as he passed her a glass of the chilled sparkling wine were, "You don't remember me."

5.

The next day's papers were emblazoned with photographs of Kim and accounts of his heroic intercession in the Pepe-Francesca-Abdul love triangle. The introduction of a new character into the already-dazzling cast sold millions of newspapers, and millions of readers who had never read a word Kim had written were now aware of him as a celebrity—a person, as someone said, who is famous for being famous. Once again, the legend grew.

"I noticed you right away," Kim told Ilona the next night at dinner. "You reminded me of someone I know."

"I realized that. Who did you confuse me with?" she asked, curious.

"I'll tell you one day. Not now," said Kim. "But I'm very embarrassed that I didn't remember you. All I can say now is that I'll never forget you again," he added with a charm so well-practiced that it had begun to be conscious.

That evening Ilona found herself telling more about herself to Kim than she had to anyone in a long time. Her childhood, with the winters in Charleston, the summers on a farm in Virginia; the engagement she had broken because she decided she wanted to go to New York and have a career; how her father, always on her side, called a University of Virginia classmate who called his brother-in-law who was a New York lawyer who knew an author's agent who was looking for a secretary; how excited she had been when she got the job, how much she loved New York, and how living there was the greatest dream of her life. She was more pleased than she could have said when Kim told her that she seemed to him to be a real New York woman, intelligent, poised, sophisticated, beautiful.

"But don't lose your accent and don't lose yourself," Kim cautioned. "There are a thousand sophisticated New York women. There is only one Ilona Vanderpoel from Charleston. If you lose her, you lose everything . . ."

Kim saw more and more of Ilona. She soothed the loneliness that ached more and more deeply within him; she was comforting and undemanding, and Kim was glad that he had met her. The feeling went deeper on Ilona's side. She saw Kim as a very, very glamorous man who wore his fame gracefully and modestly. He was an artist

338

yet he was not a prima donna like so many of the difficult and insatiable clients she had had to soothe and placate. Not as rich as many of the men Ilona had known, he was more generous with money; busier than many men she knew, he was more generous with his time and attention. It wasn't very long before they became lovers. Ilona assumed their intimacy implied a commitment.

Kim, having just finished *Plains of the Serengeti*, immediately began another book—*Memories of a Happy Time*—a post-World War I novel set in New York and Paris. His only commitments were to his work and to Nicole.

If you can sing a song that would make people forget the Depression, I'll give you a medal.
—President Hoover to crooner Rudy Vallee

CHAPTER FOURTEEN

1.

"THIS IS NOT A TIME for frivolity," Nicole wrote in 1932 in the monthly column she had been sending to Margaret Berryman in New York since the late twenties.

In fact 1932 had been a terrible year. In France, a small country, 600,000 were unemployed and they were evident on the streets of Paris, forlorn and lost, angry and confused; the President of France, Paul Doumer, was assassinated by Paul Gorgulov, a Russian Fascist; and the Match King, Ivar Kreuger, his billion-dollar financial empire in ruins, shot himself in a luxurious apartment in Paris. In England, the unemployed rioted at the Charing Cross Railway Station and a massive hunger march converged on London to the accompaniment of the "Internationale," mournfully piped on the bagpipes. In Germany, six million were unemployed and Adolf Hitler's two unsuccessful efforts to win national elections kept the country in convulsions. In America, twelve million were unemployed, former executives sold apples on the streets of New York, and Hoovervilles ringed the major cities. Twenty thousand veterans descended on Washington in a bonus march, and over two thousand banks failed.

The austerity with which Nicole had grown up and the skills of "making do" that she had learned as a child became invaluable during the critical years of severe depression. Nicole reacted to the crisis by cutting back, simplifying and economizing—all lessons drilled into her in childhood. To stimulate orders, she slashed the prices of her dresses in half. The entire staff—from Lala to the *grandes premières*, the *vendeuses* and the *midinettes*— went voluntarily on half-time. The House of Redon, like all Paris's houses of couture, had traditionally closed on Mondays; now it stayed open to receive clients. At the height of the Roaring Twenties, Nicole had shown four hundred new models in each collection. Now she cut back to eighty.

Nicole had always preferred simplicity. Now she simplified to such a degree that, without planning to, she revolutionized the way women dressed. Fashionable women until then had customarily changed several times a day: for the morning, for lunch, for tea, for dinner. Nicole did away with all that.

Kim's old tweed jacket—still hanging in her closet— gave her the idea. It was not even a new idea but one she had never been able to execute because she had never been able to get a tweed that pleased her. In the twenties she had gone to Scotland to try to persuade the fabric mills there to produce a softer and lighter tweed—one

341

that would be suitable for women—but the Scottish mills refused. When an Englishman bought a tweed jacket he expected it to last a lifetime, and that was the kind of tweed—tough and durable, not to say indestructible—that had been produced in Scotland for generations. The Scots saw no reason to change their ways and Nicole finally gave up. Now, wistfully, seeing Kim's old jacket every day, because she had moved it right to the front of her closet in order to feel closer to him, she took her problem to Roland Xavier.

"Can you make me a tweed like a soufflé?" she asked.

"You and your impossible requests!" Xavier said, only this time without his old asperity. He had learned that Nicole's brainstorms frequently turned out to be a *bonne affaire* for the Xavier mills. The French government had passed special laws to stimulate manufacturing within the country, and with that extra motivation, Xavier had a tweed that satisfied Nicole within three months.

So, with her newly invented soufflé tweed, dyed in untraditional colors of cyclamen, periwinkle and jonquil, Nicole designed an all-purpose suit. Women would put it on in the morning and wear it all day. For special evenings, Nicole made an identical suit in black velvet. While fashion even in the Depression went its merry way—first obscuring the waist and then pinching it in, first ignoring the shoulders and then exaggerating them, raising hemlines one year and then lowering them the next—Nicole made a suit that had a natural waist, un- padded shoulders and a skirt that hit at a flattering point just below the knee. Nicole's suit, designed out of the economic realities of the Depression, became a uniform for women, and for that one design, which also lent great stimulation to the domestic fabric industry, Nicole won a Concours d'Elégance in 1932.

Kim read the news in *The New York Times*, sent her a telegram of congratulations, and decided to surprise her

342

with a visit. He told Ilona he was going to Paris in connection with research on *Memories of a Happy Time*.

2.

The Depression, possibly because of the way it reiterated the poverty of Nicole's early childhood, was a spur to her imagination. Then her imagination had helped her escape Laronel; now it helped her survive the threats to the House of Redon. Out of necessity she had contracted in several directions; out of necessity she was inspired to expand in others. The design of the Redon suit was one example. The establishment of the first lower-priced "boutique" in a house of haute couture was another.

For years Nicole had known about the little sweaters Lala was making for herself. Lala had learned to knit from the peasant women who lived on her parents' country estate and, inspired by the surrealists, dadaists and cubists, she decided to make for herself, for the fun of it, a surrealist sweater. Her first attempt, in the mid-twenties, was a black sweater with a white collar, like the collar of a man's shirt, knitted right into it, with the punch of a scarlet tie knitted right down the front!

Lala was pleased with her creation and began to experiment: she knitted a white ribcage into the front of a black sweater, à la Dali; into another, sphinxes and ziggurats inspired by an exhibition of Egyptian art and artifacts. Once she made a "grocery" sweater into which she knitted green parsley, yellow lemons, red tomatoes, brown potatoes and a purple eggplant. Although Lala's exuberant sweaters were the opposite of Nicole's own restrained taste, Nicole saw possibilities in them.

"How would you like to sell your sweaters in the House of Redon?" Nicole asked. "I will give you a portion of the space on the ground floor in exchange for a percentage of the profits you make on your sweaters."

"I'd like to," said Lala, "except that my sweaters aren't *grande luxe* at all. They're not meant to be. They're just for fun."

"I think now's the perfect time for a little fun. Everything's so gloomy," said Nicole. "We can make some simple black skirts to go with the sweaters and it would make an easy, inexpensive outfit." Nicole thought the sweaters would bring in new customers and when things got better, as surely they would, those new customers, already comfortable at the House of Redon, would automatically become clients for Nicole's own, more expensive designs. "Why don't you take me up on it? It will be good for you and good for me . . ."

Thus Nicole became the first *grande couturière* of Paris to establish a lower-priced boutique with ready-to-wear clothing that could be bought and carried out in the same day. At the time, other designers considered the idea horrifying—no consultations between *vendeuse* and client! no fittings! no custom details! just pay and go!—but the sweaters and matching skirts, in three sizes, small, medium and large, became a great success.

Nicole soon added other items that could be purchased on the spur of the moment—her perfume and a selection of junk jewelry, hats bought from small independent ateliers, and scarves in colors and designs personally chosen by Nicole. The "boutique" grew so rapidly that Lala was soon spending her entire day running it and another *directrice* had to be hired.

3.

Despite the innovations Nicole had successfully introduced, the early thirties were struggle and loneliness for her. For a long time she had no personal life at all, and she wondered bitterly if she had worked so hard and struggled so long only to find herself right back where she had started: all alone and maneuvering to keep her business afloat from month to month. She sometimes compared herself with her mother. She, who had always criticized her mother so angrily, was now in the same boat: alone at night, and during the day working and working, sometimes so hard that she forgot even what her goal was, beyond surviving the day. Nicole tried not to give in to her moods of self-pity: they were not attractive, they did not get her anywhere, but the fact was that while the world was depressed, so was Nicole.

Bitterly, she counted up her losses: Cyril, Boy and now, apparently, Kim. Although their enforced separation continued, she refused to give up her dreams of the time they would be together again. They had both learned from the year they had lived together. The next time—if there ever would be a next time—things would be different.

Meanwhile, her friends warned her she was spending too much time alone. They invited her out and she was wise enough to accept their invitations. But despite the dinner parties and cocktail parties, gallery openings and theater dates, Nicole was alone and withered with loneliness.

4.

Nicole had known Mikhail Essayan by sight for years but their friendship really began one night at *Le Boeuf sur le Toit*, a fashionable Parisian nightclub. Nicole was part of a large group that included the French Minister of Economics, the same who had pleaded with her to stay in Paris in 1929, and his wife, who had since become a client; Roland Xavier, now also in the government, trying, Nicole understood, to help the French economy recover from the Depression; and Royce and Margaret Berryman. Nearby, at a table for two, were Barbara Hutton and Alec Mdivani, whose title—he called himself a prince—may or may not have been self-conferred. The poor little rich girl and the Prince would marry that June: the House of Redon was making Miss Hutton's trousseau.

"Mademoiselle, will you do me the honor of dancing with me?" Nicole nodded, and Mikhail took her by the hand and led her to the dance floor. The rhumba and the samba, with their languorous rhythms, had replaced the Charleston and the Black Bottom as the fashionable dances. As Nicole danced with Mischa, her hand resting on his shoulder and his strong arm around her, she sensed his solidity and resilience and vigorous health.

Mikhail Essayan was, she knew, attracted to her. Many men had been attracted to her in the interval since Kim had left Paris, but she had never been able to return their interest. She was, she thought in a resigned way, exactly like her mother: a one-man woman. Her mother, after all, had stayed in love with her father no matter how he had treated her, and there *had* been, from time to time, other men who had been interested in Jeanne-Marie. Like mother, like daughter, thought Nicole, unhappily. But not necessarily, she decided, and she turned her attention to Mischa.

"I have heard about your famous orchids and I have read about them," Nicole said, "I notice that although you wear your rosette, you aren't wearing an orchid tonight. In fact I have never seen you wear one, although I see you often at the Ritz. I have wondered, therefore, if your orchids are nothing more than gossip-column propaganda?"

346

She teased him with a smile and a challenge, and Mischa liked it. He liked women with character and spunk. His wife, from whom he was now separated although not divorced, had had those qualities; perhaps, in the end, too much of them to make a tranquil marriage.

"I shall have to prove to you that my famous orchids are real," he said, after explaining to her that in France, which had awarded him the rosette of the Legion of Honor for his contributions to the French war effort in World War I, he wore the rosette in acknowledgment of the honor. It would have been, in his opinion, an insult to France to replace its highest honor with a flower. "I shall send you some. They will bloom more beautifully in your company."

Nicole answered his chivalrous compliment with a smile, and the music began again. Nicole was now in her mid-thirties, just beginning to feel lonely. But only just beginning. It did not show yet.

As they danced, she smiled at Mischa, aware of the pleasurable excitement each was starting to feel.

"My father did not approve of my marriage," Mischa told her a little later that evening. "In the end, I'm afraid to say, he turned out to be quite correct."

"And have you learned from your mistake?" asked Nicole. The back of her dress was cut low, and Mikhail had moved his hand up so that she could feel the warmth of him against her bare skin. The feeling was one of great comfort. Odd, thought Nicole, how comfort had come to mean so much to her lately. She had redecorated again, using particularly deep sofas, made to her order and covered in suede and, over the suede, furs. She liked, at night, when she was done with work, to lie on her soft sofas, enjoying their embrace and remembering how much Kim had loved her oversized furniture. In a sad, lonely way she felt close to him then.

"Not in the slightest," said Mischa. "Despite my European veneer, I'm an Oriental at heart. My blood runs hot. It always conquers my head."

Nicole smiled, a smile of humor, a smile of compassion; also, she was well aware, a flirtatious smile.

"In any event, I never think of the past," said Mischa. "The past bores me. I can't change it. I can barely remember yesterday. And, for me, the day before yesterday never happened."

"You have the right idea," said Nicole, and she knew she would be comfortable with him. "I try to be the same way."

The next morning there arrived at Nicole's house a straw hamper of orchids from Mischa. There was also an engraved calling card with a brief note, from Boy. He was in Paris. He wanted to see her. Nicole was curious, flattered, indifferent. She remembered how much he had once caused her to suffer—it seemed a lifetime ago.

Boy arrived at six, at Nicole's invitation, for the cocktail hour. He had not seen Nicole since his marriage to Miranda in 1925. The Nicole of 1925 had been very, very attractive, sportive and free, glowing with health and energy, and he had been quite overcome with her. But the Nicole of 1933! She was entirely a woman now. Gleaming with assuredness, exuding a glamour and glittering sophistication that epitomized the modern ideal. Her nails were beautifully lacquered in a deep Chinese red; her hair was perfectly cut and waved, and her makeup was bold, precisely applied and immensely becoming. Her mouth—always her best feature—was painted a deep, dramatic red, and Boy, already drowning in the sight and scent of her, yearned to lose himself in her. She was really something!

"I see you took my advice and bought this building,"

he said, virtually speechless at the sight of her but compelled by a combination of nervousness and good manners to end the silence.

"Ummmm," said Nicole, smiling. It was none of his business. She was aware of the impact she was having on him and it pleased her to see him off-balance. It was nice to have turned the tables . . . very nice.

"Success becomes you," Boy finally said when his cocktail, the newly fashionable Manhattan, had been served. "You look better than ever."

"Thank you," said Nicole. "Perhaps it's the result of hard work."

"Hard work?" asked Boy. "Perish the thought. I've never, fortunately, known the first thing about it."

Nicole shrugged, used to Boy's languid pose. The fact was that although Boy liked to be thought of as a do-nothing playboy he worked hard and conscientiously at the Mellany estates. Being serious did not quite square with the portrait of himself that he wished to show the world. His attitude had been amusing in the twenties; now Nicole thought him old-fashioned.

"I hear you are the most successful woman in France. In Europe," said Boy. "Your famous suit. Your perfume. Your boutique. Your magazine column—it's being printed in London now. Everyone in London talks about you now. About Nicole. That's what they call you, you know. By your first name. There's only one Nicole and everyone knows who she is."

"It *is* nice to be talked about," Nicole said, remembering a childhood when she had been ignored and invisible. "Being a 'celebrity' seems suddenly to have become quite the rage."

"Yes, yes. It's all the rage now," said Boy.

"You look exactly the same," said Nicole. "You haven't changed at all. Your hair is the same, your eyes, your skin—you always had the nicest skin I ever saw. Even your clothes and your patent-leather pumps. Everything's the same about you."

"Thank you, Nicole. Thank you," he said, taking her words as a compliment. Now, feeling sure of his ground with her, he said, "Now, tell me, darling, where shall we have dinner?"

"Dinner?" asked Nicole. "I invited you for cocktails."

"Certainly you're going to dine?"

"Certainly," said Nicole.

"But not with me?" asked Boy, his confusion obvious. He was surprised by her rejection, and his surprise was so innocent that Nicole had to admit that it was precisely the quality she had found so appealing in him. So spoiled was he, so accustomed to having his own way in everything, that it did not anger him to be refused but rather surprised and confused him. There was something endearing about it.

"I have another engagement," said Nicole.

Nicole's cool matter-of-factness stumped Boy for a moment. Then he recovered. "Will you be free tomorrow for dinner?"

"Yes."

"Then we'll dine tomorrow evening," Boy said, his surprise past, his confidence restored to him intact. "I'll take you to Maxim's."

"What will your wife say?" asked Nicole, pleased with the calm she was able to keep in her voice.

"Say? Why, nothing," said Boy. "She's in London. She knows she's expected to stay there."

"With that attitude," said Nicole, "it seems she will make you a perfect wife. And now, please excuse me. I must dress."

Before Boy could recover himself, Nicole had gotten up and disappeared through the door that led to the stairs to her own rooms. Only the butler was there to witness his discomfort. Boy put his cocktail glass down so abruptly that he chipped its bottom, and got up so quickly that he bumped against the cocktail table, causing the bottles to tilt and clink against each other for a brief, unsteady moment. As he left through the well-lit entrance hall, so unlike the usual dimly lit foyers of Parisian buildings, he wondered what he ought to give Nicole as a present. She was obviously in a pique and he certainly wanted her again for his mistress. She had become more than ever the kind of woman the Duke of Mellany owed himself. A sapphire? No. Not a sapphire, because he remembered that Nicole had once told him that blue depressed her. And definitely not a diamond— diamonds were for wives, colored stones for mistresses. An emerald? Possibly. It would go nicely with her topaz eyes. Or perhaps a ruby? Nicole was very partial to red, with her red pajamas, her red nails, her red, red mouth. Yes. Definitely a ruby. He would put his jeweler on it first thing in the morning. She would not be able to resist.

Crossing the rue de Bretonvilliers, content with the decision he had made and already contemplating its delicious consequences, Boy almost ran into Mikhail Essayan as he crossed the street in the opposite direction. Essayan rented office space from the Mellany estates in Mayfair. The two men exchanged greetings, surprised to see each other in such a quiet, out-of-the-way street. Boy turned and followed Essayan with his eyes, and saw him ring the bell of Nicole's house. The butler opened the door to him.

Boy shrugged. Even if Nicole were having an affair with Essayan, a *petit liaison*, Boy did not really mind. He did not take businessmen seriously enough to allow himself even a moment of jealousy. But much later that

351

night, after dining with a pretty widow and spending part of the evening in her arms, Boy went home to the Ritz to bed alone, and then a frisson of jealousy invaded him. Helpless in the throes of that unfamiliar emotion, he hoped that a ruby would be enough. Something in him suggested that it might not be.

He thought he had been a damned fool to let Nicole get away in the first place. A damned fool!

5.

Jay Berlin wanted Amelia Earhart to write a book for Twentieth Century describing her hair-raising, record-breaking fourteen-hour-and-fifty-six-minute solo flight across the Atlantic. Ice formation on the wings of her Lockheed had forced her to fly low. Despite forecasts of good weather, she ran into rain, fog and wind squalls. Her altimeter failed and a broken exhaust ring trailed flames. When she landed on the coast of Ireland she said she'd flown low because she'd "rather drown than burn," and Jay had known right away that there was a book in the courageous, quotable aviatrix. He'd mentioned his idea to Kim one day at lunch and kept him up-to-date on the progress of the negotiations. One day in the early fall Kim asked if there was any chance he might get on a transatlantic flight.

"I don't want one of my best-selling writers to go down in an airplane," Jay said. "Especially one who still owes me a book." But when Kim insisted, Jay could not resist him any more than anyone else could, and he said he'd see what he could do.

That November 13, after almost thirty hours in a transport that carried nine passengers, Kim, his arms filled with red and white carnations tied with a blue bow, and a half-dozen bottles of champagne, arrived at the rue de Bretonvilliers.

"Happy anniversary!" he greeted a stunned Nicole. "Two days late!"

"Oh, my!" She had not seen him since their brief holiday in Cuba. She smiled and cried at the same time, her arms and knees trembling. She took the flowers and dropped them in her excitement. She reached for the champagne but Kim held it back out of her reach.

"Oh, no!" he said. "You might drop it and *that* would be a disaster!"

He gave the bottles to the butler, who discreetly disappeared with them. Kim took Nicole in his arms and kissed her mouth and then her face. He covered every inch of her brow, her eyes, her cheeks, her lips, her chin, her throat, with hundreds and hundreds of warm kisses.

"I couldn't stand being away from you for another minute," he said. "It was unbearable. I've never been so lonely. Never."

"Nor I." Still overwhelmed with surprise at seeing him —here in the same room with her, with his arms around her!—Nicole leaned into him, feeing that her body would fuse with his, almost swooning from the kisses that reminded her she was a woman, kisses that brought her to life again.

"This is no way to live. I hate every minute of it." He crushed her in his arms, inhaling her perfume, resenting every moment they had been apart, resenting circumstances over which neither of them had any control. "Being away from you is unbearable. I'm not even half alive without you. Would you take me back if I came to Paris?" he heard himself ask in his rash, impulsive way.

"If you came to Paris . . ." Nicole said. "Could you?"

353

"It would be difficult . . . the finances . . . the children," he said, coming back down to earth. But as he spoke, the reality of being with Nicole, of having her in his arms, of what she meant to him, of the way she and she alone could make him feel, swept over him. "But perhaps, if I plan everything carefully . . . I want to be here with you, more than anything . . ."

"If you were here everything—the struggle—would all be different. I'd be different," said Nicole. "You can't imagine how lonely I've been. How sad I've been." He tightened his embrace, burying his face in her golden, silky hair. It was longer now, more feminine.

"I'm glad bobbed hair is out of style," he said, "I love your hair and I love it long like this." He moved his lips along her hairline, from her forehead down to her ear, murmuring to her of his longing and the future. Just then the butler knocked.

"Yes?" asked Nicole, having to clear her throat. She raised her head from Kim's embrace, drowning in his scent—clean, male, healthy.

"M'sieur Essayan," the butler announced.

"Ask him to come in," Nicole told the butler. Then, to Kim, she said, "I have dinner plans. I had no idea you were coming. None! You've bowled me over!"

"That was the whole idea," Kim said. And they looked at each other and laughed out loud like children with a delicious secret.

Mischa entered the room, his robust strength a contrast to Kim's more elegant, finer-boned virility. Nicole introduced the two men and Mischa immediately invited Kim to join them for dinner.

"Of course," said Kim. "But only on condition that you will join me for champagne first."

A businessman as shrewd as his father, a great gourmet, a man who read, in the original Greek, one of Horace's sonnets nightly before going to sleep, an avid huntsman, an amateur horticulturist and a virile lover of many women, Mikhail Essayan would have been an extraordinary man at any time. In the Depression-shaded thirties, though, his brilliant business coups and his opulently sybaritic personal tastes made him a new kind of celebrity, the swashbuckling tycoon.

Mikhail Essayan had been born with the century—in January 1900—in London. By tradition, he felt himself to be Armenian, the nationality of his forebears; by education and birth, he felt himself to be British; by his marriage, he was linked to Germany; and by instinct, he was among the first of the internationals, as comfortable in Venezuela or Egypt as in Paris, as welcome in Istanbul and Baghdad as in New York. He was a darkly handsome man of medium height and solid build. His brown, almond-shaped eyes blazed with humor and intelligence, and his generous, beautifully shaped mouth revealed the Oriental sensuousness of his character. He was reliable, imaginative and well-balanced, and Nicole, who had always learned from her lovers, learned from Mischa. Under his influence, Nicole no longer thought of the House of Redon as her "little shop" but as a business enterprise whose scope could be international. It had been Mischa who had advised her to view the Depression as a challenge. The Chinese ideogram for *crisis*, he had pointed out, consists of two words: *danger* and *opportunity*. "If you think of this Depression as an opportunity," he had counseled, "you will do well.

"There are still plenty of people with money," Mischa told her, "but they are not coming to Paris right now. Why don't you take Paris to them?"

"It's never been done," Nicole said, remembering as

355

she spoke that Margaret Berryman had once suggested something similar. "And that makes it very appealing to me," she had concluded.

Innovatively, in 1932 Nicole took her collections, along with models and fitters, abroad. She went to Rome, to Madrid, to London; to Beirut, Rabat and Baghdad. Her "traveling fashion shows" were a sensation, and she had received enormous attention from the press wherever she went.

"We took orders and measurements abroad," Nicole said as the three of them sat over dinner in Maxim's, "but the dresses themselves are being made here in the place Vendôme ateliers. We are now sending finished garments to addresses all over Europe and the Near East. Our next trips will be to the Americas, North and South."

The excitement in Nicole's voice as she described the success of her innovation was the precise excitement Kim felt when his work was going so well and so easily that he felt he barely had anything to do with it. As she talked, he had been trying to think how he might possibly manage to afford to come to Paris, at least for the actual writing of *Memories of a Happy Time*.

"Other couturiers are now copying Nicole," Mischa said. "Patou is taking a show to London and Edinburgh, and Jean Desses is going to Brussels. But Nicole did it first! She was, as usual, the originator!" Mischa's pride in her, his enormous affection for her, were obvious.

"Everyone's always copied Nicole," said Kim. "From the very beginning . . ." *He'd live in a hotel; the prices, he supposed, would be about what he paid at the Algonquin . . . but there'd be other expenses. Nicole was used to Maxim's, to the Ritz, to places he couldn't afford.*

"But you've also been an instigator of trends," Essayan said, turning the conversation to Kim. "That African

356

mania that swept your country—it was a result of your novels."

Kim was surprised at how much Essayan seemed to know about everything from women's fashion to fads in the United States. He was a businessman, an oilman, after all, and Kim had usually found businessmen to be quite limited in their interests beyond the immediate concerns of their own businesses. As dessert was served —a gossamer vanilla-flavored mousse in a cage of spun caramel—Kim commented to Essayan about the wide range of his interests.

"But it's an essential part of my business," Essayan replied, "to be well-informed, to know what interests people and what they are doing. Economics is, after all, simply the monetary expression of human needs and desires."

"It's amazing how many businessmen have never thought of that," Kim said. He was acutely aware of the luxurious food, the lavishly dressed and jeweled diners, the opulent ambience of Maxim's. He remembered the six franc *prix fixe* menu at Knam's, Pharamond's in les Halles, Flo's hidden in a *cul de sac* off the Faubourg St.-Denis—they were simple places, serving delicious food at almost unbelievably cheap prices. But that was a long time ago—Nicole was not so successful then, he did not have any obligations then, they were poorer then and life was simpler. That was a long, long time ago.

"It's amazing how many businessmen don't make nearly as much money as they could," Essayan said, bringing Kim back to the present. When Kim smiled in response, Essayan did too, obviously enjoying his riposte, as he seemed to enjoy everything. He was a gracious, generous, but never ostentatious host at dinner, and what bothered Kim almost more than anything else

357

was that he not only liked Essayan but was impressed by him.

He did not see Essayan again for the next three days —days he and Nicole spent alone, rediscovering the Paris they loved, enraptured as always at being alone together, the intensity of their first attraction never diminishing but only deepening its hold as they spent time together, losing themselves in each other.

"He's your lover, isn't he?" Kim asked, suddenly and apropos of nothing, on the third night. They were in Nicole's bedroom, the room that had once been theirs. Its comfort, its familiarity, calmed Kim and beckoned him to stay, but his jealousy of Essayan had grown, gnawing at him silently, consuming him, until finally he had to speak. "You're having an affair with him, aren't you?"

"Kim, don't—" Nicole began. She was at the dressing table, brushing her hair. What she wanted to say was, *Don't torture yourself*, but Kim interrupted her.

"Don't lie about it! I'm not blind. I can see it. The way he looks at you. How you respond to him. He's more than just a friend, Nicole—admit it!" He was behind her but not yet touching her. "Admit it!"

"Kim, it's not at all what you think," she said, remembering how she had succeeded in deflecting his jealousy a long time ago, when they had first met. She had been in the tub and he had been on the chaise. She had been reasonable and he had been reasonable. "Be reasonable," she said now. "It's been three years since we were together. Kim, it's not at all what you think."

"Don't try to pacify me! Admit it! You're having an affair with him!" He had cupped her shoulders with his hands, inhibiting her movement, trapping her arms, the hairbrush in her right hand held motionless in midair. "Admit it!"

358

"If that's what you want, Kim. If it will make you happy," she said, meeting his eyes with her own in the dressing table mirror. "Yes, I am."

"Yes, you are what?" he mimicked her, tightening his grip on her, hurting her doubly: with his words and with his punishing grip. He was amazingly strong for such a slender man. Nicole made up her mind that she would not let him know that he was hurting her. "Yes, you are *what?*" he demanded.

"Yes, Mischa and I are having an affair!" she said, still holding his eyes with her own, seeing from his expression that he was not the only one who could inflict pain. He let his hands drop from her shoulders. His arms hung limp by his sides. She thought for just a moment that he would cry, and she regretted what she'd said. It was stupid to inflict unnecessary pain. Just because he'd hurt her was not justification for her to retaliate.

"How could you?" he asked. "How *could* you?" The first time he'd spoken his tone was hurt; the second time it was angry. "How could you do this to me?"

"Kim, you've been in New York. I've been here in Paris. It's been several years . . ." She could see angry red marks on her shoulders where he'd held her, see them through the dressing gown.

"That's no excuse! Goddamn it, that's no excuse!"

"Kim, Mischa is married. He and I have no intention of marrying; we have no intention of anything permanent. We have no intention of being anything other than good friends to each other. He helped me during an enormously difficult time, and I think—I know—I have helped him. He was here, Kim. You weren't."

"It wasn't my fault! It's the goddamn Depression! That's the reason. If it weren't for that, I'd have been here, too. It would never have happened. You and your Mischa!" Kim turned his back to Nicole and walked away from her across the carpeted room, part of its considerable charm produced by the contrast between the handsome but simple design of the furnishings and the elegant but complex scent of her perfume. He thought about Ilona for a moment; he was certain that *she* wasn't sleeping with anyone else while he was gone.

Nicole thought Kim was calming down, adjusting to the realities of their separation, when suddenly he whirled around, picked up a heavy crystal ashtray, and flung it across the room, smashing the dressing table mirror. Nicole had seen him in the mirror and moved in time. It had happened so fast she had not had time to be frightened.

"You couldn't wait, could you? You had to prove what a *femme fatale* you are! You've always been like that, from the very beginning. Tell me, Nicole, how many men have you had? How many conquests have you made while I wasn't looking? Tell me! I'd think you'd be happy to have the opportunity to brag!"

She was tempted to tell him that she'd had hundreds, thousands, armies of men, but she stopped herself. Kim was in a rage, almost out of control. The marks on her shoulders were still visible; the shards of the mirror glittering on the white carpet reminded her that he could have killed her with the ashtray. She was afraid of him. She was afraid of the state he was in.

"Kim, don't let this happen to us. We have the power to control ourselves, our feelings. If we don't, we risk destroying everything."

"I can't! I can't control myself!" His voice trembled. His hands tightened into fists, whitening his knuckles. They clenched and unclenched. "That bastard! That slimy two-bit phony!"

"Kim!" Nicole's voice cracked like a whip. "Stop!" She picked up a heavy silver-backed hand mirror and poised

360

it like a weapon, moving automatically, unaware of what she was doing. Behaving instinctively, she turned from the vanity bench toward him, the mirror raised, threatening.

"Nicole! Don't!" Kim seemed suddenly to understand the violence he had done to her, and the shock of recognition disarmed him. "Don't!"

"I won't, Kim," she said. "*I* don't want to destroy what we have. We'll never replace it. Never. I will do anything to save what we have."

"Will you give up Essayan?"

"If you want," she said, not understanding why her friendship with Mischa was such a threat to him. Romantic friendships between adults who had other, permanent ties were a natural part of life. Everyone involved understood. Husbands, wives, lovers, married or not. Friendships such as the one she had with Mischa were a comfort and an outlet; a way of taking pressure off marriages for married people; a consolation and a way of mitigating loneliness for those who weren't married. Kim's jealous rage was incomprehensible to her. "Of course I'll give him up, if it's so important to you."

"Promise?" he said. He was dubious. She'd given in so easily.

"If you wish," she said. "I promise."

"On the Bible?"

"On the Bible," she replied, mystified but concealing it.

"That's good," he said, visibly relaxing. "That's good." He sat down on the edge of the bed. "The terrible thing is that I like him. I admire him. He's an interesting man. If only he were ordinary."

"If he were ordinary I wouldn't be interested in him," Nicole pointed out, now secure enough to talk reasonably to Kim. He nodded and even smiled ironically. Nicole thought the storm had passed.

The next day, though, Kim asked Nicole where she'd first met Mischa and he asked her to tell him exactly how the affair had started. He wanted to know every detail: where they had dinner, what kind of flowers he sent, what the notes that accompanied them had said; what she had worn, how many friends they had in common, if he made her laugh, how much time he spent in Paris, if Nicole had ever met his wife. At first she answered his questions but after a while she asked one of her own.

"Why do you want to know all this?"

"It's interesting," he said. "That's all." Again he stopped questioning her and she thought the subject closed.

That night in bed, caressing her intimately, Kim suddenly asked, "Does he do this?" And then he kissed her privately. "And this?"

She stiffened, shocked.

"Well, does he?"

"Don't do this!" she said. "Don't ask these questions!"

"He does, doesn't he?" Kim persisted.

Nicole realized that no matter how she answered she had to lose. "Kim, put these thoughts out of your mind. You must."

"I can't."

"Yes, you can. You have always told me how strong you are. Now use your strength. Use it to control your thoughts. You'll poison everything. Everything!"

"You're right," he said, but she could not divine his tone. Had he agreed with her? Was he telling her that she was right simply to shut her up? Was he really going to try to control his thoughts and emotions? She didn't know. But he said nothing more.

The next two days passed with no mention of Mischa. But on the third day, Kim met her at eight o'clock at the House of Redon. He entered her private office, and with no kiss, no greeting, no embrace, he accused her: "You've been sneaking around during the day seeing him, haven't you?"

Calmly and deliberately, Nicole began to speak: "We are now at the end of the selling season for the fall collection, Kim. The mill is out of the blue silk chiffon for an evening dress eight clients have ordered. The mill swears they can't make more; the clients are demanding delivery or threatening cancellation. The gold buttons for the soufflé tweed suits are on back-order, and the button makers have missed their last several shipment dates. I have three shoppers doing nothing but scouring Paris for the buttons, which we need to finish a dozen-and-a-half suits that are otherwise completed. Three clients brought back rayon dresses today complaining that the hems do not hang straight after a few wearings. They were right. Seamstresses who have been working on other garments have had to be taken off them to rehang the hems. I had a meeting with Leo Severin today. A cheap perfumer is copying Nicole and selling counterfeit bottles. We have to sue him. Meanwhile, he is costing us thousands in lost sales and ruining my reputation because the fake scent is of inferior quality.

"A countess whose name I won't reveal to you, a very grand and haughty lady and a very good client over the years, brought back an evening gown, obviously worn, and demanded full credit because she claims that the dress was delivered with a cigarette burn in the front of the bodice. She was quite clearly lying, but in the end we had no choice but to accept her word and give her full credit.

"The man who drives the delivery truck got into an accident today crossing the avenue Foch, when a lorry ran into him, wrecking the whole side of the delivery truck. He was on his way to deliver a large order to a client who is sailing today on the *Ile de France*. I eventually sent the client's own *vendeuse* in a taxi to the site of the accident to rescue the dresses and deliver them personally to dockside," Nicole said, concluding her recital. She paused, looked him straight in the eye, and said, "Kim, when the hell do you think I've had a chance to sneak around?"

"Maybe you didn't do it today, but you've been seeing him every other day. Behind my back!" He stood in the door, his arms crossed in front of him.

"Kim, I told you I would end the affair. I promised and I kept my promise."

"Well, you had to see him to tell him it was all over between you," Kim was adamant. "You made love to him then. Your Armenian greaseball."

"As a matter of fact, I told him on the telephone," Nicole said, allowing his repugnant insult to pass unremarked. She was not accustomed to being so defensive; she was not accustomed to being attacked so relentlessly.

"I don't believe you. You're lying. You've been running around with him behind my back."

"Kim, what's gotten into you? I've never seen you like this! I didn't know this side of you existed. Suspicious. With no reason. None! Your accusations are totally reckless."

"So I'm reckless! Well, you're too careful. You've always been too careful. With your money. With your clothes. With yourself, Nicole. You've never really lived. You've never stuck your neck out. You've never taken a risk. And risk is what it's all about!" He was raving on, barely making sense.

"What does risk have to do with anything?" She had started her business out of nothing. From some points of

364

view perhaps that might have been seen as a risk, though from Nicole's it was necessity.

"And you're so logical all the time. So controlled and cautious!" And with that, he stormed out of her office, slamming the door so hard that it reverberated in its frame. Nicole was bewildered and, finally, furious. She walked home alone and wondered when she'd see him again.

The next morning Kim arrived at the rue de Bretonvilliers while Nicole was having breakfast in the small greenhouse she'd added to the garden side of the first floor. She had thought Kim would be chagrined and apologetic. Instead, his rage had grown.

"You spent the night with him, didn't you?"

"No, I didn't," she said. She was outraged, exhausted by the futility of the argument, the impossibility of his accusations. "I spent the night alone. I *had* planned to spend it with you."

"How could you have slept with someone else, Nicole? How could you have done it?"

"Kim—" she began, and then stopped, shaking her head slowly, not even beginning to know what to say, how to answer him, how to convince him.

"You know what you are, don't you? You're a double-crosser. You're dishonest. Nicole, you're nothing but a whore." He seemed to enjoy his fury, to revel in it, to let his ugly words inflame his rage. "Very elegant and very high-priced, but in the end, you're just a whore!"

Nicole picked up her cup of *café au lait* and threw it at him, covering him with stains from shoulder to knee. They both stood still, frozen, shocked by what she had done. And then it was as if the floodgates had opened. Kim flipped over the breakfast table, spilling coffee and warm milk, pots of marmalade, a basket of croissants, the silver shell of iced butter, the slender silver vase that held a single rose, Then he picked up one of the chairs and hurled it out through the glass wall of the greenhouse, into the garden outside. As the glass splintered and tinkled to the flagstone floor he turned to Nicole and slapped her, hard, across the face.

"I hope I never lay eyes on you again, you slut!" he snarled and crossed the room.

"Kim!" He turned, his hand on the doorknob. "And what were you doing while we were separated?" Nicole asked. "Did you spend every night alone?"

Kim looked as if she had struck him physically, his skin white, his eyes shocked. He opened the door and then turned back to her.

"I loved you from the first moment I ever saw you and I love you now and I always will!" he said. Before she could react, he slammed the door and was gone.

The party's over, the game is ended
The dreams I dreamed went up in smoke
They didn't pan out as intended
I should know how to take a joke.

I try to apply myself
And teach my heart how to sing
I'll go my way by myself
Like a bird on the wing
I'll face the unknown,
I'll build a world of my own;
No one knows better than I myself
I'm by myself alone."

—"By Myself"

CHAPTER FIFTEEN

1.

KIM RETURNED TO NEW YORK by ship. Part of him wanted to return immediately to Paris, crawl to Nicole, and beg her forgiveness, but his embarrassment at his behavior shriveled his impulse. The rest of him was consumed by jealousy. He could not get images of Essayan out of his mind—Essayan handsome, Essayan charming, Essayan a gracious host, Essayan in command at Maxim's, Essayan on top of the world and himself, and Kim, in the mediocre middle. Above all, he could not get images of Essayan and Nicole out of his mind. He tormented himself with more comparisons: Essayan was in Paris and he couldn't be; Essayan had been able to help Nicole during the difficulties of the Depression and he hadn't been able to; Essayan was rich and he wasn't any more. Rich meant free, and for the first time in his life Kim knew what it meant not to be free.

Kim's waking hours and his dreams were poisoned with jealousy. Harder emotion ruled softer emotion and jealousy won. He called Ilona as soon as he set foot in New York and saw her that same night and every night thereafter. He did not write to Nicole nor did he telephone her, although he thought of her incessantly, wondering if she would ever take him back and deciding that she wouldn't. How could she? How could she after the names he'd called her, the accusations he'd made, the torment he'd inflicted on her? Nicole, not surprisingly, did not communicate with him, and at a New Year's Eve party as 1932 turned to 1933, Kim proposed to Ilona.

"You're a wonderful girl, Ilona. I adore you and I want to marry you," Kim said. "If you'll have me . . ."

"If?" Ilona said. She would have walked naked through fire for him! "If!"

"I want to warn you: I'm not easy to live with."

"You're the most darling man in the world," Ilona said. She was a woman in love and women in love do not heed the warnings of their lovers.

That summer they were married in Charleston. Ilona, who was a good negotiator in business, insistent when it came to protecting her clients' rights, was utterly vulnerable privately, and just before the wedding Kim asked her to promise him something: that his life would be her life; that she would do everything his way because his way would be her way.

"Do you promise?" he, asked. He had decided that Nicole's business was the real problem between them. If she had been able to devote herself entirely to him, they would be together right now. He didn't want to risk the same problems with Ilona. He wanted her to belong to him totally.

"I promise," she said. She had already decided to quit her job; she just hadn't told Kim yet.

"On a Bible?" Kim insisted.

"On a stack of Bibles," Ilona had said, smiling.

Ilona could hardly believe her good fortune at having found such an extraordinary husband. He really was the most glamorous man in the world! She would wake up in the middle of the night, and wondering at her luck, would reach out and touch him just to prove to herself that he was really real and really hers. *Mrs. Kim Hendricks*, she would whisper to herself in the dark, and she would smile. Just to herself, drowning in the pleasure.

Having quit her job at the literary agency, Ilona devoted herself full-time to being Kim's wife. He had warned her that being married to him was a full-time job, and she soon found that he wasn't exaggerating. She was wife, protector, literary agent, business manager, housekeeper, travel agent, chauffeur and typist. So fascinated was she with her husband, in such awe of him and so dazzled by him, that she told friends she couldn't remember the last time her feet had touched the ground.

Nicole read about Kim's wedding in the newspapers. There were two photographs of the bride. One a formal studio portrait, the other a snapshot of Ilona smiling happily on a sailboat. Stunned, Nicole felt she had

369

looked into a mirror rather than at a photograph. Ilona Vanderpoel smiling looked exactly like herself. With no arrogance, Nicole realized that Kim must have married in reaction to the dreadful scenes that had torn them apart in Paris. For weeks Nicole went home every night and wept until she fell into an exhausted sleep, from which she awoke drained and sad. Several bleak months passed before, with a sense of bitter finality, Nicole was able to accept the fact that the great love of her life was over.

She returned with doubled energy to the narcotic she had always relied on: work. She threw herself into her business. By late 1933 she was able to re-employ all her former workers—seamstresses and tailors, cutters and finishers, fitters and *vendeuses*, bookkeepers and cleaning women, delivery men, doormen, assistants, apprentices and models—at their pre-Crash wages. By mid-1934 she found she had to add to her staff. She was surrounded by people all day long. At night she was alone.

Nicole read about Kim—and his new wife—frequently. *Memories of a Happy Time* was published in 1933 to fine reviews and went straight to the top of the best-seller lists in the United States and England. A year and a half later a new novel, *A Time for Loss*, was published to even better reviews and great commercial success. There was also frequent news of a more personal kind—the Kim Hendrickses at a Hollywood party with Humphrey Bogart; at New York's El Morocco with Marlene Dietrich; on the island of Cuba, where they were planning to buy a house; in Kenya on safari. Kim Hendricks, with the help of the international press, was established as a legend.

In all the photographs that accompanied the news stories, Ilona Hendricks smiled. It was a special anguish to Nicole to see a woman who looked like her twin sharing a life with the man Nicole loved more deeply and more profoundly than any other soul on earth. Nicole lived with sadness and loneliness, and she wondered if anyone ever got used to it.

2.

The legend grew.

Kim Hendricks had one religion—honor—and that religion had commandments—bravery, honesty, strength, integrity. Kim judged himself, and others, by how they lived up to the commandments.

In 1935 a competitor of Harry Cohn's had flown east to buy the film rights to *A Time for Loss*. The competitor's name was Isadore Selwyn, and Izzy, who had not read the novel, wanted it because Harry Cohn, who had not read it either, wanted it. Kim, so far, had refused to sell the novel to Cohn and Izzy had decided to get it for himself.

Izzy got on a plane and flew to the East Coast, which he detested because (although he would not admit it) he felt that people there looked down on him. Izzy arrived at Kim and Ilona's Gramercy Park apartment preceded by the aroma, of a fine Dunhill Monte Cristo and followed by two lackeys, one bearing a case of Perrier-Jouet, and the other a splendid 6.5 Mannlicher, a rare collector's item.

"Call me Izzy," Isadore invited and checked into the Waldorf-Astoria.

He became Kim's best friend, sharing with Kim the name of the tailor who custom made his monogrammed silk pajamas, the name of his bookie, and the address of New York's most exclusive call girl, a sultry brunette, probably mulatto, who gave, Izzy guaranteed, a no-hands blow job that put a man right into paradise. Izzy admitted he hadn't read *A Time for Loss*, admitted he was just trying to screw Cohn. "I'm a hustler," he said, "but an honest one."

Izzy talked money; every time he named a figure, Kim told him that he appreciated it, that he considered the huge amount of money a compliment to his work, but that he had no interest in selling movie rights to A *Time for Loss*.

Rejection did not stop Isadore Selwyn for a second. He'd leave, trailing fumes of the expensive Monte Cristos, return to his suite at the Waldorf, recalculate his figures, and arrive the next day at Kim's apartment with a larger, more alluring offer. On the fifth day Izzy had upped his offer to one hundred and fifty thousand dollars, more than had ever been paid for the film rights to any novel, and Kim, who shook his head in amazement and acknowledged that he was only human and therefore not immune to temptation, finally accepted. On the spot, Izzy wrote him a check for twenty-five thousand dollars against the balance.

That night, Izzy's last in New York, his business having been successfully concluded, Kim and Izzy, Ilona and the mulatto hit every saloon, high and low, in Manhattan. They were still going strong at eight A.M., when Kim and Ilona drove Izzy to Idlewild for the flight west.

"He's dead honest in his way," Kim said as they watched the plane take off. "I like him. I like anyone that persistent. Persistence is the difference between the men and the boys."

Kim and Ilona went home and slept all day long. That evening at six they turned on the radio. The plane carrying Isadore Selwyn had crashed during a thunderstorm over the Rockies. All aboard had died instantly. Izzy would never make his movie. Kim took Izzy's check, still in his wallet, put it in an envelope, and returned it uncashed to Izzy's widow.

The honorable thing was to return the money and return the money Kim did—even though it would have almost completely wiped out his father's debts. Mrs. Selwyn thanked Kim publicly for returning money that was legally his, and the legend grew even greater.

3.

It was easy for Kim to be honorable about money; it was not easy to be honorable about his girls, because he was ashamed of himself. His girls, he realized, were a way of telling Ilona without words that she wasn't enough for him. He had never, ever, been able to tell Ilona of whom she had reminded him so piercingly when she smiled at him that night at the Stork Club, but the first time he found a girl he forced himself to tell Ilona.

The girl's name was Faith. She worked for Twentieth Century as an editor's assistant and had one night been swept up in one of Kim's legendary bar crawls. When the hangers-on had disappeared only Kim and Faith were left, and the inevitable happened. They went to Faith's apartment.

"I had a little thing with Faith last night," Kim told Ilona the next morning when he came home. "I want you to find out about it from me, not from someone else." The humiliation and the pain Ilona felt were clear on her face.

"It wasn't important. It doesn't mean anything. It was just—" His voice cracked suddenly. "I don't know why I did it. It'll never happen again, so help me God. I promise you. If you can only forgive me. Can you forgive me?"

Ilona was stricken, unable to speak.

"Please?" Kim begged. "Please, Ilona . . ."

Finally, silently, she nodded.

"Please. I'll do anything to make this up to you," Kim said. "I swear."

"You don't have to," Ilona said. All she wanted was to forget the whole thing; she would have given anything if Kim hadn't told her. Why couldn't he have lied like other men? Him and his precious honesty! "Let's not talk about it. If you say it wasn't important, I believe you. Let's drop it."

Kim was gentle and considerate and for a while he was the loving, attentive husband he'd been in the very beginning of their marriage. He told Ilona that she was the stronger of the two of them and that her strength would hold them together no matter what happened. Ilona was complimented, as Kim intended her to be. She remembered how her mother had always told her that women were the stronger sex. Eventually, Ilona would come to feel a certain pride in her stoic forbearance of her famous husband's dalliances.

Faith was the first of the "girls." In the future there would be more—girls in whom Kim took a particular interest, at first always literary. His girls were editors, reporters, writers—all of them young, all of them eager to learn from the master. They were adoring pupils and they knew that their association with McKim Hendricks would not hurt them professionally. In their glowing innocence, with their awe and admiration, they threw themselves at Kim, and he was not invulnerable to their youth, their awe, their adoration. If she wanted her marriage, Ilona realized, she'd have to learn to live with the girls. It was one of the hazards of being married to a famous, desirable man.

She recognized what she had sensed from the very beginning: the old saying that in every marriage one partner loves more than the other was indeed true. In her marriage it was she who loved more. At first it didn't seem terribly unfair.

And so, bit by bit, a certain unhappiness moved into Ilona's life and, to her surprise, once she had learned to recognize it, once it had become familiar and predictable, she found she could coexist with it. Her life, after all, was an enviable one. She had a famous, magnetic husband who, she did not doubt, loved her. Her life was glamorous and exciting and there were many good things to enjoy.

Kim's expansiveness was all-embracing: his personality, his appetites, his generosity with money, his interests, his travel, his work habits. The years, except for the periods when he was actually writing, passed in a blur of restless movement, and Ilona became an expert packer, freight forwarder, organizer, keeper of lists and guardian of the files—files of Kim's contracts, publicity, press clippings, photographs. She paid the bills, ordered supplies, saw to it that they never ran out of anything from typewriter ribbons to champagne to toilet paper.

Kenya, Bali, Madrid, Majorca, Cuba, Maui, Key West, Venice, Beverly Hills, London, Dublin—the movements of Mr. and Mrs. Hendricks were similar, Ilona used to joke, to the movements of an army. There were friends to be called and written to, sporting companions and drinking companions, business associates, sportswriters, the girl of the moment, servants and, of course, the working press to record every coming and going. Except for the times they made love, Ilona and Kim were rarely alone. Kim was compulsively gregarious and there was always company for every meal except breakfast, ten for lunches that lasted until four-thirty in the afternoon, eight or twelve or seventeen for dinners that went on until the early hours of the morning.

Ilona arranged their lives so that nothing disturbed

Kim that he didn't want to disturb him. She took care of his children on their visits and made sure they didn't interrupt him when he was working; saw to it that he saw only favorable reviews and flattering photographs; made sure he saw only the people he wanted to see. His work was his life and nothing was permitted to upset him or distract him, to interfere with him or to irritate him. He wrote continuously, going from one novel to the next like an addict craving his drug. Between 1935 and 1938 he published a new novel each year, each one more successful than the one before, making him a rich man. His work was his fortress, shielding him from any unwelcome intrusions, and his wife and his friends understood that nothing was more important than the words Kim Hendricks put on paper.

4.

Fashion, although hardly immune to the worldwide Depression, did not cease to exist. On the contrary, it did what it had always done: it changed. The loose, low-waisted look of the Twenties became the slim, body-conscious silhouette of the Thirties. By the mid-thirties, led to a great extent by Nicole, who used inexpensive, easy-to-care-for fabrics such as cotton and rayon in her most elegant designs, there had been almost a complete revolution in fashion. No longer was fashion the prerogative of the very rich and leisured. The private fitting rooms, the discreet *vendeuses*, the hushed salons, the haughty models, the three fittings, the elegant accouterments of couture, had begun to wane in importance while affordable fashion for every woman was beginning to generate an enormous and influential industry whose products, advertised and promoted by the newly powerful fashion magazines, would

376

become the intimate concern of millions of people. Fashion during the thirties, brought down to earth by Nicole's simplicity and practicality, would become democratized.

Nicole, moreover, had turned out to be a stroke of genius. Its sales more than any other single factor got the House of Redon through the blackest years of the Depression. Millions of women who could not afford a new dress *could* afford a bottle of perfume and, during the worldwide Depression of the thirties, sales of *Nicole* broke every record. Nicole's early insistence on international advertising now paid tremendous dividends; people everywhere clamored for *Nicole*, with its distinctive modern bottle, its easy-to-pronounce name and, above all, its contemporary, abstract scent. In the mid-thirties the company, which Nicole now owned in conjunction with Leo Severin, employed more chemists, label pasters, bottlers and wrappers, and bought more natural essences, synthetic stabilizers and bottles than any other perfume company in the world.

Nicole's tremendous contribution to the recovering economy of France was recognized by the French government, and by 1936 she was entitled to wear her own rosette of the Légion d'Honneur. At mid-decade, Nicole was, thanks to her own efforts, a millionaire.

The greatest satisfaction her money brought her was in permitting her, finally, to take care of her mother. Nicole had once sworn she would never return to Laronel, but in the mid-thirties she did.

"The last time I saw you I swore I would never return, but I found that I wanted to," Nicole told Jeanne-Marie. "Because, as I get older, I can see how much like you I am and how, in the end, I owe my success to you. I learned from your example not to give up and not to give in. I learned to be proud of work, not ashamed of it. I learned, above all, to follow where my own instincts led me. I want to thank you for all that."

Jeanne-Marie looked at her polished, glamorous daughter and for once saw nothing to criticize.

"I have a house in Antibes and I would like to give it to you," Nicole said, thinking wistfully of the dreams she had once had of sharing it with Kim. It had stood almost empty in the years Nicole had owned it, and when her accountant told her how much money she was making her first thought was that it was too much for one person. She immediately thought of her mother. "Would you like to live there?"

"I've been thinking of retiring," Jeanne-Marie said. It was as close as she could come, even then, to acknowledging all that Nicole wanted to give her. "I'm getting old, Nicole, and tired . . ."

Jeanne-Marie accepted Nicole's gift and moved into her *mas*. She invited Nicole to visit her every summer, and attended by a butler and a cook, Jeanne-Marie, who had spent her life serving others and was now *being* served, told everyone who would listen that few women were lucky enough to have such a loving and attentive daughter. Nicole, Jeanne-Marie like to say, was one in a million.

To Nicole, her mother's compliment, of all the compliments she would receive in her life, was the one that meant the most to her.

5.

Boy Mellany had realized a long time earlier that a ruby would not be enough. In the intervening years he had come to give Nicole an entire necklace of rubies and, subsequently, a pair of ruby and diamond

378

earrings to match. The more he gave her, the more elusive and the more desirable she became to him. He contrived more and more reasons to be in Paris and in late 1937 he gave Nicole a gift of three bracelets: one of rubies, one of diamonds, one of emeralds. He would have given her one of sapphires, but he remembered that she had once said, a long time ago, that blue, except for navy, depressed her.

"I've been thinking about you, Nicole," Boy said when she had finished thanking him. "About us. About the future. I'd like to divorce. I'd like to marry you."

Reflectively, Nicole studied the smoke as it rose from the tip of her cigarette. "Is this a proposal?" she finally asked.

"Well—" Boy stammered, always uncomfortable putting his feelings into words. "Well—yes. As a matter of fact, it is."

"If you only knew how much I wanted to marry you once upon a time," Nicole said wistfully.

"We can do it now," Boy said. "Nicole, will you marry me?"

"Do you remember what you told me when you first came back to me?" Nicole asked.

"No." Boy was taken off guard. "What did I say?"

" 'There is only one Nicole and everyone knows who she is,' " Nicole said, quoting his own words back to him.

"I don't understand . . ."

"I won't marry you, Boy," Nicole said gently. "There have been many Duchesses of Mellany. There is, as you yourself said, only one Nicole Redon. Everyone knows who I am."

As Nicole neared her fortieth birthday, she would become famous for the number of brilliant, accomplished men who would want to marry her and whom she put aside in a way that only increased their admiration of her.

She would also become famous for the jewels her admirers lavished on her, and for the casual way she wore them, mixing real rubies and real emeralds and real diamonds with her own paste copies. "It doesn't matter if jewels are real," she was quoted as saying, "as long as they look fake."

The remark was printed and Kim read it. He was touched by her surface insouciance and he wondered how much pain she was hiding. He wondered if it could possibly equal his own.

6.

Ilona was a loving and loyal wife but privately, after she had been married five years, she allowed herself to admit—only to herself, to be sure—that certain things about Kim seriously upset her. Just as she shielded him from the world, she protected the image he presented to the world by never allowing herself to indicate, even to her most intimate friends, that Kim was anything but the hero-artist, a man other men might strive to emulate. And she never told a soul that now and then she and Kim talked of divorce.

There were, first of all, his compulsive, unhappy infidelities and his frightening and unpredictable periods of depression. There was also his drinking. For as long as Ilona had known him, he had always drunk heroic quantities of alcohol, able to absorb a few drinks before dinner, wine with it, and a chain of brandies after. Kim's denunciations of men who "couldn't hold their liquor" were so scathing and so ferocious that Ilona never thought of alcohol as a problem. Kim was as good as his favorite saying: a man takes a drink; drink doesn't take a man. She would never have given his drinking more than a passing thought except that the very worst argument in their marriage had not been over one of Kim's girls but over liquor.

It happened one hot Sunday in late August, 1939. Kim's newest novel, *Champagne Years*, was to be published in early September, and some two dozen people had drifted by their apartment early one Sunday afternoon for a premature celebration. Bottles of gin and scotch and rum and champagne, the staples of Kim's bar, were arranged on the sideboard, and Kim was drinking a mixture he said he had learned from the barman at the Ritz: a combination of rum, bitters and orange juice —"for the vitamins," Kim liked to say—topped off with cold champagne. Kim poured the end of the rum and went to the closet where the extra cases were stored.

"No rum!" Kim shouted. "Where's the rum?" he demanded, returning to the living room. He had a small linen bar towel in his hand and, using it as a weapon, he suddenly whipped it across the low cocktail table and scattered glasses, a vase of daffodils, ashtrays, packs of cigarettes, a gold cigarette lighter and a large bowl of his favorite pistachio nuts to the carpet, mixing ashes, remnants of drinks, ice cubes, the water from the vase and hundreds of the small red nuts. "What's going on here?" he roared, his face white with anger. "I'm the most famous writer in the world and I can't get a drink in my own house!"

The guests were stunned into silence. So was Ilona.

"Well, *say* something!" Kim thundered. He stood in the living room, seething with rage. He swung back and forth on his feet as if unsure where to strike next. "There's no rum! I want to know why the hell not!"

"I ordered some just this week," Ilona finally said. She

had stayed home to wait for the delivery from the liquor store. It had made her late for a hairdresser's appointment, so she remembered it clearly. She had watched the boy unload two cases, one of rum, one of gin, and put them in the closet for her. She had tipped him fifty cents and she clearly remembered his delighted smile of thanks for the enormous fifty-cent tip. "It's got to be in here."

Ilona went to the closet and looked. Kim was right. There was no rum. There were two new cases of liquor, both gin.

"I'm sorry," Ilona said, returning to the living room. "The liquor store must have made a mistake. Why don't you have a gin and tonic?"

"I don't want a gin and tonic," Kim said in a tight, furious voice. "I was drinking rum and I want to continue to drink rum."

"Then let's go out," Ilona suggested.

"We can go to the bar of the Gramercy Park Hotel," said one of the guests.

"The drinks are lousy there," Kim pronounced.

"We can go to 'Twenty-one'—you like the drinks there."

"Jack Kriendler is a cheap bootlegger," said Kim, stubborn, furious.

"You told me just last week how much you like him," Ilona said quietly.

"I guess I did," Kim said. Suddenly he smiled sheepishly. His tantrum, Ilona thought with relief, was over.

Everyone piled into taxis and went to "21". Kim ordered sidecars, the house specialty. He seemed to have forgotten his insistence on rum and no one reminded him. By five the party had broken up, and Kim and Ilona went home.

"I feel terrible," Kim said, and he went straight to bed.

The next morning *The New York Times* reviewed *Champagne Years*. "Kim Hendricks, equally famous for his fine early novels and his recent frequent appearances in café society circles, seems on the evidence of this new novel to have lived in a never-never land while the rest of the world coped with the harsh facts of the Depression . . . the rise of fascism . . . Anschluss, the Czech crisis, Chamberlain, appeasement, Munich . . . the increasing certainty of World War . . ."

Despite Ilona's attempts to keep them away from him, Kim insisted on reading all the reviews of *Champagne Years*. Although none of them was unequivocally bad, almost all of them reflected the opinion of *the Times* and expressed the wish that a writer as important as Kim Hendricks would address himself to the grave problems that were turning the lives of millions of people upside down, pointing out that Ernest Hemingway was in Spain covering the Spanish Civil War and that Ring Lardner was a war correspondent for the *Tribune*. Another reviewer wondered if Kim Hendricks would ever show any sign of a social conscience.

Kim stayed in bed for four days, drinking white wine, speaking only in response to direct questions.

"Are you all right?" Ilona would ask.

"No."

"Are you sick?"

"No."

"Don't you think I ought to call a doctor?"

"They're a bunch of quacks."

"Why won't you get up?"

"I don't feel like it."

"Are you angry with me?"

"No."

"Did I do something wrong?"

"No."

"Then what's the matter?"

"Nothing."

But something *was* the matter and Kim knew exactly what it was. The reviewers had been absolutely right. He had been living in a never-never land, totally removed from the problems and concerns of the rest of the world. He had been protected and coddled and catered-to. He had no one to blame but himself, because that had been what he had once wanted. It was the reason he had asked Ilona to promise that everything would be done "his way." She had done as he had wished, and now he didn't like himself any more. He didn't like the way he treated Ilona, he didn't like it that he was drinking so much, he was bored with what he was writing, he was sick of being a "celebrity," he was tired of the traveling, the girls, the interviews, the flashbulbs, the flattery. He was fed up with the legend.

The next morning, Sunday, September 3, France and England declared war on Germany. Shaky with a hangover, Kim called S. I. at home. They made a lunch date for the next day.

"Are you still interested in turning me into a newscaster?" Kim asked.

"What a question!" S. I. replied. "Ed Murrow—he's head of our European bureau—would give his right arm for you."

"I'd want to be right in the middle of things," Kim said. "I don't want a desk job."

"Good! I want someone who'll report directly from the front lines. I want listeners to hear your voice with the bullets and the cannons sounding in the background. Front-line war reporting is the coming thing in radio, Kim. It's made in heaven for you."

"One thing."

"Name it."

"I want to stop in Paris first."

"Who's stopping you?" replied S. I. "So tell me, Kim, are you going to do it?"

"I want to do it, S. I.," Kim said in an earnest voice that reminded S. I. of the eager boy he'd first known during World War I, doing anything to get a job, a byline. "I need a risk, S. I. I've been living too soft."

"One thing, Kim. We'll want you to leave as soon as possible. Things are coming to a boil . . ." *The Times* had reported that morning that a German torpedo had sunk the first ship of the war, the British liner, *Athenia*, carrying Canadian and American civilians. Hitler was with the German Army on the Eastern Front. The Poles were accusing the Germans of making aerial gas attacks on civilian populations in Polish towns and cities. "When can you leave?"

"Two weeks."

"Two weeks! That's terrific! You're like the old Kim Hendricks, an eager beaver, hungry for the action," said S. I. He flagged down a passing waiter. "Waiter! Champagne!" he commanded. "This is a real event. I've only been after you for ten years!"

"No champagne for me," said Kim.

"You're sure?" S. I. gave Kim a look of disbelief bordering on shock.

"I'm sure."

S. I. shrugged his shoulders and began outlining Kim's new assignment.

The alcohol was beginning to show in the pouches beneath Kim's eyes, in the dry flaky patches of skin on his face, in a certain blurriness around his waist. Kim didn't want Nicole to see him like that—assuming she'd agree to see him at all.

In the two weeks before he left for Paris, Kim did not touch a drop of alcohol. He did not miss it once.

385

7.

In Europe, in Nicole's world, throughout the late thirties a foreground of elegance and sharp-edged glamour had glittered darkly against a background of gathering and ominous clouds. The franc had devalued, the Bank of France nationalized: the rich were buying gold while unemployment soared and the employed went on strike: the automobile workers—Panhard-Levassor and Hispano-Suiza—the railwaymen, postel workers, bakers, textile workers and the saleswomen at Printemps and the Galeries La Fayette. They wanted employment contracts, a forty-hour week, paid holidays—all benefits Nicole had offered freely to her workers. It hadn't been entirely humanitarianism on her part, although there was certainly some of that; it was simply the kind of sensible business practice she had learned from Mischa. It was more than worth it to her to avoid a strike—Chanel's workers were striking, spitting at Coco as she tried to enter her own establishment—but still Nicole worried. Still she worried that the strikes which had plagued England and France would halt production at the House of Redon. She worried over the inevitable fabric shortages. The windows of a famous Faubourg St.-Honoré shop which sold fine leather goods had been broken by rocks thrown by anarchists, and Nicole, like all the shop owners of Paris, worried that her *maison* would also be attacked and vandalized.

There were not only shocking rumors of Nazi anti-Semitism, there was disturbing proof. Middle-class refugees had crowded Belgium; poorer Jews without the proper visas made their escape from Germany on foot. Rich Jews, who had fled in limousines, packed the fashionable hotels in Zurich and Paris.

Nicole, who had never been the least bit political, was violently anti-Nazi. She, who had suffered prejudice as a child *for no reason except her birth*, sided with the Jews of Europe, who were suffering prejudice *for no reason except their birth*.

Politics, to which no one had given a thought in the twenties, had become the obsession of the thirties. The conflicts glossed over in the Treaty of Versailles could no longer be swept under the rug. The talk along the quai d'Orsay, in the drawing rooms of the avenue Foch, in the intellectual cafés of Montparnasse, the joints of Pigalle, and the red-light districts surrounding les Halles was talk of the coming war.

By the late thirties Nicole had resumed her friendship with Mischa but on a different, more platonic basis. With the constant talk of war, annexation, Hitler, Mussolini and Franco, reality constantly intruded on the distractions of romance.

Mischa was away from Paris much of the time, traveling constantly on business. Oil, now that war was declared, was of strategic importance. He had returned from England with talk of air-raid sirens, from Italy with news of the Brownshirts, from Japan with news of massive military buildup, from Berlin with stories of decadent nightclubs where the hostesses wore green nail enamel and of Jews sent off to detention camps.

It was no longer possible to imagine a normal life as all Europe poised on the brink of catastrophe, and Nicole, lonely and exhausted, sometimes wondered how long she could go on. She was in her office in mid-September, selecting dye samples, when she was called to the telephone. It was Kim and the call was a local one! He had just arrived from New York on a military aircraft and had an hour in Paris until his escort would fly him into Warsaw.

"I'm at the Ritz," he said, his voice as familiar to

387

Nicole as her own. "I can see the awning of the House of Redon. Can you—would you—spare some time for me?"

Nicole threw down the phone and rushed out of the House of Redon while Kim flew out of the Ritz. They ran into each other's arms in the middle of the place Vendôme, and under the gaze of Napoleon, who understood such things, in the city of love they embraced as if they were alone and it was as if they had never been a moment apart.

Paris has suddenly been having a fit of prosperity, gaiety and hospitality. . . . It has taken the threat of war to make the French loosen up and have a really swell and civilized good time.

—Janet Flanner

CHAPTER SIXTEEN

1.

THEY WALKED ACROSS the place Vendôme hand in hand to the Ritz, their hearts pounding with excitement, slightly breathless with emotion. The doorman smiled, bowing slightly. He had known them for years and he had always thought that M. Hendricks and Mademoiselle Redon were the handsomest couple in Paris. Nothing in the passage of the years had caused him to change his opinion. Mademoiselle Redon became more beautiful, *soignée* and elegant; M. Hendricks became handsomer, more distinguished, more and more a *personnage*. The Ritz existed for people like them.

"I wasn't sure what kind of reception I'd get," Kim said once they had ordered their drinks. "If any . . ."

Nicole smiled. They sat at the table that had been, in years past, "their table." Nicole wore a navy blue suit with a white silk blouse, necklaces of pearls mixed with strings of colored stones, her shining gold hair untouched with gray, tied back neatly with a simple black ribbon. In the elegant, assured woman Kim could see the girl who had been sweeping the sidewalk in front of the small shop in the rue Montaigne. He held her hand in both of his, unwilling not to touch her. "I wouldn't blame you if you refused to speak to me."

"I told myself that if I ever saw you again I wouldn't—not a word," Nicole said. Kim, wearing a tweed jacket, a shirt the color of his eyes, and lean, twill trousers, his trench coat folded over an empty chair, had the elegance, the energy, that had overwhelmed her on the rue Montaigne—how many years ago? He was still the same man and she was still the same woman, and all her feelings were the same now as they had been then. She was bewitched and enchanted, hypnotized and mesmerized, unable to take her eyes from him. "I imagined how I'd look straight through you and walk right by you, my nose in the air. I consoled myself imagining how good I'd feel ignoring and hurting you. But, you see, my imagination has nothing at all to do with the way I feel. Nothing! It's really very mysterious."

"*People* are very mysterious," Kim said. He could feel the strength and capability in the bones and tendons of her hand. He stroked its skin, so smooth and so beautifully cared for. Her hands were her: strength within; soft on the surface. The intensity of his feelings for her amazed him, still caught him off guard. He was still riveted by the thunderbolt. He felt safe talking generalities; his emotions were too turbulent to risk expression. "It's the ace up the novelist's sleeve, you know—the

390

mystery of the individual. Anyone can do or think or feel anything."

"You sound like an anarchist," said Nicole. Her hand in his was so warm, so protected. She felt as if her entire life, her whole being, were in those linked hands and yet he was the man who had wrecked her house and her life with his violent jealous tantrums.

"The last time I saw you, you certainly behaved like an anarchist," Nicole continued. "Only it was more than my greenhouse you destroyed; you left my life in shards and splinters. I still haven't put it together."

The vulnerability in her expression twisted Kim's heart. Guilt and humiliation at the memory of his ugly words and uncontrollable destructiveness flooded through him. He tried to speak but couldn't.

"You weren't like yourself, Kim," Nicole said, hurt and disappointment in her voice. "You were like another person. A stranger . . ."

A *stranger* . . . thought Kim. A *stranger?* He remembered the very first thought he'd had Armistice Day on the rue Montaigne: *How do you say 'I love you' to a stranger?* But Nicole was no stranger. She had never been a stranger. She was the other half of himself, the half without which he was incomplete. He was who he was because of her. He wrote the way he wrote because of her. His heroines—idealized by the world—were inspired by her. The way he felt toward her defined love for him—and the way he defined love influenced the way millions of other people defined love. The one time he had told her he loved her was, shockingly, in anger, the time he'd last left Paris. How could he have spoken of love with ugliness in his heart? It was profoundly wrong. It was cruelly unfair—to him, to her. It was time to tell her what he had been impelled to tell her from the very beginning: *I love you.* He was a writer and words meant more to him than to most people.

I love you had the power to bind the first moment and the last heartbeat in an eternal circle. *I love you* had been there from the beginning and would be there for an infinite forever. He would tell her now . . . today . . .

"You were a monster, Kim," she was saying, "A demon possessed by your jealousy."

"It was even worse than you think," Kim said. Nicole noticed he had ordered an Evian. He sipped it thoughtfully. Nicole deserved the truth. Without the truth, there was nothing to believe in.

"Worse?"

"I had met Ilona," he said. "Ilona and I were already having an affair when I accused you."

"Then how could you?" Nicole asked, and she realized that in a way she had known all along. "How could you have been so jealous? We were apart . . . you had found someone, so had I. It was normal, human . . ."

"I was a little crazy then," Kim said. Nicole, as always, had been reasonable; he, as always, had been emotional. "I had lost everything. My father had killed himself. I had lost all my money. I was just divorced. I was even afraid I'd lose my children. When I met Mischa, I compared myself with him. He had everything and I had nothing. I was afraid I'd lose you too."

"How could you have imagined you could lose me?" asked Nicole. "It's not possible, Kim. Not possible. Nothing would ever change the way I feel about you. Nothing! I knew it the first moment I saw you on the rue Montaigne."

He looked at her, silent, amazed. Could it have been possible? Had she thought what he had thought? At the same instant? He wanted to tell her what he had thought, to ask her what she had thought, to find out if the thunderbolt that had struck him had struck her. But before he could open his mouth to begin, the military escort the army had assigned to take him to Warsaw stood by the table and cleared his throat.

"Excuse me, sir, but we're scheduled to leave now."

Kim nodded to the young man and called for the check and paid it. Nicole walked him to the sidewalk where the military vehicle waited to take him to the air base, its motor turning over. They embraced, kissed.

"Promise me something," Nicole said, her voice husky with emotion. The escort stood at the open car door, waiting for Kim to get in.

Kim was aware of Nicole's perfume. He loved her—oh God, he loved her, and when he saw her next he would tell her. He would find the right time—he would create the right time. Of course he would promise her anything. "Anything," he said.

"That you'll be careful," she said. She remembered his limp, his medal, the story she'd dragged out of him about his part in the raid on the Big Berthas in the Saint-Gobain Forest. She knew he couldn't resist being in the center of things; it was part of him, and one of the reasons she loved him. "Please be careful."

"Of course!" he said. He did not for a moment share her anxieties. There was no doubt in his mind that the Allies would emerge victorious, no doubt at all. "We'll get old and crotchety together, Nicole. *That* I can promise you."

She forced a smile to her lips. He kissed her lightly and he was gone.

2.

In September and October Kim broadcast five minutes a day, describing the Blitzkrieg that crushed Poland in a week and the agonized mopping-up period that followed. German tanks and armored trucks had ravaged Poland while bombs destroyed communications, leveled towns, scattered terrified civilian populations, smashed power plants, and blasted hospitals filled with the wounded. In defiance of the German onslaught, the Warsaw radio played Chopin's Polonaise over and over all day long to let the world know that Poland was still Polish. On October 16, when Hitler flew to Warsaw with Colonel General Wilhelm Keitel, Chief of the High Command, and Heinrich Himmler, Chief of the Secret Police, to review the victorious German troops, Kim ended his broadcast with a recording of the Polonaise gradually being drowned out by *"Deutschland Über Alles."*

When he returned to his hotel from the studio, he was greeted by two of Himmler's staff officers. They were frigidly polite but their warning was not: Herr Hendricks was to abide strictly by the censor-approved script. The playing of music had *not* been in the script. Such outrageous departure from the approved was not to happen again. It would not be tolerated. Did Herr Hendricks understand? When Kim did not answer, the question was repeated: *Did Herr Hendricks understand?* Yes, Kim finally said, he understood. But down by his side, out of sight of the two Germans, he crossed his fingers.

"Oh! You're all right!" said Nicole, tears and smiles, as he swallowed her up in his arms. He was back in Paris for a few days after the Polish debacle, awaiting his next assignment. He had forgotten all about the "warning" from Himmler's two minions and never mentioned it to Nicole.

"Of course, I'm all right!" Kim said. "You don't think a kraut bullet could hurt me, do you?"

"No," she said. "Knowing you, I suppose not. But, still, I worried . . ."

"Worry is a bad habit and you'll have to overcome it," Kim said. He smiled down at her, the laugh lines around his grayish-blue eyes crinkling, adding a seasoned handsomeness to his already handsome face. Nicole thought at that split-second, as she had so many times before, that Kim Hendricks was quite simply the most attractive man she'd ever seen in her life. "Nothing's going to happen to me from now on except good things. It's going to be a hell of a war and I'm going to be right there in the middle of it. I'm going to file the best dispatches anyone ever wrote about war and when it's all over I'm going to get at least one big novel out of it. Just you wait and see!"

"File dispatches?" Nicole asked, knowing the terminology. "But you're on the radio now."

"I know. But I write my own scripts and I still think like a print journalist. I'll probably never stop, either," said Kim. "Once an ink-stained wretch, always an ink-stained wretch." He shrugged and smiled. "How's Paris these days?"

"Surprising. Gay, busy, vital, as if the whole city's had a vitamin shot," said Nicole. "People's spirits are high and they're joking about the phony war. The Bore War, they call it. Sitzkrieg. And as for me personally, women are buying more dresses than ever and I'm designing them. This city is living from day to day. No one really thinks about the future."

"I do," said Kim. "*Our* future. I thought about it a lot in Poland. A future for us, Nicole."

"Future? What about Ilona?" asked Nicole, realizing that in the few moments they'd had at the Ritz there hadn't been enough time to say all the things each longed to say. "You're married, Kim. You can't just walk away when it suits you. Not a second time."

"Ilona's going to Reno as soon as she gets settled in Washington. She's got a good job there on Eleanor Roo-

395

sevelt's staff, as a press attaché. We've known for a long time that the marriage was a mistake. The whole mess was my fault. Ilona was a good wife; I was not a good husband, far from it . . ."

"It's not like you to do something and do it badly," said Nicole.

"I know," said Kim. He was serious, sobered. "I married her because I wanted you and felt I couldn't have you. It was as simple—and as complicated—as that," he said. "But that's the past. I want to talk about the future."

"Future?" Nicole asked softly. She resisted the abandon and the gaiety that reigned over Paris; she remembered the last war too vividly. "Europe is at war. Things will get worse, not better. How can we even think of a future?"

"*I* can. And you will, too, one of these days very soon. Just wait and see! But meanwhile, if you don't want to talk about the future, let's talk about the present." Kim's smile returned, his eyes sparkling. "Let's find a good dinner, in a place that has some real French bread, some good red wine, some strong *café filtre*. I missed all of them while I was in Poland," he said. "But not as much as I missed you."

They had thirty-six hours. Nicole had never been so conscious of time. They fit minutes into seconds, hours into minutes, days into hours. Kim's next assignment was the Western Front and when it came time for him to leave, Nicole felt that thirty-six hours was all the time in the world and no time at all.

"Oh, be careful!" she said, clinging to him. "Please be careful!"

"Don't worry!" Kim said. "I never forget my promises!"

With a last kiss, he was gone, his destination somewhere along the Western Front.

3.

He had a leave in Paris in early December. This time he and Nicole had sixteen hours—all the time in the world and no time at all.

"I have a three-day leave coming up at Christmas," Kim said. "Let's go to the country. Maybe we can even find a goose. And now that Louisette's speaking to me again perhaps she'll make us a *bûche de Noël*. My friends at the Ritz have assured me that there will be as much champagne for me as I wish."

"That's a wonderful idea! Roland Xavier has a house just outside Paris. The other day he offered it to me for the holidays, since he and his wife will be visiting his wife's family in the Dordogne."

"Then it's a deal," Kim said.

"It's a deal," Nicole agreed, and he smiled as he always did when his American slang met head-on with her French accent. "We're going to have a wonderful Christmas. A wonderful life! A wonderful everything!

"I hope so," Nicole said with her customary caution.

"We will! You have to stop worrying all the time!"

"I'll try."

"Trying isn't enough. You'll have to promise," Kim said. "Promise?"

"Promise," she said, knowing she had been bested and smiling at the loving defeat. "I promise to stop worrying."

The sixteen hours went like sixteen seconds and Kim was sent to Berlin.

In Berlin Kim had problems. He couldn't say what he wanted to say, he thought, as he read from his censor-approved script in the studio on the Wilhelmstrasse, his part of the year-end roundup. Murrow would report from London, Shirer from Helsinki, Hendricks from Berlin . . . "Blitzkrieg . . . France and England declare war . . . the Civil War ends in Spain . . . Italy invades Albania . . . Russia attacks Finland . . . Hitler offers peace proposals to stop the conflagration . . ."

As Kim read the bland script, an incident he had witnessed on the first night of Hanukkah forced its way into his mind. Jews forced to their knees to scrub public toilets in a railway station with the sacred prayer bands, the tefillin, while a black-shirted mob stood by shouting obscenities. Kim had happened upon the scene as he was returning from a trip to the countryside to report the effects of the war there. Suddenly, Kim diverged from the Nazi-approved script and began to relate the incident. He wanted Americans to know, he wanted the world to know . . .

The soldiers who guarded the soundproof studio suddenly slammed open the door and three Gestapo men walked in. The one in the lead, a lean, gray-eyed man with a dueling scar, knocked the microphone to the floor, while the other two forced Kim out of the studio.

"We've had our eye on you ever since Warsaw, *Mister* Hendricks," said the gray-eyed Gestapo officer, his eyes turning almost the color of snow. "Our patience is running thin."

Kim spent a week in Gestapo custody in a sterile cell in a black basement somewhere in the middle of Berlin. He was released only after days of American embassy negotiations with Hitler's government, and only on one condition: he had to promise in writing never to try anything like that again. Kim realized that if he wanted to broadcast from any German-held territory he had no choice but to acquiesce. He signed with his right hand and crossed the fingers of his left.

The snowy-eyed Gestapo man escorted Kim to the aircraft that would take him back to Paris, and warned him one final time: "Be careful, Herr Hendricks. You are far too provocative."

CBS's attitude was ambivalent: on the one hand, they wanted the best reporting to come out of the war and Kim was certainly providing them with that; on the other hand, they did not want to anger the Germans, whose cooperation they needed to get their shortwave transmission across Europe, and they most certainly did not want to lose a reporter of Kim's stature. Kim's nightly lead-in had become famous, an aural symbol of the darkness of the approaching war. All over America, millions of people waited for the portentous words: "Dateline," followed by the name of the place or, if even that had been censored, with the ominous phrase "somewhere in Europe." Kim's reading of the phrase made it memorable: "Dateline"—followed by a long, dramatic pause— "somewhere in Europe," uttered with sober gravity. What happened was that CBS in an official memo ordered Kim to stop such provocative behavior immediately; privately his peers and his superiors congratulated him—"You did what the rest of us wish we could do"— and S. I. sent a cable telling Kim that his work was the best to come out of Europe.

"Christmas will be a little late this year!" Kim said, his trenchcoat flapping, a bottle of Kirsch, a gift from an anti-Nazi German who'd thrust it into his surprised hands late one afternoon in Berlin, in his right hand, as he swept into the house on the rue de Bretonvilliers. He had returned to Paris, thanks to the hospitality of the Gestapo, almost a week late. It was December 26.

"Oh, my God! I was afraid I'd never see you again," Nicole said, crying.

"I *told* you worry was a bad habit," Kim said, holding

her. "Every time I come back I see you in tears. What happened to your promise?"

"But you were due back days ago! No one at CBS would tell me a thing! I was crazy with worry. What happened?"

"Top secret!" Kim said, and winked outrageously. "But I can tell *you*. Adolf What's-his-name wanted an autographed copy of *Champagne Years* and I had to wait around Berlin until the Führer could take a few moments from reshaping Europe to thank me in person."

"Kim, you're impossible!"

"Maybe," he said, shrugging. "Now let's go celebrate Christmas. I don't intend to miss Christmas just because of a minor detail like a world war!"

Laden with food that Louisette had scrounged up, with champagne from the Ritz cellars, with the bottle of Kirsch, they went to Roland Xavier's house in the country northwest of Paris. They walked in the snow under the great pines, burned fragrant cedar logs in the fireplace, feasted on the goose Nicole had managed to get in exchange for three bottles of *Nicole*, laughed at the "Blitzmas" cards that were all the rage and at the greeting from an English friend who had ended his holiday letter wishing them "anything but a Jerry Christmas." They made love in the soft feather bed and they talked about the future.

"We have to put each other first," Kim said. "It's been our big mistake all along. You were always—from the first moment I met you in the rue Montaigne—the most important thing in my life, but I kept forgetting. I kept letting other things and other people come ahead of you. I put my work first . . . I put myself first, and I was wrong. I've learned, Nicole. I've finally learned what matters to me, and what matters to me is you. I kept forgetting it. That was my big mistake."

"And mine," said Nicole, thinking of the collections

400

she'd put ahead of Kim, thinking of the times she'd put the cook and the maid and probably even the postman ahead of the man she loved. "I must have been out of my mind. But I've learned, too. Loneliness has taught me. Bitter tears have taught me. They were harsh teachers. I'll be different now."

"No, *I'll* be different," Kim insisted.

"No, darling," she said, "*we'll* be different."

As the year turned, Kim left to report on the New Year from the Maginot Line. As always when he left, Nicole reminded him of his promise.

"Be careful," she warned. "Please be careful. Remember your promise to me."

"And you remember yours!" Kim retorted. "When are you going to stop worrying and accept the fact that I'm going to be around for a long time? A long, long time!" He crushed her to him and kissed her; then, holding himself at arm's length from her and looking her in the eyes, he said, "About that promise: are you going to be a good girl from now on and stop all that worrying?"

"I promise," she said, and smiled, and he was gone again.

4.

In the early months of 1940 the phony war suddenly became real. People began to talk about leaving Paris; they began to talk about the Occupation. Nicole stayed in Paris for two reasons: one, at the request of the French government, which considered her presence essential to the morale of the city; and two, to be there for Kim, who used Paris as a headquarters. Business, Nicole noted, was good. War seemed to be good for business. At the request of clients, the House of Redon was reviving the fashions Nicole had invented during the last war, and "pajamas" became a new fashion the second time around. But the House of Redon was working with new, inexperienced staff. Nicole's *midinettes* had gone to work in the war factories. In their starched and spotless white coats and with their perfectly manicured and lacquered nails, they no longer sewed seams and placed darts but their skilled fingers did the delicate wiring of radio sets for airplanes and ships and defense installations.

Kim was in and out of Paris in the early months of the year, on his way to and from Helsinki and Montmédy, Rome and Warsaw, Berchtesgarten and Copenhagen. Every time he returned, he seemed more vital, more alive; every time he returned, the hours passed more quickly. People no longer joked about Sitzkrieg. People were taking the war seriously. War was imminent; war was certain; war would be here in Paris—any day—any hour—any minute.

So much to say and so much to feel. Kim and Nicole. Nicole and Kim. Their reunions—magical, soaring hellos, wrenching, heartbreaking goodbys, bracketing exquisite moments of love—were governed by a clock whose hands moved faster and faster.

They did not speak very much of the past. They lived in a fiercely intense present, grabbing at life, grabbing at each other, and over and over, planning their future. They would be something! Kim and Nicole! Nicole and Kim! Strong and independent, loyal and loving, free and united. Nicole finally kept her promise. She finally stopped worrying. She thought the way Kim did: of a glorious, endlessly sunny future.

"I notice you're not telling me to be careful any more," Kim said in April. "You've improved!" ·

"A promise is a promise!" Nicole answered gaily. "Anyway, you've convinced me. Nothing's going to happen to you. Nothing's going to happen to me. It didn't in the last war and it won't in this one either. After all, you survived Warsaw, Berlin, the Maginot Line. You were born under a lucky star."

"*We* were born under a lucky star. And it happened the moment I met you on the rue Montaigne," Kim said, and then looked at his watch. "Are we going to be something! You and I!" And with that, he was off.

He had almost told her—*I love you*—but he had glanced at his watch: there wasn't enough time. It wasn't the *right* time. It had to be the perfect moment—tender, intense, passionate. It would have to be a moment from which there was no return.

Next time, Kim promised himself. The next time we're together.

In mid-April Germany launched a spring offensive, pointed at Denmark, Norway and Sweden. It was ferocious and swift, masterfully coordinating air, sea and land attacks. Denmark's land border was assaulted by shock troops supported with air and sea bombardments and the tiny country, taken by surprise, outarmed and outnumbered, fell swiftly.

Kim was in Oslo when the Germans arrived. He was amazed that a city of 250,000 could be taken by a force of 1500 with barely a shot being heard. Nazi warships had steamed into the Oslo Fjord virtually unharmed. Many of the Norwegian fortifications and naval units had simply not resisted. Kim was curious, suspicious. The overnight Nazification of Norway was a mystery and Kim decided to untangle it. What he found would shock the world: the fall of Norway had not been a battle; it had been a kidnapping. Kim learned that Major Vidkun Quisling, head of the supposedly defunct Nazi party in Norway, still had enormous influence in the army and navy. When the Germans aimed their ships and guns at

Norway, orders had gone out not to fire, not to resist. Oslo and other major points of entry had been betrayed from within. He broadcast the news, in detail, and with passion.

Kim knew there would be consequences. He waited to see how the Germans would react. The mildness of their retaliation surprised him: he was ordered to leave Oslo immediately. He was being escorted to the airport in a military vehicle when a squadron of German bombers flew over the road, dropping their incendiary cargoes on the oil storage tanks that lined the roadside. In the ensuing noise and confusion, Kim's escort, a senior Gestapo official, drew his pistol and fired, missing only because an aftershock spoiled his aim. The incident was over in a flash.

"My death would have been reported as a bombing fatality, wouldn't it?" Kim asked. The ashen-faced official did not answer. He feared his superior, a frigid man with snowy eyes, and he knew the penalty for failure would be terrible.

"So you're not going to answer?" Kim said. "Well, I know I'm right, so you needn't bother."

Roaring fires raged out of control in the big oil tanks, turning the sky orange, but the vehicle rolled on toward the airport and the moment of confusion and crisis passed.

The Gestapo man, still wordless and ashen, escorted Kim to the ramp rolled up to the plane that would take him to Paris. With a contemptuous grin, Kim wished a final farewell to the man who had tried to murder him:

"Better luck next time," he said sarcastically, snapped a jaunty salute, and disappeared up the ramp and into the transport.

"That Quisling affair is a scandal," Nicole said. "The Germans must not have been too pleased with you."

404

Kim shrugged. "All they did was order me out of Norway. Frankly, I've been thrown out of better places."

Nicole shook her head and laughed. Kim's irrepressible good spirts were contagious, and as the spring weather turned balmy and beautiful Nicole shared Kim's buoyant ebullience. She remembered the intense gaiety that had accompanied World War I—the dances and the parties and the breaking down of all the old Victorian hangovers governing conduct. It was the same now: not in years had the House of Redon made so many wedding dresses and trousseaux; everyone was in a rush to marry. War brides! And babies! If women weren't getting married they were getting pregnant, and usually managing to do both in record time. One of Nicole's long-time clients, a woman who must have been close to fifty, came in and ordered a maternity wardrobe—and she wasn't the only one. Women in their thirties and forties were having babies and thinking nothing of it. Nicole, despite herself, was amazed and told Kim about the epidemic of marriages and pregnancies.

"We ought to join the crowd," Kim said, holding her, resting his chin on her golden, scented hair. Now, just forty, Nicole was a polished combination of external glamour, an unmistakable integrity of character, and a warmth of personality. She had become, Kim thought, more and more desirable with age—the golden aura of her allure, her gleaming hair, her intelligent eyes, her generous mouth, now informed with experience and self-respect. Every time he came back to Paris he reeled with the sight and scent of her.

"Why not?" answered Nicole. "Only I insist on a certain decency."

Kim pulled back, tilted her chin up, and looked her directly in the eyes. "Decency? In *this* day and age!"

"Marriage first," Nicole insisted.

"And pregnancy second!" Kim was joyous, then sud-

405

denly serious. His own children were, amazingly, almost grown: Kimjy at Yale; Christie in high school. A baby, a new life, a new beginning, a *real* beginning for them, for him, for Nicole. "I want us to have a baby. Your baby. My baby. *Our* baby, Nicole . . ."

Nicole nodded but she did not speak because she could not. The tears and the joy interfered, and Kim thought he would faint with love for her.

A little later Kim realized that that had been the perfect moment. He should have told her then—*I love you, I love you*—but he had missed it. He could have kicked himself.

On Friday, May 10, the first German bombs fell inside France when the Bron Airdrome near Lyons was raided by German planes. The first alarm was sounded at 4:25 A.M.; the all-clear at 6:45 A.M.

A week later, on May 17, the German army pierced the Maginot Line on a sixty-two-mile front, and *The New York Times* reported that President Roosevelt's preparedness message would be followed by the commencement of construction of airplane and munitions factories in the midwest, out of the reach of possible Axis bombing raids.

On Wednesday, May 22, the German army crossed the Aisne River sixty miles from Paris and French Premier Paul Reynaud, announcing that advancing German forces had occupied Amiens and Arras, called for "hope and savage energy," urging the people of France to "rise to the height of the misfortunes of our country." By May 30 the battle for Flanders had become entirely a rearguard action, the Germans attacking massively on land, in the air, on the sea, and under the sea. And then, Dunkerque: 500,000 men killed, wounded or captured.

The Maginot Line caved in. Le Havre fell. Montmédy, northern end of the Maginot Line, fell. Verdun, thought impregnable, fell. Paris would be next.

On June 11, from a studio in Paris, Kim reported that German tanks were now thirty-five miles from Paris itself. The French government and its ministries had moved south to a new capital, believed to be Tours.

Under a pall of smoke, amid the noise of rumbling cannon, life went on in Paris. The buses and subways continued to run, although on reduced schedules. The citizens of Paris went out to the suburbs on excursions to see for themselves the damage caused by German bombs. The cafés and the Bank of France were open, and American films showed in the movie houses along the Champs-Elysées. But then the air of frenzied excitement suddenly caved in and gave way to panic. An endless cavalcade poured out of Paris, jamming the highways leading from the city. An endless line of cars, taxis and buses; of trucks, fire engines, motorcycles and horse-drawn carts; bicycles and ambulances with sirens screaming impotently in the crush of traffic; pedestrians with their earthly possessions on their backs. Paris was no longer safe.

The smoke from the surrounding battlefields hovered over the city, covering skin and clothes with a sooty mantle. Nicole's old worry overcame her and she turned to Kim for reassurance: "Is everything really going to be all right?"

"Damn right!" he said. "Roosevelt's got no choice now. The American people have no choice. It's only a matter of time before the United States declares war, and then the Germans will find out what war really is!"

407

"And us?" asked Nicole. "What about us?"

"We're going to be sensational! Just the way we planned," he said. "Kim and Nicole. Nicole and Kim."

"And baby makes three?" Nicole asked shyly.

"And baby makes three," said Kim. "You betcha!"

Kim had been broadcasting from Paris, which had purposely been left undefended. As the German armies moved inexorably closer, Kim was sent to accompany them on the final few miles to the city.

"I never thought I'd live to see Paris under a German flag," Nicole said. They were about to part, as they had done so often in the last months. No matter how often they repeated the words and the kisses and the scene itself, it never lost its power over them. The actual moment of farewell wrenched them both. Kim's early romantic dream of a bittersweet ending had come true— over and over.

"Nor I," Kim admitted. "But they won't be here long. And you have Kim Hendricks's personal guarantee of that!"

He kissed her goodby and tore himself away from her. He got into the drab Citroën, one of the few autos left in Paris, and headed toward the outskirts of the city to join up with the entering German forces. He hadn't left the suburbs yet when he suddenly realized he *still* hadn't told her. There had always been other things to talk about, other pressures, other distractions, and never, never enough time.

I love you, he said to himself, the broadcaster in him practicing the tone to get it just right. The writer in him arranged and rearranged the words to get them just right: *I love you. I've loved you from the very beginning, when a thunderbolt struck me on the rue Montaigne . . . I love you now and I always will . . . I thought you were a stranger but you weren't, you were the other half of me . . . the half without which I was not complete . . .*

As the Citroën rolled toward Kim's rendezvous with the Germans, he rehearsed the words and the tone. He wanted everything—the words and the tone and the moment—to be perfect. Well, next time they *would* be perfect. He'd see to that, and that was a promise.

To himself, to her.

Kim entered Paris with the German army. Although, according to the agreement that left Paris undefended, no shots were fired, the German soldiers were nervous —and Kim said so on his nightly broadcast.

The Germans did not look like conquering heroes; they were dusty and scared and apprehensive—and Kim said so.

The Germans did not act like conquering heroes; they wanted to buy French perfume and sit in the cafés for hours and meet the Mademoiselles—and Kim said so.

The Germans had not acted like conquering heroes during their march across the Low Countries and through the countryside of France. They had raped and looted and pillaged—and Kim said so.

He kept expecting a warning, a visit from the censors, a slap on the wrist, a repeat of the "incident" that had happened on the way to the airport in Oslo. But nothing happened. Nothing. Finally Kim decided that victory had made the Germans generous.

Stranger things had happened!

Meanwhile, the Germans moved into Paris and Kim reported their progress in a series of broadcasts that made the war seem real, that put it into human terms. There were heroes and there were cowards. On the Allied side. On the German side—and Kim said so.

The weather had been beautiful—sunny and warm, a procession of perfect June days. Paris was almost empty now, the boulevards deserted, the cafés ghostly, the

409

traffic jams gone, the horns silent. The façade of the Opéra was hidden behind sandbags and so was the Madeleine. Units of German soldiers in hobnailed jackboots marched across the bridges of the Seine and down the Champs-Elysées, while gleaming Mercedes staff cars, twin swastikas affixed to their front fenders, carried the conquering officers.

Metal treads clanked against the cobblestone streets as the panzer divisions rumbled through the deserted city. Wehrmacht sentry boxes were being constructed along the arcades of the rue de Rivoli, in the place de la Concorde and in front of the Palais du Luxembourg. At Number 74 avenue Foch—now Gestapo headquarters —stood guards with the twin silver flashes of the SS on their tunic collars. The German high command appropriated rooms in the first-class hotels, the Ritz, the Crillon, the Georges Cinq. An enormous red, white and black swastika hung from the Eiffel Tower. The Occupation had begun.

June 15 was a beautiful day, a gorgeous duplicate of the ones that had preceded it. The House of Redon, like everything else in Paris, was closed. Nicole was expecting Kim at any moment and, for some reason, she didn't know why, she went to her office and stood at the window that overlooked the place Vendôme and to the portals of the Ritz, opposite.

She wondered if she would ever get used to the drab military vehicles painted with swastikas that lined the curb, replacing the Stutz Bearcats and Lagonda touring cars; she wondered if she would ever get used to the uniformed and armed soldiers posted along the façades of the place Vendôme. She did not think so.

Nicole, along with the heads of the other great houses of couture, had been told by high Nazi officials that she would be permitted to continue to operate exactly as always. The German people did not want the French people to think they were barbarians. Kim encouraged her to continue, and she remembered saying that no obstacle had stopped her in the past; the Germans would certainly be no exception.

She gazed out the window thinking of how the beautiful June weather made a mockery of the unthinkable —the swastika flying over Paris—when she saw Kim come out of the Ritz. He was flanked by two German soldiers. He looked up at Nicole's window and, seeing her, waved. She waved back, a shadow crossing her soul. Why the two soldiers? Was Kim a prisoner? He began to move at a trot across the place Vendôme, his trench coat open in the June warmth and flapping out behind him. The Germans, looking startled, began to run after him. An officer near the Ritz called, "Halt!"

Kim ignored the order and continued toward Nicole. He picked up speed, running now. The Germans, confused, looked back to the Ritz, awaiting orders.

"Halt! Halt!" the officer commanded.

Kim paid no attention but, to Nicole's astonishment, he held up a tiny French flag in one hand and made the V-for-Victory sign with the other, a triumphant smile on his face.

"You fool! You fool!" Nicole screamed from behind her window. He could not hear her. "Stop! Don't provoke them! Do what they say!"

Still, Kim ran toward her, smiling up at her.

"Halt!" the officer screamed, and Kim raised his little tricolor higher in defiance, Suddenly, he fell.

Nicole thought he had tripped. But he didn't get up. It was only later that she realized she had heard the shot. She ran down the stairs, out the door, across to where Kim lay. Blood trickled out of the corner of his mouth.

"They ordered me out of Europe," Kim said. "They were going to take me straight to Orly but I had to see

you first." He spoke with increasing difficulty. Foamy
pink froth appeared on his lips. "You'll leave Paris. We'll
meet in New York."

"*Shhh.*" Nicole gently moved his head to her lap. She
looked around wildly, searching for help. There were
only German soldiers circling the portals of the place
Vendôme, their eyes empty, purposely not seeing what
was happening under the unseeing gaze of Napoleon.
Bonaparte had seen so many men die.

Beads of sweat broke out on Kim's forehead, and the
blood began to pump out of his mouth in jets. Nicole
could feel the wetness of the bloodstain that spread
across the left side of his chest and the wet warmth of
the blood that flowed from his back onto her skirt.

"Help! Help!" she cried to the Germans lining the
place Vendôme. Each wore a gun; one of them had just
used it. "Someone help!"

No one looked at her—except one. His frozen eyes,
almost the color of snow, locked with hers and then
moved on, expressionless, to focus on nothing. Nicole
thought of all the times when she had been little and
how much it had hurt her that people had refused to
look at her. She realized it had never really mattered
then. Now it did. "Please!" she screamed. "Help!"

"Nicole . . ." Kim's voice was labored, difficult to
hear.

"Yes?" she said, putting her ear to his mouth to make
it easier for him. He was aware of her perfume.

"I love you," he said. "I always meant to tell you. I was
waiting for the perfect moment and this isn't what I had
in mind . . ." He tried to smile but the light was going
out in his eyes. "I knew it that first moment . . . on the
rue Montaigne . . ."

"So did I," whispered Nicole, remembering the thunderbolt, remembering her own very first thought. "*Je*

412

t'aime," she whispered, uttering the words she had never in her life spoken. "*Je t'aime . . .*"

He managed a smile. He had heard. Then the light was extinguished.

On the day of the funeral Nicole dyed her golden hair black. She kept it black for the rest of her life. "It matches the darkness in my soul," she said if people asked, but she refused to elaborate.

EPILOGUE

AT CLOSING TIME on Christmas Eve, 1940, Nicole announced to her staff that she had come to a decision: the House of Redon would be closed as long as the Nazis occupied France. That night, after everyone had left, she symbolically locked the doors for the last time and drew down the iron shutters. They would remain down until the Occupation was over and the French flag once again flew over Paris. Nicole was rich enough to be able to continue the salaries of her long-time employees and she herself went home to the rue de Bretonvilliers, where she endured until the war was over.

In 1945, when the Allies freed Paris, Nicole reopened the doors of the House of Redon. Christian Dior would invent the New Look; Balenciaga would be acknowledged as the master of pure line; Yves St. Laurent, a young man, still in his twenties, would burst upon the fashion scene in 1960 with a series of spectacular collections. They were all men, all gifted. But it was Nicole Redon who reigned as the Queen of French fashion, a woman who designed for other women.

She died peacefully in her sleep in the spring of 1976. She had never married. She was known as "Nicole" the world over, and everyone knew who she was.

There had been men in her life: Grand Duke Cyril, who sold a brooch so that she could open her first shop; Boy Mellany, who made her the precious gift of treating her as an equal at a time in her life when she had been persuaded of her inferiority; Mikhail Essayan, who encouraged her to think internationally and spread her influence beyond the borders of France.

But it was Kim Hendricks who freed her from the phantoms that had haunted the caverns of her spirit, and it was Kim who, believing in his own dreams, gave her the courage to believe in hers. Only Kim had viewed the world as she had: to them, men were heroes and women were heroines. Kim wrote books about his heroes and Nicole furnished her heroines with a style that went far beyond clothing. But their impact went even further than words and dresses: there were those who said that Kim Hendricks was the first twentieth-century man and Nicole the first twentieth-century woman. They were the last romantics, the first contemporaries. Kim was the man other men wanted to be and Nicole was the woman other women wanted to be. Together, they changed the way men and women all over the world thought of themselves.

Nicole was in the habit of discipline and so she rarely allowed herself to wonder what might have been had Kim lived. The only external sign she permitted herself was the simple bouquet of red and white carnations, tied with a blue ribbon, that was placed on Kim's grave every year on the eleventh of November. The card said, simply, *Je t'aime* . . .

The little bouquet, now without a card, arrived as usual on November 11, 1976, and again on November 11, 1977, and forever after, according to the first provision of the last will and testament of Nicole Redon.